The Friendship List

BOOKS BY BETH MILLER

The Two Hearts of Eliza Bloom
The Missing Letters of Mrs Bright
The Woman Who Came Back to Life

Starstruck
When We Were Sisters
The Good Neighbour

The Friendship List

BETH MILLER

bookouture

Published by Bookouture in 2025

The

Copyright © Beth Miller, 2025

Beth Miller has asserted her right to be identified
as the author of this work.

All rights reserved. No part of this publication may be reproduced, stored in any retrieval system, or transmitted, in any form or by any means, electronic, mechanical, photocopying, recording or otherwise, without the prior written permission of the publishers.

ISBN: 978-1-83525-659-6
eBook ISBN: 978-1-83525-658-9

This book is a work of fiction. Names, characters, businesses, organizations, places and events other than those clearly in the public domain, are either the product of the author's imagination or are used fictitiously. Any resemblance to actual persons, living or dead, events or locales is entirely coincidental.

To John, Milo and Saul. Thank you for distracting me. I needed it.

ONE
LONDON, APRIL 2023

Rose's seat was still empty.

The human brain can hold on to many things simultaneously. For me, right now, it was six.

1. Rose wasn't here, and wasn't answering her phone.
2. Something terrible must have happened.
3. But she was probably just late.
4. How much longer could we wait? We'd already stalled for half an hour.
5. The guests were becoming restless. It wasn't quite warm enough to be sitting outside for as long as this. And my son Edward on piano, bless him, only knew three tunes – 'knew' was a euphemism – which he'd been playing on rotation.
6. We should start, but how could I get married without my best friend there? Without knowing if she was OK?

Various members of my family had been phoning and messaging Rose. Now Stella came over and shook her head.

'No go, Mum, I'm sorry. She's not answering.' She saw I was about to speak and raised a hand. 'And no, there's no record of any traffic incident that she might have been caught up in.'

What I wanted ideally was someone to call all the hospitals between Rose's home in Winchester and here in London, but there was no one I felt I could ask who wouldn't think it over the top. Ironically, the only person in my life who would understand, and volunteer to do it, was Rose.

'She rang me last week to check the timings for today,' Stella said, 'and everything was fine.'

Edward struck up a different tune, presumably desperate to play something new. It took me a few seconds to recognise this faltering attempt as an interpretive rendition of 'Feeling Good', which was – till now – my favourite song. Five men had struggled for nearly an hour to drag the heavy old piano down from the house into the garden, and Edward wanted to show that it had been worth the effort. But he'd barely played since his childhood lessons, more than twenty years ago, so enthusiasm was his primary asset, as he delivered a wild run up and down the octaves that would have brought Nina Simone to tears.

To Stella's sisterly grimace, I said, 'It's not his fault. I did ask him to keep going till we were ready.' I looked across the garden at the rows of guests, most of whom had given up even twisting round in their seats to find out why we hadn't started, and were now chatting, or on their phones, or walking round the garden inspecting the flowers. They knew that whatever the hold-up was, it couldn't be a real sitcom-type crisis, because not only were bride and groom both present, we were already married. We got hitched this morning in a register office with just our adult children in attendance as witnesses. You weren't allowed to legally marry in a garden, and that's what we wanted.

Murray, standing under a flowery arch where our public ceremony would hopefully, at some point, take place, seemed utterly relaxed. He sensed me looking across at him and pointed at himself, meaning, 'Do you need me?' but I shook my head. He was doing a good job keeping guests in the front rows entertained.

'Ten more minutes? Give everyone more champagne?' I asked Stella. She nodded and went off to organise it. I stood a moment, wondering what to do next, and thus made myself an easy target for Alice, my ex-mother-in-law.

'For heaven's sake, Kathleen, what *is* the hold-up?'

Imogen was close behind her, nearly obscured by Alice's hat, a navy blue chiffon circle the size of a dustbin lid. The two of them were old friends from their days working for royalty in the 1960s.

'Rose hasn't arrived,' I said. 'We're a bit worried.'

'Oh, my dear,' Imogen said. She was the hostess of this wedding – it was her garden – and was such a comforting, motherly presence. I really missed my own mum right now. 'That's very upsetting.'

'It is rather,' I said, trying not to let tears come, and ruin the make-up Stella had spent so long on. The later it got, the longer there was no message, the harder I was finding it to believe that Rose was just delayed. A dread weight was forming in my stomach.

'Awfully rude to be this tardy,' Alice said, taking a swig of champagne, which I had insisted to Murray be the best we could afford, purely so Alice wouldn't have that to moan about. In a quieter voice, still likely audible to the outer reaches of Hampstead, she added, 'Perhaps she's staging a boycott?'

'Alice, for *goodness* sake,' I said.

It made no sense that Rose wasn't here, and Alice was. I'd laughed when Stella had suggested I invite Alice, told her that her grandmother would never come in a million years, but of course Alice always managed to find a way to wrongfoot me, and graciously accepted. To me, inviting ex in-laws to one's second wedding was the very stuff of *The Jeremy Kyle Show*. But to Stella, it was the sort of thing our 'blended and non-traditional' family ought to do, in order to heal whatever breach remained from my divorce from Richard. Ouch. The divorce was, of course, my idea.

Alice waved her hand dismissively. 'Very nice champagne. So why bring down the tone' – she pointed at my dress – 'in this garish colour?' So much for the expensive champagne. 'Hardly the choice for an older bride, is it?'

I dug my sharp, newly manicured nails into my soft palm and thus managed to avoid saying anything I might later regret. 'It was good of you to come today,' I said, determined to be the bigger person, while simultaneously aware of the unstoppable urge to exaggerate my Liverpudlian accent, an urge which only ever surfaced when with Alice.

She moved a little closer. 'I've something to tell you, Kathleen.'

In a gruff, Brandoesque mumble, I replied, 'So Alice, you come to me, the day of my daughter's wedding...'

It was the sort of nonsense that would have made Rose laugh, but Alice looked at me with stony irritation. 'I beg your pardon? It's not Stella's wedding.'

'I was just being silly.' Why *did* I persist in trying to be daft with her? There was nothing to gain from it.

She shook her head impatiently. 'What I was *going* to say...'

'Actually, if it's all right with you,' I said, adding in my head, *or even if it's not*, 'I have rather a lot on right now, so let's talk later.' I was surprised at my own daring. No one interrupted Alice. But after all, she wasn't my mother-in-law any more; I didn't have to comply with every request.

'Fine. I thought you'd be interested, but never mind.' She turned on her heel, the blue chiffon hat vibrating alarmingly, and set off at speed to find someone more agreeable, e.g. anyone.

I puffed out my cheeks, and Imogen smiled knowingly at me.

'That cheerful colour suits you beautifully,' she said. She was well into her late eighties, but still incredibly chic in dark green lace and matching pillbox hat. 'Your friend did definitely intend to come, Kay dear?'

'Oh yes! She...' I stopped. Well, of course Rose had said she was coming, hadn't she? She was my closest friend! But I couldn't recall her definitely confirming. Why had I been so informal? I should have sent out proper invites, not texts, should have insisted on RSVPs. I got out my phone and scrolled back through our last dozen or so messages. We hadn't actually sent each other any texts for a couple of weeks, not since my hen do. I'd been in such a whirl of arrangements, I hadn't noticed. But still, she'd clearly meant to be here. She'd phoned Stella to check timings, after all.

I sent her my fifth message of the day: – *Really hope you're OK, chick. Are you nearly here?*

'I do think we might have to make a start, Kay dear,' Imogen said, 'and surely Rose will arrive in time to raise a glass.'

I glanced for the hundredth time at the back door of the house, where any late guests would appear.

'I know you're right, Imo. But what if...?' I stopped. I didn't want to voice my worst fears out loud. 'I'm worried about her. It feels like, I don't know, a bad start.'

'Oh, now, *chérie*. That man loves you. Anyone can see that.'

I looked across the garden to Murray, and he waved and blew me a kiss. Even at a distance of twenty metres, I could see the sparkle in his eyes.

'Ready?' Richard said. He was taking the role of my father at this, my second wedding. At my first, thirty-five years ago, he'd been my groom. 'You look lovely, Kay. I like your dress.'

'It has pockets,' I said, showing him, but he didn't really get it. God, I really needed Rose. She was the friend I felt I dressed for, whose opinion counted more than anyone else's.

The photographer, who Richard had bossily told me was 'all organised' when I suggested one of my college friends do it, snapped some pictures of us standing together. She looked familiar but I had too much going on in my head to work out why. When she stepped aside, I took Richard's arm, and for a moment, this cool, blue-skyed April day was quiet and still. The only sound was the rustle of Edward rifling through papers for the walk-down-the-aisle sheet music. I prayed that he'd practised it more than 'Feeling Good'.

Into the lull, Alice's unmistakable tones were picked up by a breath of wind right across the garden. Richard's mother couldn't do an indoor voice even when sober, and everyone heard with clarity the single unignorable word, '*FINALLY!*'. A wave of giggles rippled through the guests, and Richard grinned at me. I wished I could find it funny, but I felt too anxious to relax. If Rose had got into an accident on her way here, how could I ever forgive myself? How could I look back on this as a happy day if her coming here led to tragedy?

Edward struck the first three thunderous chords of the 'Wedding March', a relic of tradition I'd been reluctant to embrace. But Imogen had suggested it, in her gentle-but-firm way, as a counterbalance to the less conventional aspects of the wedding. 'Everyone will be relieved to hear a little Mendelssohn, *chérie*.'

Perhaps she was right: it wasn't particularly traditional for your ex-husband to give you away. And I guess it was also unusual to marry someone you'd only known for six months.

'Why didn't we play this at our wedding?' Richard whispered. 'It's rather good.'

I shrugged. Our wedding was ancient history. 'Shotgun',

Alice had called it, and back then it felt like she was the one holding the gun. The main emotion I'd felt on the day was relief. Despite – or because of – the whole shotgunness of the thing, I'd been a radiant bride, barely hatched, wearing a blue polyester frock that smoothed deceptively over my stomach. Radiance was easy at twenty-one, a little harder to come by in one's fifties, outside of the periodic and unwelcome radiance bestowed by menopause. But I was undoubtedly a happier bride now than then. Apart from that one little dark Rose-shaped cloud.

I took my one-hundred-and-first check on the door, but if she was going to come, it wouldn't be when I was staring at it, a watched pot. I had to shake it off. I told myself sternly that she was undoubtedly stuck in a traffic jam with no phone signal.

'All right. Let's do this thing.'

Arm in arm, we walked slowly towards Husband the Second. Murray Garland was a fine-looking man, well-built in the Australian style, with thick hair and crinkly brown eyes that looked at me and liked what they saw. He was wearing a dark grey suit, teamed with a bright yellow shirt in solidarity with my buttercup dress. When I'd shown him the dress I felt uncertain, because his first wife had been an elegant woman with a restrained colour palette. But he laughed, hugged me and said, 'Brilliant! I'll get a shirt to match.'

Now, as Richard made a slightly jokey play of handing me over to my new husband, ugh the retro symbolism was awful, Murray smiled down at me. How tall and handsome he was! He whispered, 'I'm sorry about Rose, love.' It melted my heart that at this moment he was focused on me and how I was feeling.

I slipped my hand in his. 'I'm not thinking about anyone else but you.' It was a white lie.

'I'm one damn lucky fella.' He squeezed my hand. 'Thank you for being here.'

Very quietly, because I didn't want anyone to hear, especially not Richard, who I'd hate to hurt, even though he was hovering in an annoying way, I said to Murray, 'You don't need to thank me for falling in love.'

Because that's what had happened. I'd gone and fallen head over heels in love. I was fifty-six years old and giddy as a schoolgirl.

Edward brought the 'Wedding March' to a shuddering stop on the wrong note, and Anthony, my former colleague, stepped forward. He'd trained to be a celebrant when same-sex marriage was first legalised, and was very excited to have been asked to perform this wedding: 'My first straight one!' He started off with the traditional, 'Dearly beloved, we are gathered together here in the sight of God,' but quickly veered into irreverence, '… that's if you believe in God, which I'm guessing not everyone here does, including yours truly…'

It was as well that I couldn't see Alice's face. Although very much a rational agnostic, she would certainly not approve of *that*. Thankfully, Anthony settled down, with a sobering, 'It is not to be entered into unadvisedly or lightly – but reverently, discreetly, advisedly and solemnly.' Being giddy as a schoolgirl might count me out, in that case, but we were already on to the undeniably dramatic, 'If any person can show just cause why they may not be joined together – let them speak now or forever hold their peace.'

Years of watching films where someone bursts in at this point meant that, when the back door crashed open into the charged silence following Anthony's words, there was a huge gasp and every head, including mine, spun round. Surely Rose, at last! Would she denounce the entire business and explain exactly why we shouldn't be joined together, or was she just late and relieved to have got here?

But instead, a harassed-looking waitress stuck her head round the door, clocked us all staring at her, cried, 'Oh no, I'm sorry!' and withdrew. Everyone laughed, and we turned back to Anthony, who put his hand on his heart and said, 'Thank heavens! I'd have had no idea what to do next!'

The rest of the ceremony went smoothly, and when Anthony pronounced us husband and wife, and told us to 'Kiss, already!', Murray pulled me into his arms and we had a dreamy smooch that drew whistles and a round of applause from the crowd.

Stella twined her arms round my neck. 'How are you, Mrs Garland?'

We'd had the speeches and the cake-cutting, and now everyone was eating and drinking. Imogen's garden was full of conversation and laughter. Music played from a speaker hanging in a tree, and some people were dancing on the lawn. My grandchildren, Jamie and Finlay – Edward's boys – were charging round the garden like mad things, cute in their little jackets and kilts.

So how *was* I? I should be on top of the world, my supportive family around me, a gorgeous new husband. But I was thoroughly uneasy. 'I'm good, I loved it... do you think Rose is all right?'

'Oh Mum, don't let this ruin your day.'

'I'm trying, but it keeps bubbling up.'

Stella looked at me thoughtfully. 'I know I've suggested this a million times, but I do think you should talk to someone. Not about this, particularly, but about everything.'

She'd been trying to get me to see a therapist or counsellor for years. It was hard not to be slightly offended.

'I'll see, darling, when I get home from honeymoon.'

She went off to oversee something – her company was doing

the catering – and I checked my phone for the dozenth time. Still nothing. I sought out Edward, who was sitting with Anthony and Imogen, and thanked him for the music, but he immediately said, 'It was terrible, Mum. It's a rotten piano. Sorry, Imogen, but when did you last tune it?'

'It's hard to recall. Maybe 1978?'

They all started laughing.

'But we enjoyed it so much,' Imogen went on. 'Your *joie de vivre* was infectious.'

'I nearly had a heart attack,' Anthony said, 'when that door opened during "any just cause".'

'You were cool as a cucumber,' Imogen told him. 'And you' – she took my hand – 'look delightful. So sunny and young.'

'Young?' I laughed.

'Compared to me, *chérie*, you are a mere child.'

'Imo, thank you again for letting us use your gorgeous garden. It's the perfect setting.'

'Ah, it's my wedding present to you. I hope you and Murray have very many happy years.'

I left them and went to seek out the man in question. He'd saved me a seat at one of the long trestle tables, and put together a plate of delicious food for me. What a promising husband he was.

As the sun went down, the fairy lights went on across the garden, and the musical instruments came out, with Charlie playing guitar, Edward a little drunk and back on the piano, alas. Murray and I held hands, and I smiled across the table at Richard, who was sitting with Aileen, his own better-luck-this-time second spouse, bouncing our grandchildren on his knees. I forgot everything else, and was able to be there, in this beautiful moment of family and togetherness.

Then my phone buzzed in my pocket, and I fished it out, trying not to get my hopes up. But it *was* from Rose. At last!

Kay, I hope... was all I could see. She was alive! Thank God.

And yet, as I fumbled to unlock the phone screen, my thudding heart knew, before my brain, that things weren't right; that they would never be right again.

Kay, I hope it's a good day. Sorry not to reply to all the messages. I'm fine. Please don't contact me again. Rose.

PHOTO #1

Then

Rose is in her school uniform, a brown blazer and tunic that does not suit anybody, though with her long fair hair she makes it look better than most. She is sitting on the sofa at Kay's house. She and Kay have been best friends for a few weeks, since starting secondary school, along with Bear, who couldn't come back with them as she has a clarinet lesson. Rose is smiling broadly and holding up the go-to after-school treat in Kay's house: a Mr Kipling chocolate cupcake. She says she doesn't get anything like this at home, and Kay is never invited to Rose's house in all the time they are friends. Kay has been given a proper camera for her twelfth birthday and has already used almost a whole roll of film today. After this they will watch TV and Kay's mum will make them sausages and fried eggs for dinner.

Date: November 1978. Location: Kay's family home in Hoylake. Photographer: Kay Hurst.

* * *

Now

Rose looks at the camera with what could be interpreted as a sardonic expression. She is wearing a pretty blue dress and holding a cocktail. Perhaps her expression is more anxious than sardonic. The little frown lines between her eyebrows are particularly marked, as the slightly blurry photo has got a clear focus on them. Behind her, some women are dancing, but Rose does not look like she plans to join them.

Date: 7th April 2023. Location: Tre-Ysgawen Hall, Anglesey. Photographer: Stella Bright.

TWO

LONDON AND WINCHESTER, MAY 2023

The first disagreement of my second marriage took place as our plane taxied in to Heathrow. It was rather awkward because we weren't sitting alone. I was sandwiched between Murray in the aisle seat, and a friendly Texan called Ashton in the window seat.

The disagreement was because Murray told Ashton that we were heading straight home to Wales, and I said that actually we were going to Winchester first, to see Rose. I'd had this plan for the whole two weeks we'd been in Dallas – yes, we went to Dallas on our honeymoon, not my pick but it was a wonderful time – but I now realised I hadn't said it out loud to Murray. I'd been too busy keeping everything light and fun.

'Is that a good idea?' Murray asked.

'Well, I've given her some space. Hopefully she'll be ready to tell me what's up now.'

'But, darl, her message was extremely clear that she didn't want to be in touch at all. Doesn't turning up unannounced rather trample over that?'

Technically he was right, but of course I had to try to see her. If I didn't, I'd always wonder if I could have done more.

Murray hadn't been there the last time I'd had to rescue Rose, after all.

'Can't you contact the lady to let her know you're coming?' Ashton said.

I gave a wry laugh. 'I've sent her dozens of messages.' Dozens was a slight underestimate. 'Not had one reply.'

'We think she's blocked Katie's number,' Murray said.

'Oh, my!' Ashton said, leaning forward so he could see Murray better.

'Suppose there's really something wrong?' Now we were nearly back in the UK, the anxiety I'd squashed down was rising back up. 'I'd never forgive myself if I let her go, then later it turned out I could have helped.'

'What sort of thing are you envisaging?' Murray looked concerned.

I'd had two weeks to think of pretty much every possible scenario, and didn't want to empty the entire pot of my imaginings into his lap. I said the most likely one: 'Maybe she's ill and doesn't want to bother me.'

'So she tells you to get out of her life?' Murray raised an eyebrow. 'Kind of an extreme way to get people to stop bothering you.'

But she wouldn't be the first person to do exactly that. When Ursula, *aka* Bear, one of my dearest friends, got ill, she stopped writing to me, and was clearly willing for us never to speak again. It was only by forcing her hand, turning up unannounced, that I found out the truth. And thank God I did, because I was able to be there for her, very close to the end. Five years on, I still found it hard to believe that she had died. But she must have done, otherwise there was no way I could have married Murray. Because he had previously been Bear's husband.

I decided not to bring her into the conversation, though, and risk having to explain who she was to the overly invested Ashton.

'Rose knows she'd have to do something drastic to keep me away. I don't know, do I?' I could sense that I was raising my voice, because Ashton began to find the in-flight magazine extremely fascinating. More calmly, I said, 'I've also thought that maybe things have gone wrong with Graham...'

'Graham? That mild-mannered fellow with the leather elbow patches, who drank one small sherry at my stag do before leaving at nine o'clock?'

'I hate that I'm even thinking it. Graham's always been lovely to me. But you can never tell what goes on behind the scenes. And she didn't know him very long before they moved in together.'

'Sweetheart, *we* didn't know each other very long before we moved in together. Anyway, if that's the case, why didn't she tell you at your hen party, when he wasn't around?'

I didn't know the answer to that. It all seemed very unlikely. But then, the whole thing – her cutting me off so brutally – was really unlikely too.

'It's a welfare check, that's all. I'll simply knock on the door, say hello, and if she's OK, I'll leave her alone. We've been friends almost fifty years. Maybe she does just want shot of me, and if so I'll have to accept it, but I owe it to our friendship to make sure.'

'Fifty years! You don't look old enough, Katie,' Ashton said, gallantly.

I liked Murray calling me Katie; it was an in-joke between us, but I wasn't keen on a stranger doing it. I gave Murray a sideways glance, and he made a sympathetic face at me. 'You need to try, I can see that,' he said. 'Do you want me with you?'

'Aren't you nice. No, I'd better go alone.'

'But what if Graham really is a secret bastard? It mightn't be safe.' We both smiled at the idea of Graham being anything other than extremely polite.

'Me and Rose together can take him.'

'Yeah, reckon so.' He laughed, then turned serious. 'I don't want you to get your hopes up too much, Katie. If she's just being flaky...'

Tears immediately formed in my eyes. 'She is *not* flaky.'

'She is a bit, you prawn.' He was trying to keep it light, but I felt properly offended. That was my best friend he was talking about! 'She's spoiled what should have been a wonderful time for you.'

'She's not spoiled anything...' I whispered, keenly aware of Ashton hanging on every word.

Murray lowered his voice too. 'You have to admit, you were a bit distracted on honeymoon.'

'I was not!' I snapped. Ashton rustled pages.

'You checked your phone ten times a day.'

Damn, I'd thought I'd been so discreet about that. Actually, perhaps I had, because it was rather more than ten times. I was aware that this wouldn't make the point I wanted to make. But I honestly hadn't been distracted for the most part – we'd had a fantastic honeymoon, and not only the bedroom parts. Though the bedroom parts were pretty sensational, the sort of sex you think you'll not have again when you're looking down the barrel of becoming old. I was the luckiest woman in the world to have found someone who made me feel desirable, despite all physical evidence to the contrary. I was, apparently, 'one hot patootie'. But we also found time to visit amazing restaurants, and interesting museums, even a baseball game. Murray went out a few times on business, but I didn't mind. I was used to workaholic husbands, and I made good use of the hotel's gorgeous spa and pool while he was gone. Once or twice I might have used that time to wallow a little, let thoughts tumble through my mind.

But when he came back I always pushed it away and focused on him.

'Of course I've thought about her occasionally,' I said, my face a hot patootie, whatever that was. 'But not when we were together. I didn't let it spoil anything. I had the best time of my life.'

The plane landed at this point with a small bump, the first time ever that I'd neither noticed nor white-knuckled a landing.

Murray kissed my hand. 'Katie, I had the best time of my life too. I'm sorry. I love you and I just don't want you to be even more hurt. Suppose going to see her makes things worse?'

'I can't see how it could, but anyway, I have to try.' I kissed his hand in return. 'I love you too.'

'Phew!' Ashton said, blowing out a stream of air. 'Glad that's sorted.'

'Cheers, mate!' Murray gave Ashton his most charming smile. 'Sorry for the ringside seat.'

'Not at all. I think you're a terrific couple. Now take it from an old married man, life will turn to beige soon enough.' He did a comedy wink. 'You guys should try and continue the honeymoon a little longer, know what I'm saying?'

'Can we please not...' I mumbled to Murray, but he was reaching across me to high-five Ashton, and they started chatting about romantic gestures their 'ladies' tended to appreciate, Australian to American, while the embarrassed Brit in between pretended she wasn't there. Ashton looked very pleased with himself. I imagined him calling his wife when he got to his hotel, saying perhaps he should retrain as a couples counsellor.

It was good to get out of the stuffy airport and into the light drizzle of a classic English spring. There was the usual stress of trying to remember which far-flung field I'd left my car in, and the extra stress of getting shot of Ashton, who looked for a while as if he'd be joining us for a mini-break to Winchester. When he finally, reluctantly, said his goodbyes, Murray and I spent the shuttle journey to the car giggling and making up increasingly daft scenarios in which Ashton infiltrated himself into our lives. My favourite was him applying to be our butler.

'What will you do while I talk to Rose?' I asked Murray, as I drove us towards the M3.

'Drop me in the city, I'll find something to do. We can meet up whenever you're ready.'

'OK. God. I haven't thought what I'm going to say.'

'Say what you told me. That you want to make sure she's OK, then you'll leave her be.' He stroked my hair. 'I'm sorry. I know how hard this is. Call me as soon as you're done. And listen. If she says anything weird, don't take it to heart.'

'Weird? Like what?'

'Well, she's been acting strangely, right? So maybe there's, you know. A mental health thing.'

This was one explanation that hadn't crossed my mind. What if it was something like that? What would I do?

'You also have to be prepared for her refusing to see you.'

'Of course.' But I absolutely couldn't imagine that. When she saw me, I knew she'd relent.

Murray hugged me before he got out of the car, and wished me luck. Then I drove on to the outskirts where she lived. I was grateful for the satnav, as I was definitely not up to route-finding. I tested my opening statement out loud: 'Rose, whatever it is that I've done, I'm sorry. I just want to make sure you're OK.' It sounded cheesy and not the sort of thing a person would say, outside of reality TV.

I'd spent some of my honeymoon downtime searching for clues in the texts she'd sent before that final one. I had to scroll a long way back, because I'd sent so many unanswered messages, ranging from bewildered (*What on earth is going on?*) to contrite (*I must have done something awful, please tell me*) to bargaining (*Whatever it is, we can work it out*). How persecutory silence was! It was the most extraordinarily powerful weapon. Into her silence I couldn't help but read every single failing I had as a person, every mistake I had ever made.

But there weren't any clues. The last messages, sent before my hen do, were breezy and factual: *What time you getting there?* and *Can Graham have Murray's number?*. Murray had organised a low key 'stag' type drinks at the same time as my hen, and because he didn't know many fellows here, Graham had stepped in to make up the numbers.

Steeling myself, I looked again at her final text. Even though I knew it by heart, it was still a punch to the guts. *Please don't contact me any more.*

The most likely explanation, as I'd said to Murray, was that she was ill, and hadn't wanted to tell me and ruin my wedding day. But there were many other possible reasons:

1. Did she hate Murray? If so, why?
2. Did she think it in bad taste to marry my dead friend's ex-husband?
3. Did she think we were rushing into marriage?
4. Had Murray said something unforgiveable to Graham at the stag do?
5. Had I offended her somehow, maybe at the hen do?
6. Was she upset that I hadn't asked her to be my matron of honour? I'd not even thought of it in all the rush, but wished I had. I could hear her response: 'Bit long in the tooth for it, chick, but if you want me in pink tulle I'll do it.'

I turned into her familiar street. There was The Eagle pub on the corner, where we had so often gone for a pre-dinner drink, or a Sunday lunch. There was the house opposite Rose's, owned by a strange woman called Filomena, where we'd once gone for a barbecue. Filomena's elderly mother had tripped on the patio and banged her head, and I called an ambulance while

Rose covered the lady with a blanket because Filomena panicked and locked herself in the downstairs lav. The mother was fine, and Rose and I later cried with laughter doing impressions of the incident, and had ever since referred to any example of someone burying their head in the sand as 'doing a Filomena'.

I pulled over and did some calming yoga breathing. I hadn't been to classes for years but still remembered the instructions to breathe slowly in for five counts with your mouth open, or possibly shut, then out for five with your mouth shut. Or open. Hopefully it didn't matter which way round. Rose's house was far enough outside town not to have parking restrictions, and I remembered her saying, when she'd put in an offer on it, 'I don't want to have to faff about with visitors' parking when you pop in to see me, chick.'

Those were the days, when she wanted to see me.

How dear her house was to me, with its dark blue front door and patch of cottage garden which she'd filled with pots of flowers. I was the first person she took to see it. Could that really be twenty years ago? She'd viewed a lot of houses after leaving Tim, but had a good feeling about this one. Near – but not too near – her sister. And not big or fancy, like that insane place she'd walked out on, littered with Tim's expensive little flourishes that made it a nightmare to look after. There was not a single surface in that house in Suffolk you could put a cup on without ruining it, and by the time Rose left she owned the world's biggest collection of coasters. She once said that the two things she was really glad she'd left behind were Tim and the coasters. Together, we agreed that the Winchester house was perfect, and that the furniture she'd cobble together to fill it – some of which came from my and Richard's house – would be of the sort that could tolerate an un-coastered cup.

When I couldn't put it off any longer, I told myself to man up, and got out of the car. I'd borrowed 'man up' from Anthony, who often said it when we worked together. Scared of using the new computer tills? 'Man up, Anthony,' he'd tell himself. Worried about confronting the shop assistant who'd been late every day that week? 'Man up, Kay!' My heart was thudding out of my chest, useless yoga, my eyes darting about, scanning for anything new or unusual. The bay tree in a pot at the side of the doorstep was in poor shape, with curling brown leaves, but I shouldn't read too much into that. I counted to five, then rang the bell. I could hear it echoing inside the house, and it felt like a very long time before the door opened.

It was Graham. 'Hello, Kay!' he said. 'This is a surprise.' But he didn't sound surprised.

'I'm sorry just to rock up…'

'No, that's OK. How are you?' He was, as always, very polite. Not polite enough to invite me in, though, I noted.

'I'm not great, to be honest.'

'I'm sorry to hear that. Er, did you have a nice wedding?'

It was a little hard to answer that, given the situation. I settled for the award-winningly bland, 'Lovely, thank you.'

'And your honeymoon?'

OK then, small talk it was. 'Very nice. We went to Dallas. A lovely luxury hotel.'

'Unusual choice, but lots of history there. The Texas School Book Depository…'

'The what?'

'Where Lee Harvey Oswald shot Kennedy from?'

'Believe me, it was right at the top of my honeymoon must-sees.' I really didn't want to stand on the doorstep talking about assassinations. 'So… is Rose here?'

'No, she's, er, out.'

I didn't believe him for a minute. 'I can wait if she won't be long.'

'Well, see, she's away for the night, she's gone to Manchester to see Will.'

There was an awkward silence, during which I considered

accepting this lie, turning round and getting back in my car. It was tempting, because I had never been a big fan of confrontation. But if I went back without seeing her, nothing would have changed.

My hand shook a little as I gestured to the street. 'How come her car's still there?'

Graham's face went red. He'd be rubbish at poker. 'She's borrowed mine.'

Quietly, I said, 'Graham, I know she's here.' I didn't really, not for sure, but I could sense her presence, if that didn't sound odd.

He stared at the floor, mumbled that he was sorry, that he didn't know what to say. I waited, letting him find his way to a decision, and finally he looked up and said, 'OK, she is here, but, well, you can't come in. I'm sorry.' It was obvious how much he hated this, hated having to stand there, blocking my entry.

So it hadn't all been a horrible nightmare; she really didn't want to see me.

I wondered what would have happened if Rose herself had answered the door. Would she have shut it in my face? Then I realised that of course she wouldn't have answered it, that the delay in the door being opened was them looking out of a window and seeing who it was. That's why Graham hadn't been surprised.

'I'll go then. But, Graham, before I do. Could you please tell me truthfully if she's all right? I'm so scared there's something wrong with her.'

'There's nothing wrong, Kay, honestly.'

'She's not ill?'

'No, she's fine.'

Christ, what was it then? 'In that case I've clearly done something terrible. I wish you'd tell me so I could at least try to make it up to her.'

'Kay, it's not... I can't... it's not for me to say.'

'Well, who *is* it to say, then? Cos I'm sure as hell not getting any information from anyone else.'

I saw a tiny flicker of something like anger cross his face, and that's when I knew that this was not Rose's idea, could not be, Rose would never do this to me of her own free will! This was all Graham's doing, supposedly placid Graham standing here in his PE teacher's fleece, Graham who had been so helpful and supportive when I was trying to get myself together after leaving Richard. Oh, what a long game he'd played, pretending to be so kind. And Rose had a history of picking these men. Her ex-husband, the wretched Tim, had treated her so horribly, she'd had to actively escape from him, as I remembered only too well. Like Tim, Graham seemed so nice at first, but that's what everyone said about those coercive control people, they love-bombed you until you were well and truly suckered in, isolated you from everyone who loved you, told you lies until you...

Graham was looking at me funny. I might have been staring at him a bit too long. 'Kay, she doesn't want to...'

'Get out of the way,' I said, and pushed past him. It was easy; he might be a controlling bastard but he wasn't exactly a rugby forward. 'Rose! Rose!' I yelled as I ran through the house. 'Where is she?'

Seemingly involuntarily, Graham looked at the stairs, and I ran up them fast.

'Rose!' My panic was rising. Had he killed her? All the doors off the landing were shut. I threw open her bedroom door, fear prickling down my spine, who knew what I would find in there? But it was empty. I whirled back into the hall and ran to the spare room, where I had so often stayed, and opened that. No one. I ran back out into the hall and...

'Kay?'

'Rose!' Her voice! Her wonderful voice! Thank God. 'Where are you?'

'Bathroom. I've locked it.'

'Ah ha, doing a Filomena? I don't blame you...' I leaned against the bathroom door, my heart thumping. 'Let me in, I won't let anything happen to you, I promise.'

Graham had come up the stairs while I was hurtling about. He called out, 'I'm sorry Rose, she pushed past me.'

'Go away,' I told him. I turned back to the door. 'Rose, listen. Are you OK? You maybe don't feel free to talk, but if you come out, we can go somewhere safe.'

'Somewhere safe?' She let out a bark of laughter. 'What the hell are you on about?'

Graham interrupted, 'Please, she really doesn't want to...'

I turned to him, furious. 'Can you give us some privacy here?'

'I'm sorry, Kay. I don't think Rose wants me to go anywhere.' He spoke so gently that it was momentarily hard to maintain the idea of him as a controller. But that's how these people fooled you.

'No I bloody don't!' Rose called out. 'Kay, I couldn't have been any clearer.' Was she crying? 'I need you to leave.'

'Listen, chick. If there's something going on with Graham...' God, it was so awkward that Graham wouldn't budge. 'Can I text you? He's standing right here!'

'Well he lives here, you know? And I've blocked your number. Please, just go. I can't bear it.'

'All right. But I'm here for you, if anything's happening, you know, *domestically*.'

'You think Graham is a domestic abuser?'

'Thanks a lot,' Graham muttered.

'He really isn't. Kay, it has absolutely nothing to do with him. I just can't see you any more.'

I started to cry. 'Can't, or won't?'

'Can't, and won't.' There was a silence, and I thought she was going to say something else, but she didn't. Now I could definitely hear her crying.

I launched into my planned line. 'Rose, whatever I've done, I'm sorry. But at least tell me why. Don't I deserve an explanation?'

That frightening bark of laughter again. 'I tried, you know. I really tried.'

'When? You didn't!'

'She did, Kay,' Graham said gently. 'It's costing her a lot, if you only knew, she needs...'

'Costing her a lot?' I took a step towards him, and he took one back. 'It's costing me everything. Rose. I'll do anything you want, anything at all. Please...'

'Really? Anything I want?'

'Yes, I promise.' I leaned my face hard against the door.

'I. Want. You. To. Go.' She let out a sob. 'Please, Kay. Please go.'

I'd only once before heard her sound so sad, so weary: when things with Tim were at their absolute worst. She'd felt hopeless then, before I got her away, and she sounded like that now. I could hear the truth in her voice. She meant it. I was in the playground, six years old, and my best friend said she didn't want to be friends any more.

I lurched away from the door so wildly that I almost fell down the stairs. Graham steadied me, but I shook his hands off my shoulders, pushed past him and fled downstairs and out of the front door. I could hear him calling out, 'Kay, I'm sorry,' but I didn't stop, I ran to my car, locked myself in, and with shaking hands drove myself away as fast as I could.

PHOTO #2

Then

Helena is sitting on a desk, face towards the camera. She is holding her own camera, ready to take a photograph of Kay. Her hair is spiky and black, emulating her hero, Robert Smith of The Cure. The ends of her hair are dyed red, and she has thick eyeliner on. Her denim jacket is covered in badges. She is laughing because she hasn't yet had time to pose properly.

Date: circa October 1987. Location: Photography studio at The London Institute. Photographer: Kay Hurst.

* * *

Now

Helena and Kay's faces are close together as they smile at the camera. Helena's hair is short and brown, and her face is unmade-up. Kay's straight hair is in an up-do and she is wearing party make-up. Alice, Kay's former mother-in-law, is out of frame but the edge of her shoulder can be seen. Kay's smile is the bigger of the two. Helena is ready to leave.

Date: 4th June 2023. Location: Richard and Aileen's home in Richmond. Photographer: Kay Garland.

THREE
NORTH WALES, MAY 2023

When Murray proposed marriage, one of my few concerns was where he'd want us to live. I dreaded that he'd suggest a big city, because when I told him I lived in a remote part of North Wales, he thought I was kidding. But I needn't have worried: the first time he came to stay here in my little cottage, this beautiful place worked its magic. Now he said he couldn't imagine being anywhere else.

Bryn Glas, my white-walled, slate-roofed house, actually belonged to Imogen, though she hadn't lived here for decades. It was nestled by itself, in a valley overlooked by the craggy, magnificent grey-blue Carneddau mountains which lent their name to the cottage – Bryn Glas meant 'blue hill'. I'd first stayed here nearly thirty years ago as an exhausted new mum, on my knees with a baby, toddler and absent husband. Back then, Imogen let the cottage out casually to her friends. Luckily for me, she was friends with Alice, who pretty much ordered me to come here alone while she watched the children. That precious weekend was one of the shimmering memories of my life, though I spent most of the time here in glorious, healing sleep. It stopped me losing my mind. After that, the cottage always seemed to be available when I needed it. For school holidays, it was an easy place for solo-parenting when Richard was working. I'd catch glimpses of Edward and Stella running past the kitchen window, safe in the large contained garden, hear them laugh as they rocked back and forth on the swing-seat, free in the mountain air.

Later, there were the hilarious, magical visits I made here with Rose. Thinking about any of these used to make me laugh. Now she was no longer in my life, they made me want to cry. That time she brought three pounds of spuds to make dauphinoise potatoes, as if one couldn't get potatoes in Wales, but left them on the train and made crisp butties instead. Her fortieth birthday when I put candles in every room and set off the smoke alarms. The time we finally climbed up Yr Wyddfa – Snowdon – and could barely walk back down afterwards.

Bryn Glas became even more important five years ago. It was where I came after walking out on my marriage, the place that opened the door into my new life. Imogen agreed to a long let, and I'd been here ever since. I spruced it up, and converted the barn in the garden into a one-bedroom apartment for holiday rentals. While living here I'd got divorced, gone back to college, fallen in love with Murray.

The cottage was a small space for two people, but Murray slotted into my life as easy as pie. We created an office for him in the spare room, and to give him wardrobe space I packed my woollens in the loft, a brave move in North Wales, where winter could reappear at any point. And he reorganised the kitchen to make it 'properly ergonomic'. He did have the grace to call himself a pretentious figjam for that, whatever a figjam was. Different from a patootie, I think.

Organising our finances was straightforward. He didn't want to have a joint account, which surprised me, because it was all I'd known with Richard, but Murray said we should retain our independence, and I appreciated that. We agreed that he'd pay the rent, and I'd pay bills, which was pretty equitable. Making these mundane arrangements was more interesting than it sounds, because we never knew when, in the middle of a conversation, one of us would suddenly come over a bit *stirred*, and decide that now was the perfect moment to make love. If you'd told me, when I was in my arid forties, exactly how much action I'd be getting in my mid-fifties, I'd have laughed you out of the building. The honeymoon was most definitely not over, and I had the kitchen tile marks on my backside to prove it.

Murray's work involved managing rich people's boats for them, which meant a lot of travelling. Until I met him I didn't even know that was a job. He explained it to me, of course, in the early days of our courtship, but I didn't take in a great deal, unable to focus on anything other than the excitement of being with him, the joy of unexpected love. It already felt too late to ask some of the more basic questions. He said he wouldn't always have to be away so much, but spring was his busiest time, everyone wanting to refurb their boats for the summer season. Each time he returned, even if he'd only been gone a couple of days, we'd run into each other's arms and kiss like we were in a Hollywood movie. It was addictive. I don't think I had ever liked kissing anyone as much.

The sort of money his clients tossed around on fripperies was astonishing. They'd replace perfectly good fixtures and fittings because they were last season's colours, or purchase wildly expensive gadgets for a kitchen they never cooked in. A Lalique pepper grinder for £1,000? A multi-coloured Dolce and Gabbana fridge for £5,000? I loved hearing about his work, a glimpse into another world, and Murray had the happy knack of making everything into a funny story. Most evenings after dinner we just sat and chatted and laughed together. Maybe that sounded smug, but didn't I deserve this? I'd done my time with a long boring first marriage.

Only two dark clouds hovered over my lovely new life. The smaller cloud was that my photography degree was hurtling to an end, and though I'd given it my all over the last three years, I'd unsurprisingly dropped the ball lately. In a few weeks I had to hand in a proposal for the final exhibition, and I had no decent ideas for it. I'd thought of piecing together something about Dallas, but my honeymoon pictures were uninteresting, other than the ones of my handsome husband. I could hear my tutor Vanessa now, if I presented 'Dealey Plaza: Sixty Years On' using stills from the JFK assassination alongside my shots of what it looked like now (hardly any different). 'What's the relevance?' she'd say. 'What does it tell us about the world, or about you?' Well, nothing really, Vanessa, but I had to hand something in, so maybe it told us that I was in a slight panic after spending all my research time planning a wedding instead?

The big cloud, of course, was Rose. I thought about her every day, her voice through the bathroom door telling me to leave her alone playing on repeat in my head. To not be able to just pick up the phone and talk to her was… well, it was like she'd died. Like Bear. Every so often, I'd ring her number, to check I was still blocked. I did this now. The phone rang once, then gave the engaged tone and a robotic voice intoned, 'User unavailable.' Well, that was certainly true. I dropped the phone onto the table. By now I ought to have had a dozen conversations with her at least. Rose, what did you think of the wedding? Wasn't Alice awful! Did my dress work out, tell me honestly. What about Richard's speech, isn't he the giddy limit?

I imagined telling her now. Richard, standing near the wedding cake, abruptly banging his spoon against a glass. My eyes meeting Murray's, and he raising an eyebrow; me responding with a tiny shake of the head. No, I emphatically did *not* know that we were breaking convention so far as to have my ex-husband give the first speech. I prayed he wasn't planning to say something like, 'Look out, Murray, after twenty-nine years she gets restless.'

'No one has asked me to give a speech,' Richard began, and everyone laughed.

Edward called out, 'So don't, Dad!' but as you know, Rose, Richard was never short on confidence.

'Well, someone has to!' he said. 'So I want to say how honoured I am to be involved in these unusual nuptials. I've never been to a wedding in a garden! And a celebrant, not a vicar! I myself have played a part in the strangeness by taking the part of Kay's father. But there's nothing wrong with unusual, is there? So on behalf of me and my good wife, Aileen, I'd like to propose a toast to the happy couple: Kay and Murray!'

'Kay and Murray,' everyone said, raising their glasses, and despite clenching my teeth at the awkwardness of Richard's words, I enjoyed the sound of those names together. Aileen smiled adoringly at Richard, and I felt utterly grateful to her for being married to him, instead of me having to be.

Now Murray was tapping a spoon against his own glass. 'Friends, family, thank you so much for being here. Richard, thanks for kicking us off' – Murray held up his glass to Richard – 'and being so kind as to play such an important role in this wedding. Your support to Kay, and the support of the rest of our families, has taken my breath away.'

Lots of people clapped here, though not Alice.

'When my first wife, Ursula, and I separated, I thought I'd had my one shot at finding a life partner.' Murray looked briefly at the ground, then continued, 'Several years went past, and I was busy working, sharing the care of our wonderful son, Charlie. And then, as most of you know, Ursula passed away. You wouldn't think that something beautiful could come from something so terrible, but when Charlie came over here to study, we connected with Ursula's dearest friends, Rose and Kay, at a memorial dinner.'

How grateful I was to Murray for mentioning you, Rose. You were with me at the wedding in name at least. He scanned the faces for mine – I would never tire of the way he looked at me, a thirsty man who has found water at last – and raised his glass. 'I don't know what Kay sees in an old dag like me, but I'll always be grateful for it, and for her. To the lady in yellow, my beautiful bride, Kay.'

'To Kay!' everyone repeated.

Murray and Bear's son, Charlie, though pretty shy, had insisted on doing a best man's speech. Visibly uncomfortable, poor lad, he mumbled, 'Um. I can't add much. I really miss my mum, but I'm glad my dad's got another chance at happiness, and Kay definitely makes him happy.'

'Thank you, Charlie,' I whispered, wiping under my eyes quickly to deal with any rogue mascara.

We all cheered and he went even more red. Murray pulled him into a hug.

'I guess it's my turn now,' I said, tapping my own glass.

'Oh my dear, no one ever wants to hear from the bride,' Alice murmured, supportive as ever.

Ignoring her, I went through a long list of thank yous, concluding with: 'To all those who can't be here, for whatever reason, we miss you so much. Rose, I'm going to give you such a talking-to! And Ursula. Bear, I will never stop missing you.'

There was a lot more I could say about Bear, but Murray had asked me to keep to myself her expressed wishes on the matter of his remarriage. It would make a funny speech, and help explain my butter-yellow dress, but I had promised not to share it; he felt it was too personal. Instead, I finished with, 'To Murray. Thank you for...'

I wanted to say, thank you for making me believe in marriage again, or showing me what romantic love really feels like, but, mindful of who was here, I just said, 'believing in and loving me.'

. . .

As I thought of what Rose would have made of all that – how she would have laughed, and cried – a tear splashed onto my phone. I wiped it off and opened my email, to check on the unlikely possibility that she'd got in touch. She hadn't, of course she hadn't, but there was a message from the wedding photographer, enclosing the photo files and asking which ones I'd like to have prints of. Her name was Helena Chen. I knew I'd recognised her, but hadn't thought about her since Rose's text brought my wedding day to a juddering halt. The surname was different, but I knew exactly who she was. 'Helena Goodwin!' I said out loud. We'd been at university together, first time round. Almost forty years ago. How amazing! Helena Goodwin back then had been thin as a pencil, with spiky hair and a heavy hand with the eyeliner. Now she was quite curvy, with short brown hair and little make-up.

I knew I must have some old photos of her. I dragged out all my archive boxes of prints, scrabbling through them till I uncovered pictures from my distant youth. Yes! Here was Helena in the photography studio at university, circa 1987. Quite a good picture, if I said so myself. We were always using each other as models. She was sitting on a desk, her own camera held loosely in her hand, looking straight at me and laughing. I'd remembered the spikiness of her hair correctly, but not that the tips of it were dyed red. I smiled, thinking about some of the wild nights out we'd had – one in particular just before I left, with Rose and my cousin Stacey...

As if it had been staring me in the face the whole time, a fully formed plan dropped into my head. It seemed obvious, all at once, that to find out what had happened with Rose, I needed to speak to the people who knew us.

Helena.
Richard.

Cousin Stacey.

Stella.

Luca, my boyfriend before Murray.

Finally, here was something productive to tackle the big cloud. The small project cloud could wait. I took a photo of student Helena's picture and emailed it to her, explaining who I was, asking if she had time for a catch-up. Once I'd spoken to her, I'd work my way through the rest of the list.

I returned to the box of photos and found more of Helena, looking even more goth, as well as amazing ones of Rose and Bear, and cousin Stacey looking glamorous in fake fur. It was quite the trip down Memory Lane, and I got so absorbed that I practically jumped out of my skin when the front door opened and Murray called out, 'Hellooo!' Surely he couldn't be back from work already? But, my God, it was almost six o'clock. I'd lost a whole day sitting here, communing with ghosts.

'Hello, darl. You look very serious.' He put his arms round me. Ah, the warmth and comfort of him, after a solitary day navel-gazing. 'Have you managed to come up with your proposal?'

'Nearly... got some ideas brewing.' That was true, even if the ideas weren't about the project. 'How about you? Good meeting?'

'Great!' He took off his coat, then went into the kitchen, calling over his shoulder, 'I'm gagging for a decent coffee, you shoulda seen the shit they gave me. Want one?'

One of the few things Murray had brought to the marriage – he'd left nearly all his belongings behind in his house in Sydney for his tenants – was the most complicated coffee machine I'd ever seen. It had been passed on by one of his clients who'd presumably upgraded to a superior Dolce and Gabbana version. I loved the smell it produced but coffee was not my caffeine of choice.

'I'll have tea.' I followed him into the kitchen. If I left it to him he'd insist on trying to make my tea the 'proper' way in a pot. He was as bad as Rose in that regard. Damn you, Rose, would you please stay out of my head for five minutes?

'Hey, you'll like this,' Murray said, pottering about. 'This guy I met today, guess what his richest client asked for last year? Platinum towels.'

'Towels the colour of platinum?'

'Sure, that's what any sane person would think, right? So he goes to loads of trouble, gets them specially commissioned the exact Pantone shade, cost a fortune. Anyway the client goes, excuse me but what are these shitty grey things? Turns out, he thought platinum was this soft pliable material you could make towels with.'

We both laughed at the ceaseless folly of the super-wealthy.

'These rich fellas, Katie. I've said it before and I'll say it again, they're a strange bunch.' The coffee pot started bubbling and Murray poured the black liquid into a tiny glass cup. 'So, are you excited about our presents?'

We'd agreed to open the wedding presents this evening. The stash of gifts under the living room table gave me a little lurch of anxiety every time I saw them. How cross Mum would be if she knew I hadn't yet sent out thank you cards. It felt particularly important to get on with it as we – all right, me – hadn't exactly given people a wonderful day to remember. Murray tried to reassure me that most of them hadn't even noticed I was in a bit of a state towards the end of the day. I hoped he was right.

As I unwrapped a set of whisky tumblers from Anthony and his husband Kiernan, I told Murray about Helena, and my plan to meet with her. 'It feels rather providential that she's popped up now.'

'Does this have something to do with Rose-gate?' He took the box from me. 'These are nice. Crystal.'

'Rose-gate, is that what we're calling it? Yes. I'm thinking of speaking to a few people, trying to see if there's a pattern. Have I always been a rubbish friend...?'

'No way, Katie!' He kissed me. 'None of this is your fault, you're the best person I know.' He picked up another present and started opening it carefully, pulling the sticky tape off as though planning to save the paper. How cute! 'Has it ever occurred to you,' he said, working away at a stubborn piece of tape, 'that Rose might have dropped you because of me?'

Of course it had occurred to me, but it made no sense. If she had something against him, surely she would have told me up front.

'Absolutely not. You're objectively wonderful. It must be me. You just haven't known me long enough to see how rubbish I can be.'

How well do you know each other?

Unbidden, this audio-memory from my hen party flashed into my brain. *How well do you know each other?* I couldn't remember who'd said it; the party was almost entirely a blank in my mind.

'This is nice, from Charlie,' Murray said, handing me a wooden chopping board.

'That's properly useful. Hope he's getting on well.' Charlie was studying for a master's in Oxford. 'Anyway, after Helena, I'm going to contact my cousin Stacey. Do you remember I told you she turned up unexpectedly at the hen party?'

'Yes, didn't Stella invite her as a surprise?'

'It certainly was that.' Poor Stella, I'd not exactly responded the way she had hoped.

'That's why you got so thoroughly tanked that night, right? Wow, that was one hell of a hangover.'

I winced at the memory of how sick I'd been. 'A weird night all round. I feel really bad that I didn't speak to Stacey properly.'

'It must have been a shock, seeing her after so many years.'

He opened Alice's present, a set of blue towels. 'Bit dull but at least they're made of fabric.'

I examined the label – Selfridges, naturally, did Alice ever shop anywhere else?

'It was a shock, but I was incredibly awkward. Rude, really.' I opened an old-school set of dinner plates, bright pink and covered with unlikely looking birds. 'I need to apologise.' And Stacey, like Helena, would be able to give me her take on Rose-gate.

'Crikey, those are brutal,' Murray said, catching sight of the plates. 'That thank you note will be a challenge.' He looked at the tag. 'With love from Hattie and Isla. Who?'

'Aileen's daughters.' Murray looked blank. 'Richard's wife,' I clarified. His memory was almost as bad as mine. 'Talking of Richard, I'm going to ask him too, if he has any insight into Rose. He knew her pretty well. And Stella, of course.'

'I understand where you're coming from, but...' Murray hesitated. 'Well, we don't want you being sad all the time, Katie darl, do we? Look how you were after Winchester. Bloody inconsolable. If you keep picking the scab, it's going to keep bleeding.'

Had I been banging on about Rose too much? Yes, probably. I didn't want my lovely new husband thinking I was a misery-guts. I should keep it to myself a bit more. I picked up a blue gift bag and read the label. It said: *To be opened by Kay only when she is on her own.* I stared at it, confused.

'On the subject of Richard...' Murray held up a tartan woollen blanket, presumably chosen by Aileen. 'Rather nice for these cool Welsh nights.'

I looked round for my tea which would now be the right temperature, but I'd left it in the kitchen. 'I'll get my...'

'Sit down. I'll heat it up for you in the microwave.'

'Oh there's no...' But he had gone. I shook my head, resigned to scorched tea, and looked again at the puzzling label. I didn't recognise the writing. It was probably something embarrassing in the vibrator or saucy underwear line from my student friends. But no – inside the bag was a large envelope, which I nearly dropped in astonishment when I opened it to reveal a massive wad of red fifty-pound notes. I'd never seen so much money in one place; it must be several thousand. It was like something from a heist movie. I blinked, but it was still there. What the hell?

I read the instruction again. *To be opened by Kay only when she is on her own.* I turned the envelope over, and in the same unfamiliar hand, the sender had written: *Every new bride needs a secret account. Don't tell him!*

What?!

I sat there dumbly, money in one hand, envelope in the other, not a clue in my head. Then I heard the microwave ping, and shoved everything back in the bag and slid it under a cushion. My immediate thought was Rose. It wasn't her handwriting, though she could have got someone else to write it for her. But Rose didn't have that sort of money. She'd let Tim keep everything when they divorced – 'I just want to be free' – and Graham was a schoolteacher before retirement, not an investment banker or something. And anyway, it would make no sense to cut off ties with me, then send such a gift.

Who, then? Imogen was the only really wealthy person I knew, and giving me a nest egg was the sort of darling thing she might do. But why would she want me to keep it secret from Murray?

Richard? Surely not. He'd have made a big deal of it, ideally with an audience. He'd have written a cheque with his Montblanc fountain pen, while cracking jokes about the cost of getting shot of wives these days.

Murray came back in with my tea which was sending up alarming steam signals. 'Here you go, sweetheart. Right, where were we?' He picked up another gift and started opening it. 'It's like Christmas, isn't it?'

Should I tell him about the money? I didn't know. I took a confused gulp of tea and nearly took the roof of my mouth off. Thoughts were ricocheting around my head like a pinball. When we'd finished, and Murray turned on the TV to watch the news, I took the envelope upstairs and buried it at the bottom of my T-shirt drawer. I had more than enough already on my mind. It could wait there until I had the capacity to deal with it. Whenever that might be.

FOUR

LAST ENCOUNTER WITH HELENA: LONDON, JULY 1988

Though the floor and tables were sticky, and the queue to get drinks long, the Rezz was the most popular Saturday night student hang-out. It was cheap and buzzy, with disorienting flashing coloured lights that made a drunk person feel even drunker. Being there while stone-cold sober was not ideal, but Stacey was determined to have a wild night out in London and I didn't want to disappoint her. The minute we got into the club, Stacey ordered me to get her a 'very strong' drink. She tried to drag Rose and Helena onto the dancefloor, but they both resisted, so Stacey tottered off on her own, flinging herself into the writhing mass of dancers, behaving exactly as you'd expect from someone who'd sunk half a bottle of vodka before coming out.

At the bar I had to shout my order three times to get heard. Beer for the others, lemonade for me. I hoped Helena wouldn't notice my soft drink as I brought them to our table, but she did, of course. She was, as our photography tutor Howard often said, extremely observant.

'No booze?'

'Taking it slow.'

'Fair enough, you've got to look after your cousin. She's quite the handful.'

Stacey had turned up out of the blue yesterday afternoon. 'Finally got Ma to fucking babysit for a whole weekend and I am ready for action!' It was terrible timing, but it wasn't her fault – she didn't know it was my last weekend at university. Hardly anyone knew. And actually she was a useful distraction, stopping me having to think too much about the fact that I was leaving for good.

She'd made no end of fuss about the 'boring' evening I gave her last night at the student bar, and Richard and I had taken her to lunch today in an allegedly 'elderly' restaurant. She'd been loudly insistent that we go somewhere more happening tonight. I'd brought Rose and Helena in for backup, but I was starting to regret this, as they didn't know each other well, and the conversation was stilted. Throw in Stacey at her loudest, wearing a tiny skirt and boob tube, and the whole evening felt weird and difficult. I wished I *was* drinking.

Stacey flopped back into our booth, all mussed-up hair and sweat. 'So hot out there!' She glugged down half her beer in one go.

'Isn't that the bloke you used to go out with?' Helena said to me, nodding towards the club's entrance, where a group of lads were coming in.

'Ooh, where?' Stacey gasped.

Helena pointed out David Endevane while I attempted to make myself invisible. Rose sent me a sympathetic look – she was the only person who knew how upset I'd been when we split.

'He's *gorgeous*,' Stacey said.

'But you know, Richard's a lovely bloke,' Rose said, loyally.

'Bet those cheekbones photograph well,' Helena said.

My eyes bored into Rose, willing her to change the subject,

and she started talking about her relief that the exams were over.

'Dunno why you'd actually *choose* to do exams,' Stacey said. 'Had more than enough at school.'

'But we get the long summers,' Helena said. 'I'm going to Italy for a month, taking photos and drinking wine.'

'You lot are so lucky,' Stacey said, knocking Rose's drink over. 'Whoops. I get one crappy weekend, then I have to go be Mummy-Wifey again. Oh, I love this song!' She jumped up, and we watched her weave back to the dancefloor.

'She's hammered,' Helena said, shaking her head. 'We could sneak out, go somewhere quieter. She'd probably not notice for ages.'

Rose laughed. 'I was thinking the same.'

'You two go, I'll stay,' I said. 'I feel responsible for her.'

'She's eight years older than us!' Rose said.

'Only in actual years, not in maturity,' Helena said.

I was glad they were bonding, but felt bad for Stacey. 'She's been feeling cooped up. She's just letting her hair down.'

'That's the thing if you have a kid so young.' Helena got up. 'I'll get another round. Beer this time, Kay?'

'Um, sure.'

When she'd gone, Rose gave me a look. 'I thought you were going to tell her?'

'I am. But she's going to be so pissed off. We're meant to be doing the final year placement together.'

'Well, don't say that bit then, soft lad. But at least tell her you're preggers, so she stops buying you alcohol.'

Rose knew nearly everything. She knew I was pregnant, she knew I was planning to marry Richard, she knew I was going to leave university before the final year. But there was one thing she didn't know. Only Richard, David and I knew.

'Quick, while she's gone. What did your tutor say yesterday?'

'He wasn't happy.'

Howard was a strident feminist who generally made most of us women in his class feel that they were constantly letting down the Pankhursts. 'Now come on, Kay. I can't have promising women photographers dropping out on me just because they've got a bun in the oven!'

I couldn't look at his disappointed face. I stared instead at the photos on the walls behind him. Some were his, extraordinary portraits where he had gone right into the soul of the sitters. And a few were favourite pictures taken by his students. There was one of mine, a black and white portrait of David. The lighting was excellent, though those cheekbones would look good no matter who was behind the camera. Ironic to have him staring down at me, given the situation.

The more Howard outlined my many options, ranging from abortion to the university creche to taking a year off, the more it felt like we were talking about someone else. Imagine Richard's face if I said, thanks for stepping in and marrying me, Rich, and by the way, I'll be leaving the baby soon as he's born so I can go back to being a student. Hardly!

Anyway, most people who studied photography didn't even go into it as a career, why should I be one of the lucky few? I wasn't anything special, I had a good eye but little else. I'd probably end up working in a shop anyway, so I might as well do that in the stationery shop that Richard was planning to open. At least then we'd be supporting each other and our new little family. My future was with Richard, who'd rescued me, not here, playing with film and developing fluid.

'Howard asked if I wanted him to arrange for me to see a medical professional,' I told Rose now.

'And what did you say?'

'Well, Rose, you know I couldn't...'

She didn't say anything, and I hoped she didn't feel I was judging her. She'd had a termination last year and I'd been totally supportive. It just wasn't right for me. It was partly being Catholic, though of course, Rose was Catholic too. But I also couldn't bear to upset Mum, particularly not now, when she was still grieving Dad. Rose would say that I didn't have to tell her, but I found it impossible to keep things from her.

There was another reason, one I couldn't tell Rose, because she naturally thought, as did everyone, that Richard was the baby's father. The only person I could potentially tell was Bear, but I could imagine her response, furiously scratched biro on the letter that landed on my mat every other month. She'd press so hard she'd likely rip the flimsy blue airline paper. *Can't bear to get rid of David's child? When he didn't think twice about dumping you when you told him? Christ, Kay, you are the crown princess of idiots! What the hell is the matter with you?* or words to that effect. What *was* the matter with me? I suppose nothing more unusual than that predictable old malaise, unrequited love.

Helena returned and we clanked our drinks together, a toast to having finished the second year. I hoped Helena's legendary observation skills would be dulled enough by beer to not notice that I didn't touch mine, and that whenever she looked away, Rose took a big glug from my glass.

There was a huge upsurge of noise from the dance floor, and we all turned in its direction. It was centred round a woman who was dancing wildly, dementedly, on the stage next to the DJ.

'Kay, that's not... is it...?' Rose said.

I stood up to see better. The woman's boob tube was pushed down to her waist. 'Oh no, no, no.'

The three of us ran towards the stage. A large group were surrounding Stacey, cheering her on. As I tried to push through the crowd, the DJ pulled the plug on the music, but Stacey kept on dancing to some inner tune. A bouncer moved me out of his way as easily as if I was a blade of grass, and did the same to everyone else in his path until he reached the stage, vaulted onto it, grabbed Stacey round the legs and flung her over his shoulder. She kicked and flailed but he didn't react at all, simply jumped down from the stage with her, walked through the baying crowd and dumped her onto a chair. I followed them, along with dozens of rubberneckers, arriving in time to hear the bouncer shouting at her, 'No tits! Do you want to cause a riot?'

Stacey covered her chest with folded arms and stared at him defiantly. 'Everyone's got tits!' she yelled.

I handed her my denim jacket which she reluctantly put on.

The DJ started to play some quieter music and, sensing the show was over, the people around us wandered off.

The bouncer turned to me. 'Get her home, please.'

'We only just got here,' Stacey cried. 'You're a massive spoilsport!' She tried to pull the two sides of my jacket together – it was too small for her – and said, 'What the fuck's this in your pocket? S'heavy.' She pulled out my red Swiss Army knife which I took everywhere.

'You can't bring in knives,' the bouncer said, grabbing it out of her hand. 'What the hell is the matter with you?'

'It's mine.' I held out my hand.

'It's confiscated.'

'But it was my dad's...'

'Shouldn't have brought it in, should you?'

'Is everything all right, Kay?' a male voice said next to me, and I turned to look into the stunning blue eyes of David Endevane. Could this night get any worse?

'I'm fine,' Stacey told him, as though he'd asked her. She grabbed my arm. 'You're right, he *does* look like that whatshisname, from that band you like, Kay.'

My face flared in shocked embarrassment. 'Let's get you out of here.'

'You remember! You told me he looks like him. Japan!' she

said triumphantly. 'You know who I mean, don't you?' She grabbed the collar of David's shirt.

'David Sylvian?' he said, his eyes on me.

'That's it, Kay, isn't it?!'

The earth sure was taking its time in swallowing me up.

'Well, Kay looks like Jane Birkin, don't you think?' David said.

I didn't know who that was, and he'd never said it before, when we were dating, if you could call it dating if you never left the bedroom. And I also didn't know why he was acting like everything was fine between us. I felt like screaming.

David was basking in the attention from Stacey, an older, half-naked woman, and puffed himself up. 'Maybe I can help.'

'Yes! Help me!' Stacey pointed to the bouncer. 'Can you tell this dickhead that I only want to dance?'

'You've had your dance, love,' the bouncer said. 'Now I need you all to fuck off.'

'Come on, man, she was only having a laugh…' David said, as if he was really going to square up to this enormous bloke. The bouncer took one step towards David and he backed away. 'All right, all right.'

The bouncer pulled Stacey to her feet, surprisingly gently, then began walking her towards the exit. He didn't even seem to notice her hitting out at him while yelling, 'Gerroff!'

I turned my back on David. 'You don't have to leave,' I said to Rose and Helena. 'I'll go with her.'

'No way,' Rose said. 'You'll need help.'

'Let me…' David said.

'Please don't,' I said, but too quietly for him to hear. Helena did, though.

'I'll be along in a minute,' she said. As Rose and I followed Stacey, I heard Helena say to David, 'Get lost, there's a good fellow. No one wants you.'

Rose and I caught up with the bouncer as he was escorting

Stacey outside. 'Look after her, yeah?' he said, as he went back into the club.

We each took one of Stacey's arms and tried to get her walking. She didn't make it easy, wriggling like a bag of eels, constantly turning round to try to go back the way we'd come. When she wasn't making steering impossible, she was yelling into the night about how London was 'as shit as Hoylake!'

Rose laughed. 'We never got thrown out of a club in Hoylake.'

A car slowed down alongside us and an older man leaned out of the window. 'All right, ladies, want a lift?'

'Yeah!' Stacey said, weaving towards him. 'Back to the Rezz!'

I pulled her back. 'No thanks, we're OK.'

'She looks cold,' he said, his eyes all over Stacey's inadequately dressed body. 'I can warm you up in here, honey.'

'Go away!' I yelled, but the man laughed.

There were running feet behind us, and Helena's voice called out, 'Hey, you! Piss off and leave them alone.'

'Lezzers, are you?'

'Yes!' Rose and Helena yelled together.

'I'm not!' Stacey cried.

'Don't fucking dress like tarts if you're not tarts,' he said, and drove off with a screech of brakes.

'He was nice,' Rose said, making Helena laugh, but Stacey was too far gone for sarcasm.

'He had a car, it would be nice to be in a car.'

With Helena behind Stacey, a hand on her back keeping her steady, we moved considerably quicker, though every time a car went past, Stacey waved and yelled as though she were being kidnapped. Finally, Helena told her to stop, in a voice that brooked no argument.

'Hey!' Stacey said abruptly. 'What happened to that man? The dishy one?'

Rose glanced at me. 'David? The blond idiot?'

'No, the one in the jacket, with the funny laugh. He bought me chicken salad.'

'Richard,' I said. 'He told you at lunch, Stacey, he couldn't come out. He's got to study for his exams.' Not that Richard would have been seen dead in the Rezz.

'He was nice to me. Hey, Kay. Kay's friends. Shall I tell you something. A little secret?'

'Yeah, go on then,' Rose said.

'If you keep walking in a more or less straight line,' Helena added.

She twisted in our grasp so she could see my face. 'I don't love Steven.'

'Oh Stace, of course you do! He's your husband.'

'Don't be so naive.' It came out, in her slurring, as 'snive'. 'I don't. I don't like him. I love someone else.'

'No, you don't.'

'I do. Ivan, my boss. I really, really, oops!' – she stumbled and nearly fell over – 'really love him.'

'Lucky he can't see you now,' Helena muttered.

At last we got her back to the house Rose and I shared with four others, and we tipped her into my bed. I'd sleep on the sofa. I made tea and toast for Helena and Rose, and we sat in the kitchen laughing about our wild Saturday night. After a while, Rose went up to bed, giving me a look – tell her! – as she went out.

'Sorry it was such a terrible evening,' I said to Helena.

'Not your fault. And it was nice to get to know Rose a bit better. Hey, nearly forgot – I got this for you.' She took the Swiss Army knife out of her pocket.

'Oh Helena, how did you manage that?' I felt myself well up; it was such a precious object, one of the few things of my dad's that I had.

'Asked politely,' she said, with a grin.

Her calm, firm voice had worked wonders on Stacey. I could see how it might have worked on the bouncer too.

'I have something to tell you,' I said, putting another piece of toast on her plate. 'I'm pregnant.'

'Well, honey, I'm pretty sure it's not mine.'

I laughed, not only at her joke but at her calm response. How I wished I could be as unruffled, as sure of myself, as her. 'It's Richard's.' I barely blinked as I said those words.

'The fella doing the MBA who looks like a banker?' She looked surprised.

'They're encouraged to wear suits on their course.'

'That's why you weren't drinking, right?' So she *had* noticed. 'I guess you're planning to keep it?'

I nodded, and wondered how to tell her I was going to be leaving tomorrow, and not coming back.

Then she said, 'Don't turn your life upside down, will you?'

'Well, I...'

'Look at your cousin. Cautionary tale if ever I saw one. Married to a husband she can't stand, got a kid she doesn't like, falling all over town with her boobs out because life didn't turn out like it says in Mills & Boon.' Helena stood up. 'Men come, and men go. You have to put your friends first, cos without them, you got nothing. Sisters before misters.'

I'd not heard that phrase before and it made me smile. 'Sisters before misters,' I repeated. I stood too, and impulsively gave her a hug. Rose was right; I didn't have to tell Helena I was leaving, but it did mean that only one of us knew that we wouldn't be seeing each other again for quite a while.

FIVE
RICHMOND, JUNE 2023

Remember during Covid when you couldn't hug and kiss people? Those strange days of keeping your distance, bumping elbows? There was little I missed about that time, but occasionally one did wish for a bit less social embracing.

Murray and I were back down south, and in my old marital home, no less. Stella and her business partner, Nita, were moving to Italy for six months to attend a prestigious cookery school, and Richard had declared he'd give them 'a jolly good send-off'. The scene that greeted us as we entered the house was the exact opposite of lockdown: more like a student party, in vibe, if not age group. The hall was jammed with middle-aged women, awash with Prosecco and good cheer, and there were people all the way up the stairs. I didn't recognise anyone, but that didn't seem to matter; squeezing my way along the hall was one rolling passage of being boozily kissed and exclaimed over. There was absolutely no possibility of offering up a hopeful elbow to bump. I lost sight of Murray, and when I eventually made it to the kitchen, I was as damp around the cheeks as if I'd been through a car wash.

'My God,' I spluttered as I hugged Stella, the first person I'd seen that I actively wanted to kiss. 'Who are all those people out there?'

She opened the oven door. 'I told Dad not to overdo it. Next thing he's telling me we need food for two hundred.'

'Wow, he's changed his tune about entertaining. What's happened to the man?' But I knew the answer: Aileen, his second wife. It was hard not to feel offended, as though I'd been responsible for holding him back.

'I made him cap it at a hundred, but they all seem to be in the hall for some reason. It's mostly Nita's family, though Aileen's also invited loads.' She put a tray of stuffed aubergines in the oven.

'A bit rum you're stuck with the cooking at your own do, darling.'

'Oh, I wanted to – I love it.'

'This is a banging party,' Murray said, laughing as he came into the room, pink-faced. 'I've just been snogged by a dozen drunken ladies in spangly frocks.'

Stella greeted him warmly and handed him a plate of arancini. 'I know you like these.'

'I do, very much,' Murray said. 'Delicious, Stella. You should be a chef.'

'Haha. These are poor imitations. Wait till I've learned the authentic version in Naples.'

'It's wonderful that your business is doing well enough to leave while you're away,' Murray said.

'The catering will be in Yelena's safe hands.' Stella nodded at an earnest-looking young woman slicing spring onions. 'And Newland will keep an eye on the admin.'

Newland was Stella's long-term boyfriend. I was terribly fond of him. 'He's not going to Italy with you?'

'He can't leave his job for six months, Mum. That was never the plan.' Stella turned to greet Nita, who'd just come in, her arms full of coats.

'My relatives all think I'm the cloakroom attendant,' Nita said, laughing. 'Oh, hello Mrs Bright, sorry, Mrs, oh no, I don't know your new name!' She blushed as she dumped the coats on a chair and gave me a hug.

'To be honest, I'm not completely used to my new name either. It's Garland, like Judy,' I said, but she looked puzzled at the archaic reference. 'You've known me long enough to call me Kay, anyway. How are you, Nita?'

'I'm fine.' She looked at Stella, who shook her head. I was briefly caught in the middle of this non-verbal exchange, then Stella went to the fridge.

'I'll top you guys up,' she said, pulling out a bottle.

'Let me get that,' Richard said, as he came into the kitchen. He had an eighteenth-century belief that a woman shouldn't have to deal with the tricky business of pouring wine. 'Ah, Kay! And Murray! So glad you could come.' Richard went straight into the blokey bonhomie mode that Murray seemed to trigger in him. He actually slapped him on the back before kissing my cheek. 'Gracious, Kayla, your face is sweaty.'

'Actually it's sweat mixed with other people's saliva.'

'Charming.' He poured so much wine into my glass that it spilled down the side, and my ex-wifely instincts told me he was already a couple of sheets to the wind. 'So this is lovely, isn't it? Sending our girl off in style.'

I glanced at Stella – she always appreciated an ironic wink at Richard's more bombastic tendencies – but she was looking at Nita. As I watched, she reached out and touched Nita's arm, and I hastily turned back to Richard. He easily took over the crowded room, and oh God, now here was Aileen, floaty in pastels, bustling in bosom first like a schooner. I was trapped against a wall, and couldn't avoid a squashy hug from her. Oh elbow bumping, wither art thou? What with all the people, and the ovens blasting away, I had to hope I wouldn't get one of my occasional hot flushes, or I'd have no choice but to shove everyone aside and climb into the freezer.

I half-listened to Richard and Aileen chat to Murray about his upcoming trip to Monaco, but my focus was on Stella as she gave instructions to her sous chefs. What was going on between her and Newland? Surely living apart from him for half a year was not a good sign. She might be nearly thirty, but I'd always been watchful of her, making sure to check in regularly. Of course, those check-ins had lately fallen off a cliff. What had I failed to notice these last few months, while I was caught up in the whirlwind of courtship?

'Sparkle.' I grabbed her hand and pulled her into my corner. 'Are you OK? You look stressed.'

'Of course I'm stressed! We're going in two days. I only found my passport yesterday after turning the flat upside down. At least Piet's finally found the three of us a decent apartment.'

Piet was Nita's boyfriend. How come he got to go, but not Newland? That made it seem even worse, that it wasn't just the girls together.

'Kayla,' Richard called over to me. 'Do make time for Mum, won't you? She wants to talk to you, and has some idea that you'll try to avoid her.'

'I probably will, to be fair.' I hadn't seen Alice yet in the melee, but no doubt she was holding court somewhere.

'Oh, Kay, honestly!'

'Do you know what it's about?'

He shook his head. 'No idea.'

But suddenly it came to me. The mystery cash! Though not properly rich like Imogen, Alice was extremely comfortable. Those boomers and their savings! Though why would she give me money? She'd never been my biggest fan. Perhaps she wanted to pre-empt the possibility of me claiming my share of the family home. Because where would she go, if Richard sold up? It must be cushy here, Aileen doubtless indulging her in a way I'd never been willing to do. Or maybe it was less self-serving. Maybe she felt bad about her behaviour towards me, regretted her decades-long and loudly articulated belief that I'd trapped her son into marrying beneath him. Could the money be an overdue attempt at reparation?

I took a steadying slug of wine and went to find her. As I forced my way out of the kitchen, Richard and Murray were talking about yacht specifications, and Aileen was looking from one to the other, ready to jump in if Richard took a sudden notion to buy a boat. The living room was crowded but a lot cooler, and I could see Alice in the corner, talking to someone. When I reached her she grabbed my arm – no damp kisses from her, mercifully – and pulled me down onto the sofa next to her.

'Kathleen, *finally*,' she said, an echo of her big moment at my wedding. 'Now sit there and don't move.'

'Sorry, Mrs Bright. Please don't put me in detention.'

Alice made a rolled-eyes, I'm-going-to-rise-above-this face – I'd seen that expression a lot – and introduced me to the woman she'd been talking to. But I already knew who it was.

'Helena, this is my ex-daughter-in-law. How modern that sounds! In my day we didn't have ex-daughters-in-law, or if we did, we certainly didn't mingle with them socially.'

'Helena!' I burst out. 'I'm so bloody pleased to see you at last.'

'*Must* you?' Alice shook her head. 'I'm so sorry, Kathleen enjoys the shock of the swear.'

I turned to Alice. 'Helena and I were friends at university! My first time, back in the eighties.'

'I *know* that,' Alice said impatiently, though I didn't see how she could possibly have.

Helena looked uncomfortable. 'Sorry I didn't reply to your email.'

'I expect you're incredibly busy with work, aren't you?' I

had of course looked at her website, which was full of her gorgeous photos of beautiful places and famous people.

She waved a modest hand. 'I'm doing OK.'

'There's so much I want to ask,' I said.

I glanced at Alice and she took the hint. 'I need a top-up.' She pointed at me in her imperious way. 'We'll speak shortly.' She walked off remarkably quickly for someone in their eighties.

'She's a scream, isn't she?' Helena said. 'Like someone playing a dowager duchess. Well, this is wild, isn't it! How long has it been? Thanks for sending that amazing old photo.'

'You look exactly the same,' I fibbed.

'I don't at all, but you really do,' she said.

Well, if that was true, surely she must have recognised me at the wedding?

'We're the "don't look it" generation, aren't we?' she went on.

'Don't look it...?'

'Our age! When my mother was in her fifties, she was already an old lady. We're very different.'

Rose had once said the same thing about her own mother, who had descended into premature old age by means of a woollen shawl. All those shared memories, and no one to share them with.

I asked Helena if she was here to take photos, and she smiled. 'No, I'm here on a social basis. I got friendly with Aileen a couple of years ago, when she hired me to take pictures for the website. Then she asked me to do your wedding. I didn't know it was you, of course – I had no idea you were Richard's ex-wife.'

'What was Aileen's website that you did photos for?'

'Oh, for their online shop.'

Well, that was a slap in the face. For almost three decades,

I'd been the manager of the biggest of Richard's chain of stationery shops. And for about fifteen years, I'd failed to convince him to set up an online store.

'Aileen's project, really,' Helena said. 'She's a force of nature, isn't she?'

'Did you take any photos at Quiller Queen?' I asked. There was a lump in my stupid throat, but for God's sake, why? I had been *thrilled* to walk away from that bloody shop, an albatross around my neck.

'Yes, most of them as it's the biggest of the shops.'

I fought back the urge to say, I bloody well know that! I know every square centimetre of it! I swallowed down the lump and said, 'It's so wonderful that you made a real career in photography.'

'Oh, yes. It's what I always wanted to do.'

It was what I had always wanted to do too. I'd thought that maybe at last it was starting to happen, but who was I kidding? You needed years of experience, like Helena, to make a decent living at it.

'I restarted my degree a few years ago,' I told her. 'Nearly finished. Better late than never!'

'Gosh, good for you. It can't be easy going back to the classroom.'

'Most of the others are young enough to be my kids. And it's very different, all the digital stuff, Photoshop. And no final year placements, alas.'

'That's a shame. My placement with Zander Parkes was my big start. Shit, you were meant to do that with me, weren't you? Zan was a star. He hired me after graduation, and I had ten fabulous years travelling with him, before I set up on my own in New York.'

It was lucky she couldn't see the jealous green mist swirling inside my head. But probably she'd had this glittering career at the expense of a private life. 'Did you ever marry?'

'Yes, and then some! Three times. Third time's the charm, I hope. He and I moved back here, we live in Stoke Newington near my photography studio, and I teach at the University of East London, oh and we've a child, Martha, bit of a late one, I was forty-three, so she's nearly fourteen, what a nightmare, wants a tattoo already...'

As she burbled on, I had to hold on to the edges of my chair to stop myself falling headlong into an alternative universe. This was *my* life, if I hadn't got pregnant and abandoned my degree. Helena launched a proper career, and had a whole life before having a child. I'd done everything the wrong way round, and was trying to have my interesting life now when it was, if not too late exactly, then certainly close enough to be able to read the 'It's too late' sign from here.

As I came out of my green-mist reverie I heard her say, 'Have you approached photographers for internships?'

'At my advanced age?'

'It's about the person, their talent. One of my best assistants was in her sixties,' Helena said. 'Her end-of-year degree show was superb.'

'Oh blimey, my show's in a couple of months, and it's still a bit under-baked.'

'Well, you ought to crack on with it. It's your calling card, you know?'

I hadn't thought about it like that. I told myself firmly I would 'crack on' the minute I got home.

Helena sat back in her chair. 'I often wondered what happened to you.' Her tone had lost its lightness. 'You disappeared off the face of the earth.'

She was right: I'd ghosted her. Not that ghosting was a concept back then. I'd completely dropped out of her life, after being very close.

'I'm really sorry, I didn't mean to, I just couldn't face telling you I was leaving.'

'We were young.' She did a sort of half-laugh. 'It's a self-obsessed age, isn't it, the early twenties.'

Oh God. She still seemed sore about it. 'I was very self-absorbed, you're right,' I said. 'Absorbed' sounded better than 'obsessed'.

'I did see that friend of yours around occasionally, after you left. Rose, wasn't it? She told me when your baby was born.'

My heart started beating faster. So Helena remembered Rose.

'The baby must be completely grown up now.'

'He's over there, talking to Alice.' I pointed at them.

Helena gasped. 'How is that possible? He's almost middle-aged!'

At the wedding I'd reflected that Edward had also been present at my first one, admittedly only in bump form. Extraordinary that he was now thirty-five. How fast things went. You blinked, and your baby was an adult.

'He's got two children, twin boys. My grandchildren. There's one.' I waved at Jamie, who was sitting under the table, demolishing Stella's homemade doughnuts. He hadn't noticed me before, so intent was he on the food, and he came haring over, threw sticky arms round me, planted a strawberry-jam kiss on my nose, told me he loved me, and ran off. Laughing, I dabbed my face with a tissue, and was surprised when I looked back at Helena to see that she seemed emotional, her eyes glistening.

'Talking of friends,' I said. I needed to be quick; Alice had begun her stately way round the room. 'I've got a bit of a situation. With Rose, in fact. Long story short, she's dropped me.'

Helena raised her eyebrows. 'Sounds familiar.'

Ouch. 'She didn't disappear; she told me not to get in touch with her ever again.'

'Wow!' Her eyes widened. 'What did you do?'

'I'm trying to find out. And I'm wondering... you knew Rose a little, you knew me. You and I didn't have a proper end to our friendship.' I stopped. It seemed daft to think she'd have any insight into two people she'd last seen more than three decades ago.

'What are you asking, Kay?'

'I'm not sure...' What I really wanted to ask was, how much of an arse was I to Helena, and did she think I might have been a similar arse to Rose? But Helena was looking at me with something like disdain.

'This sounds the sort of thing you should explore in therapy.'

I rolled my eyes. 'My daughter's always saying that.'

'I don't think I'd be here now, if not for my therapist back in the 2000s. Best thing I ever did.' Helena smiled broadly. I started to smile back, then realised she was looking behind me to Alice, who had silently joined us. 'Afraid I have to head off. Early start tomorrow. A baby blessing, followed by a celebrity chef I can't name, for their latest cookbook.' Helena stood up without catching my eye, though I was desperately trying to catch hers. She must think me a complete crazer.

'That sounds fascinating, doesn't it, Kathleen?' Alice said, putting a bony hand on my shoulder.

'I'm in London for a couple more days, if you fancied meeting up,' I said urgently to Helena, trying to signal that I was sincere and not bonkers. Whatever her opinion of me, I didn't want this to be the final word. She'd known me when I was young, and I had so few people left who I could say that about.

'I'm afraid I can't.' Damn it. I'd been too intense, and put her off for good. 'Heading to Leicester tomorrow for a few days – a dull but lucrative job for a building society.'

Let no one say I could take a hint. 'Could we get a quick selfie?' I asked, partly because I wanted evidence that we had reconnected, even if she couldn't get away fast enough, and partly to shake the bony hand of doom off my shoulder.

'Now there's a clear sign that we're in different photography generations!' Helena's smile was a little patronising, but she graciously put her face next to mine, and we smiled performatively into my phone camera.

'Great to see you,' she said, looking at Alice, and then she went out.

Alice sat in Helena's vacated seat, her back as straight as a ruler. 'Extraordinary that you two were contemporaries,' she said. 'She's so vibrant, isn't she? Well, at last we're *finally* getting to chat.'

Despite everything, I felt a bit sorry for Alice. She was starting to look her age, and her hand shook as she picked up her glass. She'd made some of my life miserable, it was true. Though Richard and I had made it to almost thirty years together, I knew she saw our divorce as vindication of her initial opinion that I wasn't good enough for him. But she had been kind, in her brisk way, when the children were little, and been a terrific grandmother, especially to Stella. Without her, I'd never have met Imogen, never have found my life-long home in Bryn Glas.

'I'm here now. What was it you wanted to tell me?'

'Oh, at your rather odd nuptials?'

'We call it a wedding in this century.'

She raised an eyebrow. 'It's utterly passé now. I was going to tell you that the photographer was your old friend, but we have rather moved on from that, haven't we? Now there's something else I want to discuss.'

'Hang on, you knew about Helena at the wedding? How come?'

'Well, when she arrived I offered her a glass of champagne, and we were sitting together when she saw you walk past with your Australian gentleman, if that's not an oxymoron, and she went quite white. She asked your name, then insisted I try to recall your maiden name, which I must confess, was not close to the front of my mind.'

'Hurst.' Bloody hell! I'd been right that Helena had known who I was from the start.

'Luckily Richard was able to furnish us with that detail.' Alice smiled, a cat toying with a nearly dead mouse. 'Helena indicated that you had been rather a swine back when you were students together. Dropped her, apparently, with no more consideration than one drops an orange rind into the compost.'

'Colourful analogy,' I said. I wondered why, if Helena was still annoyed with me, she'd come here tonight, when she knew I'd be attending?

'When she left the wedding, after your histrionics...'

'After my *what*?'

'Kathleen, dear, you must know that after you received that curt message from Rose, you went rather Violetta at the end of *Traviata*.'

'I was upset, Alice.'

'We all got that. Anyway, Helena said she would reconnect with you at a more felicitous point. And that brings us neatly to tonight.'

'So *that's* what you wanted to tell me at the wedding? That Helena was my old friend?'

'Yes, but you really didn't want to be bothered with me.' Alice put on such a woebegone expression that I had to bite my lip not to laugh.

'I'm terribly sorry.' I straightened my face. 'Actually, there's something I want to ask you.'

'Oh yes?' She leaned forward.

'About the money.'

'What money? What are you talking about?' Her eyes were popping out of her head, and I could immediately see exactly how wrong a tree I was barking up.

'Nothing really. I was sent some money as a wedding present, but...'

'For heaven's sake, you thought I'd give you money?' Alice sat back and croaked out one of her rare laughs. 'One of us is crackers, and I don't think it's me. How much?'

Though I hadn't counted it yet, I certainly didn't want to give her a sense of how much it might be. 'About a grand.'

She laughed again. That laugh was getting way more exercise than usual; I hoped she'd done a warm-up first or she'd do herself a mischief. 'You thought *I'd* send *you* one thousand pounds?'

Cross with myself more than her, I said, 'You're right, Alice. It was a very silly thought from a very silly person.'

Her smile turned off like a light switch. 'That's hardly headline news, is it? "Kathleen is being silly." You could announce that every day. I cannot believe you are talking about money when right under your nose there is something extremely troubling, in your *very own family*.'

She sipped her wine, eyes boring into mine. Great, I was absolutely in the mood for a guessing game. 'What am I meant to have noticed?'

'I see I will have to spell it out.' I'd known Alice so long, I could tell, despite the exasperated expression, that she was enjoying herself. 'Have you not noticed what's going on with your daughter?'

'What about her?' I sat up. What did Alice know about Stella? Why did she know more than me?

'You don't think there's anything odd about her leaving her partner for six months?'

'Well, yes, I have been thinking it's a bit...'

'You haven't noticed how touchy she is? Regularly close to tears?' Alice examined the small amount of wine left in her glass. 'Mind you, you have been rather *unavailable* lately, haven't you?'

'Have you spoken to her? Has she told you she and Newland are having problems?'

Alice leaned away from me in mock alarm. 'Heavens, Kathleen, must you be so *Play for Today* about it? Of course I haven't asked her, I wouldn't dream of intruding. If she wants us to know, she will speak up.' She drank the last of her wine. 'You're having rather a time of it, aren't you, with your nearest and dearest? Any word from Rose yet?'

Hard to believe I'd been feeling sorry for her ten minutes ago. I stood up, wanting to ask Richard if Stella had said anything to him. But Alice grabbed my wrist. 'Try not to barge in with both feet, won't you, dear?'

I pulled out of her grip – she was remarkably strong – and hurried back to the kitchen. Richard was still there, being ebullient with Newland. There was no sign of Stella. I greeted Newland warmly, and scanned his face for evidence of domestic problems. But he seemed his usual urbane self.

'I was just saying' – Richard turned to me, breathing alcohol into my face – 'these girls don't need to learn Italian cuisine, do they?' He patted Newland on the back with enough force to make him stagger slightly. 'Did you taste that pannacotta? Incredible.'

I could see that Richard had descended from a couple of sheets to the wind to the full linen cupboard. 'Rich, could I have a word?'

Newland, the soul of discretion, melted away, but I couldn't risk speaking here, with Stella likely to appear any moment.

'Talk away,' Richard boomed, waving his glass around and spilling wine on the countertop. 'Always got time for my lovely first wife.'

I took the glass out of his hand, on the pretext of topping it up, then left it on the counter. 'Can we go somewhere private?'

We went upstairs, past the aunties in the hall, who were having a considerably better party than me. Richard led me, not into our old bedroom, thankfully, but into what had once been Edward's room, and was now apparently Aileen's sewing parlour. There were rolls of fabric everywhere, and the bed was covered with reels of thread and other haberdashery items.

Richard gave me the chair and he sat on the bed, shoving aside piles of stuff to make room, not noticing that he was pushing most of them onto the floor. 'Aileen's such a creative person. You know, synonym for messy.' He said this fondly, then abruptly went into serious mode. 'I know what this is about, Kay.' He gave me his most sympathetic face.

'You do?'

'Thought I could make her see sense, you know.' He looked at his hand, surprised. 'Where did I put my wine?'

'Make Stella see sense?'

'I went there, you know.' He got awkwardly onto the floor, one slowly lowered knee at a time, and looked under the bed. 'Winchester.'

'What? Not to see Rose? Oh God, Richard, what did you say...?'

'No one was in, I rang and rang. Sorry.' He climbed back onto the bed, stumbling on the fabric rolls he'd dropped. 'Can't think where I put my damn glass!'

I pictured Richard banging on Rose's door. Her and Graham peeking out of the window, waiting for him to go away. 'What were you planning to say to her?'

'Well, I've known you a long time. I was going to explain that you didn't mean to be a bad friend.' He looked round helplessly for his missing drink. 'I know, I know, you can't help it. Aileen's always saying, well...' Even drunk, he recognised the unproductiveness of this pathway and swerved away. 'It doesn't matter what she says, of course. But I've been thinking about things lately. One does when one gets older, does one not?'

'One definitely does, one can absolutely agree.'

He smiled. 'Think you're taking the piss. Anyway, s'occurred to me that the reason you caused such a stink at the wedding when Rose sent you that text...'

'I caused a stink?' Bloody hell. I was really getting to hear it tonight. Stink. Histrionics. *La traviata*.

'Gosh, Kay, we all ran out of tissues! You were, what was the amusing phrase Anthony used, oh yes, you were a "hot mess". Funny. Anyway, I realised that you've always been the one to say goodbye. Lucky you, says I! But you know. Relationships have always been very much on your terms. Could even say you take people for granted?' He raised his hand as though I'd interrupted him, but how could you interrupt when your mouth was hanging open? 'When Rose called time first, you didn't know what to do, cos it's not happened before. Don't blame you, it's horrible being the one who gets left. I'm gen-in-ly, genly, damn it, *gen-u-inely*, sorry for you.'

I felt like I'd gone six rounds in a boxing match. First a double-header of Helena and Alice had knocked me about, now Richard delivered the final blow. He was plastered, yes, but clearly he did really think this of me.

'I mean,' he went relentlessly on, 'you have had a needy few years. Rose probably just had enough of being expected to run when you whistled.'

'Oh Richard! What an awful thing to say.'

Wasn't that what friends did for each other? I'd gone beyond the call of duty for Rose in the past. That night I got her out of her house. Remember that, Rose? You were shaking with terror and I was absolutely there for you. I needed to remember that it was Richard who was dishing this stuff out; after all, the least truthful account in the world would be titled: *Your Flaws, An Unbiased Account by the Man You Walked Out On*.

But even as I railed against his words, a tiny voice in my head was pointing out that I had in fact made a lot of demands of Rose in the last few years. I'd thought she was fine with it, but maybe thinking it was OK without checking was the very definition of taking someone for granted.

'Hello, parentals.' Edward stuck his head round the door. 'Wow, what's Aileen done to my room?'

'You don't need it tonight, do you?' Richard said.

'No, me and the twins are staying with Stella. Are you OK? I could hear Dad shouting.'

'I wasn't shouting!' Richard shouted. 'Animated discussion, is all.' He spotted the glass in Edward's hand. 'Don't suppose that's my drink, is it?'

I nodded at Edward behind Richard's back, and he smiled conspiratorially at me and handed Richard the glass. I hoped this might cause him to break off our conversation, a kitten distracted by a ball of wool.

'You're a fine boy, thank you for looking after it for me.' Richard took a big gulp of wine. 'Fine boy.'

Edward's appearance reminded me that I had actually come up here to talk to Richard about Stella. Not in front of her brother though. 'Could you check on Murray?' I asked Edward. 'He doesn't really know anyone.'

'Yes, sure. I'll go find him.'

When Edward had gone, I readied myself to move on from What a Bitch Kay Is, and on to What Is Up With Stella. But Richard started talking again before I could say a word.

'So, Kay, talking of Murray, why's he banging on about the house, eh?'

'What do you mean?'

'Is he short of money or something? I have been worried about you, finanshully, you know.'

'You have?' All at once, it occurred to me that perhaps *Richard* had given me that money. I mean, that was crazy. He was my ex-husband! But was he opening a door, trying to tell me it was him?

'Someone gave me money, actually. For a wedding gift. Quite a large sum.' I watched his face but he didn't blink.

'Oh yes? Who?'

'I don't know. I was wondering... it wasn't you, was it?'

'We gave you a lovely, what was it? Aileen sorted it. Glassware, was it?'

'A blanket.'

'Thass right. Charming. Little weaver in the Highlands, or some such. It was probably Imogen. She's your fairy godmother, isn't she? You're a lucky girl, Kayla! But as I say, do ask me any time you're a bit short. I know some ex-husbands would have to pay maintenance or whatnot and you've been very good about that.'

It was true that I'd never asked Richard for money. Rather like Rose saying she only wanted to be free after leaving Tim, I'd always considered my relatively easy exit from my marriage reward enough.

'So what was Murray saying?'

'Telling me how big my house is, as if I'd never seen it. Asking how many bedrooms it has. Dropping hints about downsizing. Love Aussies to bits, don't get me wrong, but they're not known for their subtlety, are they?'

'He was making small talk, Richard.' He'd clearly inherited his Australian xenophobia from his mother.

'Bruce, I said to him, Bruce' – Richard laughed at his hilarious wit – 'I still regularly have a house full of people. I don't want to sell up just so you can buy yourself a nice little pied-à-terre. If it's not Edward down from Glasgow with the boys, it's Stella and Nita staying here every other week.'

Richard chugged down the rest of his glass. Was he more of a drinker than he used to be? Ah, I couldn't be worrying about that too. He wasn't my responsibility. 'Why do Stella and Nita stay here?'

'Well, not tonight, but they often stay when they're working in London. It's more convenient than slogging back to Essex, isn't it?'

I thought of Stella's tender gesture when she stroked Nita's arm. Was *that* what was going on?

'They love staying in Stella's old room. They say it's like sleepovers when they were kids.'

Jesus, how could Richard be so blindly Queen Victoria? Did I really have to ask Stella if she and Nita were having an affair now? My tired brain was not equipped for this amount of drama.

'Look, Richard, I'm sorry if Murray's questions bothered you. We're very happy in Bryn Glas and have no plans to buy a pied-à-terre, or anything else.' I was hopeless at managing husbands. If it wasn't the first one rocking off to Winchester unasked to interrogate Rose, it was the second one winding the first one up. Maybe Husband Number Three would be more docile? I should ask Helena if she'd found this to be true.

'Good, long as there's no trouble in paradise,' Richard said. How smug he looked, his face flushed red, like an old Tory grandee after a five-course dinner. He'd put on weight since marrying Domestic Goddess Aileen, with her cakes and her before-dinner snifters and her sewing. And no, I didn't know what sewing had to do with it. I was annoyed with him, and all at once felt disinclined to share confidences about Stella. He clearly didn't know anything.

'Well, talking of my gorgeous husband, I'd better go find him.' I hurried out before Richard could remember that I hadn't actually raised any topic. How typical that was of the man. He always did take over every conversation.

The hall was still full of people chatting and laughing, and most of them now had full plates and glasses of wine. When I was halfway down the stairs I saw a woman near the front door drop her plate and, in the confusion of trying to save it, splash red wine up the wall. I was about to rush to help when I remembered, with a rush of joy, that this wasn't my house any more. I smiled to myself and unfortunately came immediately face to face with Alice. She put on her disgusted expression, and I whisked past her into the kitchen where my beautiful (bisexual?) daughter was ladling food into dishes.

'Can I help, darling?'

'No, I'm fine.'

I took a breath, and said in a low voice, 'I've been thinking about you and Newland, and I realise there's...'

'Not now, please, Mum. I'm up to my eyes.'

'OK, Sparkle. Shall I come over tomorrow?' She'd be off to Italy in a couple of days, and then there would be no opportunity to make sure she was all right.

'Christ no, I'll be packing.' She dropped a ladle-full on the floor. 'Damn! Let's talk another time, all right?'

'If you're sure.' I bent down to clear up the mess, but she moved me out of the way.

'Can you please leave it?' She threw a towel over it, then turned her back on me and started vigorously beating cream.

I knew better than to try to talk to her when she was in this mood. I went out, and the Hall Aunties parted to let me through. I stepped outside, closing the front door behind me. The noise from the party was muffled out here, and it was lovely and cool. I sat on the bench by the front door, inhaling the aroma of the beautiful night-scented nicotiana I'd planted years ago. I should take a cutting for Bryn Glas. I told myself not to worry about Stella. She knew where I was if she needed me. But it was hard not to worry about one's children, however grown up they were. And on top of that, Richard had got into my head, so that all I could think of were the times when I hadn't been a good mother, a good friend. It had always bothered me, for instance, that Bear had never told me that she was ill, that she was dying. I'd thought we were really close. And whatever was going on with Stella, she didn't want to tell me.

Why didn't people talk to me about the important things in their lives? What did that say about me?

I could feel the tears start. I should be embarked on my beautiful new life with my wonderful new husband, but every day, thanks to Rose, I spent time dwelling on everything I'd ever done wrong. Maybe Stella and Helena were right: I should see someone. I certainly didn't seem to be able to unravel all this on my own. Therapy was the best thing Helena had ever done, apparently.

I wiped my eyes, pulled out my phone, and filled in a form to request a GP appointment. There were dozens of questions about breathing and heart pain before I reached the 'give more details' bit, and by then it seemed lame to ask for counselling on the grounds of inadequate friendships. Nonetheless, I started typing, and then I wasn't able to stop.

> I'd like to be referred to a counsellor please because I've recently got remarried and at the same time, I've been dumped, it sounds silly, by my best friend. My other best friend died five years ago and I still really miss her, we used to write every month and anyway it's her ex-husband I've married, sounds a bit odd maybe, and my other best friend told me not to contact her ever again but I don't know why, if she won't see me how will I ever find out what I've done, and my ex-husband said—

At this point I couldn't add any more; underneath the box it said: *500 character limit reached.*

I deleted it, and wrote: *I think I'm a little depressed*, then pressed 'submit' because I was already sick of the whole thing. An automatic message popped up, promising a response within a week, which seemed unlikely. I sat back, feeling equal parts pleased with myself for being proactive, and a little ashamed to have nearly poured out so much personal detritus to a stranger, or worse, a robot. Then I saw Murray walking along the street. What was he doing out there? He was whistling to himself, and didn't see me till he turned towards the house and pushed open the gate.

'Hello, sweetheart!' he said. He was in high spirits.

'Where have you been?'

'Just stretching my legs. Stuffy in there.' He sat down and kissed me, his lips warm on mine. 'Why are you out here?'

'Taking a moment away from the loving bosom of my family.'

He accepted this with a nod. 'Ready to face the fray? Or shall we clear off?'

My heart filled with love for him. 'Can we really clear off?'

'You are such a good girl, aren't you? Course we can. A short Uber away we have a lovely Airbnb waiting for us, with a nice big bed.'

'Oh, my coat and bag...'

'I'll get them.' He gave a salute, and went inside. I walked over to the gate and leaned against it, looking back at the house. All the lights were on and music pulsed gently out. It should be utterly familiar to me as the place I had lived for so many years, but it looked alien and unknown.

A few minutes later, the front door opened, sending shafts of light onto the path, and Murray came back out, Richard close behind him. Murray shot me a look which I understood meant, sorry, couldn't shake him off.

'Kayla!' Richard slurred, putting his arm round Murray. They stood there looking at me, like some weird husband salt-and-pepper set. 'Don't go without saying goodbye!' He hugged me. 'I'm sorry about what I said about the thingy.'

The hug went on rather, and I patted Richard's back in an attempt to bring it to a close. He didn't smell the way he used to; under the top notes of booze and sweat he wore a new cologne I guessed Aileen had chosen.

'Actually I don't think you're right.' We broke apart, and I took my coat from Murray. 'I wasn't the one to say goodbye to David, remember?' The minute it was out of my mouth I regretted it.

Richard looked at me with distaste. How he resembled his mother at that moment. 'Yes, funnily enough I do remember.'

A car pulled up in the street outside.

'That's our Uber,' Murray said. 'David who? Your old boyfriend?'

'Oh, Bruce knows about him, does he?' Richard said, staggering slightly.

The front door opened again and Aileen stepped out onto the path. 'Everything OK?'

'Richard's a little the worse for wear,' Murray said. How I admired – was aroused by, let's be honest – his quiet, authoritative tone.

Aileen looked from me to Richard, and back again. 'Come inside, Richard. Kay and Murray want to leave.'

Her soft voice was so calming. If only she and Murray had been the ones to fall in love, what a lovely sensible life they'd be leading. Richard waved a careless hand, and stumbled back towards the house. 'I'm going, I'm going.' Aileen, the consummate host, thanked us for coming before going inside and closing the front door.

'What was all that about?' Murray said.

I shook my head. 'Let's go.'

In the car I reached for Murray's hand, and told him about my worries about Stella, her not wanting to talk to me. 'What with her, and Rose, I really am *persona non grata*.'

'Not with me. You're my top *persona grata*.' He squeezed my hand. 'Richard was in a funny one, wasn't he?'

'I shouldn't have mentioned David. Bit incendiary.'

Murray knew that Edward's biological father wasn't

Richard, but David Endevane, my student boyfriend back in the day.

'You've had quite a romantic past, haven't you, Mrs Garland?'

'You knew all that when you married me, Mr Garland.' I gently kissed his lips. 'And you also know that none of that matters, because you are the love of my life.'

I felt him smile in the darkness, and he leaned down and kissed me back.

PHOTO #3

Then

It's after the ceremony. Richard stands with a glass of wine in one hand, his other hand resting on the back of a chair. Behind him is wood panelling and the edge of a gilt-framed painting of horses. He is wearing a dark blue wide-lapelled suit in the fashion of the time. He has a red rose in his buttonhole. He looks serious; he is listening to someone. The only other person in the picture, half cropped out, is his mother, Alice.

Date: 24th August 1988. Location: Royal Battalion Hotel, Richmond. Photographer: Rose Nolan.

* * *

Now

Richard's head is back, and he is laughing. He has a glass in his hand. His suit is dark blue, with a modern cut, and he has an orchid from Imogen's greenhouse in his buttonhole. His hair is grey and a little sparse on top, and he is stockier than in his youth, but otherwise he is recognisably the same person as in the first photograph.

Date: 22nd April 2023. Location: Imogen Gray's garden, Hampstead. Photographer: Helena Chen.

SIX

NORTH WALES, JUNE 2023

We were scarcely back from London and Murray was off again, to Monaco.

'Busy season,' he reminded me. 'Make the money while the going's good.'

Of *course* these insanely wealthy people he dealt with would just adore hanging out on their superyachts in Monaco. He explained that there was a big boating scene there, and I replied there was also a big lack of individual tax there, and he laughed and said that my cynicism was 'bracing'. I was learning a little of the lingo and methods of Murray's working life, though if I was suddenly invited onto *Mastermind* with 'Murray's business' as my specialist subject I would do very badly.

After I'd seen him off at the station, and we'd shared a proper weak-at-the-knees goodbye kiss, I was finally ready to face the mystery money. It felt wrong that I hadn't told Murray about it, but that weird little message – *Don't tell him!* – was stopping me. It was as if someone was watching me, someone who knew things I didn't know. It took a long time to count, because it was, unbelievably, £10,000. What an insane thing.

Having counted it, I didn't know what to do with it, and shoved it back in the drawer. Doing a Filomena.

I had plenty to get on with while Murray was away. Neither Helena nor Richard had been wildly helpful in my quest for Rose intel. Still to go: Stella, my ex-boyfriend Luca, and cousin Stacey. I could kill two birds with one stone by visiting Stella in Naples, if she'd let me, and seeing Luca at the same time. He was likely still living in Milan. So outside of the Italian contingent, the only other person on my list was cousin Stacey. I rummaged in the sideboard drawer till I found the card she'd sent after Mum died, her contact details listed neatly down the left-hand side in her curvy schoolgirl hand. I picked up my phone, tapped in half her number, then pictured her face as it was when I last saw her, at my hen do two months ago. Upset, disappointed, bewildered. I deleted the numbers I'd typed. Another day, perhaps.

There were more pressing deadlines anyway, such as the one for my proposal. So of course, I decided that now was the perfect opportunity to clean the cottage from top to toe. I was sitting in the bath trying to remove a Victorian-era stain, muttering to myself, when I was startled by the phone ringing in my pocket. It was the GP. Wow, they really did call back within a week.

'Mrs Bright?'

'It's Garland now. Sorry, I haven't updated my records yet.' I tried to get out of the bath but it felt like too much effort so I sat back down.

'I'm following up your online appointment request. How are you feeling today?'

'Er... fine.' I was glad she couldn't see me, sitting in an empty bath having a psychologically questionable cleaning spree.

'You said you were feeling a little depressed.'

'I don't know if that's right, exactly.' Had I really said that?

'It's just... things have been a bit difficult.' I couldn't believe I was blurting this stuff out. Stella would be proud.

'Oh dear. Well, if you come in for a face-to-face appointment, I can prescribe something that might help.'

Straight away, we were onto tablets. What happened to talking? 'I was hoping to see a counsellor.'

She did that sigh GPs do, when they're asked for the moon. 'The waiting lists are months-long for an NHS counsellor. If you're able to pay, it'll be a lot quicker. I can text you a list of accredited private therapists.'

I agreed to that, and the text came through almost as soon as we'd hung up, along with the opportunity to provide feedback on my recent experience with my medical practice. I randomly chose a name from the list, mainly because the town she lived in wasn't too far away, but I'd be unlikely to see anyone I knew there. And also because she had a melodious name: Louisa Madubueze. The small act of sending her an email made me feel as if I had already sorted everything out.

I got out of the bath and drove to the university for a lecture on 3D capture I'd intended to skip. Afterwards I went for coffee with my student pals, and showed them the best of Helena's wedding photos. After the group had analysed the photos intellectually ('excellent depth of field') and aesthetically ('your bum looks nice in that one, Kay'), we took turns to discuss our proposals, or lack of proposals in my case. Emily, at twenty the baby of the group, was planning to travel round the UK taking photos of bus shelters. I secretly thought it was a boring idea but she was an intimidating and very pierced young person; there was doubtless something in her proposal that I could not understand, given my decrepitude. Most of the others' ideas were more comprehensible to me – one was photographs of the sea at Newborough Beach on Anglesey at different times of day, which sounded lovely, but which its creator, Dylan, had been told had a 'lack of narrative'.

'What, are we meant to have a narrative?' Padma said. 'Vanessa never said anything about that to me.'

When they realised I had not only no narrative but no proposal, they piled in with advice. Emily suggested I do something about how photography styles had changed since my first, abandoned, degree. She probably thought I'd used a Box Brownie back then. Actually she'd never have heard of a Box Brownie. But when I mentioned that I'd got old photos of Helena, they all sat up excitedly.

'Then and now!' Padma exclaimed, at the same time as Dylan said, 'Today and yesterday!'

It seemed obvious when they said it. I had an enormous archive (e.g. a few cardboard boxes) of old photos, and the thought of pairing those with more recent photos of the same people felt both interesting and doable. Not to mention, given my current self-reflective phase, rather therapeutic. I thanked them and rushed home to get on with it.

I started with the box I'd found Helena's picture in and spent a couple of hours sorting through hundreds of old photos. My initial excitement didn't last long, as it was a melancholy business looking at all the bright young faces of people who'd since died, not to mention the many photos of Rose. Here she was, aged eleven, on the sofa at my childhood home, massive smile, holding up a cupcake. I could date it to autumn 1978, shortly after we started secondary school and became friends. Here she was again, circa 1986, waving a wooden spoon while I cooked something in a pan on our disreputable student stove in London. Here were both of us, this time with Bear, all in tiny T-shirts, the Australian sun making our hair gleam like gold. So young and lovely, with everything in front of us. No hint in Rose's face that one day she would turn her back on me.

By the time I called it a day I was feeling rather flat. Thank goodness I'd contacted a therapist. Talking of which, I checked my emails and yes! There was one from Louisa Madubueze;

things sure did go at lightning speed if you went private. It said she was booked up, other than one slot at 7 p.m. on Fridays. Mine if I wanted it, and starting this very week – tomorrow, in fact. Presumably it was available because it was an unpopular time. It felt way too soon, but on the other hand, I had started talking to myself while cleaning the bath. It was only after I'd replied to confirm that I read through her terms, and nearly choked at the price: £90 an hour! Not even a whole hour – fifty minutes. But I had the mystery money, after all, and as I didn't know what its purpose was meant to be, the benefactor could scarcely object to how I used it, could they?

The next evening I found myself in Louisa's street ten minutes early. As I waited in the car, the doubts crowded in. This was all happening a bit fast, wasn't it? I only mentioned counselling to the GP at the start of the week and now I was here, actually seeing one. It took me longer than this to decide whether to buy a pair of trousers! I turned the ignition back on and drove down the street. What was I thinking? That I was a Hollywood star who saw their therapist in between their nutritionist and their personal trainer? How big was my ego, anyway? Paying someone to listen to you, talking about your silly first world nonsense about friends, when half the world was on fire. For goodness sake! I turned right, and headed back towards the Menai Bridge. Of course, for some people, who had mental health problems, therapy was an essential part of treatment. Seeing a therapist had been life-saving for Stella, when she was so knocked back after university. But for someone like me, who was relatively stable, I didn't need this. I'd never needed it. Sitting there, banging on about your problems as if you were the most important person in the world...

My eyes filled with tears so abruptly that I couldn't see, and I pulled over into a bus stop. I was such a bloody idiot. Of course I'd not needed a therapist before now. Not because I was the most stable woman in Britain, but because I'd *had* someone to sit with, to gas away about my problems to. I'd had someone to talk to since I was eleven years old. Someone who listened to me properly, considered all angles, and then sympathised, or told me I was being a soft lad. I didn't know what it was like to not have it. Until now. Not having it led you here, to a stranger's house in a strange town.

Richard was right – I'd taken Rose for granted.

By the time I'd pulled myself together enough to drive back, I was almost late. I hurried up to the house and Louisa greeted me at the door. She was swathed in neutral layers, a long ruby-red scarf round her neck the only point of colour. Her hair was white and she looked somewhat older than her website photo, reassuringly so. I didn't want to be set straight by someone young, it was bad enough with my tutor Vanessa at college, who looked about twelve.

Louisa said, 'How *are* you?', her years of training showing in that emphasised 'are' which meant: You've been crying, haven't you?

I opened my mouth to say I was fine, then caught myself on, as Rose might say. What a foolish instinct to say I was fine to the very person I was paying to tell how un-fine I was.

'I was crying in the car about my friend, how much I miss her.'

'I'm sorry,' Louisa said, sounding as if she genuinely meant it. She showed me into a handsome sitting room full of books and cushions, the soft furnishings in deep greens and blues. We sat opposite each other on armchairs, and I waited for her to ask something, but she sat quietly, waiting. This morning I'd calculated that a minute of her time cost £1.80, so I'd already had about ninety pence worth, and needed to get on with it.

'Um, thanks for seeing me so quickly.'

She didn't say anything.

Awkwardly, I rambled on, 'In fact, I'd been wondering if it was too quickly, because I haven't had time to prepare.'

'What is it you would have liked to have prepared?' Oh thank God, she spoke. It wasn't just going to be me talking into a void for fifty minutes.

'Erm, well, the reason I'm here, I think, is because I've messed up an important friendship, and my ex-husband, Richard, says it's because I take people for granted.' I could feel myself gabbling. 'So maybe I need to do some reckoning on the way I treat people? I don't know why things went wrong with my friend, but if I could find out, maybe we could make things up.'

Louisa nodded. She was used to crazy people, of course.

'Is this the friend you were upset about, in the car?' she said. 'Can you tell me about her?'

It turned out I'd been worrying unnecessarily about silence in the room. The floodgates opened and I spoke for twenty minutes without taking a breath. These were the Rose highlights, as presented to Louisa's impassive face:

1. Meeting Rose and Bear on day one of secondary school and the three of us being inseparable after that, until Bear and her family moved to Australia when we were sixteen.
2. Rose and I going to university in London together because we didn't want to be apart.
3. Me getting pregnant and flunking out before my final year.
4. How Rose supported me when my kids were little, how she picked up the pieces when my cousin Stacey, who had promised to help, called me a judgemental cow and walked out of my life.
5. How I helped Rose and her boys escape from Tim, who was abusive and controlling.

6. Rose and I sneaking off for weekends of laughter and talk at Bryn Glas when the children were teenagers.

'Is this the sort of thing you want me to tell you?' I asked, as I came to a natural stop. Was Louisa embarrassed for me, pouring out all this detail? She'd been nodding a lot as I talked, but maybe she was being polite.

'Tell me whatever you like,' she said, unhelpfully. Fine then. I carried on.

Rose highlights, part two:

7. If the biggest thing I'd done for Rose was extricating her from Tim, the biggest thing she did for me was be there when I left Richard. She looked after me, liaised with my family, and helped me get back on my feet.
8. Then last year I met Murray, my new husband. He used to be married to Bear, my friend from Australia, who died.

Louisa looked at me more intently, I felt, and I started gabbling: 'Well, he was her ex, they divorced years before she died. So it wasn't completely weird, me marrying him. Maybe some people think it's a bit odd, especially how quick it was...'

Still Louisa sat there, unreadable as the sphinx. Her silence was clever because it made me want to fill the space with talk. Knowing it was a tactic didn't stop me doing it.

'Anyway, last year Murray and Charlie moved to the UK because Charlie was starting a course here.' It was hard to know what was and wasn't relevant. I was on an unstoppable roll of speaking now, purging myself of words, and I tell you something, I was never coming back here again. I would reveal everything about my life to this stranger and then leave it here, in this overstuffed room, and she could do with it what she wanted.

'Murray contacted me and Rose, her oldest friends, so Charlie could talk to us about Bear, and we all went out for a meal.'

That night sparkled in my mind like a diamond. From the moment I walked into the restaurant and saw Murray, I was gone. Lost. Of course I'd met him before, but rarely, and not for years. I had only a vague memory of him when he was married to Bear. I hadn't gone to their wedding as my children had been so little, and when Bear came to Europe on one of her whirlwind tours, he rarely accompanied her. All I knew about him was the little she wrote in her letters.

This meant that I was not prepared for the physical impact of him. When I walked into the restaurant and he stood to hug me, I was properly shaken. I couldn't remember the last time a man had had such an impact. Probably never. My only boyfriend since my divorce, Luca, was a lovely chap, but we had rather a cerebral connection. Perhaps Murray reminded me of my first love, David. Not in looks, but in, let's call it what it was, sexual attraction.

By the time Rose joined us I was, as Anthony might say, a hot mess. Luckily it was a messy occasion; Bear had raised Charlie to be a sensitive fellow and he had already cried twice while I recounted some of the details of his mother's final trip abroad, with me in Venice. While talking to him I was never not conscious of Murray at Charlie's side, watching me intently with his dark brown eyes. How intoxicating it was, to feel completely *seen* by a man. I was aware of him and his body in a way I never normally was with people, and unusually aware of my own body too. I was wearing a grey silk shirt which I'd thought looked nice, but now felt too prim and contained. I had an overwhelming urge to undo the top two buttons, slowly, while looking straight at Murray. When he was studying the menu and I knew he wasn't looking at me I stared openly at him, taking in the way his hair fell over his forehead, the width of his shoulders underneath that jacket...

Rose, of course, knew immediately that something was up. She sent me little glances all through the meal, and at an appropriate juncture invited me to accompany her to the ladies.

'What the bloody hell is going on?' she said, laughing, the minute we were in the safety of the bathroom. 'It's like you're both on heat.'

'Is it him too?' I wasn't sure, my brain was so addled.

'Chick, if the temperature between you goes up any more, I'll need to call in the burns doctor.'

She said she knew Murray was attractive, which seemed a wild understatement. But she warned me to be cautious, in the interests of Charlie's feelings. 'That poor young man is still bereaved, and does not need the hassle of a stepmother.' I laughed a little hysterically at that, secretly thinking how amazing it would be to marry this gorgeous man. Rose also reminded me that I was already in a relationship. I knew she really liked Luca – she once described him as 'the perfect man' – but he and I only saw each other a couple of times a month. I'd never really thought of it as a long-term prospect.

Nonetheless, for the rest of the evening I kept my attention on Charlie, and behaved impeccably as the upright middle-aged woman who'd been friends with his mother. There was only one moment when I nearly lost my self-control, which was when Murray, asking Charlie to pass me a menu, referred to me as 'Katie'. I raised an eyebrow and he laughed, and explained that when he'd first heard Bear talking about me, he had misheard my name as 'Katie', and it had become a kind of joke between them.

Very few people called me 'Kathleen', and certainly no one

ever called me 'Katie'. But on his lips it sounded like the sexiest name I'd ever heard.

'I'm really sorry,' he said. 'I know it's Kay. I will remember from now on.'

Astonished at my daring, the verbal equivalent of undoing my top buttons, I looked him straight in the eye and said, 'I like you calling me Katie.' OK, it might not sound like much but I assure you, it was *sizzling*. His eyes widened; he knew what I was saying.

'So you and Murray married when?' Louisa asked.

'April. So yes,' I added quickly, in case she was thinking it, 'only six months between meeting and marrying. A proper whirlwind. Not my usual style.'

'What is your usual style?'

'I'm pretty cautious, careful. I don't rush into things.'

She said nothing.

'I don't, honestly!'

She still didn't speak. Bloody hell. 'OK, I did rush into marrying Richard, but that was decades ago.'

'You're questioning yourself?'

'You're questioning it, not me!'

'I don't think I said anything.'

Bloody bloody hell. This was infuriating. Though also energising, electric. I reminded myself that I wasn't coming back, I could say whatever the hell I liked. 'It's only been the last few years that have been a rollercoaster. My life was steady for decades. Dull, really. But then, in my fifties, just when you're meant to settle down for a quiet drift into old age, I shook it all up. I left Richard, left my job, moved here from London, lived alone for the first time in my life, went back to university, and then I fell in love.'

'That's a lot of upheaval, isn't it?'

'The point is, Rose was the best friend anyone could have, she wouldn't describe me as someone who rushes into things, I can tell you that for nothing! But suddenly she decided she hated me, and told me to leave her the fuck alone. So.'

I wasn't sure what the 'so' was doing there. I seemed to have slipped into adolescent mode.

'That must have been very hard,' Louisa said gently, and now I was a blubbing wreck, tears and snot leaking down my face.

'It seems so stupid but it's one of the worst things that's ever happened to me,' I wailed. 'And I've lost people, Mum died, Bear died, but Rose abandoning me seems even worse.'

Louisa didn't say any more, just sat calmly and waited until I was through the worst, then pushed the tissue box towards me. I took a handful and mopped myself up.

'I'm so embarrassed,' I muttered.

'Why is that, do you think?'

'I don't know, crying over a friend like I'm back at school, it's so silly.'

'You don't feel that your feelings of loss over your friend are valid? Yet friends can often be one of the most significant relationships of our lives. What was it Emily Dickinson said? "My friends are my estate." You've lost Bear, and now you've lost Rose. It sounds pretty devastating.'

How strange, how compelling it was to hear her say my friends' names. She didn't know them, but in this quiet room, I had shown them to her, and now she showed them back to me. And quoting Emily Dickinson to boot. I looked at her through blurry eyes with increased respect.

'But I think you know that already,' she went on, 'because you have sought help.' She smiled for the first time. 'We have five minutes left...'

I couldn't believe that. I felt like I'd only just arrived.

'...and we can continue next session.'

What next session?

'Richard saying you take people for granted – I wonder if you think that's true.'

I thought for a few seconds, about eighteen pence worth. 'It struck a chord. The last few years have all been about me, I suppose. I'd thought that me and Rose were really close. I checked in with her regularly, texted, all that. But maybe all that was superficial? Maybe I wasn't a good friend when it really counted? For her to cut me out of her life is simply ridiculous. It only makes sense if I've done something unforgiveable.'

'Is taking people for granted unforgiveable?'

'Yes... well I... I don't know... isn't it?'

'It's a very human trait.'

'But maybe I keep repeating it. I think Bear as well, I wasn't the right sort of friend for her when it counted. My mum, I've been having dreams about her...' The tears threatened to start again, and I shook my head to rid myself of them. I was crying an insane amount lately. 'Luca, my partner before I met Murray, I dropped him abruptly. Richard. Probably lots more.'

'Hmm. We all have them, don't we? People who are no longer in our lives. Friends we lose touch with, family members.'

People started crowding in my mind. Friends from primary, who went to different senior schools and who I never saw again. Teachers, like lovely Mrs Kemp, my art teacher, and Howard at university. Various aunts and uncles on my dad's side, who drifted out of my life after he died. Colleagues from Quiller Queen. Friends I made at the school gates because we had children the same age. Why, there must be hundreds of people who had passed in and out of my life.

Louisa smiled again and said, 'We have to stop now. I'll see you next week, same time.'

She stood up, and so did I, though I felt as if my head wasn't on straight any more. Things looked different. The rich jewel colours of the cushions on her sofa, of her ruby scarf, seemed more vibrant than before. I muttered something about payment and she said she would invoice at the end of four sessions. We said goodbye and then I was on the other side of the closed front door. Bloody, bloody, bloody hell! So much for only having one session. I had somehow agreed to at least four.

Back home, in a tidal wave of energy, I went straight to my photos on the living room table. The one on top was of cousin Stacey, misleadingly Madonna-like, holding tiny baby Edward on her lap. It would have been the last time I'd seen her, before she rocked up to my hen do thirty-five years later with a nervous smile, and I blanked her like a complete cow.

I grabbed my phone, and dialled the number on her card.

'Stacey? It's Kay. Cousin Kay. Can I come and see you?'

PHOTO #4

Then

A moodily lit interior, all dark shadows and yellow glow. Stacey, in her late twenties, holds Kay's baby boy, a few days old, on her lap. He does not yet have a name. Her auburn hair is lit through with gold streaks from the lamplight, and she is looking tenderly at the baby in her arms. She is wearing her coat.

Date: February 1989. Location: Richard and Kay's first flat in Richmond. Photographer: Kay Bright.

***

Now

Stacey is standing in front of a half-timbered shop. She is leaning against the wall and is looking to her right, away from the camera. She is in her mid-sixties and her grey hair is tied in a ponytail. Her pose is reminiscent of the young Julie

Burchill in the famous 1978 photo of her and Tony Parsons, taken by Pennie Smith on the roof of the *NME* building in London. Stacey has one hand wrapped round her body. The other is near her mouth because she has just taken a drag from her vape. Her face is half-obscured by vape clouds.

Date: 14th June 2023. Location: The Rows, Chester. Photographer: Kay Garland.

SEVEN

LAST ENCOUNTER WITH STACEY: RICHMOND, FEBRUARY 1989

'Where is he, then?' Stacey pushed past me the minute I opened the door. She stood in the middle of our living room, where the light was on low. The gloom made her appear a statuesque, almost mythical figure. 'Why's it so dark?'

I considered saying, 'What, no hug?' but knew I wouldn't be able to make it come out casually enough. Instead I pointed to the Moses basket by the armchair. 'He's asleep.'

'They don't need dark quiet rooms, you know. Petra slept through everything. Took her to Eric's on Matthew Street for my nineteenth, and Echo and the Bunnymen played so loud my ears pretty much bled. She was spark out.' Stacey bent down to peer in to the basket, and her face unfolded. 'He's very sweet.'

'Thank you.'

A half-laugh. 'It'd have been fucking easy if Petra had ever slept like this.'

Well, she must have slept at some point, I wanted to say. Like during that gig you just mentioned, for instance. It seemed impossible, somehow, for me to mention the lack of sleep I was barely coping with at night.

'Any wine on the go?'

I poured her a large glass from a bottle that Richard had started last night. She was still standing by the Moses basket in her coat.

'Have a seat?' I gestured to the armchair.

'Just for a minute then.' She perched on the edge of the chair, and sniffed the wine suspiciously.

I knew I should sit down too. I avoided it if possible, as it still hurt. Lying down was much better, but I felt it was too look-at-me to lie on the sofa in front of Stacey. Instead I lowered myself carefully onto the doughnut cushion I'd borrowed from a weird breastfeeding group up the road, trying not to wince.

Her face half in shadow, she said, 'Stitches,' with no question mark, which meant she didn't want me to go into detail, which was a shame, because she was the person I most wanted to tell.

'A few.'

'You need wine, then. Why aren't you drinking?'

'Breastfeeding.'

'I drank when I was feeding Petra, and she turned out fine.' She laughed. 'More or less. Bloody needed wine, those first few months. It's bullshit them telling you that you can't.'

'How is Petra?'

'She's all right. If it wasn't for her I'd have left by now. I don't know what my ma's told your ma. She always twists things.'

'She hasn't said much.' I wanted to ask if she'd done what she said she was going to, last time we met, but I didn't want to mention Ivan, or his poor wife.

Stacey sipped her wine. 'So, can I hold him?' She was already getting him out of the basket. How tiny he looked, in her long arms. He didn't stir.

'I've still got the skills,' she said, rocking him gently.

I wanted to tell her that I didn't know what I was doing. She was eight when I was born, the big sister I never had. She and

Aunt Jean lived in the next street to us and we were always in each other's houses, from the moment I could toddle. It goes without saying I looked up to her.

At eighteen – even younger than me – she'd had Petra. She was an expert on babies, and whenever I panicked about becoming a mother, I'd clung to the thought that we'd be here, sitting together, her telling me what to do. But this was a washed-out version, cloaked in the shadow of our last, brittle, conversation. I'd already done a week of baby that felt like a year. I couldn't think more than a half hour ahead. Half an hour was pushing it. I just wanted her to stay. But she was here under sufferance, because I'd been so pathetic on the phone.

'Can I take your picture?' I asked. My beloved cousin, holding my baby. I wanted a record of it. My camera was on the side table next to the sofa.

She shrugged. 'You still doing that photograph thing then? Thought you'd gave all that up.'

'I'm taking a lot of photos of the baby.' I played around with the aperture to allow for the low light in the room, and took a few quick shots in which she looked, deceptively, the epitome of maternal love.

When I lowered the camera she shivered, and I thought she might be cold, even though she was still wearing her coat.

I said, 'Shall I make a fire?' I wished I'd made one before she arrived. Fires were cosy, they made you want to stay.

'No, I'm fine. Baby is a little hot water bottle.'

Three months ago, I'd stayed with Mum in Hoylake for a few days while Richard got the shop fittings sorted. He was so busy, he'd taken a sleeping bag into the shop so he could stay there at nights and get going first thing. It coincided with the time I'd have gone back to university for my third year, if I'd been going back, and with Richard out I needed a distraction. I'd been married two months, was six months pregnant, been the joint owner of this small flat in London for one month. I'd taken everything I knew about my life and thrown it into the air. When it came down it was all in a different order.

Mum and I went round to Aunt Jean's, and Stacey suggested she and I go to Café Marco to talk. I already knew things were frosty between her and her mum, because of her affair with a married man, the one she'd mentioned the night of the Rezz Club. I got a sense that Stacey was pleased because now I'd messed things up almost as much as she had; we'd both got pregnant way too young. She said that us Catholic girls had no chance because no one told us how babies were made, or how to stop them.

In Café Marco she let me talk about my pregnancy for a while, but she was only waiting so she could tell me about Ivan. He was a senior manager, and ten years older, apparently the love of her life. She said he was going to leave his wife very soon. I hesitantly mentioned Petra and she said, what about her? She would obviously live with her and Ivan once they'd got together, Petra was the easy part. The sticking point, she went on, was Ivan's idiot wife who really ought to be told what was going on. Stacey outlined her plan to make an anonymous phone call to Ivan's wife. She had worked out the best time to do it – when Ivan was on a late shift and their children would be in bed – what to say – she was a friend who thought Ivan's wife ought to know – and how much to deny it when Ivan asked if it was her – take it to the grave.

Surprising both of us, I blurted that this would be an awful thing to do, that Ivan's wife didn't deserve it, and Stacey called me a judgemental cow and walked out before I'd finished speaking. When I paid for our hot chocolates I started crying and the girl behind the counter gave me ten per cent off. I didn't see Stacey again for the rest of my stay with Mum, and after that I was busy homemaking in London, and getting bigger and bigger.

In January I had the baby, a straightforward hospital birth that left me stunned and sore. The day after we got him home, Richard had to go out to the shop because the temporary manager he'd hired hadn't turned up. I felt sure I was going to accidentally kill the baby. I laid him on the floor so I couldn't drop him, sat as far away as possible on the other side of the room and rang Stacey, my hands trembling so much I misdialled the first time. I don't remember what I said, other than I really needed her help and didn't care about anything else.

Now finally she was here, but it wasn't how I'd imagined.

'Where's Rich, anyway?' she said.

'At work.'

'Fucking hell, Kathy, it's gone seven.'

'We've only just opened the shop.'

'We?'

'Well, I'll be getting involved when the baby's a bit older. It's only these first few months Rich will be working flat out, then he'll do more normal hours.'

'I'll have to go soon.' Gesturing with her glass, closer to the baby's face than I'd have liked, she said, 'What's this business with not naming him, then?'

What a can of worms it was, naming a child. Richard didn't know I'd heard him yesterday, crooning to the baby, in the half hour he was home to wash and change. He thought I was asleep. 'Edward, oh Edward.' He sang to the tune of 'Lydia the Tattooed Lady'. He had a nice voice. 'Edward, oh Edward, say have you met Edward? Edward the lo-ove-ly baby.' Edward was his grandfather's name, his mother's father. He hadn't pushed it too hard in our discussions, had merely proposed it as an option. It ought to have been a no-brainer; given Richard's decency in taking me and the baby on, I ought to call it the name he chose. But I didn't feel any attachment to Edward as a name.

'We can't come to an agreement,' I said.

'You did all the fucking work, you should decide,' Stacey said.

I remembered her, sitting up in the hospital bed with baby Petra, saying the same. 'Steven hates it, but it's up to me, I'm the one whose foo-foo's been shot to bits.'

'Is Petra named for anyone?' I'd asked.

She laughed. 'Yeah, the dog on *Blue Peter*.'

'What do you think I should call him?' I said now.

'Ivan,' she said immediately, blazing out a challenging smile. Because I hadn't asked after her lover.

'How *is* Ivan?' I tried to bring the conversation back to a normal social setting.

'Good. He's driving round a bit then he'll collect me.'

'Oh! He brought you here?'

'Course he fucking brought me. He's my *boyfriend*.'

'He could have come in. It would be nice to meet him. Or' – and an idea came to me – 'he can come in when he gets back, and you two can stay for dinner. We can get a takeaway.'

She was smiling. 'Kathy, I'm not being funny but we hardly ever get to have a night away together. We're not going to spend it with you and the baby having chicken chow mein.'

I nodded. It was important not to show her how hurt I was. 'What are you going to do?'

'He's booked us into this hotel in Tottenham. We're going to fuck each other's brains out.'

'Sounds delightful,' I said, with a flash of my old spirit.

'Ivan's angry with you, you know.'

'How can he be? He doesn't know me. I've never even spoken to him.'

I'd given birth a week ago. I didn't feel like anyone had the right to be angry with me, but especially not this infuriating-sounding man I'd never met, though I knew his name, his job, his wife's name, his children's names, the size of his penis. I knew he'd promised to tattoo Stacey's name on his arm after his divorce came through.

'He says every minute away from me is like being tortured.'

'Well, I'm sorry I inconveniently gave birth and asked my cousin to come and see me. You're making him sound rather silly.' I held my breath at my own daring.

'Yeah, I know. He's a bit of a twat, sometimes. He just can't get enough of me. We can't get enough of each other. It's incredible. Have you ever had sex like that? Where you want to lick them inside out?'

I didn't know how to answer this. Sex with Richard certainly didn't feel like that.

'What even is sex?' I said, putting on a smile. 'Can't imagine having it ever again right now.'

'I remember that, feeling like razor blades down below. Don't worry, it does eventually heal.'

'Good to know.' I felt my shoulders drop a little; we were talking at last like our old selves.

The phone rang, loud in the quiet room. 'Sorry. I'd better answer, don't want to wake the baby...' I got to it as quickly as I could. 'Hello? Oh! Hello, *Steven*.'

I looked at Stacey as I said his name, and she made a surprised face, a round circle of red mouth.

'Yes, she's here. She's holding the baby. Do you want to...? Hang on a sec.'

I eased carefully out of my chair to pass the cordless phone over. I couldn't face trying to sit again so I leaned against the wall.

'Hey, Steve. Yes, absolutely gorgeous. So tiny! Brings it all back. Oh, early night I expect. Not wild times here, breastfeeding, you know! Enjoy the film, give Petsy a kiss from me.'

She handed me back the phone, and I played my part: 'Thanks, Steven. Yes, everyone says that, ha ha! It doesn't feel like it's flashing by right now. Bye then.'

I hung up, and the small silence that followed was broken by a car hooting outside. Stacey gently put the baby back into the Moses basket.

'What a great sleeper, you are so lucky. Well, glad I've seen him. Hope he gets a name soon.' She came over and brushed her cheek with mine. I smelled her scent, the one she always wore. I remembered buying her a bottle of it for her twenty-first birthday. I saved up my pocket money for months so I could say I'd paid for it myself. She had given me a massive hug, told me it was perfect, that she'd just run out of her previous bottle. She knew back then how to make me feel good about myself.

I followed her to the door.

'Am I the cover for you seeing Ivan tonight?' I didn't know I was going to say this until I said it. My body and brain felt so battered, I was so outside myself, that it seemed that my mouth was saying things without me being completely on board.

'Kind of.' For the first time, she looked less than confident. 'Kathy, he's outside...'

'He can wait a minute, he's already cross with me, anyway. So... what would have happened if Steven had rung after you'd left?'

The car horn sounded again. There was a small noise from the Moses basket, the baby stirring.

'I'm not sure.' She looked at her watch.

'You told him what time to call, didn't you?'

'I gave a rough estimate. I wasn't sure...'

'Well, he's rung now, so you're free to go.'

Finally, she looked at me properly. 'It's not like that.'

'It's exactly like that. When you see Steven tomorrow, you'll be able to update him about the baby, about me.' I smiled. 'Not everything you tell him will have to be a lie.'

'You don't know what it's like. With Ivan.'

'You told me. Licking each other inside out. Can't say I fancy the sound of that much.'

The baby was making little whimpering noises, ones I realised with a startle that I knew how to interpret. I picked him up and he nestled against me, warm, his mouth damp on my cheek. I felt his breathing slow down.

Stacey hesitated at the door. For the first time, I wanted her to go. The horn sounded again.

'Go on.' I gestured towards the front door. 'If he wakes the baby up with that hooting, I'll kick his headlights in.'

'All right.' She moved to embrace me, but I stepped back, holding the baby in front of me.

She paused a moment longer, as if she wanted to say something. Not 'sorry', she never said 'sorry', but something. But then she opened the door and closed it behind her. Moments later I heard the car speed away.

'I do know my baby's name,' I said quietly, though there was no one to hear me but Edward.

EIGHT
CHESTER, JUNE 2023

It was lucky I'd seen Stacey recently, because otherwise I'd have found it hard to hide my shock at the old lady who sat down at my table. At my hen do she'd been wearing make-up, so the contrast between Current Stacey and Stacey In My Head was even starker: today, her face was bare, her silver hair pulled back in a ponytail, which seemed to accentuate her wrinkles. She was doubtless thinking how much *I'd* aged, of course. But I'd never had that beautiful bloom she'd had in her twenties, a vibrancy that attracted attention wherever she went. Was it harder to have had beauty and lost it, or never had much of it, like me?

Get over it, soft lad! I heard Rose's voice. People aged. That was one of the few things you could be sure of, if you didn't live in a plastic filtered world of smooth cheeks. Don't be so superficial.

Stacey said, 'Passing of time's an absolute bitch, isn't it?'

I laughed, embarrassed that she'd guessed what I was thinking. 'You mean I'm ancient, dear cousin?'

'I mean me. I'm eight years older than you. You look pretty much the same, with your Jane Birkin hair.' She nodded at the waitress as her cappuccino was placed in front of her, then asked me, 'Is this place OK?'

I'd offered to come to see her in Liverpool, but she, trying to make things easier, I think, suggested this café in Chester, roughly halfway between us. It was a modern place, pine floors and a noisy coffee machine, popular at this time of day with mothers and babies, and a few been-here-for-hours laptop people hogging the plug sockets.

'It's fine. It's really nice.' I felt compelled to reassure her because after her bold opening, she began tearing a napkin into little strips and there was an awkward silence. Quickly, before I lost my nerve, I said, 'I'm so sorry about the way I behaved. At my party.'

'It's OK...'

'It's really not. I was just so shocked to see you. I didn't know Stella had invited you.'

'Yeah, I worked that out.' She laughed. 'You fucking avoiding me the whole night was the giveaway. Actually you didn't completely ignore me. You said, "Christ, what the hell are you doing here?" and, "I need a drink".'

'Oh my God, that's unacceptably rude, I'm so sorry.' My face started to flare up.

'Don't worry about it. It was pretty cool to see you as blasted as that.' She grinned. 'Is that why you rung me? To say sorry? You could of just sent me a massive bouquet.'

'It's not the only reason.' I took a breath. I knew that if this, well, whatever it was, quest? That seemed a ridiculously pompous term for it, this reckoning I was on was going to have any meaning, I needed to be truthful. So I explained that I was doing some personal housekeeping, trying to find out what had gone wrong with relationships over the years. She jumped straight in.

'Ha, you've come to the right place. I'm the expert on crappy relationships.' She threw up her hands, and I saw a flash of the vigorous girl she'd once been. 'I fucked up every single one.'

'I'm sorry things didn't work out with Ivan.'

'Jesus, he was the least of it.' She stirred her coffee.

I knew from Mum via Aunt Jean that the great affair had only lasted a couple of years, but by the time Stacey had come back to Liverpool with her tail between her legs, her husband, Steven, and daughter, Petra, had moved to Canada. She followed them, to see if they could reconcile, but it didn't work out. She stayed anyway, to be near Petra, and because, according to her mother, she couldn't bear to return and face everyone. What a mess.

'Who've you seen so far, then?' she asked. 'Relationships you screwed up, like.'

I hadn't thought I'd be sharing this outside the therapy room. 'Er, my old uni friend Helena. You met her once, you might remember...'

'Oh yeah!' Stacey cackled. 'She was so pissed off with me. Belter of a night, though. So, what did you get out of seeing her? Did you make up?'

It was a good question. What *had* I got out of meeting Helena? An acknowledgement that I had been a lousy friend at twenty, but then, who wasn't a bit flaky at that age? Maybe this whole thing was a fool's errand. I changed the subject, asked Stacey when she'd returned from Canada.

'Three years ago, when Petra moved back. She's divorced now and decided to start again. She's doing a nursing degree in Brighton.'

'Wow, good for her. Do you see her a lot?'

'Not really. We don't get on great. My fault, obviously. You can't just walk out on a child and expect them to forgive you.'

This seemed to still have the shock of revelation to her; she said it as if it was something I might not know. My heart went out to her. She'd made one terrible decision – to leave her family and run off with a great love – and, as terrible decisions tend to do, it had ruined everything.

'That sounds very hard.'

'It's all right. When my ma died she left me her house, so at least I had somewhere to live. Other people have it worse. I've a boyfriend, Keith, he's low maintenance. I work for John Lewis and they're a good company.'

I found this summary of her life unbearably poignant. She'd never been one to accept the mediocre.

'What about you?' she said. 'I'd get your news when your ma was alive but I'm ten years behind. Thought I'd catch up at the hen party but... well...'

'Can I ask – why *did* you come to it?'

'I was pretty chuffed to hear from your Stella.' She shrugged. 'Thought a lot about you when I was away, I suppose. Me ma's gone, and I lost touch with all my old mates here yonks ago. Don't know anyone who'd known me when I was young.'

'I know exactly what you mean.' How weird that we were on similar trajectories. 'I can't remember much about the hen night, to be honest.'

'You was too bladdered. It was a bit of a shit night, can't lie.' Stacey stared at the table. 'I dragged myself to the back arse of beyond because I was so excited to see you.'

I felt terrible. She'd come all that way to see me, and had a lonely and miserable night in North Wales, because I'd been an unwelcoming, selfish cow. I asked if she'd stayed in a hotel, said I'd reimburse her. But she told me it was already sorted.

'Your Stella said it was the least she could do after you was such a twat. She didn't really say "twat", you raised her nicely.'

Oh God, something else I'd have to make up to Stella. I really was leaving a mild trail of devastation wherever I went. It didn't feel like the right moment to ask Stacey if she'd spoken to Rose that night. Anyway, she'd warmed up now and was ready to do a little crowing.

'Couldn't believe it when I heard you left Richard. Makes me feel a bit less of a fuck-up, that you've got divorced.'

What could I do but laugh. 'Glad if the end of my marriage helps in any way.'

'Were your kids upset?'

'They're fine now. Stella took the divorce quite hard.'

'She's lovely. She looks like you.' She hesitated, then: 'I'm sorry I wasn't around when you had babies.'

Sooner than I'd thought, we were on to the last time we'd seen each other.

'Do you remember that evening?' I said, sure she must do. 'You came to our flat...'

'You'd just had your baby boy, he was gorgeous wasn't he? Jesus, you were a bitch back then.'

'Oh!' I braced myself, but this was partly what I was here for.

'You told me to my face that I was doing everything wrong. You were so judgemental.'

'I'm really...'

'And you were spot on.'

'Pardon?'

'Everything you said, I remember like it was yesterday, you turned out to be right. I left Petra behind, I left everyone important behind. Worst decision of my life, and you were the only person who told it to me straight.'

'I wish I hadn't been right, though.'

'You should of locked me in a room until I'd come to my senses.'

'Like you'd have consented to be locked up! I've always wished I hadn't said anything. I'd been counting on you being around.'

'You wouldn't have had me around anyway. Ivan moved us to Skopje. Macedonia.'

I knew this from Aunt Jean. Ivan's family was from there. 'Was it difficult to leave him?'

'No, we both knew it was a mistake.' She moved her confetti-making business onto my napkin, hers having been decimated. 'So what about you? You was saying about relationships going wrong. Your second marriage isn't in trouble already, is it?'

'God, no. It's wonderful.' I showed her one of Helena's wedding photos on my phone. I certainly wasn't going to tell her that I'd lately found myself wondering what impact my Rose quest was having on my marriage. I'd not had the experience of being married to Murray without Rose anxiety bubbling under the surface – the two things had happened simultaneously. If my head wasn't filled with Rose, would I be more available? Might I be in Monaco with him right now? I felt a brief flash of anger at Rose. My new life with Murray, which should have been the happiest time, had been tainted right from the start.

'Ooh he's fit, isn't he? Congratulations. Shame I couldn't of been there.' She smiled as she said it, but I could sense the neediness.

A harassed-looking woman bumped into the back of Stacey's chair, trying to get a buggy through.

'Oi!' Stacey snapped.

'She's trying to get past,' I said. 'Can you pull your chair in a bit?'

'I'm already squashed.'

The woman had got her wheels stuck under the table behind us, and I got up and helped move them out. She finally got through, with a grateful smile at me.

'Right old Mother Teresa, aren't you?' Stacey said, as I returned to my seat. 'They should have separate cafés for buggies and babies, people don't want to be bashed about, and the bloody noise of them.'

'I like the mix of ages.' I signalled for the bill and then, trying to erase the impression I'd given that I didn't want her around, invited her to my photography degree show. 'I know it means dragging yourself back up to Wales but I'd really appreciate it.'

'Your life's pretty fucking amazing, isn't it?' She looked down at the table. 'Gorgeous new husband, grandkids, doing a degree. Got to say, I'd be scared if I had it all, I'd always be waiting for the other shoe to drop.'

There was no end to how sorry I felt for her. 'I'm very lucky, yes, but not everything's perfect, and I've been questioning a few things. I've always wondered, with you. We were really close, and then we fell out of each other's lives. What should I have done differently?'

She sipped her coffee. Surely it was cold by now. 'Honestly, nothing. You were judgy, yes.' She smiled. 'But like I said, you was right, and I was never going to listen to you. I saw a counsellor for a bit...'

'You *did*?'

Yeah, John Lewis offer it to staff. Partners, we are. And one thing it's taught me is, you couldn't have done anything different, Kathy love. No one could of. It wasn't just you I walked out on, it was everyone. I hated being a mum. I'm sorry, I know you're not supposed to say that, but I hated it, the nappy years, the toddler years, I was bored shitless. And I most definitely didn't want to start helping with your little babies.'

'But you said...'

'I know I said I'd be there. But I didn't want to.' She put down her cup. 'It's not very nice coffee here, is it? When things went tits up with Ivan, I did really miss you. But by then Edward was older, and you'd got Stella too, it was too late to come barrelling back into your life, you know? Too much water under the fucking bridge.'

I sat back, stunned. Our falling-out hadn't been my fault after all. And that was scarcely the point, anyway. My cousin had thrown her life in the air, like I had when I left Richard, only way more damagingly, and had lived with the regret ever since. I was barely a bit player in her story, let alone a driving force.

As if she could see inside my head, Stacey grinned and said, 'It's not always about you, Kathy.' She looked briefly like the outspoken, sassy young woman she'd been. 'Shall we go round the shops?'

We strolled along the famous Rows: two tiers of shops, beautiful with their ancient half-timbered walls. I asked if I could take her photo for my project. She didn't require any explanation, simply nodded and said, 'Ooh get you,' when I took out my camera. I stood her in front of one of the most photogenic of the old buildings, but the decision to lean against a wall like an 8os punk, serious expression, smoking her vape, was all hers.

In every shop we went in, Stacey picked up something and looked at it longingly. I found myself offering to buy her gloves, a pen, a bracelet, a sweater. I wasn't sure why. For all I knew she had plenty of money. I supposed I was trying to make up for something, even now she'd absolved me. She refused every time, until we went into a deli and conceded that I could buy her a tub of fancy olives. While we waited for them to be weighed, I asked if she could tell me anything about the hen party, anything I might not have remembered.

'Dunno. I only talked to a couple of people. Some girl with her face covered in metal who said she was on your course, and that old friend of yours from school, Rose.'

So she *had* spoken to Rose. I tried not to be too pushy. 'What did you talk about?'

'You was the main topic of conversation. You and your menopause marriage.'

'My *what*?'

'I came up with it!' She looked pleased with herself. 'Funny.'

Funny, but also a bit disheartening. 'Rose didn't call it that, did she?'

'No, I told you, I made it up. Keith says I should be a stand-up. Me and Rose mainly talked about how smashed you were. How you wasn't so goody two shoes as you used to be. Pissed up, divorced, marrying some bloke you only just met.'

I couldn't go chasing after every scrap, so I decided not to dig into whether the 'only just met' jibe was direct from Rose, or Stacey's take on it. I paid for the olives, and almost missed what she said next.

'Oh yeah, and Rose talked a bit about Tom?'

'Who?'

Stacey looked at me like I was daft. 'Her ex-husband, of course. You must have known him?'

'Tim?'

'Yeah, Tim, not Tom. That's right.'

I handed her the olives, feeling confused. 'Why was she talking about him?'

'I don't remember. Anyway, after a bit she said she had to go. I went soon after, it was nice in that Premier Inn and I lay in bed and watched *Love is Blind*, have you seen it?'

We went outside, and started walking towards the river. My head was spinning.

'That's bloody weird, Stacey. Rose *never* talks about Tim.'

'All right, Kathy. Chill out, babe.'

'You must have asked her about him, surely?'

'Why would I do that? I never heard of him.' She glanced at my face. 'You look pale. Shall we get a drink? I'd like one. Look, there's a pub.' She dragged me into a bar and ordered two large gin and tonics, standing in silent expectation when the barman brought over the card reader until I tapped it with my card.

We sat in a corner and I begged Stacey to try to remember

every detail and nuance of what Rose had said. But she couldn't come up with anything else.

'You're quite sure she mentioned Tim?'

'Definitely.'

'Because at first, you said Tom.'

She rolled her eyes. 'If I'd known how important this was going to be, I'd of filmed it. Why's it such a big deal?'

'I've fallen out with Rose. But Tim was awful, a controlling arse. She hasn't seen him for twenty years. We never discuss him. If he's come back into her life, she might be in a state, maybe he's threatening her...' Could *this* be why Rose didn't want to see me again? She didn't want to drag me into anything more to do with Tim? Damn it, why couldn't she have made this Delphic-like mention to anyone else? She just had to leave it in the ears of the most unreliable person I knew. Probably Stacey had completely misheard.

'You two was proper good pals. What did you do?'

'Why are you assuming it was me?'

Stacey shrugged. 'You said you was trying to work out what had gone wrong in relationships. You wouldn't be doing that unless you was the problem.'

Fair point. I looked at her with fresh eyes. She was pretty sharp. Maybe she could help. I gave her a potted history of the last couple of months, from wedding text to permanent radio silence, taking in the disastrous trip to Winchester.

'But you've been back there, right?' Stacey said.

'To her house? No way, she made it pretty clear that...'

'You give up too easily, Kathy.'

'I've sent her a couple of short letters.'

'Letters? Like *Pride and* fucking *Prejudice*? You need to be more proactive.' She stood up and held out her hand. 'Give us your card, I'll get more drinks and we'll sort this out for you.'

Another gin and some cheese and onion crisps later, Stacey had somehow convinced me to text Rose from her phone. 'She hasn't blocked *me*, has she? So what do you want to say to her?' She handed me her phone, and I stared at it, my slightly soused brain coming up blank.

'I don't know...'

'Jesus, Kathy, you must of thought of what you want to say a hundred times!' She took the phone back and tapped away using her thumbs, like a teenager. 'What about this?'

I read her text, expecting the worst, but it was rather good: 'Rose, it's Kay on Stacey's phone. I miss you. Say hi if you want me to call you or pop in.'

'Your punctuation is excellent.'

'Don't sound so surprised, I got an A in English O level. Give me her number then.'

'No, Stacey, I can't send it. She told me to leave her alone.'

'That was two months ago. She's probably changed her mind. Too proud to make the first move.'

Knowing I'd regret it, but unable to stop myself, I read out Rose's number, and Stacey sent her text. We sat and stared at the phone for a few minutes, but there was no response. Of course there wasn't.

'Want another?' Stacey said, nodding at my glass. 'My round.'

'I've had enough.' I stood up. I was not at my steadiest.

'Don't be sad, Kathy love. You know what, you should really just go back to Winchester. Don't knock or anything, just camp outside till she comes out, follow her a bit so she can't run back home. Then politely ask her what the fuck's going on.'

I laughed. 'I can't, Stace. Don't think I haven't thought about turning up at her door again. I've thought about it every which way. But you didn't hear her when she told me to go away. She really meant it. I have to respect her wish not to be contacted.'

'You sound like a lawyer.' Stacey put on her coat. 'Anyway, you have contacted her now.' She nodded at her phone, which sat silently in a ticking hand grenade kind of way. Why had I let her send that text? It was the hope that killed you. I felt tipsy and dislocated, and I'd had more than enough Stacey for one day. I made up some business about needing to get back for a tutorial, and we walked to the station. My train was due first so she waited with me on the platform. I wished she wouldn't.

She asked what had happened to Mum's house – she didn't know that Mum had ended up in a care home. 'You must really miss her, you was always very close.'

'I do. Every day. I dream about her a lot.'

'Do you? Ooh, I'm glad I don't dream about mine. She'd probably be disappointed in me, like in real life.'

'Both our mums would be pleased, don't you think, to see the two of us together again?'

'Probably. I weren't so close with mine. My fault, of course. I think I made it up to her in the end. I was there holding her hand when she went.'

'Oh, me too, with mine,' I said, without hesitation. One day, I would unpack all that, but today was not that day. I'd already unpacked what felt like a hundred suitcases.

'My phone went!' She grabbed it out of her bag, and my heart started thumping. 'No, stand down, it's just Keith asking when I'm getting back.'

How many times over the coming days and weeks, I wondered, would I curse myself for being talked into sending that text.

She hugged me when my train came in, and said, 'I'll keep in touch, don't worry. I'll message the minute she replies.'

I sat at a window seat so we could wave goodbye. Just before my train moved off, she held up something with a triumphant look on her face. It was the silver bracelet she'd liked in one of the chi-chi shops on the Row. She must have pinched it. I made a shocked face, and she laughed, and thankfully the train went then, leaving my delinquent sixty-five-year-old cousin behind.

I wasn't expecting Murray back till the evening, so it was a thrill when I arrived home to find him already there, cooking up something delicious-smelling in the kitchen. This was one of the many things I loved about him – he was not a man who sat around waiting to be fed.

He didn't hear me come in because he was singing along to music, his favourite old-style blues, which I was catching on to myself: those bluesmen with amazing names like Lightnin' Hopkins, Howlin' Wolf, Mississippi John Hurt. I watched as he swooshed onions and garlic around in a pan with a wooden spoon, and felt a rush of love for this big rugged fella filling my kitchen, all the new and wonderful things he had brought into my life. God, he was gorgeous! I'd told Stacey I was lucky and by golly, I was. I went over and pressed myself against his back to his startled surprise, put my arms round him.

'I love you,' I told him.

'I love you too,' he said fiercely. 'You won't forget that, will you?'

By way of an answer, I snaked my hands down to his belt buckle, and started to undo it. He leaned against me as I teased and coaxed him until he turned round and swept me into his arms, literally picked me up off the floor in a way you only ever saw in the films, carried me into the living room and laid me down on the sofa.

'The onions!' I said, sexily.

'Fuck the onions.' He knelt beside me and started undoing my shirt.

'Won't they burn...' I trailed off as his fingers moved gently across my breasts.

'I turned the ring off...' he said, easing down my jeans and kissing the base of my stomach. 'You're so beautiful.'

'Come here,' I said, pulling him on top of me, and what ensued was by some distance the most satisfactory part of the day.

NINE

NORTH WALES, JUNE 2023

Four sessions in, and I still wasn't sure about therapy. I didn't know what Stella liked about it so much. I could see, logically, that exploring why I had alienated my closest friend would hopefully help me be a better person, and a better partner to Murray. But we didn't seem to be making much headway with finding out why. Still, I supposed it contained things a bit, in Louisa's slightly stuffy living room. I didn't want to keep bothering Murray about my 'quest'. Louisa was at least getting paid to let me bore her, whereas I'd noticed Murray changing the subject a couple of times when I mentioned Rose. He'd been taken aback when I told him I'd started seeing a counsellor, which made sense: we were newly-weds in love and I should be on top of the world. If it had been the other way round, maybe I would have felt it as a slight on me. But his concern was more about me repeatedly returning to excavate something painful.

'I hate the thought of you searching for what you've done wrong. You haven't done anything wrong, in my opinion. It's not your fault you're surrounded by dickheads.' His smile showed me that he was referring to himself, but I knew he did also think that Rose was flaky.

'It's not just about trying to see what I did wrong,' I said. 'I've had a lot of losses, and not properly processed them. My mum, for instance...' I welled up, which took me by surprise.

'Kay, Jesus, I'm such an idiot.' He pulled me into his arms. 'It's brilliant to want to sort this stuff out. I should do it myself, shouldn't I, then I wouldn't be such a drongo.'

'I don't want you to change. You might be a drongo, but you're my drongo.'

He hugged me tighter. 'I hope you always feel that way.'

One thing that surprised me about therapy was that Louisa wasn't always wholly on my side. For instance, she wasn't keen on my project idea to approach people from my past for an up-to-date photo.

'I do wonder,' she said, in her understated way, 'if it's entirely healthy to confront people this way.'

'Wow. Am I really confronting them?'

She didn't answer, so of course, muggins filled in the space. 'You mean it would be more honest to see if they want to take part only once I've made things right with them?'

'Hmm. That puts rather a lot of pressure on "making things right", doesn't it?'

This wasn't the first time I'd noticed that maddening little 'hmm'.

'Well, meeting up with my cousin definitely helped heal a few old wounds.'

'Hmm.' Aaaargh! 'It also sounds like it opened a new one.'

I wished I hadn't told Louisa about Stacey texting Rose. You should have heard the length of the 'hmm' in response to that one.

'Still no reply from Rose to your cousin, I assume.'

'None.' I didn't mention that Stacey had taken the opportunity, several times a week, to update me on there being no news. I already knew what an idiot I was; I didn't need Louisa to tell me.

'You said you wanted to include Rose in the display. Are you thinking of approaching her?'

Well, of course I'd been thinking about it. 'I could write to her, I suppose, and explain the project. Apologise for Stacey while I'm at it. If you think it's a good idea?'

'Do *you* think it's a good idea?'

Oh come on Louisa, why was I paying nearly two quid a minute for you to repeat my questions back to me?

'I could ask if she'd be willing to send me a photo?' I said, tentatively. 'If she was ready to forgive me, it might be a way in?'

'Hmm.'

We'd spent ages trying to work out why Rose had mentioned Tim, if one trusted Stacey's account, but it was all just guesswork. Louisa pointed out that even if Tim was back in Rose's life, things were very different for her now, with their children now adults, and her new partner, and I knew I had to be comforted by that. If she didn't want me to know, there wasn't much I could do about it.

'Perhaps for now,' Louisa said, looking at her notes, 'we should come back to the hen party.'

'You still think it's important?'

'Well, it was the last time you saw Rose.'

'Maybe you should hypnotise me, see if I can dredge anything up.' I was joking, but she didn't smile.

'I don't practise hypnosis. But the brain has a way of slowly revealing memories, if you give it time.'

Whenever I thought about the hen do, my mind slipped on to the morning after, waking with the hangover from hell, and a shoe missing its heel. The night itself seemed destined to float forever out of reach of my memory. We were drinking French 75 champagne cocktails, deceptively harmless, and they kept on coming. Thank goodness I didn't have to go straight into the wedding the next day. The hen do was a couple of weeks before it so that – oh, the irony – Rose could come, because she and

Graham were going on one of their middle-aged hiking holidays, booked a sensible year in advance.

'Perhaps a little earlier, then?' Louisa said. 'I've been wondering about Rose's reaction when you told her your marriage plans.'

'She was delighted for me, of course.'

'What exactly did she say?'

'Really, marriage?' Rose stared at me, her half-pint of Guinness arrested on its way to her mouth. 'To Murray?'

'Of course to Murray!' I giggled like a schoolgirl. 'It's so exciting and romantic.'

'But...' She put her glass down. 'What about Luca?'

I'd been so preoccupied with falling head over heels, I'd scarcely given Luca a thought. 'He was only ever a casual thing.'

'You've been seeing him for five years!'

'It's not serious. You know how little we see each other.'

She drank half her Guinness in one go before replying. 'Wow, it's fast, isn't it, chick?'

'Yeah well, when you know, you know.'

Louisa nodded. Was her normally impassive face a little sceptical? 'So when you said that she was delighted for you...'

Like I said, I still wasn't sure about therapy.

'She was eventually, once she understood how I felt.'

'She was surprised that you were marrying Murray, rather than Luca?'

'I suppose, yes.' Though goodness knows why. She was the first one to point out the sizzling chemistry between Murray and me. But then, Rose had always liked Luca. She described him as 'a keeper' last summer, when he and I spent a few days with her and Graham. 'She thought Luca was my ideal man.'

'Why was that?'

I fidgeted in my chair. This wasn't getting the baby washed, was it? 'I suppose he's handsome, intelligent and kind, ticks all the boxes.'

'And Rose didn't see those qualities in Murray?'

'She must do, because he has them in spades. Hang on, you're not suggesting that Rose has dropped me because she thought I was mean to Luca?'

Louisa didn't respond. We sat in silence, her calmly, me fuming at her, and at Rose. Finally I said, 'Rose was so pro Luca, she'd probably have been against anyone else I chose to marry.'

'Hmm.'

Did we need to talk about the 'hmm's? And how come there were so many questions today? What happened to me pouring out my heart without intervention other than sympathetic nods? She still wasn't done – there was one more question.

'How did the conversation end?'

'Well, I told her I was really happy with Murray, and she said she was pleased for me.'

There was a short silence, then Louisa glanced at the clock, and said, 'We're out of time.'

Good. I didn't want to tell her the rest of the conversation, which I could now recall in startling clarity. It was none of her business, after all. Nosey cow! I replayed it in my head as I drove home.

'I'm pleased if you're pleased,' Rose had said. 'I just...'

'Just what?' I tried not to sound as irritated as I felt. 'You're not going to wheel out "marry in haste, repent at leisure", are you?'

'Well I...' She clocked my face, and said, 'Couldn't you date for a while longer? Have a lovely affair and see what happens? You only met him a few months ago.'

'I know!' Why couldn't she see how thrilling it was? 'It's a complete rollercoaster. And really, I've known him for years, when he was married to Bear...' Why was she raining on my parade? 'What are you trying to say?'

'Nothing. I'm sorry, I don't want to upset you.' Clearly, she was not willing or able to tell me. 'If you're happy, I'm happy.'

As I drove home I tried to let my mind float free, see if I could capture some of these memories that were allegedly floating just out of reach. Nothing. But then, as I pulled up onto the gravel outside Bryn Glas, I had a flash of an image: Rose giving me something... a present. Louisa was right! The memory came whooshing back: Rose handing me something small, wrapped up... white paper, a wisp of red ribbon... Then I could see her standing, holding up her phone, squeezing past the other women in the booth, a hand pressing my shoulder, a kiss on the cheek. Were her eyes wet or was I embroidering detail now? But I wasn't making up the gift, or her words as she gave it to me: 'Something blue.'

I raced into the house and rummaged through the pockets of my fancy coat, the one I'd worn that night, but turned up nothing except tissues and, alarmingly, the heel to my shoe. I shook my head. How had I broken it? Stacey must have left too early to witness how that came about, because there's no way she'd have missed the chance for a good old gloat. If only Stella wasn't in Italy and barely responding to my texts, I could have asked her.

What sort of ass was I, to have lost what might be the last thing Rose would ever give me. I was getting ready to have a solid sob when I remembered that I'd taken a bag with me, a daft little evening bag that Stella had lent me. Did I still have it? I dashed upstairs and looked in all the feasible places, finally finding it under the bed where I must have flung it when I came home that night. Please let Rose's gift still be there, let me have put it in the bag and not left it in a puddle of beer on the bar, or dropped it in whatever vehicle got me home. I tipped the contents onto the bed, and there, in amongst a tangle of comb and lipstick and coins, was a little package of white tissue paper, a piece of red ribbon loosely around it. It looked like I had opened it on the night, then wrapped it up again. I scrabbled to get to what was inside, and stabbed my hand on something. It was a small silver brooch, its pin unmoored from the clasp. I impatiently dabbed the little bud of blood on my palm with a tissue – not now, body. The brooch was in the shape of a spray of blue flowers, old-fashioned in style. I put the pin into its catch, then held the brooch tight, trying to get a message from it. Come on, Rose, what had I done? You loved me well enough at the hen do to give me this gift. But the brooch wasn't talking.

TEN

NORTH WALES, JULY 2023

I was noticing a pattern to Murray's trips away. The first day I'd miss him like blazes, the second day a little less, and by the third day I'd be used to having Bryn Glas to myself again. Murray could be a larger-than-life presence, and our attraction to each other was very consuming; him going away so regularly was good for our balance.

That said, I couldn't wait to see him. I'd been working hard on my exhibit while he was away in Sheffield, and was excited to show him. My proposal had been approved – in fact it had got a rather good grade, to my surprise – and I'd allocated one wall of the living room as my gallery space. I was tacking up photos, working out where everything might go, when there was a knock on the door. Murray! Though why he hadn't used his key I didn't know. I ran to open it, and was astonished to see my dear landlady, Imogen, standing there, with her son Simon. How bizarre to see her here, so far from her London milieu. At my wedding she'd mentioned that she hadn't visited Bryn Glas in more than twenty years.

'Hello, *chérie*. Sorry to land on you like this.' She kissed my cheek, and Simon shook my hand. It was Imo's cottage but

Simon did all the practicalities of rent and contracts. He was rather dour; though he was probably around the same age as me, he seemed older.

I ushered them into the kitchen and offered them tea, and freshly baked lemon cake I'd made for Murray's homecoming, though only Simon accepted a piece.

'I must say, Kay, you've done a beautiful job with the cottage,' Imogen said. 'The photos didn't do it justice.'

I thanked her, though I couldn't hide my worry. Why was she here? 'Is everything OK? Are you well?'

'You are a sweet thing. I'm not completely well, I'm afraid.'

'Oh, Imo, I'm sorry.'

'It's an awful drag, but people seem to think I can't live in my house any more.'

'Come on, Mother, you did agree with us.' Simon put his hand on hers and she smiled at him fondly.

'It is a big place to manage, to be fair,' I said, trying not to look shocked. I'd imagined her going on for ever in her Hampstead house, living in bohemian splendour. I thought of my wedding day there, one of the watershed days of my life, and for more reasons than the obvious fresh start. Nothing since had been quite how I'd imagined it. And Imogen's expression made me suspect that something else wasn't going to go my way.

'I wanted to tell you face to face, my dear.' She closed her eyes briefly, and I knew before she said it. 'I'm afraid I'm going to have to sell Bryn Glas.'

She was old school: the landlady always delivers the eviction notice in person. My stomach lurched with homesickness, my body already processing the shock of the news before my brain could comprehend it. My home, my beautiful home.

'I'm really sorry,' I managed to say on automatic. 'I've loved living here.'

'I can't stop falling over, you see. Isn't that silly? Usually just a little bang, a tiny bruise. But two weeks ago I fell through the glass door in the conservatory.'

'Oh no, Imo, that's awful.'

'Simon was terribly cross with me.'

'Yes, because I only found out when the hospital phoned.'

'Against my wishes, might I say. Some silly business about next of kin.' She smiled at me. 'So you see, I've agreed to move into a care home.'

'It makes sense,' I croaked, my throat dry. But I didn't think it did, actually. She was fiercely independent. Wouldn't she go mad somewhere like that, being told what to do?

'We've found a very nice one, insofar as these places are ever nice,' Imogen said. 'It has quite the cachet in care home circles. But of course, it is hideously expensive. Several thousand pounds a month.'

'Goodness! Well, I can see that you'd need to sell up, to cover that.' I wondered why she wasn't selling her London home, which would bring in far more money, but she immediately addressed that.

'I don't want to give up the Hampstead house, because after a couple of years being looked after I might be well enough to go back there.' She looked at me with a pleading expression. 'That might be possible, mightn't it?'

'Of course, Imo.' No, not at all. My mum had deteriorated quickly once she lost her autonomy. 'So when do you need us out?' Pull the plaster off quickly.

'There's not a huge rush,' Simon said. 'We don't want to put the house on the market until September.'

'Simon is explaining things in a funny order.' Imogen looked at him fondly. 'We wanted to ask if *you'd* like to buy it.'

'Oh, Imo! Yes, of course, yes!' From despair to sunshine, that was the order of the day. I'd been so stunned by her selling the cottage, it hadn't occurred to me that I could buy it. If only Murray would come home now, so we could say yes together, as a couple. I glanced at my phone, and saw there was a message from him, but it would be rude to read it in the middle of this important conversation.

Imogen patted my hand. 'I know you adore it here, and it would warm my heart if you'd be the new owner. Simon is willing to give you first refusal, so if you can let us know by September we won't put it on the market, of course.'

'No, Mother, by the end of July, so we have time to decorate.'

She winked at me. 'I can't get much off the asking price, I'm afraid, his sentimentality only goes so far, but I do hope you'll say yes.'

'We've got to get a good price for you, haven't we?' Simon said. 'You're going to need every penny.' I wondered that Imo didn't mind his patronising tone.

I thanked them fulsomely, and reiterated that we very much wanted to buy it. Imo looked delighted, and put her hand on my arm. 'This house should be yours.'

Simon stood up. 'In case you don't buy it...'

'She will, of course,' Imogen said.

'I'll take a quick look round to see what might need doing if we put it on the market.'

I was so relieved I could have kissed his grumpy face. 'Actually I was meaning to let you know, there's a little spot of damp in the spare room. Shall I show you?'

'Thank you.'

I took him upstairs and was no more than five minutes, but when I came down, leaving him to examine the rest by himself, Imogen was sitting on the kitchen floor by the back door, half in and half out of the garden. 'Oh my God!'

'I'm fine, *chérie*. Nothing broken. But I don't seem able to get up.'

One leg was awkwardly under her, the other stretched out in front. She looked like a tiny, ancient rag doll.

'What were you trying to do?'

'I wanted to sit outside and look at the flowers. I'm so silly!'

'I'll get Simon...'

'Please don't bother him, Kay, I'd much rather not.'

Remembering some traces of manual handling skills from my Quiller Queen days – Richard had a manic phase of making us do a corporate training programme – I hooked my arms under hers and managed to get her up and onto the bench outside the back door. She was barely bones but still weighed enough, and my arms and shoulders ached by the time she was sitting comfortably. I brought her a glass of water and insisted she give me a verbal check through all the places she'd hurt herself. She claimed only a small ache in her knee, but I knew how unforgiving the kitchen's terracotta tiles were.

'You see?' She managed a wan smile. 'I can't be trusted on my own.'

'I really ought to ask Simon to take you to hospital, get you checked out.'

'Shush! Absolutely not, Kay. I'm completely fine. I'm sick to the back teeth of hospitals.'

'But, Imo, if you're hurt...'

She took hold of my arm, reminding me of Alice's hand on my shoulder at the party. Where did these old ladies get their strength from? I couldn't have pulled away if I'd wanted to.

'If you send me to hospital, Kay, I will never forgive you.' Her expression was pure steel. 'I mean it.'

'Fine.'

'*Fine.*'

We both started laughing.

'I'm like the old lady in the poem who wears purple and doesn't care,' she said.

'You're making me feel sorry for poor Simon. I only hope he has power of attorney so he can veto all your bonkers decisions.'

'He does, but did you know that power of attorney cannot

be used, however "bonkers" the decision, if I am still considered capable of making my own choices?'

'I did not know that. Trust you to know.'

'Sit next to me, we can admire the alliums together.'

I did as she told me, and we shared a moment's companionable silence as we looked out at the garden, the lawn leading down to the large trees at the end, the big-headed purple alliums, the pretty ox-eye daisies and the euphorbia, all overlooked by the majestic Carneddau mountains. It was a sight I never tired of.

'If you're needing money...' I thought of Simon saying that she could do with every penny, but hesitated, because it felt indelicate. 'Do you want your gift back?' She looked confused. 'The money?' I clarified.

Her watery eyes held mine. 'I gave you money?'

Maybe it wasn't her after all? But I'd ruled out pretty much everyone else who it might have been. 'Ten thousand pounds for a wedding present, in a blue bag? The note said it was only for me, and not to tell Murray? I'm so sorry I haven't thanked you properly. But it's such a lot, I must give it back if you're in need.'

'Gracious, someone is suspicious of Murray, aren't they?!' She laughed. 'I wonder why.'

I sat back. 'It wasn't you?'

'I wish it was, I love an intrigue. But no, my dear, forgive me, but I had hoped that hosting your wedding was gift enough.'

Nope, not muddled at all. Sharp as a tack, as usual.

'I'm so sorry, forgive me. Of course it was. I just don't know who else has that sort of money.'

'When I'm feeling stronger I'd love to play detective with you. I'm sure we can uncover your secret patron, if we put our heads together.'

'I'd like that.' I glanced at her; she was looking very wistful as she gazed at the garden. 'Is there really no option but the care home, Imo?'

'Alice was first to propose an alternative. She rang to commiserate, and to offer a bolthole with her in your old family home...'

'Oh, you should definitely do that! Aileen already looks after her, I'm sure she wouldn't mind an extra lady.' I could feel Imogen's eyes boring into me. 'What?'

'Nothing, dear. Merely amused at your generously offering up Richard's new wife as a full-time carer to the elderly and infirm.'

'Fair enough. You can't blame me for wanting you to be with people you know, though, can you?'

'Everyone's offered. Simon said I could live with him, goodness only knows what it cost him to form the words. What he means, of course, is that his wife and daughters will look after me. Have you noticed how carers are always the womenfolk? It never even occurred to you, good feminist that I know you to be, that Richard might look after me, rather than Aileen.'

Ugh. Out-feministed by an octogenarian.

'No, I'd rather pay my way and know that my carers are at least getting financially rewarded, however small.'

I nodded, thinking of how Rose and I had once agreed that we'd live together when we were in our dotage. So much for that.

Imogen slowly opened her handbag and took out a lipstick and a small compact mirror, decorated with brown and gold swirls. 'Have you heard from your friend?'

How did she know I was thinking about Rose? 'Unfortunately not.'

'I'm sorry. You were so upset at the wedding, I did feel for you. But whatever it was that she didn't like about your marriage, I'm sure she'll come round.' She opened the mirror and examined her face.

'You think it was definitely something to do with the marriage?'

'Well, don't you, dear?' Imo said, in her maddeningly gentle way. 'The timing would suggest so, no?'

'Yes, of course, but I thought perhaps it was something I'd done in the run-up to the wedding, been a bad friend, you know.'

She ran her lipstick a little tremulously around her thin lips. She had worn the same shade of dark pink since the 1960s. '*Have* you been a bad friend?'

'Maybe. I've certainly been rather needy lately.'

For a hopeful moment I thought Imogen was going to tell me exactly what was going on with Rose, and provide a step-by-step guide to solving it. But she shrugged. 'We all have phases of being needy. Look at me now! I'm going to have to ask you to help me into the house.'

'May I take your photo first? The light's lovely and I'm doing a project for my degree...'

'Of course,' she said immediately. I fetched my camera and took a few shots of her sitting with her eyes closed, her face tilted to the sun. How radiant she looked. Then I helped her to her feet, and arm in arm we made our stately way into the cottage. I settled her into a chair, and she winced as she moved her legs slowly into position.

'That's a charming brooch you have there,' she said, I think simply to distract me from registering her every little tremor of pain. She pointed to Rose's Last Gift, which I had decided to wear every day until we were friends again. It was a bit of a rash decision as it looked daft on my M&S hoodie. 'You don't often see that forget-me-not design any more.'

I looked down at the brooch. 'They're forget-me-nots?'

'Yes, the language of flowers, you know. Ladies used to wear jewellery that had a message, back when they couldn't speak for themselves.' She laughed.

Simon came in. 'Looks good up there.' Thank goodness I'd tidied up this morning. 'Everything OK?'

Imo and I glanced at each other. She had that same furious expression as when she'd gripped my arm. 'Yes, absolutely,' I said.

As Simon helped her up, she held her head high, so he couldn't see the pained expression on her face. How magnificent she was. I'd never thought of her as a friend, not exactly, because she was so much older, my mother-in-law's contemporary. But in these weird days of re-evaluating what a friend was, I realised that of course she was. She had been a good friend to me almost my whole adult life.

When they'd gone, I read Murray's message. *Katie, I'm such a drongo*, it began, and I had to smile at that. *I need a couple more days to get everything done. Can you spare me? I'll make it up to you.* I was disappointed, but too elated about the cottage to be downhearted for long. I dialled his number.

'At last! I thought you were mad at me,' he said as he answered.

'No, Imogen was here and I couldn't text. Listen, Murray, she wants to sell Bryn Glas...'

'Katie, I'm sorry, that's a blow. But you know, every cloud, that could work out great, because a fellow I know here, same line of work, he has a flat in Sheffield, said I could use it whenever I'm here. I'm sure he'd be up for both of us moving in, peppercorn rent, he wants it looked after, it would be so much more convenient than Wales, much less travelling for me...'

I felt myself curl up inside. All the little comments he'd made about the cuteness, the tininess of the cottage, the charming remoteness of North Wales, the adorably patchy phone signal, read different. How quick he was to move on. To him, Bryn Glas was just the place we happened to be for now, a temporary arrangement. He didn't know the extent of my attachment to it.

But how could he? I'd not told him about it, not talked about those years when I had little kids and little support, and Bryn Glas was my sanctuary. Or the weekends I had here with Rose, walking in the day, drinking and talking all evening by the fire, laughing till we cried. My love of this isolated little cottage was one of the things Murray and I ought to have discussed before we married, along with what a figjam was, what actually he did for a living, and why he and Bear divorced.

How well do you know each other? I heard it loud and clear, and this time, as if my session with Louisa yesterday had turned a key and I had only to push against the door, I could hear Rose's voice saying it. Of course it had been Rose, who else? I saw her face as she said it, half-smile, raised eyebrow, silver bracelet slipping down her arm. Her eyes crinkling at the edges. Her blue dress.

That knowledge had been in my brain all this time and chose now to resurface. Maybe therapy plus time was, after all, as good as hypnosis.

'Katie, are you there?'

I returned to the present with a bump. 'You didn't give me a chance to finish, Murray. Imogen is giving us first refusal on buying the house, and I want to.'

'Oh, mate! I'm *so* sorry. I went straight into problem-solving mode. I didn't want you to think that we might be homeless for even one minute, but if you'd like to buy it, let's make that happen.'

'Do you really want to move to Sheffield?'

'Not if you don't. I didn't realise.'

You didn't ask; you just talked.

'It doesn't sound like it's what you want, but for me it would be a dream come true.' My head ached. Back and forth it went: the cottage will be sold... but you can buy it! Murray doesn't want to... But then he says OK...

'Katie, if it's your dream then it's mine too. Let's sit down when I get back and work out the figures. I'm sure we can pull a deposit together.'

'Well, I've got that ten grand in my T-shirt drawer!' The moment it was out of my mouth, I remembered he didn't know about it.

'You've got what *where*?'

I made light of it. 'Big ol' stash of cash upstairs.'

'Where did that come from?'

'Oh, it was a late wedding gift, you were away when it came and I forgot to tell you.' I didn't want to hurt his feelings with the whole 'keep it from him' thing.

'You forgot to tell me about ten grand?! Who was it from?'

I thought fast. 'Richard. He said I'd been good about not asking for anything in the divorce.'

'Damn right – he owes you, doesn't he? But, sweetie, you shouldn't keep a huge sum like that at home, it's not safe. What if someone broke in?'

'What, here, in the middle of nowhere?'

'Seriously, I'm not messing. Promise me you'll put it into the bank tomorrow.'

'It's Sunday tomorrow.'

'First thing Monday then. I mean it, Kay.'

'I will. I just liked having it to look at and feel rich.'

'You're a funny one, and no mistake. Well, when I get back, I'll consolidate my accounts and see what I've got.'

This was great news, but also, why did Murray never seem to know how much money he had from one month to the next? Yes, he was a freelancer, but the amounts he talked about getting from clients seemed huge to me. Was he not putting any away for a rainy day?

Add this to the list of questions I ought to have asked pre-marriage: how much do you earn and how much have you got saved? Or perhaps start with a broader question: what is your attitude to money? Whenever he had some he was beyond generous with it: meals out, concerts and plays, clothes, flowers, wine, but other times he seemed concerned about relatively small sums.

'Are you sure it's what you want?'

'I'm really sure. I jumped in way too soon. I'm a double drongo today. Forgive me? I'm totally Team House Buy.'

I needed a quiet sit-down. I made winding-up-the-call noises: 'OK. Thank you. I love you.'

'I love you too. I'll be back soon. Get that money into the bank, OK?'

We hung up, leaving me feeling faintly relieved to stop talking to him, and rather guilty about that relief. Then I saw that Stacey had texted while I'd been on the phone. Ready to roll my eyes at another 'no news' update, I was surprised, and anxious, to see that it was a longer message than usual.

Just heard from Rose and she says – my heart was in my mouth – *that she has blocked me. I sent her a few extra texts yesterday, and she probably got pissed off. Sorry!*

I chucked my phone on the floor. Stacey was a complete liability, but the fault was mine. I should have told her no, refused to give her Rose's number. However, on the plus side, we now knew three things:

1. Rose was alive.
2. She had the same phone number.
3. She still didn't want to be in contact with me.

I was so tired. I closed my eyes, maybe even drifted off for a few minutes. Then my phone started ringing with my special 'family' ringtone, and I leaped to scoop it up off the floor. Stella! My exhaustion evaporated, and I was immediately on high mother-alert. We rarely rang each other. Her generation, she'd often lectured me, didn't use their phones for actual talking.

My generation were the ones who thought that calling from

overseas was a huge extravagance, but it wasn't, of course, any more. I pressed 'answer' with a trembling finger. 'Darling! What's up?'

'Hey, Mum.' She sounded subdued. 'Hope I didn't worry you.'

'Little bit... Are you OK?'

A small pause. 'Not really.'

'Sparkle, what is it? Isn't Italy what you were hoping?'

'No, it's amazing.' There was another pause. 'I'm just not coping very well.'

'I'm so sorry. It can be discombobulating, can't it, being in a different country?' I wondered if she was missing Newland.

She lowered her voice. 'It's harder than I thought. I don't suppose...' Her last words were so faint I couldn't hear them at all.

'Say again, Stella?'

'I said, I don't suppose you could come?'

'To Naples?' What was going on? She hadn't asked for my help for a long time.

'Sorry, forget I said anything. You've got your degree to finish. You're busy.'

'I'm never too busy for you, darling. Of course I'll come. I'll get a flight tomorrow.'

'Oh, Mum. Are you sure? Thank you, thank you.' Again quietly, she said, 'I don't know who else to talk to.'

What was going on that she couldn't talk to Nita and Piet?

'Don't worry, I'll be there as soon as I can. I love you.'

'I'm so grateful. Love you too.'

We hung up, and I sat for a moment, possibilities ricocheting round my mind. But I would find out tomorrow. Powered by adrenaline, I booked a flight, then ran upstairs to pack.

PHOTO #5

Then

Luca stands by the canal outside a palazzo. It's the morning after the first night he spent with Kay. Though he's wearing the same clothes as the previous evening, he still looks effortlessly stylish, with his coat open, sunglasses on, one hand pushing back his dark hair from his forehead. He is smiling at the photographer. He looks hopeful, as if this new relationship might be the start of something.

Date: June 2018. Location: Venice. Photographer: Kay Bright.

* * *

Now

Leaning against one of the creamy-yellow columns, Luca looks away from the camera, towards the fountain. His hair is less dark, flecked with grey, but he otherwise looks as louchely urbane as always. He is wearing a chic wool jacket and a green patterned scarf. He is posing patiently but he is running late, and is ready to go as soon as the photographs have been taken.

Date: July 2023. Location: Pantheon, Rome. Photographer: Kay Garland.

ELEVEN
NAPLES, JULY 2023

You haven't known fear until you find yourself in the passenger seat of a tiny Fiat 500, being driven along an ancient narrow street by a very tall Dutchman with absolutely no sense of danger. Even the hair-raising taxi ride I'd once taken with Luca in Lisbon, till now my high watermark for terrifying car-based experiences, didn't seem so bad; at least there the roads were wide enough for vehicles to pass each other in the normal fashion.

'Piet!' I cried in genuine terror as we rounded a corner at speed, barely missing three cars all going in different directions. 'I know Neapolitan driving has a certain reputation but there's no need to put on a show for me.'

'I know, it's crazy, right? It is always like this.' His knees were almost up around his ears in the toy-like car, but as we zipped along tiny passageways I could see why he'd ended up with this one. Anything larger would get wedged between the walls which loomed close to us on either side. He drove calmly, one hand on the steering wheel, as though it was completely normal to beep strolling pedestrians out of the way.

'I guess they're used to it,' I said, slamming down a braking foot and hoping Piet hadn't noticed.

The deeper we drove into the old town, the narrower the streets became, till they were more passageway than road, and when a pedestrian appeared ahead of us in Piet's headlights they had to press themselves flat against the black stone walls. It was impossible to conceive that the hotel I had booked hastily at random, described in reviews as 'lovely', could possibly be down here.

'What an, er, colourful neighbourhood,' I said.

'Yes, wonderful.' Piet didn't do irony. 'We feel at home here.' He turned to smile at me, which meant his eyes were now not on the road. 'It is the exact change we are in need of.' He turned back just in time to avoid a moped racing towards us, apparently being driven by a small child. By the time I saw that their parent was sitting behind them, I'd grown a few more grey hairs.

'So how are the girls getting on at cookery school?' I asked, to distract myself from the carnage. I wondered what Piet was doing while they were busy.

'Very well,' he said, and then, answering my unspoken question, added, 'My job is to look after them. The course is very full-on and when they come home they are exhausted. I cook and clean.'

'Wow, that is good of you.'

He made a 'no big deal' gesture, his driving hand briefly leaving the steering wheel. I closed my eyes till it was back in place. 'You may not know that Nita's mother comes from Rome, and they used to holiday here,' he went on. 'Nita and I had such a plan...'

There was a silence as Piet negotiated a group of teenagers weaving across the street.

'Yes, we planned to move here, the two of us, when Nita and Stella had sold the business.'

'I didn't know they were going to do that.' Something else I'd missed while preoccupied with wedding plans.

'It was not to be for a few years. They would develop a franchise, sell the overall holding and then Nita and me would...'

He broke off again but there was no obstacle to negotiate this time – at least, no physical obstacle. I glanced at him and saw that he was choked up. How I wished I knew what was going on. What was Stella's role in this apparent abandonment of their plans? If she and Nita were an item, how did Piet fit in to things?

Recovering, he said, 'We can leave your bag in the hotel, then walk to the apartment, OK?' He pulled over and turned off the engine.

I looked doubtfully around us as we got out of the car. There was nothing resembling a hotel or apartment, only the forbidding dark walls. Piet rang a bell on a small wooden door, and after a moment, a buzzer sounded and the door opened. Even I had to duck to get through, and Piet had to practically bend double. As I straightened up, I found myself standing in the most gorgeous courtyard. There were little café-style tables with candles flickering on them, and lights were strung across the trees. Behind them was the glowing sign of the hotel. The contrast between this hidden space and the down-trodden street on the other side of that door could not be more stark. It was like a magic trick.

'How on earth do people know this is here?' I said. 'You can't see it from the street.'

'Many of the houses and hotels in the old town are this way,' Piet said. 'Concealed behind walls. Our apartment also, and the cookery school. On the first day Nita and Stella could not find the building and had to knock on many doors!'

He carried my bag into the hotel, which was indeed lovely. My room was small but spotless, and I gazed longingly at the comfortable-looking bed. It had been so hectic getting myself packed and on a flight after Stella's call. But I was keener to see her than to sleep. We returned to the darkening streets, only walking a hundred yards or so before Piet stopped outside another inauspicious-looking wooden gate. This led into a handsome building with a wide external white marble staircase, and I felt hugely relieved when I realised that this was where Stella was staying.

'There is no lift, I am afraid, but it is only on the second floor.'

'That's fine,' I said. I was eager to get there, see my girl, and I trotted behind him with renewed energy.

Piet unlocked a door at the top of the stairs and led me into a large, warmly lit sitting room. Stella came running in, a tea towel over her shoulder, and threw her arms round me.

'Mum! I can't believe you're here.'

'Darling, it's so lovely to see you!'

Still in my embrace, she said to Piet, 'Nita's lying down but said you should go in.'

I heard him go out, and a door open and close somewhere, and still Stella clung to me. As I held her, I thought of embracing Bear in Venice, when I'd realised how very thin and ill she was. It wasn't that Stella seemed ill, exactly; but there was an emotional fragility to her. Oh, my darling girl, what was going on? I'd read an article recently about the actors who played characters at Disneyland, and how they were instructed to keep a hug going for as long as the child wanted. What was the longest hug ever recorded on Disney soil, I wondered, and was it longer than this one? I closed my eyes, leaned into it, let Stella decide when it was over.

At last, she pulled away. 'Wow, I needed that! I expect you could use a cuppa?'

'Real tea? They only had lukewarm coffee on the plane.'

I followed her into the kitchen, where she set a pan with water on the stove. 'Sit down,' she said. 'You must be exhausted.'

'I'm still benefiting from the cortisol rush of having booked and arrived within twenty-four hours.'

'Maybe I should make a calming tea? Valerian? Camomile?'

'Absolutely not. English Breakfast please.'

She grinned, and got down some cups. As she pottered about, my motherly eye flitted over her in what I imagined was a discreet manner, a fancy sadly dashed when she said, 'You can stop looking at me as though I'm about to break.'

'Sorry, Sparkle. I don't mean to.' Of course I was worried; she'd asked me to come with no notice, then hugged me like her life depended on it. But before I could ask anything, she changed the subject.

'Was Murray OK about you darting over here?'

'Lord yes, he's away himself anyway, but told me to give you his love. I think he found my spontaneous trip rather charming.'

'Being a newly-wed suits you, Mum. You look very well.'

'Do I? I suppose I am still a newly-wed, but I'm past the honeymoon stage now, and ready to see all the people I've neglected. You're the most important of those, and I'm sorry I've not had as much time as I used to. I've been in bit of a whirl.'

'Not at all. For goodness sake, I'm a grown-up.' She poured boiling water into the cups. 'Murray swept you off your feet, and you were ready to be swept. I get it completely.'

'You really are a grown-up.' I smiled at her. 'So. Want to tell me?'

She gave me my tea. 'I do. But not right now.' She raised her eyebrows at the door and mouthed, 'I don't want them to hear.'

So I was right, there was some horrible tangle between them. 'Shall we go out somewhere?'

'Not tonight, when you've just arrived. I'm making you spaghetti alle vongole. But there's no cookery school tomorrow, so we can spend the day together.'

'I'd love that.'

'In fact, I've got us tickets for something special.' She smiled properly for the first time.

'What?' Then I realised. 'Oh, Stella, not Pompeii?'

She nodded, delighted. How amazing of her to remember that Pompeii was on my 'things to see before sixty' list! I'd taken Latin at school, and the whole class had been very invested in the story of poor Caecilius in our textbooks, who lived in Pompeii at the worst possible time. We studied him for two years and Rose sobbed at the end, despite it being the most signposted tragedy in history. I'd been pretty upset myself.

While we talked, Stella put an amazing-smelling sauce together, and knocked up fresh pasta from dough she'd made earlier. She rejected my offers of help, because apparently I was a 'rank amateur' who threw salt into everything 'without tasting it first'. I loved how relaxed she was as she cooked, and felt reassured that whatever the problem was, it couldn't be too bad.

When the food was ready Piet and Nita came in. Nita gave me a hug almost as eloquent in its intensity as Stella. When she finally stepped away – I followed the Disney principle again – I saw both Piet and Stella looking at her with great fondness. I wondered how difficult it was for the three of them to be together, navigating various complexities and uncertainties.

As we ate the delicious pasta, they told me about life in Naples. They were all clearly completely in love with the place. 'My favourite thing is the chaos on the streets,' Stella said. 'You're in the apartment, all quiet, then step outside and whoosh! You're pulled along into the mayhem.'

'Isn't it scary?' I said, thinking of the streets I'd been driven through.

'Maybe we've been lucky, but it feels like a very unthreatening kind of buzz,' Nita said. 'It's so... alive. Don't you think so, Piet?'

'Yes, it is a beautiful city that lives its loves and losses on the street.' He looked thoughtfully into his glass. There was a silence, and I was aware of the three of them having a conversation of facial expressions over my head. I let them get on with it, busying myself with my food.

'You'll see tomorrow,' Stella said. 'We'll walk through the old town to the station.'

Once I was back at the hotel and alone, I messaged Luca. He was one of the last names on my Rose quest list. He'd got on well with her and had seen the two of us together fairly recently. Of course, I needed to speak to Stella too, but only if I could find the right moment; her problem, whatever it was, had to come first.

She collected me at ten the next morning, looking exhausted, with dark rings circling her eyes. It gave me a chilling flashback to how she'd looked during that awful time after her degree, when she was trapped in what Richard referred to as 'the slough of despond'. Those dreadful, endless, flattened days when she could scarcely get out of bed. I was lucky – I'd never suffered from depression, despite what I said in my request to the GP. But it wasn't hard to imagine how Stella felt, back then. I'd not been particularly happy with my own life, and understood how it felt to have messed up a degree. She got what she not-jokingly referred to as 'a devastating third', while I, of course, had dropped out. Getting my photography degree this year, more than thirty years after my first abandoned attempt, would be one of the great milestones of my life. But I knew how it felt for things not to have worked out as you'd planned.

Stella saw a therapist, which helped turn things round. It was such a joy when she felt able to move out, met nice friends like Piet and Newland, reconnected with her oldest friend, Nita, and made a success of her life. I could be forgiven, couldn't I, for having taken my eye off the ball, for thinking that she was fine now?

We plunged into Naples old town, teeming with intriguing

little alleyways and interesting shops. The streets were crowded with beautiful dark-haired young people, and elegant older ladies whose timeworn faces made me long to photograph them. Stella stopped at one of the many coffee stalls that were decorated with murals of Diego Maradona. When I commented on this, she said, 'Look up.' High above our heads, strung across the narrow streets like lines of washing, were yards of fluttering pennants bearing Maradona's image.

'He's the Hand of God guy, isn't he?' I asked, dredging up my meagre knowledge of football.

'He's a secular saint here. He played for Naples, when he could have had his pick of the world's greatest teams.'

She handed me a takeaway coffee, and a paper bag with a delicious pastry – sfogliatella, she called it – and we took the rattling but charming train on the Circumvesuviana line to Pompeii, gazing at the incredible views of Vesuvius looming over the city. Though it was gorgeous weather, the sun shining in a piercing blue sky, there were few other Monday visitors. As we made our way up the stone path that led into the ruined town, Stella said, 'Amazing to think we're walking where people walked two thousand years ago, isn't it?' and I felt the full impact of her words. It wasn't a stretch at all to imagine people living here, people not so different from us, buying food at the shops, going to the theatre to watch a show.

We went into the bath house which was nice and cool, and decorated with rather rude wall paintings of people *in flagrante* in a variety of combinations. I didn't remember being taught about *that* in Latin O level. I stepped forward to take a closer look, wondering if it might be a golden opportunity to let Stella know that she could tell me whatever she needed to. But she didn't pick up the cue, even when I said, all innocent, 'Is this two women, do you think?'

Not subtle, but she just looked at it blankly and said, 'Hard to tell.'

We walked along the straight streets, with the aim of finding Caecilius' house, and, trying again to create an opening for Stella, I said, 'By the way, as per your bullying, I've started seeing a therapist.'

'At last! I'm so pleased. How are you finding it?'

'I'm not sure. She's a nice woman but she doesn't really tell me what to do.'

'The point of therapy is for you to come to your own conclusions.'

'I could do that at home on my own, couldn't I?'

'Could you?'

Hmm, as Louisa might say. Maybe I couldn't. 'It is good to have a place to talk about Rose. I've been thinking about the time she ran away from Tim. Do you remember that?'

'Not really. I do remember her boys staying with us for a few nights. I had to share a room with Edward. Oh look, it says they sold bread here.'

The shops were roofless but otherwise you could see how they must have looked. This one had a big central oven, and a counter to one side where people would have sat to wait, or eat. We pretended that Stella was baking bread, and I was a customer, until a serious-looking older couple walked past and we stopped, embarrassed.

'Anyway,' I said as we resumed walking, 'I was thinking about something Stacey told me...'

'Ugh, I'm still so sorry for inviting her,' Stella said. 'It was stupid, I wanted it to be a nice surprise but I didn't think it through.'

'You've already apologised, and you shouldn't have to; I was the one who was awful. What's more, I owe you for her hotel. I was thrown by seeing her but it was inexcusable to ignore her. I was so awkward, and I drank way too much after that and then...'

Stella stopped walking and looked at me. 'That's not right. You were already absolutely blotto by the time she arrived.'

'I was? But... I thought it was because of her, being so shocked to see her, that I got so drunk.'

'Nope. I must say, I was confused by that at the time. Why did you drink so much?'

'I don't know, in that case.' That bloody hen party! Would I ever get to the bottom of it? 'I'm embarrassed by how little I remember.'

'But you remembered something Stacey said?'

'No, but I met her a couple of weeks ago for coffee and humble pie. And she said that at the hen party, Rose mentioned Tim. Did she say anything about him to you?'

'No. How strange. She never talks about him.'

'Exactly. It's a tiny thing but it's the closest I've got to a clue right now.'

'Well, maybe it was something to do with that which made you so angry with her.'

'Angry with who?'

'Rose, of course.'

I felt lightheaded. 'What? When was I angry?'

'When she was leaving. You must remember! You walked her to the door, then you swore at her...'

'Are you *kidding*?'

'Christ, Mum, don't shout.' Stella looked around but the serious couple were out of earshot.

'Sorry.' I got a grip on myself. 'What did I say?'

'You don't remember telling her to eff off?'

The light-headedness got worse and I stopped walking, leaned against a wall.

'You were spitting feathers. I've no idea why. I didn't hear the run-up to it, only the "eff off" bit.' Stella looked at me, concerned. 'Have you really lost that whole night? I'm worried about you. You've burned away a ton of brain cells.'

'I'm worried myself. You're quite sure I said that?' My God, what wouldn't I give to have a video of that night. Louisa was correct – it held the key.

'Yes! I was right there. After that she went, but she was going anyway. Graham had rung, she said she had to go.'

'Graham was at Murray's stag do. Why was he ringing her?'

'Ugh, these stupid gendered nights out, why did you do them?'

'Thought it would be fun,' I said, deadpan.

'Yeah, a riot.' Stella consulted the map. 'Come on, the house is just up here on the left.'

'I can't believe I said that. How could I be so vile?' No wonder Rose didn't want to hear from me. No wonder she didn't come to the wedding. 'Did she say anything to you about me that night, about getting married?'

'Nothing really. Apart from maybe you were rushing a bit?' Stella raised a hand. 'I hate to say it, but we were all saying the same, she wasn't the only one.'

'Oh, bloody hell!'

'Come on, Mum! It was pretty weird, you have to admit. You'd left Dad, you said, because you didn't want to be married any more. Then five minutes later you were marrying Murray. And *that* was only a short while after his wife – your friend! – had died.'

'His ex-wife.' I wasn't as bothered by this as you might think. Bear had died four years before Murray and I got together, and of course, they'd divorced several years before that. And while it was true I hadn't wanted to remarry, I didn't factor in falling madly in love with someone who really wanted to get married. I obviously wasn't going to say this to my daughter, whose father was my ex-husband.

'Here it is!' Stella said, stopping outside a house, almost completely intact, which bore a plaque stating: *Domus L Caecili Iucundi*. There was a beautiful mosaic of a curled up black dog in the entranceway. Canis! We'd learned about him. You couldn't go inside, but I stood by the grey stone walls, pointing at Caecilius' name plaque, and Stella took photos. When I got home I'd print them, add the legend, *Caecilius est in horto*, and send them to— Oh.

There was no one who'd studied Latin with me to send them to.

Stella took my arm and we walked on. 'Are you cross about me saying that the wedding was a rush?'

'Not at all. It's interesting how differently people see things.'

'And anyway, Mum, I don't feel that way any more. I love Murray. He makes you happy.'

I thanked her with a shaky voice, grateful I could hide behind my big sunglasses. Murray did make me happy, more than almost anyone. I thought of his face when we wrote our vows together, the jewelled droplets of tears on his thick eyelashes as I read mine out to him. His hand on my waist as we cut the cake.

Nita had handed Murray a knife. 'Just pretend to cut it together for photos, then I'll cut it into portions afterwards.'

'How did we end up with so many fusty old traditions?' I'd asked Murray in a low voice. 'Cutting the cake, the "Wedding March", bloody annoying old relatives. I thought we were eschewing all that.'

'It makes me hot as hell to have married a woman who chucks round "eschewing" in casual conversation,' Murray said, giving me one of his sexy looks, and despite everything else that was juggling for attention in my head, I felt my body respond.

'There's one tradition I'm looking forward to,' I muttered. 'The wedding night.'

Under the guise of kissing my cheek for the camera, he said, 'Let's slip away right after this.'

'Where?'

'We can lock ourselves in the bathroom.'

'I'm in.' I could feel my insides melt.

'All right, people,' Murray said, handing the knife to the caterer. 'That's yer lot. I'm going to take a little stroll with my stunning bride while you get tucked in to this fine cake.' He put his arm round my shoulder and we walked as quickly as possible without actually running towards the house.

Afterwards, as we lay quietly in each other's arms, I said, 'I hope Bear would feel that we did her proud today.'

'Well, not necessarily this bit on the bathroom floor. But certainly the rest.' He kissed me. 'It's lovely that you can think of her at a time like this. Generous.'

'It doesn't feel like that. I feel like she generously gave you up so that someone else could have you.' I stroked his hair. A handsome head of hair he had, dark brown, threaded with strands of silver. 'I think it's OK if we both miss Bear sometimes, isn't it?'

Now it wasn't just Bear I was missing. I couldn't face reflecting any longer about my stupid self, the self who'd apparently told my last remaining best friend to 'eff off'. I had to put it aside; there'd be plenty of time to cringe myself every which way later. I needed to focus on Stella. I pressed closer to her. 'Is this a good moment to tell me what's going on?'

'This conversation would be easier with a coffee.' She consulted the map. 'Come on.'

'What, here? But... How can we...?'

'Unbelievably, there's a café the other side of the Forum.'

'There can't be.'

But there was, crouched anachronistically in amongst the

ancient stones. Now we knew where all the other sightseers were; the place was teeming with people clutching takeaway cups.

'OK, this is weird,' Stella said.

'Very. You wonder how on earth they got planning permission... oh great! There's loos here!'

'So much for your stand for archaeological integrity.'

We sat with our drinks on a low stone wall in the Forum, the sun on our backs. It didn't say you couldn't sit on the wall. Probably one day soon this whole thing would be roped off, like Stonehenge. They'd say, rightly, that the millions of people tramping everywhere, touching everything, were causing the place to fall apart, that it had to be preserved. But for now, you could still put your hand on a warm stone column where perhaps a woman had placed her hand two thousand years ago. I did this now, feeling the shiver of history, the then and now of human life.

I took a picture of Stella, the sun overhead making her glow like an angel. She liked the idea of my photography project, but did wonder if it was a bit miserable 'having to reflect on the past, about people who aren't around any more?'

'Yes, now you mention it. Wish I'd done landscapes instead.' We smiled at each other. We were in the right place for reflecting on the past, that was for sure.

We sipped our coffee, and I kept quiet, giving her space.

'It's Nita,' she blurted at last, her face desolate.

'Oh, darling.' I put my arm round her shoulder. 'I did wonder.'

'Really? She thinks she's hiding it so well, but I thought you might guess. After all, it's not that long since you went through it with Bear.'

'Er...' I was lost. Went through what? Did Stella think Bear and I had been lovers? I almost laughed aloud at the thought.

Then the cold realisation hit me. You bloody idiot, Kay. 'Nita's ill, isn't she?'

'Cancer. Stage four.' Tears started pouring down her face.

I pulled her in close and let her sob it out. Let us both sob it out, because I couldn't hold back my own tears. Nita was only thirty, she should have her whole life ahead of her. It was so bloody, horribly unfair. Being in this place really rubbed your face in the relentless randomness of everything. All those people here, two thousand years ago, going about their lives, worrying about petty things, having silly rows, and then one ordinary day it was all rendered meaningless by a single violent act of nature. The families, their belongings, their pets, their houses, their day-to-day concerns, were gone.

On a far smaller and undramatic scale, the same thing played out in all our lives. Nita, or Bear, finding out that they were not going to carry on for several more decades, or infinitely, as we all secretly felt sometimes, but were going to stop soon: really soon. That the things they felt so deeply about, that they thought were important... they all came to nothing in the end.

I don't know how long we sat there, holding each other in the sunlit ruins, but it might have set a new record for Disney. When at last Stella pulled out of my arms, sat up straight and busied herself with tissues, I was ready for whatever she wanted to say, or not say. One of the hardest things about parenting grown-up people was knowing when to wade in with advice, and when not. But I was getting better at it. I didn't ask questions, or try to solve the situation. All Stella needed was someone to hold the awfulness of it with her. How grateful I was, how touched, to have been the one she called when she couldn't cope any longer with the secret burden.

'She found out a few months ago,' Stella said. 'She's had all the chemo she can take. We'd been talking about coming here for years and she said, let's go.'

'That's what she wanted to do, and how lovely that you were able to make it happen.'

'You should see her in the classes! She loves it.' She wiped her eyes. 'But things were a bit tricky with Newland.'

'Surely he understood?'

'Yes, he was great. Told me to go straight away. But there was something we were going to do, we'd waited ages for it, and we had to put it on hold.'

It took all my self-control not to ask what this was. She'd tell me if she wanted to. I silently begged her to want to.

'I'll tell you another time, if that's OK?'

'Of course, darling.' Ah well.

'I can't talk to Piet, and of course not to Nita. They're both determined to stay in the here and now. I was so wobbly when I rang you, I didn't know if I could be strong for them in the way they need me to.'

'Do you think you can now?'

'I hope so. I feel lighter. Talking helps, doesn't it? Though I think I've passed it on to you; you look really sad.'

How could she see that, behind my sunglasses? I attempted to reorganise my face. 'Well, who knew we'd feel so melancholy in a place where thousands of people lost their lives?'

'Ha!' Stella looked at her phone. 'Mum, would it be OK if we head back? I know there's loads more to see, but I don't like being away from Nita for too long.'

'I've seen plenty,' I assured her. We hadn't been into the museum, but I didn't have any desire to see those awful plastercasts of real bodies, Pompeii citizens caught at the actual moment of death. There was already more than enough talk of death today.

The little train was almost empty, and we had the carriage to ourselves. I put my arm round Stella's shoulder and we gazed out of the window.

'I feel better now,' she said as we arrived back in Naples. 'You won't worry about me, will you?'

'Of course not. Since when do I worry?' I smiled, but my heart was breaking for her. For all of them.

That evening I took the three of them to dinner. I guessed that Nita had been told that I knew, and there was a relieved feeling among the company. We drank wine and there was a lot of laughter. Nita still looked in the flush of youth, but her body seemed weighed down with an impossible load. It made me think – how could it not? – of Bear. Of her last evening with me in Venice, the night I finally realised that she was ill, the heightened beauty and sadness of it. I couldn't help but compare the two situations. When Nita found out she was ill, she turned immediately to Stella. But when Bear knew she was ill, she pretended everything was fine. Even when I flew across the world to see her, still she didn't tell me. Maybe I simply wasn't the sort of friend people confided in. Bear didn't tell me the truth, not till it became too obvious to avoid. And nor did Rose, whatever was going on with her. It all seemed to point to me being a lousy friend, but I didn't know why. Well, I would bloody well try to find out.

After the meal we walked through the dark streets, me arm in arm with Stella, Nita and Piet holding hands. The town was pulsing with families, couples, groups of friends. An old man was leaning against a wall playing an accordion, and two ladies in fur-collared coats walked past with tiny dogs on leads. It was like being on a film set.

'I can see why you like it here,' I said to Stella as we queued at a gelateria.

'I love it.'

'How long will you stay, do you think?'

'The plan is six months, remember?'

'Yes, but with Nita...'

'Mum...' Stella pulled her arm out of mine.

I knew I should shut up, but I felt anxious about what Nita's future looked like. 'I'm not trying to be an interfering old mum. I'm just concerned about her. And you...'

'My friend needs me, and I'm supporting her.' Stella glared at me, her face red. 'You've got quite the cheek, you know that? It's barely five years since someone, not so far from here, left their husband with no warning and ran off to Wales. Ring any bells? And no one had a clue why or what was going on. So don't start badgering me about *my* plans. It's one sodding day at a time here, OK?'

'Yes, you're right, I'm sorry.' It didn't seem the moment to point out that when I left Richard, she and everyone else pestered me non-stop, demanding to know what was going on. But I did need to back off.

We walked back to the hotel with our ice creams, not saying much. That was another thing about parenting grown-ups: they really needed you, until abruptly, they really didn't. At the gate of my hotel, Stella told the others she'd see me to my room. My phone was pinging away in the lift, punctuating the awkward silence, and when we got to my room Stella said, 'Feel free to check it.'

'It's OK...'

'I need a drink, anyway.'

I sat on the bed with my phone, and she poured us some wine from the minibar.

'Oh, it's a text from Luca. He's in Rome. Is it far?'

'No, there's a quick train.'

'I'll go tomorrow, perhaps?'

'Good idea.' I could hear her relief.

'Stella, I know you're still angry about me leaving your father...'

'For heaven's sake, Mum, it was years ago.'

'But you mentioned it just now, when you were upset.' I certainly hadn't forgotten that when I left Richard, Stella was so distressed, she'd gone to a support group for, what was it called now? It had a daft name. ACODs, that was it. Adult Children of Divorce. Although she herself had taken the mick out of it, the fact that she'd sought out such a group showed how affected she'd been by our split. It had taken months for us to get back any semblance of a decent relationship. Perhaps there would always be a scar there.

'It wasn't about that, it was about you expecting me to have plans all signed, sealed and delivered, when you never do. Leave Dad, marry someone you've known five minutes...' She stood up. 'Honestly, I don't have bandwidth for anything that isn't about Nita right now. Have a good day in Rome. Make sure you get the fast train, but here...' She rummaged in her bag, then handed me her headphones. 'Take these in case you get the slow train by mistake. It's *really* slow, you'll need a distraction.'

'Stella, I'm sorry.'

'I'll see you tomorrow evening, when you get back.' She left her undrunk wine on the dressing table and went out. Somehow I'd managed to alienate yet another important person in my life. I really was sorry about everything, but neither Stella, nor Rose, wanted to accept my apology.

I could only hope that Luca was in a more forgiving frame of mind.

PHOTO #6

Then

Baby Stella is facing out, perched on Rose's lap, her arms in the air, her face a picture of delight. Kay, behind the camera, is making her laugh with silly noises. Stella's big brother, Edward, aged six, is next to them on the sofa, sitting up straight and solemn as though for a school photo. Rose is smiling at Stella, not the camera. Rose does not yet have children, but is engaged to Tim and is looking forward to starting her own family soon.

Date: February 1995. Location: Richard and Kay's house in Richmond. Photographer: Kay Bright.

* * *

Now

The golden light bouncing off the wide expanse of stone means Stella is backlit, her hair aglow. She is sitting on a wall in the Forum at Pompeii, an incongruous takeaway cup of coffee in her hand. Behind her are limestone columns and arches, and behind those, Vesuvius glowering down. Vesuvius was originally three times the height it is now, and Stella is trying to imagine what it must have been like to live in Pompeii before the fateful eruption. That is not the only reason for her sombre expression.

Date: 3rd July 2023. Location: Pompeii, Campania. Photographer: Kay Garland.

TWELVE

LAST ENCOUNTER WITH LUCA: LISBON, NOVEMBER 2022

Despite the cold weather, a few customers were eating on the terrace, next to outdoor heaters. I knew they were an environmental scourge, but I rather liked their festive warmth. However, I hoped Luca was inside the restaurant as I felt chilled to my bones.

He was – I spotted him straight away, sitting in a corner reading the menu. He and most of the other customers were wearing masks. In the UK lots of places had stopped expecting them. I put one on myself now so we weren't divided by that, at least. Actually, given what I had come to say, perhaps avoiding a greeting kiss would be a good idea.

'*Tesoro!*' Darling! He stood and we hugged. 'It's wonderful to see you. How long has it been?'

'Since we met in person? Oh, months. Early summer, when you came to Winchester?'

We'd done a lot of Zoom catch-ups, of course, but even those had fallen off in the last few weeks. I owed it to Luca to tell him straight, had come to Lisbon for that express purpose, but now I was here I felt nervous.

'I have a very nice hotel booked, can you stay two nights or three? You weren't sure?'

'I've booked my own hotel, Luca, I'm sure I told you.'

'Maybe. I forget. Well, once you see my room, you might want to cancel your booking. It has a view of the Castelo.'

'Did you know that Lisbon is on my list of places to see before I am... *un certain age*?' It was silly to be coy, he knew how old I was, but I hated saying 'sixty' out loud. I was still a few years away from it, anyway.

'Really? I'm even more glad you could come, then. My conference does not start for another two days. Such a relief that there are not so many obstacles to jump through this time.'

'You jump through hoops, over obstacles.'

He smiled. 'There were so many, maybe I will use both terms. That symposium in Brussels last year, oh the tests I had to purchase, at such expense! The paperwork! It was wildly bureaucratic. I felt at times like Josef K, caught in an infinite loop. It seemed to have been organised by an old communist state.'

'It was the same to get on a flight. When I came to see you in Berlin, the nurse who gave me a lateral flow test at the airport had definitely been an East German shot-putter in her youth.'

Our lunch arrived, and the masks came off. Which made practical sense – you couldn't eat in a mask – but didn't make sense from a risk perspective. I'd come to understand that a lot of pandemic precautions were about theatre, not efficacy.

Luca spoke about where he would live, now he no longer had to stay in Milan to care for his father, who'd sadly passed away. He was thinking of returning to Venice, where he'd grown up, and where he and I had met. Or Lisbon, where we were now, because the food was so delicious, and it had the pizzazz of an up-and-coming city. But Luca could not get on with the language. So maybe London... or even Wales...? He looked at me expectantly, but his expression changed as he read something I didn't know was on my face.

'*Cara*, what's wrong? I sense you have news.' He smiled, but his eyes didn't twinkle in his usual Luca way.

'Not really... it can wait till later.'

He was, objectively, an extremely attractive man. In the last couple of years his slight resemblance to Sacha Distel had faded. He was less tanned, his hair less richly black, and these changes suited him. But since falling in love, I could no longer recall what I'd once seen in him.

'I usually like your air of mystery, Lady Kathleen of Hoylake,' Luca said. 'But today, I think I would like to know now, if possible.'

The waiter cleared our plates, and I ordered a second bottle of wine. It was my turn to pay for the meal – we had a strict alternating system – and I was glad of it. I didn't want to owe him anything today.

'Where to start,' I said, and shivered. Luca asked if I was cold.

'I'm too warm, if anything. It's stuffy in here.' My menopause was mostly relatively light, but there were moments when I was unexpectedly suffused with boiling heat.

'You need silk underlays, they are very good for different kinds of temperature. I will buy you some if you like.'

'They sound expensive.' In my fifties I had suddenly found myself in the company of men who liked to spend their money on me. It was probably fortunate it hadn't happened when I was younger as my head would have been completely turned.

'Fine silk threads for beautiful women are never wasted.'

I laughed. 'You are still such a cheesemeister, aren't you?'

'I know you enjoy my old-school charm. Or at least' – and he looked down at the table – 'you used to.'

'I still do.' I could feel the tears welling up. 'You're a wonderful man.'

The waiter brought our second bottle and I practically snatched it out of his hand, filling both our glasses almost to the brim.

'So, tell me, Kathleen. Quickly. What is that expression you use, tear away the plaster.'

My heart started to beat more quickly. I took a large gulp of wine, and did as he asked. 'I've fallen in love with someone.' In case this was ambiguous, I added, 'Someone else.'

'I see.' He picked up his glass, which was so full, he spilled a little onto the table. 'In that case, a toast: to love.'

I should have known he would take it well. Somehow, that only made it worse.

'It's OK, Kathleen. Don't cry.' He passed me his pristine serviette. 'Thank you for telling me.'

Crying in public was awful. The two women at the next table were looking at us with undisguised interest; one, a redhead in a burgundy blouse and matching face mask made sad eyes at me, presuming, I suppose, that the dowdy English mouse had been let down by the handsome Italian lothario.

'Can we go?' I asked. I would love to have just thrown down a wad of euros and rushed away, but of course we had to wait till the waiter came with the bill, then a separate trip for the card machine, all done in excruciating silence with me sniffing and dabbing my eyes, Luca inscrutable and calm.

When at last we could escape, I walked fast across the square, no idea in my head about where I was going. Luca caught up with me and put his hand on my arm.

'It's all right, Kathleen, it's all right.'

'I feel terrible, you've done nothing wrong, you've been the loveliest person...'

'Take my arm, like you always do. Come on.'

I linked my arm through his, and he said, 'I know somewhere we can go, out of the cold.'

We walked, not speaking, along the side of the river, our

breath clouding out in front of us. I was relieved that I had spoken, said what I had to say, but mostly I just felt sad.

He took us into a large modern white building, an art gallery. 'There is a wonderful painting in here,' he said. 'I would love for you to see it.'

He led me up some wide stone stairs and into a room with vibrant canvases. There was no one else in there.

'How do you know about this place?' I asked, as we walked through this room into an adjoining one.

'I am often in Lisbon for work, as you know. Where can a man wander when he does not wish to eat or drink? I always look for a gallery when I am away. Ah. Here we are.'

We stopped in front of a large painting, quite abstract, of two people talking together, one leaning intently towards the other, an elbow resting on their knee. The colours were gorgeous, dark olives, blues, and a spray of yellow and orange flowers behind.

'It's beautiful.'

'You know, I think this painting has a flaw in it,' Luca said.

'It does?'

'Yes, look there.' He pointed to the black hair of one of the figures. 'That little smudge of orange is from the flowers, it should not be there. But every work of art has a tiny flaw in it, making it unique.' He reached for my hand. 'The flaw in our beautiful work of art is that you don't love me.'

'Oh, Luca. You don't love me, either.'

'Do you know that for sure, Kathleen?'

'I'm sorry.' I squeezed his hand. 'I really liked our thing, this thing, whatever it is. But neither of us ever spoke about love, did we?'

'You would not have liked it if I had.'

I wanted to protest, but he was right. Had he said anything, I would have felt uncomfortably obliged to respond in kind. I liked him, very much, and would always be grateful for him being there when I needed someone. I met him the day after Bear had told me her diagnosis and flown back to Australia – the day after I had, on her urging, considered trying to reunite with Richard. It was one of the bleakest times of my life. Luca made things bearable again.

'You know in the summer, when we stayed near your friend Rose?'

'Yes, it was such a lovely week.'

'One night, after you and Graham had gone to bed, she asked why I hadn't asked you to marry me.'

'She did?' I was a little surprised, she'd never mentioned this to me, but I did know how fond she was of Luca.

'I told her that I was not sure you would say yes.'

'Luca...'

'She said that she thought you would, and I replied that this was the first time she had ever been wrong.'

I didn't know what to say, and we stood silently, side by side, staring at the painting.

After a minute or two, he said, 'Seen enough?' and I nodded. We went downstairs and back out into the frigid November air.

'Let me walk you to your hotel. Where is it?'

'You don't want to...' I started, then faltered.

'Don't want to what?'

'You know, talk, and...'

'You want to hang out?' He took a step backwards. 'Maybe you want to tell me all about the man you have fallen in love with.'

'It's a stupid idea, I'm sorry.' What had I thought, that I would finish things with him and he would still want to shop, have a coffee, go to dinner?

'Oh, Kathleen, why did you come to meet me?' I'd never seen him cross before. 'Flights, hotel, expense. You could have told me it was over in a Zoom call.'

'You've always been so kind. It felt so impersonal not to speak face to face.'

'Maybe impersonal would have been better. It does hurt, I can't pretend.'

'I wish it didn't have to be like this. But I'm not the sort of person who can juggle two men.'

'Perhaps I have been juggling other women.'

I'm not sure what impact he wanted this to have. When I was young, I was the jealous type, but I really wasn't any more. It was something that had faded with age and experience, like caring about one's underarm hair. 'Well sure, you easily could have, we don't see each other very often.'

'What I am saying is, I don't mind if you juggle two men.'

'That is good of you, but *I* mind. It isn't who I am.' I didn't say, and I don't want to, anyway.

He didn't know me when I was young, when I was jealous. How I sobbed for a week when I saw David Endevane with another woman. I was a different person now. What was that thing about cells renewing themselves every seven years or something? I didn't think I had any of my cells left from my twenties. I was literally someone different.

'So. Your hotel?'

I told him, and he set off confidently, but we were soon lost. We walked in silence for what felt like a long way before I hesitantly asked if we were nearly there, and he came to a standstill.

'I don't understand,' he said. We were in a deserted square that had five streets leading from it, none, clearly, the one he wanted. 'I have walked this place so many times.'

'It's no problem, I'll look it up on my phone.'

'Let us try this avenue here. It is familiar to me.'

Sighing, I trailed after him. Men could be so boring in their unwillingness to ask for help. He was walking faster than usual, and I had to half-chase him to the end of the road. When we turned into the next street, he stopped again.

'This is not right.'

'OK, I'm looking at my phone now.'

'Always this phone. You are obsessed, like a teenager. It's always up close to your nose. So we don't know something immediately? We must ask our phone.' In a silly, high-pitched voice, presumably intended to be mine, he said, 'Oh, Mister Phone, please tell me, what should I do now?'

I was reminded of Stella and Edward's teenage strops. I ignored him, as I had ignored them, and typed in the name of my hotel. 'Look. It's almost thirty minutes from here. We've gone the wrong way.'

He glanced at the screen, then turned and started walking in the opposite direction. 'Fine. This way, if Mister Phone says so.'

I shook my head. 'Luca, let's get a taxi.'

'No need, I know where it is now.'

'I'm too tired and cold to walk that far.'

'Those phones put long estimated times on for old people. It is not more than fifteen minutes from here.' He walked even faster back across the square, and I had a choice of running to catch him up, or stopping completely. I stopped, then turned in a different direction, towards a busy street where I could flag a cab. It only took him half a minute to realise I wasn't following him, and he came hurrying back.

'You don't need to wait with me,' I said. I raised my hand, because I could see what looked like a taxi in the distance.

'This is a waste of money, Kathleen.'

He was right; I should have finished things by Zoom.

The taxi screeched to a halt next to us, and the driver wound down his window. I showed him on my phone where I wanted to go. He nodded and I got in. There was a moment when I thought Luca might not join me, that this would be the last time we ever saw each other, but he did get in, and the car set off as if it had a rocket up its rear end. I could immediately understand why Lisbon was regularly cited as the car crash capital of Europe. However, by staring out of my side window, I managed to avoid seeing a good proportion of the many near misses we encountered.

By some miracle the taxi pulled up outside my hotel with us in one piece, and I got out, but Luca stayed in the car. I offered him money for the journey, but he waved it away, and the driver revved the engine. Was this it then? Our last conversation was to be about a taxi fare? Then Luca said something to the driver and he turned off the engine. Luca put his arm out of the window, and I took his hand.

'*Cara*, I'm sorry. We are old, we cannot afford to be angry with the people we like. There aren't so many of them left.'

'I'm not angry with you, and I hope you won't stay angry at me for long.'

'I am not angry, I'm sad. Our relationship has been important to me. But I want to let you go. *Arrivederci*, Kay.'

I kissed his cold hand. 'Bye, Luca. Take care.'

He sat back in his seat. I began to walk towards the welcoming lights of the hotel. I wasn't sure, but I thought I heard him say, '*Ti amo.*'

I love you.

I turned back, but the taxi was driving away.

THIRTEEN
ROME, JULY 2023

The woman in the sequinned black and silver cowboy hat held my gaze way longer than was socially acceptable. I turned away, looked out of the window, but could feel her eyes boring into me. Seconds later, the most godawful music started up, making me jump: it was wailing more than singing, and set to a frantic heavy beat. I looked back at the woman, who was still staring at me, a victorious smile on her face as she held up her phone like a weapon. No prizes for guessing where the music was coming from.

Everyone in the carriage turned to stare at us. It was an older crowd on this train, people who, I imagined, were not particularly tolerant of loud public music. One had reluctantly learned to expect it of young people, but Cowboy Hat Woman was my age, maybe even older. Certainly post-menopause, which is how I tended to divide my middle-aged tribe: peri, meno, post. I'd accidentally caused the situation by asking CHW, in gestures and broken Italian, if she would mind moving one of her many items of luggage so I could sit down. She huffily recruited a sweet young Frenchman to put some bags on the high shelf, while sending a great many evil looks at me. I'm not sure at what point it occurred to me that she wasn't quite all there, but I certainly got that now.

I slid my eyes away to my own phone, and started writing a text to Rose: *Help! A woman in a sparkly cowboy hat and vest top is starting a fight with me!* Then I remembered that I couldn't tell Rose about it, or about anything. That she'd taken me at my word when, for some reason, I'd told her to eff off.

There was a hostage situation on the news once, in which the police played terrible music – Engelbert Humperdinck, I think – to try to break the terrorists' spirits. If only they'd known my cowboy-hatted friend, she could have provided them with something far worse. The obvious thing was to move, but there weren't any other spare seats, and anyway, I was damned if I was going to be Humperdincked into submission.

Before I got into my own weird private hostage situation, I'd been full of the romance of foreign train travel. The thrill when the huge train came thundering into the station, the linguistically astonishing staff slipping in and out of Italian, English, German as they guided people to their seats, beautiful scenery, time to think... I hunched into my seat and messaged Luca my arrival time. I hoped this meeting wasn't too soon after we'd parted, almost eight months ago. I hated that I'd hurt him, but it had been unavoidable. Sometimes you did just hurt people, without wanting to.

The guard came into our carriage and spoke to Cowboy Hat Woman. She shrugged as if it was no big deal, why, he only had to ask!, and turned the music off. The abrupt silence was wonderful. But of course, the instant the guard went out, she turned it back on, with a look at me to say, what now? The woman on the other side of the aisle let out a groan when the music restarted, but neither she nor I were brave enough to say anything. Sadly, as in the UK, a battle of this kind was to be carried out with the inadequate weapons of tutting and eye-rolling.

Then I remembered Stella last night, who, though cross, was thoughtful enough to lend me her headphones. I put them on and connected to a random playlist on my phone, immediately and blissfully drowning out my unwanted DJ. I kept my eyes fixed firmly on my phone, praying that the woman wouldn't find some other, perhaps worse, way to express hostility, and took the opportunity to check my emails. I was always slightly hoping for something from Rose, but there was nothing other than a boring-looking one from Drive Friendly, the car hire company we'd used in Dallas. No doubt they wanted me to rate their service on various five-point scales. If I gave all the feedback requested of me after every purchase, it would be a full-time job. I was old enough to remember when you were allowed to buy something or be provided with a service and not have to rate it. No, seriously, young people, you could walk out of the shop or restaurant with nothing more than a thank you! I know! As I said to Methuselah...

When the train pulled into Rome I glanced warily at CHW, but she simply gathered up her many bags and hurried off without a glance. I'd been no more than a small, passing part of her ongoing drama. Sometimes life just happened, without any real beginnings or ends.

I walked along the platform, wondering when Luca would message to say where to meet. I'd never been to Rome before. I slowed down to avoid following Cowboy Hat Woman too closely, and watched from a distance as she attempted to corral various men into carrying her bags, reaching out her arms beseechingly. Most shook their heads or pretended not to see her, but one stopped to listen. He looked faintly like Luca, dark grey-flecked hair, that same sort of jacket he favoured, a patterned scarf, and as I got closer, I realised that it *was* him. He turned, saw me hesitating nearby, and in one suave movement, handed the woman and her bags over to a passing station guard and walked towards me, calling, 'Kathleen! I'm here!'

My nemesis glared at me furiously, as if I'd planned this entire thing, then stalked off with the four biggest of her bags perfectly balanced in each hand, the station guard trotting behind her, perhaps wondering why he was needed to carry a tiny handbag.

'*Cara!*' Luca pulled me into his arms – I'd been wondering if we'd still do this, or if we were now in handshake territory – and kissed me three times: once on each cheek and then the first cheek again for good measure. He looked, and smelled, exquisite as ever.

'How kind to come and meet me,' I said, 'though you nearly got pulled into a drama with my train enemy.'

He roared with laughter once I'd explained. 'I had forgotten about the chaos you bring wherever you go! I love it.'

I puzzled over this as we went out of the station and got into a taxi. Was that how he saw me, chaotic?

'Regrettably, this must be a fairly quick lunch,' he said.

'No problem. Are you at a conference?' Of course he was – did he do anything else?

'Yes, and I am speaking this afternoon.'

'Luca, you should have said. You don't have time...'

'I always have time for you, Kathleen.'

Uh-oh. I sank back into my seat. It hadn't occurred to me till now that he might think I'd contacted him to see if he wanted to get back together. Bloody hell. Maybe I was an agent of chaos, after all. But I needn't have worried. As soon as we were sitting in a charming little restaurant near the Trevi Fountain – Luca always knew charming little restaurants – he put my mind at rest. Raising a glass of wine, he said, 'Congratulate me, won't you? You're not the only one who is having a late marriage.'

'Oh, Luca, wonderful news!' What a relief! We clinked glasses. 'Tell me everything.'

He grinned. 'It is a simple love story, as timeless as La Gioconda's smile.'

'Dating app, was it?'

'Silver Seekers, no less.' His grin broadened. 'Romance for the over fifties.'

'Sounds amazing. Is she Italian?'

'She is indeed, a Milanese beauty.' He handed me his phone to show me a picture of a stunning blonde who did not look as if she would qualify for Silver Seekers for at least fifteen years. No wonder Luca had been so keen to meet up; if my new partner looked like that, I'd get all my exes together in a room and have her parade round. But actually, Murray was kind of her male equivalent: gorgeous, kind, sexy. I hadn't had time since arriving in Italy to properly miss him, but I did now, with a physical pang. His warm eyes, crinkling as he smiled at me, the solid feel of him as he held me in his arms.

While we ate, Luca told me all the details: their early dates, the things they had in common, their forthcoming wedding this summer at Lake Como. I was genuinely pleased that he was happy and so very much over me. Honest, I was. But he could damn well buy our lunch.

It wasn't till coffee that he asked about my life. I gave him some edited highlights, then, taking courage from Stacey's trick of dismantling a paper napkin, strip by strip, and looking at that instead of him, I said, 'I want you to know how bad I feel about the way things ended between us.'

'Kathleen, there is no need.'

'You've moved on, and I'm really glad, but I could have handled our break-up better.'

'Not at all. You were kindness personified. And I am a man of the world, I understand these things.' He reached across the table and put his hand on mine, stilling it. 'The napkin is deceased.'

'Can I ask you something... it's about Rose.'

'Your friend? Ah, a lovely woman. What a fine time we had

in Winchester with her and her man... *Cara*, why are you crying?'

'I'm sorry.' I fumbled in my bag for a tissue. 'I've managed not to cry about Rose for a while but it crept up on me.'

Luca handed me a pristine white cloth handkerchief, of course he had one, and said, 'I'm terribly sorry. I had no idea she was ill.'

'Oh, no,' I spluttered, half crying, half laughing. 'She's not dead. Well, she is to me, I suppose.'

He looked puzzled, as well he might. I dabbed my eyes and quickly explained. But the more I spoke, the sillier my intention to ask him about it seemed. Why would he have any insight into Rose's mind, any more than Helena? They'd got on well, but only met a few times. 'I don't suppose you might have any ideas why she...?' I trailed off, lamely.

He still looked puzzled. 'Why she has cut off with you?'

His English might not be flawless but that was a good description. She had cut me, and I could still feel the sting of it. 'Yes. She really liked you, and I wondered...'

'You think she was angry because you left me for your Australian man?' He laughed. 'I think you overestimate Rose's interest in me. Also, she did not cut you when you left Richard.'

No, she hadn't, that was true. She'd been incredibly supportive. But maybe she'd felt I had a second chance with Luca, who on paper was perfect, and was throwing it away on a man we both knew might have a lot of baggage.

I told Luca my latest theory, that Rose might have pushed me away because she was back in contact with Tim.

'Well, there is your answer,' Luca said, signalling to a waiter. 'You must talk to this Tim.'

'I can't, Luca, he was awful! A very difficult man. I helped her get away from him years ago. The last thing I want to do is see him again.'

The waiter held out the card reader, and Luca suavely paid the bill without looking at it, his eyes fixed on me. 'Well, Lady Kathleen, I can only tell you what I would do, if I was a detective.'

How on earth could I go about it? I could hardly call Tim up – not that I had his contact details anyway – and ask whether he'd been hassling Rose lately. But perhaps Luca was right; it was the only lead I had.

Outside, I asked if I could take his picture, and being arty he got the concept of my project straight away. He suggested we use the nearby Pantheon for a backdrop. The light was terrific, and as he posed, he was the epitome of urban Italian charm.

'I'd better go,' he said, looking at his watch. 'Can I walk you somewhere?'

'No, I'll find my way,' I said. I had the Gen-X willingness to ask passing strangers for directions, plus his least favourite app, Google Maps. 'Can I ask one more thing…?' I'd saved this question up for the last minute, so that no matter the answer, we could be out of each other's lives very quickly. 'When we were together? Did I take you for granted?'

He frowned, looking confused. I started to offer definitions – 'Was I careless with you?' – but he raised his hand to stop me. 'I know the meaning, but I am puzzled by the question.'

'It's something that was said about me. That I take people for granted, that I am not always a good friend.'

'*Ma va!*' He threw up his hands in a so stereotypically Italian way I almost laughed. 'Which of us is always a good friend? No, *cara*. You did not take me for granted. You were always good to me. And when you let me go, you did not break my heart. Even if it was bruised for a short time.'

'I'm sorry.'

'I am not. We had a lovely thing for a while, did we not? And now we have two different lovely things.' He stepped back. 'Now I really must go. It would be embarrassing if the keynote speech was late.'

'Jesus, Luca, you're doing the keynote?' I had to laugh. He was too cool for school. 'Go, go.'

We kissed each other and he raised his hand as he hurried off. '*Ciao!* Call me next time you're in Italy.'

'I will,' I called after him. 'Happy wedding!'

Happy wedding? That wasn't a thing, was it? But luckily I don't think he heard.

I wandered around the centre of Rome for a while, marvelling at the extremely famous landmarks all bunched in a small area. Then I took a long walk to the Vatican – it didn't look far on the map but it really was – and had an afternoon alternately admiring and then feeling furious at the ostentatious displays of gilded wealth there. Mum had often reminisced about coming to Rome when she was in her twenties, an inevitable stop for a Catholic student on a European tour. In fact, only last night I'd dreamed about her being in Italy with me, though frankly it looked more like Hartlepool than Rome. She'd loved seeing the Vatican, of course, and even got to meet the Pope, whichever one was in post then, I didn't know. I ought to look it up.

Back at the station I accidentally got on the slow train. Stella was right not to trust me. But at least there was no one to get into a ruck with; the carriage was half-empty and very quiet.

So Luca had either forgiven me or there was nothing to forgive. That was a comfort. I sat back, and took the opportunity of my long journey to read through my messages. There was an uplifting one from Murray, a picture of a flattened sequinned cowboy hat, accompanied by the words, *you shoulda seen the other guy*. A foolish one from Stacey, suggesting we hire a van and sit outside Rose's house for a few days. The ideal way to go from a friendship breach to a police matter, I couldn't help thinking. And a heartwarming one from Stella, asking me to come to the apartment for dinner whenever I was back. Out of boredom, I even opened the email from Drive Friendly, and discovered that it wasn't a feedback request, but a list of charges for driving on toll roads. They were apparently going to take payment in the next five business days, and from my account, because I'd insisted on paying for the car. Murray had covered every other honeymoon expense.

There was a long list of tolls, all between two and three dollars, but so many of them! It made no sense – we'd hardly done any driving at all apart from a day trip to Waxahachie. Murray had gone out a few times for business meetings but those were within the Dallas city limits. I emailed back, telling them they'd made a mistake. It was a shame they didn't ask for feedback, as I was poised to award them a devastating one star.

I enjoyed walking out of Napoli Centrale station and onto the streets like a native. After just a couple of days here I felt at home. I understood what Piet meant when he said the city was beautiful – life in all its mess and vibrancy, the people rushing by, their expressive faces as they gesticulated in that southern Italian way.

Stella was finishing cooking when I arrived at the apartment. I was nervous about seeing her after our argument, but she kissed me, and asked about my day. She seemed distracted, though, and when we sat down to eat with Piet – Nita was resting – she barely touched her food. She kept jumping up to get things that we didn't need, and at one point Piet put a gentle hand on hers and said, 'It's OK.'

After we'd cleared away and Piet had returned to Nita, Stella and I took our coffee out onto the balcony. It wasn't much of a view, surrounded as it was by other buildings, and lines of laundry flapping nearby, the air awash with cooking smells from the nearby apartments. But there were two comfortable chairs where we sat and watched the sky fade from blue to grey. I was pleased to be able to make her laugh about Cowboy Hat Woman and Luca's model girlfriend, though I will gloss over what I said as I might have conflated them in a slightly bitchy way. When it was dark, we went back inside. The air was oppressive in the apartment, heavy with sadness and worry. We could hear Piet's lilting voice; it sounded like he was reading to Nita.

Stella walked me to my hotel, and when we got to my room I thought we might have a replay of the previous night, sitting far apart from each other. But she said, 'Will you hold me like you used to, when I was little?'

We lay on the bed, she with her back to me, my arm round her waist. I pressed my face against her hair. 'Sorry I was horrible yesterday,' she whispered.

'You weren't. I deserved a good old telling-off.' She grunted in acknowledgement, and snuggled in closer. 'Was Nita bad today?'

She nodded. 'It all seems so pointless, doesn't it?' she said after a few moments.

'What does, Sparkle?'

'Life.' She gave an ironic laugh at her statement. 'You get attached to people, you love them. Then they disappear, or die, and leave you in pain. And you wouldn't have been in pain if you hadn't got attached to them. And then you die too. I mean, what's it all for?'

'Gosh, darling, I only wish I knew. It's a very profound question and I'm not a very profound old mum, am I? But I suppose there's something about the fleeting bits of love that we feel for each other, those are what make it worthwhile. I know "better to have loved and lost" is an old cliché, but it's true, I think. Better to have known the love, than to not feel anything much at all?'

'I don't how to get through the next months. I'm scared.'

'You're right in the thick of it, it's awful.' I held her tighter, and kissed her hair. How did you help people say goodbye to someone they love? It was the hardest thing there was. And yet, I did have experience of it, did perhaps have some things to say that might be of use. Now, finally, I knew why she'd asked me to come out here, what she really needed from me.

'You can be guided by Nita for the most part,' I said. 'Try to meet her where she's at. If she's high energy see if you can match it, and keep it lower key when she's tired. But also look after yourself, because you're no good to her if you're burned out. She's trying to pack in a lot of life while she can, and the best thing you can do is help her with that. If she wants to do something mad and life-affirming, don't try to protect her.'

I'd learned this from Bear, who chose to run away to Venice with me for a final few days of beauty and joy.

'I did wonder if it was a mistake to come here, but you're right. It's life, it's living, it's what she needs.' Stella shifted a little. 'What else?'

I thought of Bear, of my mum, of the things they did, and didn't, ask of me in their final days. What I wished I'd done differently. 'Spend time with her, even if she's being awful. And she might be, because this is really hard. Take lots of photos of her. Write down some of the things she says, or even keep a diary of things you do together. She might like to have it read back to her later, when she can't... when she's more tired.'

I could feel how intently she was listening.

'But, you know, death really is final.'

I felt Stella smile against my arm. 'I do know that, Mum.'

'We all know it, intellectually. But not always emotionally. When someone dies they aren't going to reappear in a few months or years to give you a second chance, no matter how much it feels like they should.'

'I thought you said you weren't profound.' She kissed my hand. 'Anything else?'

'One last thing. When the time comes to let her go...' I stopped, because I felt a little overcome, and it was a minute or so before I was able to continue. 'When the time comes, try to let her go without thinking about yourself. Later, you can think of yourself, and celebrate her beautiful life. But at that moment, let her do whatever she needs to do, even if it means...'

'Yes? If it means...?'

Bear didn't tell me she was dying, and she didn't want me to be there at the end. I had been taking that personally, and I absolutely shouldn't. 'Even if it means putting your own needs and your silly old ego to one side.' I hadn't done that. Sorry, Bear. 'She might only want to see Piet. Or she might lash out, be angry with you.' I thought of poor Mum, all those the invasive hospital routines and bedpans and catheters she underwent. It was no wonder that her irritation sometimes spilled out at me. 'People do sometimes get angry when they're actually feeling scared or upset.'

Stella nodded, and I knew we were both thinking about her shouting at me at the gelateria.

We were quiet, and after a few minutes I felt her become heavier. She'd fallen asleep, the way she used to when we hugged like this when she was a child. Back then, I sometimes felt impatient to be trapped in a sleepy hug. So many jobs to get on with, I couldn't just lie there! But now, I relaxed into it, Disney-style. After I left Richard, I'd feared that Stella and I would never be close again, and now look at us. Of course, the person who brought us back together was Rose, that day on West Kirby beach when we scattered Bear's ashes.

I closed my eyes. Rose, I know I've fucked up. I still don't know how, but I'm going to keep trying to find out, and I hope that one day you'll be ready to let me back in.

I must have fallen asleep too, because the next thing I knew Stella was getting off the bed. 'Mum, it's gone midnight!'

'I'll walk you back to your apartment.'

'No need, it's scarcely a step.' She stood at the doorway. 'We'll take you to the airport tomorrow.'

'Oh good, another rollercoaster drive with Piet.'

She laughed, and went out. I lay back down on the bed. I

meant to do my teeth and get undressed, but within minutes I was fast asleep.

In the morning, I took a final walk round Naples, and drank a coffee at a sunlit pavement café table. I'd miss this place. But when Piet and Stella pulled up outside the hotel, where I was waiting with my bags, I knew I was ready to go back, to push forward with my three projects: 'Then and Now', 'Buying Bryn Glas' and 'What the Eff, Rose?' I felt like I had new perspectives on all of them.

Piet drove in his usual oh-my-God-we're-about-to-crash style. Being in the back seat, unable to see all of it, was an advantage. 'Nita apologises for not coming,' he said, 'but she is resting.'

Good Lord, like Nita needed the stress of a car journey with Piet! I leaned forward, and said, 'I am unbelievably sorry about Nita.' It was the first time I'd said anything directly to him about it, but it felt too pretendy not to speak up. 'Life's just so shitty sometimes.'

'It really is, you know, Mrs Garland.' His voice broke in the middle of my name.

'You're such a good aaaargh!' I said, as the car swerved wildly to the left.

'Sorry, sorry,' Piet said, raising a hand. 'I did not see that pedestrian.'

'Jesus, Piet, are they OK?' Stella cried, looking behind us.

'Yes, I missed them by easily 125 millimetres.'

The pedestrian in question was yelling something robust and unintelligible as we drove on. My heart was thudding at a thousand miles an hour at the near miss; I don't know how Piet managed to avoid crashing into the wall when he pulled out of the way. Presumably he missed that by some weirdly specific amount of millimetres too.

'Are you OK, Piet?' I asked.

'I am fine, thank you. How are you?' He spoke as if we were meeting at a dinner party.

'That was so scary,' Stella said. 'Ought we have stopped?'

'They were perfectly all right,' Piet said. 'I would know if I had hit them.'

It felt all at once extremely important to get home to my lovely husband in one piece.

Stella came into the airport with me while Piet waited in the car. In the departure lounge, we clutched each other, giggling in relief and shock.

'We need a drink,' she said, and dragged me to a bar and ordered us each a gin and tonic. We chugged them down, standing at the counter.

'Piet is so weird, sorry to say it,' I said.

'I know! I'm living with him! And now I have to drive back with him.' Stella doubled over laughing.

'But he's so lovely, despite everything.'

'He really is.' She stopped laughing. 'He's wonderful with Nita. Do you know what she said the other day? That she thinks her last year might actually be her best.'

That wiped the smile off my face. 'You're being truly amazing.'

'So are you. I know things are complicated for you, and you dropped everything to come here.'

'That's what mums do.' Thank God she'd forgiven me. I don't think I could have handled another person I loved cutting me out of their life.

'Anyway, I was thinking about Rose, and I wondered, why don't you talk to the boys?'

'Rose's boys?'

'Yes, hasn't Will had a baby recently?'

'Earlier this year. Rose sent me a photo.' I showed Stella the picture of Will and his partner with their tiny baby, and Stella misted up.

'So sweet.' She wiped her eyes.

'You're not normally soppy about babies.'

'No, but I knew Will as a kid, it's lovely to see him with a kid of his own. Anyway, it would be perfectly normal to check in, ask how he's doing, then see if he knows anything. About his mum, about why she mentioned Tim.' She kissed my cheek. 'I'd better go. Are you going to be OK?'

'I am. Tell Piet to drive carefully, it's important that both of you are around for Nita.'

A final hug, and she hurried off, looking back once to wave. I started missing her the minute she disappeared.

FOURTEEN

LAST ENCOUNTER WITH TIM: SOUTHWOLD, 2003

'Has he definitely gone?' Rose's face at the door was gaunt. Those hollows in her cheeks weren't there the last time I saw her.

'Yes, he's driven off. Are you OK?'

She looked behind me to the dark street, her eyes wide and watchful, then stepped aside to let me in.

'How long were you waiting in your car?' she asked me.

'I got here about an hour ago.'

We went into her immaculate kitchen. 'Where are the boys?' I asked.

'In bed. I won't get them till the last minute.'

'Let's get you packed.'

'I don't know what to take.' Rose leaned against the wall. 'I don't know what to do.'

'Just bring enough to tide you over for a few weeks. How long have we got before he comes back?'

'He's usually out for a couple of hours.'

'Bloody hell, Rose. I can't believe it.'

'I can. Bastard. Do you want tea?'

'I'll make it, you go and start getting your things together.'

She hugged me, then went out. I could hear her running from room to room, could sense her panic. I made tea, then went to find her. She was sitting on the floor outside Jay's room, surrounded by piles of stuff. 'I can't, I'm sorry, I don't know what I'm doing.' I had never before seen her like this, heard such hopelessness in her voice.

I sat down next to her and put a mug of tea in her hands. 'You do. You told me on the phone. You're getting the boys out to a safe place. It doesn't mean you can't ever come back.'

Rose looked up at me with tear-filled eyes. 'What do I bring?'

I snapped into efficient mode. 'A few sets of clothes for everyone. Two pairs of shoes each. Toothbrushes. Any jewellery. Any precious belongings. Passports and birth certificates. Bank cards. Kids' favourite teddies. If you tell me where things are, I'll do it.'

'I can't, I don't know, I can't think where anything is.' She started crying again.

I put my arms round her. 'I'm here. I'll help.'

I fetched some suitcases and bags from the hall cupboard, and put the piles of clothes into them. Rose managed to pull herself together, and we methodically worked through my verbal list, then put the bags in my car. Had she left anything she'd regret? We scanned the various rooms, but it seemed there was very little.

'Never liked this house, never liked anything in it apart from my children.' In the dining room she opened a cupboard and pulled out armfuls of coasters. 'This stupid table. A dining room table that marks if you put so much as a paper plate on it. Yeah, that's relaxing.' She poured coasters over the table, and spread them out till every inch of it was covered. It looked like an art installation.

'Right, I'm ready.'

The boys were heavily asleep and we each carried one

downstairs. Will woke up when we went outside and the cold night air hit him. He sleepily looked into my face.

'Hello, Auntie Kay.'

'Hello, gorgeous. We're just going for a little drive.' I settled him into the back seat next to his brother, and watched his eyes close again. Rose pulled a duvet over both of them and went back to lock the house, and it was then that Tim's car pulled up. Damn it, he'd been gone less than an hour. Had he suspected something like this might happen?

'Rose!' I hissed.

She came running back, and I opened the passenger door so she could jump straight in. The second she was safely inside, I slammed the door closed and pressed the 'lock' button on my key fob. Then I walked round to the driver's side. I won't pretend I wasn't scared. I was.

Tim left his engine on and ran over. 'The fuck?' He stared in at my car windows at his sleeping children, his terrified wife in the passenger seat. Then he turned to me. 'Your fucking idea, I suppose.'

'Hardly.'

He came up close enough that I could smell the alcohol on his breath. 'Open the car, Kay, and bring them back into the house.'

'Rose doesn't want to.'

'She doesn't know what she wants.'

'I bloody do!' she yelled. Thankfully the boys didn't stir.

'You're an idiot, aren't you?' Tim said to me. He spoke quietly, more menacing than if he'd shouted. 'If you drive off in that shit heap, you know I'll follow you.'

'I'll phone the police,' I said, fear and anger giving me unusual clarity; I could see the immediate consequences of him doing that. 'They'll be thrilled to catch a drink driver in the act.'

Tim could see that I meant it. He stepped back, and looked

entreatingly through the window. 'Please, Rose, don't take my children away. I can't live without them.'

'Should have thought of that before you raised your hand, shouldn't you?' Rose said. She was calmer now, a little less frightened.

'I'm really sorry. Don't go, please.' He straightened up. 'Wait, just wait five minutes, Kay. If you're really going to take them, let me give them something. I bought the boys Lego kits for Christmas, at least let me get them.'

'OK,' I said.

He ran to his house and stumblingly unlocked the front door. As soon as he was out of sight, I got in the car.

'Drive,' Rose said. 'Lock the doors, and drive.'

I turned on the engine. 'You sure you don't want to wait for these Christmas presents?'

'Drive!' she screamed, waking the boys finally, and I didn't need telling again. My heart was still thudding several roads later, but he didn't come after us. I was right that he wouldn't risk me calling the police.

Rose talked soothingly to the boys, told them we were going on holiday to Auntie Kay's house. They were excited to see Edward, who was nine years older than Will, and something of a hero to both boys, but they were still unsettled, not surprisingly. I put on a CD of Stella's, children's songs set to a reggae beat, and got them singing along with me to 'Baby Beluga' and 'My Grandfather's Clock'. Eventually, they both drifted off again.

When I was completely sure they were asleep, I asked Rose if she wanted to talk. I hadn't asked any questions when she'd called a few hours ago to say, could I come straight away? I'd not asked anything when she told me to wait outside in the car until I saw Tim drive off. I'd not asked why she wanted to get out so fast.

'Yeah, what do you want to talk about?' she said. At least she hadn't lost her sense of humour.

'What did he do?'

'What did he do now, or what did he do in general?'

'Whichever you want to answer.'

'I don't really want to answer any of it.'

That was fair. I just drove. That was my job.

'I'm sorry,' Rose said after a while. 'I don't know where to start.'

'You've got absolutely nothing to be sorry for.' I navigated us onto the motorway. 'Is he, has he been... he was scary tonight.'

'You know, he's never once bought the boys a present. Not once. It's always left to me.'

'Er...' I was confused. That was annoying, sure, but was it enough reason to leave someone the way she had? Then I realised what she meant, and a chill went down my back. '*That's* why you told me to drive. Because you knew he hadn't bought them Christmas presents.'

'No. Whatever he was going to get in the house, it wasn't that.'

'Oh my God, what... a weapon?'

'Maybe. I don't know.'

How narrowly had we escaped someone being hurt, or worse? I tightened my trembling grip on the steering wheel.

'Rose, I can't believe it. I knew you weren't happy but I had no idea...'

'Ah look, it was OK. He was out a lot. He never hit me, you know. He sometimes acted like he would, but he didn't actually do it.'

'The man's clearly a prince.'

She laughed. 'Goodness knows how you can make me laugh at a time like this. Anyway, I've been thinking about leaving him for a long time.'

'You never said.' But as I spoke, I knew it wasn't the sort of thing one said out loud. I knew only too well that one could think for a long time about leaving one's husband without actually acknowledging it to oneself, let alone anyone else.

'Earlier today he was yelling at the boys. They'd left a mess in the living room or something. Jay answered back. Not unusual, he's a cheeky little bugger, but this time Tim raised his fist to him.'

'That bastard, Rose. Jay's three years old!'

'I ran faster than I have ever run in my life and put myself between them, yelled, and he stopped. I don't know if he really would have hit him. My baby. I told him to go out, but he wouldn't, not for hours. He was all upset, how could you think I would do such a thing, I was only pretending, all that. When Jay stopped crying Tim made the boys watch a kids' film with him, got me to order a pizza, all cuddled up on the sofa playing at happy families.'

'And that's when you phoned me?'

'Yeah.' I felt her hand on my arm. 'I'll never forget this, as long as I live.'

'You'd do the same for me.'

'You'd never be stupid enough to marry an arsehole like Tim.' She let out a long breath of air. 'We won't stay long, don't worry. When I've got my shit together we'll get a place in Winchester, near my sister. I've always wanted to live nearer her.'

'You can stay as long as you want. I hate that you've gone through this, that I didn't know.'

'You're the best friend a girl could have, chick.' She stretched her legs out, and yawned. 'Would you mind if I closed my eyes? The adrenaline's worn off and I'm exhausted.'

In a few minutes I could tell by her breathing that she was asleep. I drove on through the night, carefully, looking after my precious cargo.

FIFTEEN

BIRMINGHAM, JULY 2023

When I got home from Naples the cottage was clean, with flowers on the table, a delicious meal in the oven, a bottle of wine in the fridge, and a gorgeous husband on the sofa. And if the meal got a little overcooked while we were, er, getting reacquainted on that very sofa, then so be it.

Having spent our passions, as the romances my mum used to read might put it, I told Murray about Stella and Nita. He held my hand and listened as I talked it all out. He was wonderful – maybe I didn't need Louisa after all. We also discussed buying the cottage, agreeing to split the £20,000 we needed for the deposit. What a wonderful use for my mystery money! Murray asked if I'd put the cash in my account yet, but of course I hadn't had time; I'd rushed off to Italy the day after we discussed it.

The next morning Murray went into town to speak to his bank. He was the one who earned actual money, so was our best asset for getting a mortgage. I was just a poor scholar, in his phrase. My job was to ring Imogen to confirm that we would like to formally offer on the house; she was delighted.

Then it was straight on to the next job on my Rose-gate list:

phoning Will, Rose's oldest son. I'd been close to him and his brother when they were young, but we'd naturally drifted apart as they grew up. This was a tricky call, because I had no idea how much, if anything, Will knew about the breach between me and his mother.

'Auntie Kay, oh shit, is everything OK?' Like Stella, he was a young person who regarded phone calls as emergencies or scams. How sweet that he still called me 'auntie'.

I reassured him all was well, and asked after his partner, Edith, and baby Janis – Edith was a Janis Joplin fan, apparently. It quickly became obvious that Will didn't know about me and Rose, which was a relief. He said Edith was away on a girls' holiday and he was literally holding the baby. 'She's asleep now but not for much longer.'

'I'm so sorry to have interrupted your precious quiet time. I'll get to the point. Bit weird, but I wanted to ask you something about your dad.'

'Uh... sure.' He laughed. 'Do you want to ask him direct? I can give you his phone number.'

I resisted the urge to blurt out, 'God no!' Will and Jay had been so young when Rose left Tim, they doubtless had little memory of my role in it, and thus no idea how much Tim must despise me. I started to say that wouldn't be necessary, that I just had a couple of questions...

'Blast, I knew she'd wake up once I was on the phone. Hey listen, I'm actually taking Janis to see Dad next weekend. He doesn't get on great with Edith, or the other way round really, so it's a good time to see him, while she's away. You should join us, he lives in Birmingham, that's not far from you, is it?'

'Well, actually...'

'To be honest, it would be nice to have some adult company. I get on OK with Dad but he's hard work.'

'Thing is, I was wondering...' The baby started wailing.

'Bollocks, can you hear that? Lungs like an opera singer. Looking forward to seeing you. I'll text you the details. Bye!'

The phone went dead and I stared at it, wondering what I had got myself into.

And that is how, a week later, I was sitting in a gloomy carvery in one of the less nice suburbs of Birmingham, right across the table from Tim Swift.

It was hard to accept that this was the same man who'd loomed over me full of rage twenty years ago, reeking of alcohol, as I prepared to take his family away from him. If I'd passed him in the street I wouldn't have recognised him. He was hunched and prematurely old-looking, no trace of the vigorous, frightening man he'd been. He looked ill, with some kind of Parkinson's type tremor in his hands.

I was surprised that he greeted me warmly, with a mercifully brief hug I didn't want to have. He smelled of cigarette smoke, but not alcohol. I readied myself for him to refer to our last encounter, but his conversation was entirely centred on his current life. He did ask me a couple of questions, and seemed not to have known that Richard and I were no longer together. But mostly he wanted to talk about the home improvements he and his partner, Zoe, were making, including a thorough list of everything they'd done to eliminate damp in their kitchen. He was incredibly boring. I could sense from Will's manner that this was Tim's usual level of chat. Thank goodness for adorable baby Janis, who was an excellent distraction from the damp coursing. I ordered a large glass of wine, feeling that I was going to need it, but Tim asked for cola.

'Don't drink any more.' He smiled. 'Saves a fortune.' Although a dull conversationalist, he was an attentive grandfather, helping give Janis her bottle, and being gentle and charming with her when she was in his arms. Had this leopard changed his spots? It wasn't a small thing that a father who'd had violent tendencies could nonetheless maintain a relationship with his sons into their adulthood. Most of that must be down to Rose, who'd made every effort to keep the relationships going as the boys grew up, despite not ever seeing Tim herself. I knew she'd insisted on supervised visits with Tim's sister till the boys were in their late teens, to protect them. But some grudging credit must go to Tim, for sorting himself out. Surely Will wouldn't let him hold his baby if there was even the faintest suggestion that he couldn't be trusted?

Tim wasn't particularly interested in the food, but was very focused on his soft drinks, which he filled up constantly, taking advantage of the 'bottomless soda' offer. He seemed to hate for his glass to be empty, tapped his trembling fingers on the table while waiting for a new drink to be brought over.

Finally, after a gruelling anecdote about finding discontinued stair rods in a local recycling centre, I posed the question I'd come to ask. 'Are you in touch with Rose at all?'

Tim looked surprised. 'Not really. Only the occasional email, you know, couple times a year.'

'Though I'm hoping they'll both come to Janis' naming ceremony,' Will said, looking hopefully at his dad. 'Not that we've managed to organise it yet.'

'Up to her, isn't it?' Tim said. 'It's fine with me.'

So this looked like another dead end; Tim wasn't back in Rose's life after all. Why had she mentioned him then? If she even had.

When he went to the bathroom I asked Will if I could take a photo of him and Janis for my project. I didn't say, but he clearly understood, that I didn't especially want one of Tim. While I snapped away, I remarked that his relationship with his dad seemed very solid. Will agreed. 'He's mellowed a lot.' He said that some of the credit for that should go to Zoe. 'She likes him to arrange outings while she's away; he's still not great being on his own.'

He would have been very on his own after I drove Rose away from their house, but not for long; I knew he had got together quickly after that with a new woman, much younger, and they'd had a child, but that relationship had also ended acrimoniously after a couple of years. 'He seems happier than he used to,' I said.

'For sure. He's had money troubles, and his health isn't great. But he's working, you know. He's assistant manager in a timber yard near here. Good with customers, apparently. He's very different from when I was a child, always yelling. Rehab was brilliant for him.'

'Rehab?'

'Yeah, a few years ago.' Will rubbed Janis' back and she let out an enormous belch that made us both laugh. 'Oh, and heads up, he's going to insist on paying for the meal. Please let him. He doesn't have much money, but it makes him feel good.'

Presumably that was why we were in a carvery rather than somewhere more expensive. Some men managed to rearrange the world round them so that they could be kings.

'Would you mind holding Janis?' Will held her out to me. 'I want to finish my food before it's completely congealed.'

'Of course!' I took the baby in my arms. She was full of milk and sleepy. I snuggled her against me, her head in the crook of my neck, my hands supporting her, the old skills coming right back. I framed, and rejected, several possible ways to ask after Rose before settling on, 'How's your mum, Will? I haven't heard from her for a while, she's been so busy.'

'Yeah, she's feeling a lot better since hospital, thank goodness.'

I hoped my face was neutral. 'Ah, good. Big relief. Er, what was she in hospital for again?'

He looked up, frowning. 'Actually, if she hasn't told you, I'm not sure I should say anything.'

Oh go on, Will, for God's sake. 'Of course not,' I said, stroking the baby's back. Forgive me for this fib, Janis. 'It's just, she was quite vague when she told me about it.'

He didn't suggest I was lying, so he definitely didn't know about our estrangement. But he wasn't budging. 'She hasn't told many people, so I'm not surprised she kept it vague.' He shovelled in the last of his roast turkey.

Oh Rose, my Rose. What was wrong? This was like with Bear all over again. I blurted out, 'It's not cancer, is it?'

Will stopped chewing. I could see that I'd given myself away. 'No, Auntie Kay, it's not cancer. But it's up to Mum to tell you, so you'll have to ask her, OK?'

'Yes, but…'

'And like I said, she's much better now.' He put his cutlery down. 'Do you want to pass Janis back? I'll put her down for a nap.'

Damn it. I watched as he gently laid the baby in her fancy buggy, which went flat like a bed, and pulled a cover over her. And then, before I could think of a way to find out more, Tim returned to the table, and Will steered the conversation on to a topic almost as dull as his father's – a workplace situation of Edith's, with a host of characters who all seemed to be called Kyla and Kyle.

I hadn't wanted to be here in the first place and now I was desperate to get away, but there was a painfully protracted business with the bill, because Tim wanted to pay most of it in pound coins. Finally I said goodbye and made it to the door, only to hear Tim calling my name. Christ!

He stepped outside into the sunshine with me. 'Will's changing the baby's nappy,' he said. 'Never did that stuff when I was a young dad.'

I nodded warily. Did he want to talk about back then? Yes, it turned out.

'I was a shitty father.' He leaned against the wall and lit a cigarette.

'I remember.'

He let out a hoarse smoker's laugh. 'Best thing that ever happened to me, that night, you know.'

'Seriously?'

'Not at the time, of course. Hated you.'

I wanted to tell him that I'd hated him too, but I wasn't so sure that was completely in the past tense. 'I was only doing what any friend of Rose's would have done.' As he was here, and I would likely never see him again, I decided to find out what he knew about Rose. 'I hear she's not been well?'

'Really? No one told me. What's wrong with her?'

Damn. I'd gone and spilled beans I didn't even have myself. 'Just flu, I think.' I moved quickly on to Rose-gate – could he at least shed some light on that? 'It's a funny thing, but she and I have fallen out.'

'Oh yeah? Will didn't say.'

'I don't think he knows.'

'I suppose she can be a volatile lady.' He blew out a plume of smoke.

'She isn't usually, Tim. Not with people who aren't you.'

He had the grace to smile. 'Why did you fall out?'

'I don't bloody know, and it's driving me mad.' I told him briefly about the hen do, her allegedly mentioning his name, me telling her to eff off.

'She mentioned me?' Now I had his attention. 'Why?'

'I thought maybe she was in touch with you again.'

'Told you.' He laughed his raspy laugh. 'Rose won't go near me with a bargepole. So why'd you tell her to fuck off?'

'If I knew that, Tim, I wouldn't be talking to you.'

'Bit pissed, were you?' He screwed up his papery face. 'Well, I know all about that.'

He embarked on a long and unpleasant coughing fit, then took another drag of his cigarette, clearly having no appreciation for cause and effect.

'Rehab wasn't for smoking then?'

He laughed. 'Nah, you can't give up everything, can you?'

Well, this conversation wasn't going anywhere. 'Where's Will got to? I should go...'

'Maybe she was saying that your new bloke was like me.'

'No offence, Tim, but that doesn't seem very likely.'

'Likes a drink, does he?'

'Not particularly. Maybe a whisky or two in the evenings.'

'Whisky.' He sighed. 'Don't half miss it.'

'I don't even know for sure that she did mention you. I've only got one erratic witness.' Come on, Will, hurry up! 'More likely, she was saying that Murray was nothing like you. Again, no offence.'

'None taken.' His eyes looked alive for the first time. 'But if so, why would you have told her to fuck off?'

Damn it! 'I don't know.'

'Makes sense, she says your bloke reminds her of me. That would piss you off, wouldn't it?' He shrugged. 'You know, you should ask Rose.' His eyes were dull again.

Duh, wish I'd thought of that. 'Good plan.'

'And listen, I want you to know I've turned things round. I'm working hard. I'm doing my best. I don't want to always have to be on my knees apologising for what a shit I was.' He dropped his cigarette butt on the ground. 'I wasn't going to hurt them that night, you know.'

'The boys?'

'I was gutted you went off without letting me give them their Lego.'

Had he really gone back inside to get presents after all?

'But anyway, I mean it, I'm grateful for what you did, for looking after my family and for the wake-up call back then. Without it, might have been years before I got help.'

I decided not to point out that it *had* been years before he got help, and it looked like he'd done himself irreparable damage in the interim. It could be dangerous to poke too many holes in people's versions of their own story.

Will joined us, his baby tucked comfortably on his hip. Fatherhood came naturally to him, which was impressive when you cast an eye over his role model. We said goodbye and I drove home, puzzling over six things:

1. What health issue had Rose been through, serious enough to require hospital? Graham had said she wasn't ill, but of course, he'd say whatever he had to, to get rid of me.
2. Was this why, like Bear, she'd dropped out of contact with me?
3. Could I stop worrying about that because Will said she was better, or was it something that might recur?
4. Whether Tim was on to something about why Rose had mentioned him, or whether his brain had been completely decimated by alcohol.
5. How ironic it was that he thought Murray might have a drinking problem, when I'd been too far gone to remember why I'd told my dearest friend to fuck off.
6. Whether it was time for me to stop drinking.

SIXTEEN
NORTH WALES, JULY 2023

It was surprising – and very touching – how many people made it to my show. North Wales was a long way for most of them, but Stella came over from Italy, and stayed with Newland in our Airbnb barn. Edward flew down from Glasgow, and Charlie travelled up from Oxford. Richard and Aileen came, bringing Alice with them, presumably because of her long-standing arrangement to inappropriately attend all my major life events. You had to hand it to her, she really was committed to the bit. Cousin Stacey was there, looking awkward, though not as much as her boyfriend, Keith, who slightly broke my heart because he was wearing an interview suit, complete with tie and pocket square, Stacey clearly having drummed into him that it was a dress-up occasion. To my surprise, Helena also showed up; I'd emailed her an invitation because I'd sent one to everyone who was depicted in 'Then and Now', but didn't expect for one minute that she'd come. We'd not exactly managed much of a reconciliation, and she was very busy. Still, here she was. Watching her and Stacey chat together made me smile; the only other time their worlds had collided had been that mad night before I left university.

Back in Chester, Stacey had asked what I'd got out of meeting Helena, and I hadn't been able to think of anything, except perhaps that she'd galvanised me to get on with my proposal. But seeing her here, I realised I'd got an answer after all, which was that though people didn't always forgive you, sometimes they did, just on their own timescale. I knew that Helena being here was her way of saying that she was over it.

We'd have had a full reunion of the Rezz Club boob tube night if Rose had been here. Though I hadn't asked her for an up-to-date picture, I still went back and forth over whether to send her an invitation. Louisa kept bouncing it back to me, but sometimes you wanted a grown-up to tell you what to do. Finally I asked Murray, my resident grown-up, and he said, sensibly, that inviting her might get my hopes up too much, that I ought not spend this important day wondering whether she'd come through the door. I realised that at some point, I had to respect her wish to be left alone, and perhaps I was starting to get to that point. Nonetheless, she was very present – indeed, being in three pairs of photos, she was more represented in the display than anyone else.

There was so much to get ready for the show – mounting and layout, writing a small piece for each pair of photos, putting together an overall background and theme, plus the 200-word project manifesto on a separate placard – that I didn't have much time to brood about Rose. Getting those manifestos down to 200 words took weeks. I pretty much lost my mind trying to justify in writing why some photos had been curated, rather than actually taken by me, even though Vanessa said it was fine. Carys and I sat up one desperate night working on each other's manifestos, and though we solved my curating issue, we nearly came to blows at 2 a.m. over whether she could cut the word 'unimaginable' without losing all sense of herself as an artist.

There was such a lovely feeling of achievement, and of camaraderie, as we set up our displays this morning in the

Neuadd Fawr, the Great Hall, all of us frantically tearing round with staple guns and mounts. The Neuadd Fawr was the grandest building in the university, a beautiful space with wood panelling, a gilded ceiling, and artwork filling the walls. Once we'd finished, we had to step out while Vanessa and the other tutors walked round inspecting and, God help us, grading our work. These displays contributed a hefty percentage towards our degrees. This afternoon, the room was opened to friends and family.

I stood in front of my display now and tried to see it through fresh eyes. Each photo pair was marked with dates, and the overall impression was of a long life punctuated by last encounters. I found it difficult to look at now it was finished. Luckily, Murray was by my side and, with his usual ease and charm, handled the lion's share of the interactions with people who came to look at it. I wasn't sure I really liked the attention. The culmination of three years' work had emptied me out.

'It's terribly funny to see myself in an exhibition,' Richard said. He'd spent a long time at the display.

'You haven't changed at all,' Aileen said to him fondly. What a sweet, good fibber she was. How lovely that they had each other's backs. I thought of the time, ten years ago or more, when I rang Rose in despair over Richard, and she praised divorce as the greatest pillar of a civilized society. The legal right to have a beautiful second chance: how right she was.

I'd decided, rather late, to put Alice in the display, partly because I felt bad excluding her, and partly because she was already in one of the 'then' photos, the one I was using for Imogen. It was a professional photo of the two of them outside Rules restaurant in London circa 1962, taken for the 'About Town' pages of *Tatler*. They were in their twenties, both gorgeous in skirt suits with matching hats, looking as if they were off to the races.

I asked Richard to send me an up-to-date photo of Alice, but of course he fobbed this off onto Aileen. Following my texted instructions she'd done a beautiful job: Alice at the kitchen table, looking down at her hands, her imperiousness offset by an unexpected vulnerability. It was interesting to see the way Aileen saw her. I remembered Howard teaching us, thirty-something years ago, that so much of a good portrait was in the eye of the beholder. Perhaps I would try to find an address for him, send a picture of my display, tell him that I'd finally finished my degree.

Alice clearly hated the photo that Aileen had taken, which was an extra bonus.

Edward put his arms round me and Alice. 'It's an amazing piece of work, isn't it, Grandma?'

'*Amazing*, that's exactly right, Edward,' Alice said, making the word positively shimmer with disdain.

I asked after Imogen, who I'd invited, though I wasn't surprised when she graciously declined. Alice waved an airy hand. 'Diminishing by the day, I'm afraid. Once your relatives get the notion to put you into a home, there's a clock ticking down the minutes till your inevitable demise.'

'Bit bleak, isn't it?'

'Just realistic, Kathleen dear.'

'She hasn't moved yet, has she?'

'No, but soon. Tick, tick, tick.'

I was terribly sorry for Imo, but quietly excited that Bryn Glas was almost ours. The mortgage would be approved next week.

'There's some strong work here,' Helena said, joining us after having looked all round the show. My student friends were very impressed that I'd got a professional photographer to come. They'd have conniptions if they heard what she whispered to me: 'I'm actually looking for a new assistant at the moment. There are some possibilities here...'

Vanessa, looking very pleased with everything, jumped up

onto the stage and made a short speech, first of all addressing kind words to our proud parents (most of the other students), or our proud children (me). Then she addressed each of us in turn. When she got to me, she said that it had taken me some time to work out that the gap between the past and the present wasn't quite as large as it sometimes seemed, and that what my work showed was that some relationships had a season, while others renewed and returned. I put my hand on Rose's brooch, pinned to my dress. Would she and I ever renew our friendship, or had our season come to an end?

I'd invited everyone back to Bryn Glas for cake and champagne, and as the crowds were thinning out, I looked around for Murray. It was strange, that disappearing act he sometimes did. I eventually found him and Charlie in the corridor, talking intensely, but they stopped when I joined them.

'Sweetheart,' Murray said, giving me a hug. 'What a fantastic day, everyone loves your display.'

Charlie nodded. 'Yours is the best, Kay.'

'I guess we need to get people back to the cottage, don't we?' Murray said. 'Who are we taking?'

'Stacey and Keith. You can squeeze in the back with them, can't you, Charlie?'

'I guess so.'

'What's wrong?'

'Nothing,' he and Murray said at the same time.

'That sounded rehearsed. What's going on, Garland guys?'

'It's nothing, darl,' Murray said. 'Just a silly misunderstanding, which we've sorted out now.'

I looked at the almost empty glass of wine in his hand. Was it something to do with that? Since my lunch with Tim I'd been on the alert for signs of excess drinking, but I was either barking up the wrong tree or Murray was an expert at hiding it. I'd asked him, of course, if he'd ever worried about his alcohol intake – I couched it in terms of both of us needing to keep an eye on it – but he'd seemed utterly nonplussed by the suggestion.

I led them along the corridor to some seats outside an office. 'Tell me, please, or I'll only worry.'

Charlie sat down. 'It's your special day, Kay. Dad's sorted it now.'

'It's certainly not worth being late for your own party for,' Murray said.

'For goodness sake!'

'Fine.' Murray sat next to me. 'It's about Charlie's university money, but like I say, it's sorted.'

'What money?'

'My trust fund,' Charlie said, staring at the floor. Had he deliberately put an emphasis on the word 'trust'? I'd never seen Charlie like this. Not that I knew him well, of course, but this frowning young man was very different from the shy fellow who'd been best man at my wedding.

'The fund your mum set up for you?' My heart was thudding, my body seeming to know, not for the first time, that something was wrong before my brain caught up.

'Yes,' Charlie said, staring at Murray. 'Dad's been borrowing from it.'

'And paying it back straight away!' Murray said impatiently. 'It doesn't impact on him in any way, honestly, and...'

'Why on earth have you been doing that?' I raised my voice enough for a woman walking nearby to look over at us. 'Explain, please.'

I said this in the voice I sometimes used when, as manager of Quiller Queen, I saw a kid slip a pen or eraser into a pocket. 'I can see you,' I'd call out, loud and friendly. 'Pop it back, will you?' Nine times out of ten they did replace the item and slope off sheepishly. The occasional yob gave me a mouthful of abuse and swaggered out to a life as a hardened criminal, I imagined. Anyway, Murray was no match for the voice. I doubt he'd heard it from me before.

'All it is, the nature of my work means there's occasionally a cash-flow situation, and it makes sense to borrow money from the account Ursula set up, rather than pay bank fees for a loan. There's plenty in there, and Charlie isn't using it all at once, are you?'

'No. But you should ask me, Dad. It was a real shock when I saw last week how much was missing.'

'I don't understand.' I thought of Stacey saying how blessed I was, how in my position she'd fear that the other shoe might drop. Was this the other shoe dropping? 'Why do you need loans? Why have you never mentioned this cash-flow problem?'

'This will take more explanation than we have time for right now.' Murray stood up. 'Let's join our party, and talk properly when everyone's gone.'

Stella came over to us. 'Mum, people are leaving, are you coming now or shall I let them in and sort out the refreshments?'

I thought fast. 'Yes please, darling. Could you and Newland take Murray and Stacey? There's fizz and elderflower in the fridge, and the cakes...'

'I can handle it, Mum,' Stella said. With a curious glance at Charlie's solemn face, she went off to find Stacey.

'You head over with Stella, be your lovely hostly self,' I said to Murray, 'and Charlie and I will come shortly.' I started walking to the door, and he had no choice but to follow me.

'But, everyone's come to see you, not me! What are you going to do?'

'I'll just have a quiet chat with Charlie, make sure he understands that there's no problem,' I said. I was aware that, for the first time in our relationship, I needed to manage Murray. Resisting the urge to shove him on his way, I said, 'Go on, darling, go save our party. We'll be there soon, OK?'

'I'm not sure this is a good idea,' he said. 'He doesn't really get it...'

Stella reappeared, with Stacey and Keith, both of them with their hands clasped behind their backs, like King Charles. 'Come on, Murray,' Stella said. 'People are going to arrive and there will be no one there.'

'All right.' Murray, outflanked, gave me the car keys. 'You haven't drunk too much, have you?'

The irony! 'I haven't had any.'

'It's good of you to look out for Charlie. It honestly is fine, whatever he says, I promise you.' His face was tense with worry, perhaps reflecting my own. 'You won't be long, will you?'

'Of course not – it's my party, after all!' I kissed him and said, 'Tell everyone I'll be there in a jiffy.'

When he'd finally gone, I returned to Charlie. He gave me a tentative smile. 'He was freaking me out a bit, I'm sorry, Kay.'

I sat down. 'Listen, whatever this is, I need to know. Don't sugar-coat it, OK?'

He nodded. 'It's not usually a problem.' He wiped his face with the back of his sleeve. 'Dad does sometimes borrow money from my trust: a few hundred here, a grand there, but he always pays it back within a week. He's right, it's silly it sitting there if it can be useful.'

Useful for what? If Murray, like Tim, had a drink problem that caused him to fritter his money away, would Charlie know, or would he have been protected from it?

'But when I looked in the account last week I almost had a heart attack. He'd taken twenty grand.'

'Oh *no*, Charlie.'

'Way more than usual. I panicked that he was in trouble or something, but when I rang him he said it was a mistake, he'd put an extra zero. I didn't believe him. Sorry. I feel bad dragging him. Eventually he said he'd had a big expense, and he's paid it back now anyway.'

What could that expense have been? We needed a sum like that for our mortgage deposit, but not till next week.

'So what were you arguing about today?'

'I was telling him he should ask if he wants to borrow that much.'

'Damn right.'

'He was acting like it was no big deal. I mean, maybe it isn't.'

But maybe it was. My memory of Bear's letter was that no one was meant to touch that money but Charlie.

As if reading my thoughts, he said, 'Mum did always say...' He paused, for long enough that I could see him trying to work out a diplomatic phrasing: 'Dad's not brilliant with money, is all.'

I was desperate to know exactly what it was that Bear used to say, but didn't want to interrogate the poor boy. What was I facing here? Had Murray simply made a stupid error of judgement – several stupid errors – or was something awful going on?

'Charlie...' How to ask? 'Has your dad ever had problems with, er, drinking or anything?'

'Nah, he's really good at it.' Charlie laughed uproariously, reminding me that he was, for all his sensible ways, a student.

'OK, but are you serious?'

'I don't know. It was just something someone said...' I thought of Tim, the glass of soda in front of him, his gaunt face.

'Well, sure, he likes a drink. He's an Aussie bloke!'

This wasn't terribly reassuring, but I didn't want to worry him any more. As I drove us out of town, I thought about how protective Bear had been of Charlie. A couple of years before she died, when she knew she was ill, she'd sent a letter to Murray, which he showed me. It was called 'If You Should

Remarry', and was written purely with Charlie in mind, an attempt to protect him from an evil stepmother. In her position I might have done the same, though when we were planning the wedding I did silently question whether we really needed to stick to all of her directives now that Charlie was a grown man. The instructions varied from sweet – the bride should wear yellow, because it was, at the time of writing, young Charlie's favourite colour, and the wedding should take place in a beautiful garden – to the infuriating: an insistence on the old-fashioned tradition of the bride being given away by her father or other respectable male figure, which is how Richard ended up being involved in our wedding. Neither Murray nor I could imagine why she'd specified that. Perhaps because she felt it would bring an air of legitimacy to proceedings that Charlie would find reassuring? I'd never know now.

There were also financial stipulations in the letter: *You and your new wife must respect the money I've put away in trust for Charlie's university education and not attempt to guide or influence him in any way on its use.* This wasn't just addressed to the hypothetical evil stepmother, but also, I now realised, to Charlie's father. Oh Bear, I really hoped I hadn't let you down.

I couldn't stop the 'why' of it churning round my head. Why had Murray needed money? Cash-flow issues, he'd said. But what did that mean? Was he in debt? Having a breakdown? Being blackmailed? Having an expensive affair? Had he lost his job, and not wanted to tell me? You heard about men who got fired but continued to put on a suit each morning and go out, because they couldn't bear to tell their wives. Did an alcohol problem lie under all this? Christ, Bear, why had you been so discreet about Murray? After he and I slept together for the first time and I knew I was in deep, you can betcha I went right back through her letters scouring for information. Shortly after they'd met, in the late 1990s, there was mention of his handsomeness – I hear ya, sister! – and later, some descriptions of the hikes they'd taken together. After the divorce there was a small amount of bad-mouthing him about his lax attitude to child-rearing, but little else.

'I'm sorry if this has spoiled your day,' Charlie said as we pulled up in front of the cottage. 'Your artwork was brilliant.' Such a sweet boy, Bear – you should be so proud.

'It hasn't been spoiled it at all,' I fibbed, and pulled him into a hug, expecting him to resist but he didn't at all; he held me tight. Disney style, I let him decide when to stop, and then we went into the cottage and into a rather lovely party, in celebration of me. I did my best to put all of this out of my head until later, when I could talk it through with Murray properly, but inevitably it was hard not to let it cloud things.

Murray hadn't told me much about his and Bear's divorce, other than to say it was precipitated by Bear's affair. I'd never known about that, and her letters gave no hint, unless the teaching colleague she mentioned a few times was the smoking gun. However, Murray was very understanding about what might have driven her to have an affair: his absences from home, working away, his acknowledgement that he didn't really get what it was like for her, trying to juggle a home and job while looking after a young child. How I'd like to ask Bear about that, and whether he was as understanding about it at the time.

What did she know about Murray that I didn't? In all the months we'd been married I'd seen no evidence of him 'not being brilliant with money'. But hang on... I excused myself in the middle of a conversation with Stella and Newland, and dashed into the loo to think. I absolutely *had* seen evidence of it. A couple of months ago, Simon, Imogen's son, had called me, terribly apologetic, saying that the rent hadn't been paid for the previous month. Said he hated to chase because I'd always paid bang on time before. Mortified, I assured him it was a bizarre oversight and hastily paid it as soon as I hung up. Murray was meant to be on rent, while I was bills. He was horrified when I asked him about it, slapped his head, called himself a flaming idiot, said he'd clean forgotten. That puzzled me; I asked why he didn't have the rent on a standing order, surely that was a no-brainer, and he said… actually, I wasn't sure what he'd said now. My rotten memory was becoming less a joke and more a complete liability.

SEVENTEEN
NORTH WALES, JULY 2023

It was well into evening by the time our guests left. Murray and I had both been on hosting duty and hadn't had a chance to talk. I made a speech thanking everyone for their support, then Murray stood quickly, presumably wanting to make sure he got in before Richard, to propose a toast to me and my 'sensational exhibition'. As I raised my glass to him in response, this man I adored and trusted, I wondered what he was thinking, and realised that I really had no idea. It was a funny old business, marriage, wasn't it? You could be completely intimate with a person, yet scarcely know a thing going on inside his head.

How well do you know each other?

All *right*, Rose!

At last, when everyone else had gone, I took Stella, Newland and Charlie over to the barn to get settled. Stella asked quietly if I was all right, said that I seemed 'a bit far away'. I reassured her that it was nothing but the excitement of the day.

When I returned to the kitchen I stopped at the door, watching Murray washing up glasses. I stood there for a long, peaceful moment, as I had done not so long ago, watching him cook. No complications then, just love.

Murray, sensing my eyes on him, turned and gave me his biggest smile. 'A lovely party,' he said, rinsing off a glass, 'though I thought they'd never leave!' He seemed absolutely his usual self. He dried his hands, and said, 'We need to talk, don't we?'

Despite myself, I admired his willingness to face this tricky conversation head on. We sat opposite each other at the table, and he put his hand on mine.

'Don't look so gloomy, Katie. You were brilliant today and everyone had a good time. This is such a little thing with Charlie.'

'Maybe, but I've been feeling pretty weird about it.'

'I'm so sorry.' His eyes were full of sympathy. 'The absolute worst part of this is that your day's been spoiled.'

'I don't care about "my day". It's not important compared to me worrying that you're in financial trouble and haven't told me. Or that you might have broken Charlie's faith in you. It's not like you, but I'm worried that maybe it *is*, and I don't really know you.'

'You know me, sweetheart.' His voice was gentle. 'I'm your Murray, I always will be.'

'So tell me. This cash-flow problem. Is it because you've run out of work?'

He looked astonished. 'Good heavens, Katie, don't you think I'd have told you if that had happened?'

'I'd like to think so, yes.'

'OK, look. Do you understand how my business works? I know I've explained some of it but you always did look a little glazed, frankly. No shade, there's nothing so boring as the minutiae of other people's jobs.' He grinned.

'I did not glaze!' I grinned back, I was too used to us being grinny together to keep my serious face going. 'I just didn't really follow it.'

'Well the crucial part is that for a lot of my clients, the majority of what I earn is commission. Say I sell a nice boat upgrade to someone, that's a good day because I get a solid fifteen per cent of it.'

'Like when you had a meeting with that millionaire from Singapore, who wanted a total refit...'

'Well, he was a billionaire, but other than that, exactly. I sold him a whole new bedroom kit-out on a fifty-footer. An hour's conversation and bam, you and me were eighty grand richer. But, here's the thing, we weren't *actually* eighty grand richer. Not till the client pays for the kit, then I get my cut from the supplier.'

I could feel myself wanting to glaze over, exactly as he'd said. 'So it takes a while for you to get the money.'

'Ages, sometimes.' He nodded ruefully. 'Truth is, I've been playing catch-up since our honeymoon.'

He'd been so generous in Dallas – restaurants, flowers, champagne, shopping trips. Was that money he didn't actually have? 'So you earn commission for some of your clients, but what about the others?'

He explained that some clients were charged for his time, and they didn't all pay promptly. That in his business it was common for an invoice not to be paid for months, but he'd still have to fork out for things clients needed. He'd often described the ridiculously expensive items he'd be asked to source, but it was only now that I realised he had to pay out of pocket for them.

'So you're owed a lot of money, basically.'

'That's the long and short of it.' He ran a hand through his hair. 'The money is always coming in, but not always when I need it.'

Him not paying the rent must have been one of those times. 'Why didn't you tell me?'

'It's how I've always worked, it's a juggle, I don't see it as an issue. And there's money sitting in Charlie's account, of no use to anyone. I borrow from it occasionally to tide me over, then as soon as I get paid for the outstanding work, I put it back. With interest, I should say. And he's been fine about it.'

'Until now.'

'Well, that was a bigger sum which I stupidly forgot to mention to him. But I'd never do anything to risk his wellbeing, or his education. That boy is my life. Even ahead of you.'

I wanted to trust him, I really did.

Then he said, 'But, Katie, I have to tell you, there is now a bit of a problem.'

'Oh, God.' I got up and put the kettle on. Of course I did. I am British.

'I've tried really hard to sort it on my own, without bothering you. The timing's rotten because you've had your project, and the exhibition...'

'Tell me quickly.'

'All right. The reason I borrowed the twenty grand from Charlie is because I've been having trouble getting the mortgage.'

'What? But you said...' I cast my mind back; he'd gone to talk to the bank weeks ago. 'You said it was fine.'

'It was, but then they wanted proof of my assets, and my self-employed records weren't up to scratch. So I needed to put together a big sum to show I was good for it.'

'So you had the twenty grand from Charlie...'

'That was the limit of what I was allowed to withdraw from that account. And another ten grand or so.' He stared at the table. 'I was hoping not to have to tell you this bit.'

For a long moment, I couldn't think what he meant. Then I realised. 'You used my money.'

'It's in my account.' He still couldn't look at me. 'I had to show the bank yesterday. If you want it back in cash I can get it out tomorrow, or I can transfer it directly into your account...'

He was still talking as I ran upstairs and opened my T-shirt drawer. The envelope was there, but it was empty. My money was gone.

I sat on the bed for a few minutes, feeling dizzy. When I went back down it was with a heavy tread. He was still sitting there, his face unreadable.

'Well, go on then. Talk.' I could hear how cold my voice was.

He nodded. 'I'm going to get this all out of the way in one go. So the bad news is...'

'More bad news, on top of you taking my money?'

'I didn't want to worry you...'

'That worked out well.'

'OK, the bank still said no.'

'Fuck, what?' I sat down. I felt cold all over.

'They won't give me the mortgage because even with that lump sum, it wasn't enough to make up for my crummy accounts.'

'For God's sake, Murray!'

He'd poured two tumblers of Scotch for us while I was upstairs. He pushed one towards me, and I shoved it back at him so hard that it fell to the floor and shattered into a thousand pieces of crystal. It was one of the glasses Anthony and Kiernan had given us for a wedding present.

He looked at me with wide, alarmed eyes.

'Why the *hell* have you been trying to sort this on your own,' I said, enunciating every word so he couldn't miss it, 'and in doing so, pretty much resorting to criminal acts?'

'I didn't want to drag you into it. We both agreed that I would arrange the mortgage... I wanted to get it all sorted for you.'

'Well, ten out of ten for intention, minus a million for outcome.'

'I've let you down. I'm the biggest idiot who ever lived.'

'At least you got something right.'

What was it with men, letting their stupid pride not only get in the way of what needed to be done, but actually making it worse? I'd thought Murray was more modern than that, enlightened, but it seemed not. I blamed his father. And patriarchy, obviously.

'Well. I had no idea I'd accidentally married a don't-tell-the-little-woman caveman.'

He attempted to smile, then thought better of it. But despite my anger, I could feel myself relenting. He *had* been a stupid idiot, a desperate man. But he'd tried to sort things out for us, tried to be the man of the house. And he wasn't really a caveman, was he? I thought about how much blustering and self-justification there'd be if it was Richard sitting across from me, whereas Murray had laid his cards on the table and was now quietly waiting for me to pass judgement, decide our next steps.

'Oh, Murray, what a mess. I love this place, it's my home. Our home. We shouldn't have to lose it because you don't know how to manage your accounts.'

'I wish I could turn time back. I can't bear how badly I've let you down.'

'A drongo of the first order, I'd say.'

'Can I take any comfort in you calling me a drongo?'

I stood up to get my phone, but he thought I was intending to clear up the glass, and leaped to his feet.

'At least let the caveman deal with the mess.'

'Fine. I'm going to find out if we can get any leeway.' I went into the living room and rang Imogen's number, my hand shaking. I didn't tell her any of the bad stuff, said only that something had come up and we needed more time to secure the mortgage.

'I know Simon was hoping for the sale to go through next week, *chérie*, but I'm sure I can get a bit of an extension. We have enough put aside for my care home fees for a year so there isn't a huge rush.'

'A year would be amazing...'

'I doubt he'll agree to as long as that, but I'll talk to him in the morning, see what I can do. Kay, is everything all right?'

'Yes, completely fine.' How I'd have loved to blurt out the truth, but I reined myself in. It wasn't fair to her, and I didn't want her to think that Murray was unreliable. Even if he was.

'The show went well today? I was so sorry not to be there, but Alice has already sent me a photo of your display. I loved seeing my portrait.'

'I'm glad. Yes, it went really well...' I put on my most upbeat voice, and she told me she would let me know once she had spoken to her son.

I couldn't see Murray when I returned to the kitchen, and for one wild minute I thought he might have left, or done something crazy. Then he said, 'Glass gets everywhere, doesn't it?' and I realised he was under the table with a dustpan and brush.

I found myself beyond relieved that he was still here.

'You can't strengthen a marriage without smashing a few tumblers,' I said, re-boiling the kettle. I could feel myself going into recovery mode. I'd seen the worst, and it was bad but not devastating. We could get through it. We just needed a plan.

He looked like he was going to cry. 'I don't deserve you.' He stood up and tipped the glass into the bin.

'No, you don't.' I handed him a mug. He didn't drink tea, but we were doing things my way now. 'Right, here's what we're going to do. I need you to agree to it and then carry it out.'

He nodded, sipped his tea, and managed not to wince. This was a new dawn.

'First, we agree that nothing like this will ever happen again.'

'Jeez, yes.' He looked, if it was possible, even more upset than before. 'I'm so sorry I've fucked things up.'

'I don't think it has to be a permanent fuck-up, does it? As long as there's no more mad borrowing Peter to pay Paul.'

'It doesn't have to be a massive fuck-up,' Murray muttered, as if repeating a mantra.

'How much of a lump sum does the bank want to see?'

'Hundred grand, I'm afraid.'

'*How* much?'

'Or fifty grand plus my business accounts to show a healthy profit.'

'Right, that's got to be easier. There's no way we can get a hundred grand in a short time. Or even a long time, come to that, unless I force Richard to sell the family home.' I briefly flirted with how it would feel to tell Alice that she had to move out, perhaps even into the same home as Imogen. Tick, tick, tick. But it wasn't right to turf three people out of a home in order for us to have a home, however annoying those three people might be.

'I think you've been taking the breadwinner role too far, and we're a team. So another thing I'm going to do tomorrow is call Helena and see if she has any work for me. Then you and I are going to sit down and go through your accounts, chase up invoices and turn your business into a model of pristine bookkeeping.'

Murray gaped at me. 'You know how to do that?'

I laughed. 'I did the books for Richard's shops for nearly thirty years. I think I can manage a one-man band like yours.'

'That's amazing. I used to have an accountant years ago, but... well, I guess he moved on. But listen, before all that, I need to put your money back.'

'Yes you do. And maybe you were right that I shouldn't keep all that cash in the house. You never know when some bastard might take it.' I threw him a stern look, but now that the immediate horror of it all had passed, I was – I don't know why – slightly enjoying myself. There was something sexy about this new, vulnerable Murray, and it had to be said that I was rather liking the awed way he was looking at me. This was not the other shoe, Stacey! This was, at worst, the slight slipping of a sock, which would soon be pulled back up.

Murray took my hand. 'You're being too wonderful. I couldn't feel more of a swine. Are you sure you don't want to wallop me, or make me sleep in the garden?'

I don't know why, but Rose's voice swam into my head. 'Come on, soft lad,' I could imagine her saying. 'It's bad, but not that bad. If I'd deliberately smashed a glass with Tim, he wouldn't have cleaned it up, he'd have made me walk on it.'

Murray might have been an idiot, but he'd been an idiot for the right reasons. And he was a kind, gentle man, who said sorry when he was in the wrong. All of that counted for a lot. 'Actually,' I said, 'I think we should go upstairs.'

It had been one of the longest days of my life, and I just wanted to lie in bed, my infuriating, confusing, unknowable, sexy husband in my arms, and start our marriage, with its new rules, afresh in the morning.

PHOTO #7

Then

Three young women, a tight head shot in faded colour. Rose is on the left, smiling and looking sideways at Ursula, aka Bear, who is in the middle, laughing. Kay is on the right, looking a little harassed because she has set the timer to take the picture and had to rush back into place. Behind them, a glimpse of sea. Sunshine bleaches out their faces a little but they are radiant. Rose and Kay are visiting Bear in Sydney during their gap year before they start university in London. All three are in T-shirts; Kay's, a light blue with a rainbow design on it, has been borrowed from Bear and she will not remember to give it back when she returns home.

Date: 16th December 1985. Location: Coogee Beach, Sydney, Australia. Photographer: Kay Hurst using thirty-second timer.

* * *

Now

Rose is on the left of the photo, and Kay on the right. In between them is Stella, who has joined them to say goodbye to Bear. They have thrown her ashes into the sea at West Kirby, because one of Bear's last wishes was to return there, a place she lived till she was sixteen. They have tried to get as close as possible to the place where, as teenagers, Bear fell off some rocks into the sea. They are all smiling, though it looks as though all of them have cried at some point during that day. There is a glimpse of a grey sea behind the women.

Date: July 2018. Location: West Kirby Beach, Merseyside. Photographer: Kay Bright using thirty-second timer.

EIGHTEEN

NORTH WALES, OCTOBER 2023

'How are you, Kay?'

A simple question, but to answer fully would take the entire session. My life was so busy. In the three months since 'money-gate', Murray and I had been working flat out. But I wasn't complaining; collaborating on a common goal, supporting each other, was actually really lovely. I felt that at last, we were properly getting to know each other. Since that tumultuous day he had done nothing to make me question my trust in him, and kept reassuring me how much he loved me, how lucky he was to have me. Our shared goal was to save money for our future home, and outside of his work trips, and visits to Charlie, we led a quiet life.

In a text to Stella a couple of months ago, I'd mentioned that in the interests of belt tightening, I was going to ditch therapy. She'd replied, *Therapy is not a luxury*, and I'd come round to her way of thinking. I valued how truthful I could be here, could say things I couldn't say to my husband.

'Today is the first anniversary of the day Murray and I met,' I told Louisa now.

She nodded. Not for her, the easy small-talk of 'happy anniversary'.

'And are you planning to celebrate?'

'Yes, I feel like there's plenty to be joyful about. Our relationship feels even stronger than it did at the start.'

Tonight I'd make a ribollita bean soup from a recipe of Stella's, with homemade bread. Fancy meals in restaurants were out; eating at home was in. Our favourite activities now were watching films on TV, going for walks, and of course, bed was free. Murray was always ready for a lie-down; he was working every hour he could. He had a lot of ground to make up.

We were incredibly fortunate that Imogen convinced Simon to agree to a six-month grace period. We'd had to accept several compromises, including Simon withdrawing the discount he'd been willing to offer us as tenants. But none of it mattered – at least we wouldn't lose Bryn Glas.

We were fortunate too that Helena agreed to try me out temporarily as her assistant. She'd told me I was the best photographer at the exhibition, and we were both pleased to have this confirmed when I was awarded a First in a low-key degree ceremony in August. But she hadn't offered me much work yet, other than touching things up on Photoshop. So I'd also taken a job at Snap-No-Chat, a photo development shop in the centre of Bangor, dusting off my retail skills from my Quiller Queen years.

When Murray paid me back my mystery wedding money, we used it to open a new joint account, on my insistence. I said it would allow us both to keep an eye on how the lump sum for our deposit was building up. Of course, we both knew I meant that *I* could keep an eye on it.

Going through his business accounts, I was astonished that the problems had taken even as long as they had to come to light. It was in such a mess. His office in the spare room was a crazy place full of papers in no order whatsoever.

'How did it get into this state?' I kept asking, as I gradually shaped mountains of paperwork into a coherent system.

'I've always been able to square the circle before,' he said, his head in his hands. There was a lot of this, him castigating himself and apologising, me muttering 'for better or worse' to myself.

I chased outstanding invoices, put in penalties for late payers, and set him up with a proper business account, but I still didn't completely understand how he managed his finances. Charlie was right that his father wasn't brilliant with money. Even after we sorted everything, Murray would *still* sometimes spend large sums up front, and we'd be back to being in a hole. He nonetheless tried to insist that I step away, that he had used way too much of my time and energy, and that he would be 'a model of financial probity' from now on. Seeing the look on my face, he hastily added that he would go through the books with me at the end of every month.

There were a few other things I couldn't understand about his accounts. For instance, there was a large payment from last year, made only a couple of weeks or so before he and I met, from someone called Oriana de Damas. It caught my eye partly because it was such a striking name, and partly because so few of his clients were women – they didn't seem to be the ones who owned the boats, who'd have guessed? But mainly because the money had come in, then been returned to her in full a few days later. Bit odd. When I asked him, he said it was simply that she'd paid for some boat upgrades, then changed her mind. Which was fair enough, except when I looked her up later on the internet, yes of course I did, she didn't seem to own a boat. She was wealthy enough, for sure, and very glamorous, but in all the many pictures she and her husband posted, there was not one sniff of a boat, which was unusual amongst Murray's clientele. They liked very much to show-boat, if you'll pardon the pun, on social media. Still, it was just one transaction; I had to learn to let go of some of the things I didn't completely understand, or I'd drive myself mad.

So when Louisa asked me now how things were, there wasn't a short answer. I suspected she felt I'd forgiven Murray too quickly. But mostly, I just felt happy to have him. I'd married a flawed man, but was there such a thing as a perfect one? There wasn't a day when I didn't look at him across the table, or walking in the hills, or in bed, and feel anything less than utter contentment. He was a man who needed to learn to share difficulties better, for sure, but as we worked together on a common goal, I fell in love with him all over again. And it was deeper now. As we talked about what had happened, why he didn't tell me when things got out of control, I learned a lot about the man I married, and how protective of me he felt.

It was a year since we'd met, which meant it was six months since Rose had sent *that* text. I was discovering that you could get used to someone not being around, more or less. Any kind of loss, from death to desertion, seemed to follow a similar trajectory. At first there's a hollow ache, homesickness, a lurch every time you think of them. You can't believe you won't see them again. Every time something happens you go to message them, then with a sickening feeling, remember you can't. But as time goes past, slowly, imperceptibly, you don't think to text them any more. The homesickness fades, till things are almost normal; you almost stop noticing they're not there.

Therapy was now the only place I really let myself focus on Rose. Louisa and I chewed all the fat out of the hospital/Tim/Murray/alcohol business but got nowhere. We also explored the embarrassing 'eff off' business from every angle, but without a time machine, it was nothing but speculation.

'You've said several times that your hen party was the drunkest you'd ever been,' Louisa said. 'Why was that?'

'I've told you. A perfect storm. Delicious drinks that didn't taste alcoholic. Exhausted. Hadn't eaten anything. Cousin

Stacey turning up, throwing me for a loop.' Then I remembered what Stella had said in Italy. 'Though apparently I was already plastered when Stacey arrived.'

'Hmm,' Louisa said. I was getting used to the 'hmm's. 'So it does seem likely that something happened with Rose that caused you to start drinking.'

'Like what, though?'

'I don't know.'

Nor did I, damn it. All at once, I felt bone weary. 'You know, either I've done something unforgiveable to Rose, or I haven't. There's no way of knowing unless she tells me, and I'm starting to accept that she might not, ever. That I may never really know what happened.'

Louisa nodded emphatically, as if I had passed a test, and said, 'Have you dreamed about your mum again?'

I was startled by the change of topic. 'Now and then.'

'I'm wondering... you almost never talk about her, you know.'

'Yes I do.'

'Not really. You only mention the dreams, not the real person.'

I was always taken aback by the shift from 'how do you feel' to Louisa's more interrogative methods, learned from the Spanish Inquisition.

'Kay?' Louisa said. 'We have fifteen minutes left. I wonder if this would be a good time for you to tell me about the last time you saw your mother.'

NINETEEN

LAST ENCOUNTER WITH MUM: LIVERPOOL, 2017

Even as recently as a couple of weeks ago, I'd been able to wheel Mum out into the overgrown garden for her to get some air. Despite her stroke, she'd passed eyebrow-raised judgement on the neglectful state of the roses. If you could judge a restaurant by the state of its toilets, could you judge a care home on the state of its garden? I had to hope not, because moving her into that home and leaving her there each time I went back south was the hardest thing I'd ever done.

Now those garden trips felt to be from a golden age. She had deteriorated fast, and was, even my untrained eye could see, close to the end. She was propped up in bed in the high dependency unit, her face as grey as the walls, drifting in and out of consciousness, and I held her hand, hating every miserable second. Where had my funny, caring, sarky mother gone? Who was this old lady? The skin on her hands and arms was thin as paper, and her fingernails were unkemptly long, something she would never ordinarily have allowed.

When Marie, one of the nicest carers, came in to check on her, I asked if I might trim Mum's nails.

'Ask her,' Marie said, brightly. 'I need to give her a drink so let's wake her.' She gently raised Mum up along the pillows and her eyes fluttered open. Marie picked up an insultingly toddler-like sippy cup with an orange lid and expertly put it to Mum's mouth.

'Bet you're thirsty, aren't you, Theresa?' Marie said, and Mum drank greedily, the water going down in the cup. 'Did you know your lovely Kay is here?'

Mum's eye flickered over to me and she said faintly, 'Hey, our kid.'

Marie went out, and I shifted closer to Mum. One of the advantages of her failing memory was that she probably had no idea how little I'd been here lately. Coming up here, staying in a faceless hotel nearby, the stuffy care home, the disintegration of a life – I didn't tell anyone how gruelling I found it. Only Rose knew a little about how hard I was finding it. To Richard, the kids, I managed to be breezily practical. But when I was here I was so miserable I could hardly stand it.

'Sorry I haven't been here for a while,' I said now, to assuage my guilt.

'Don't worry. I had company.'

'You did? Who was that, then?'

There was a silence, and when I asked again, she looked confused. 'Some very nice people, I think.'

'You could do with a manicure, is that OK?'

Mum nodded, so I got the little scissors out of my bag, gently took one of her hands in mine and cut the soft nails into a square shape, the way she liked them.

'I've never cut your nails before, have I?' I chuntered away. 'Of course, you used to cut mine, when I was little. What did you do when I was a baby? I remember when Edward was tiny I was too scared to use scissors on him, so I nibbled the nails off. Did you ever do that?'

'I don't remember.' Her voice was scratchy. 'Soon I won't be me any more.'

I stopped cutting, and looked at her. 'Course you will. You'll always be you.'

She did something with her mouth that might have been an attempt at a smile. 'The only one who won't know I'm dead is me.'

'Oh Mum...' I moved on to her second hand, trying to keep mine steady.

'Can't believe the stupid things I used to worry about.'

'What things?'

She sounded exhausted. 'You think there's always more time, then there isn't.'

'You've made wonderful use of the time that you've had, Mum.'

'Have I really? That's good.' Her eyes started to close, and I quickly cut the second-to-last nail. She made a noise.

'Did I hurt you?'

She shook her head, and mouthed, 'Uh ooh.' At least, it looked like that. Then she did it again, this time getting a little breath behind it to form the words. 'Uv you.'

'I love you too, Mum.'

I put down the scissors, and moved from my chair to the bed. I sat as close to her as I could, kissed her and held her hand, and told her how much she meant to me.

And that's what I wrote in my letter to Bear, what I told Rose, about my final goodbye to Mum. It wasn't a lie, it really did happen like that.

But that wasn't the day she died.

The following morning, I was woken before seven by a call from the home. The care manager said they were pretty sure it was going to be in the next twenty-four hours. I thanked her for letting me know, and said I'd come soon.

But I didn't.

I went straight back to sleep, and when I woke, it was gone eleven. I checked my phone, but there were no messages. I stayed all day in that crappy hotel room, watching TV. I didn't get dressed. I ordered sandwiches from room service, and made tea with the little kettle, and I sat in bed and I didn't go.

I didn't go because I didn't want to see her like that any more, her Mum-ness lost to old age, to stroke and dementia.

I didn't go because I'd had my fill of it. The emptying her house, shedding almost all her possessions, sewing name labels into all her clothes so they wouldn't get mislaid in the home, the horrible wide plastic seats on top of normal toilet seats, the dining room full of ancient people wearing bibs, staff pretending everything was lovely.

I didn't go because I knew I wouldn't regret it.

The call finally came at four thirty, while I was somewhat immersed in an old episode of *Escape to the Continent*. I listened to the care home manager's platitudes, and I said a number of platitudes myself. I apologized for not being there but said something urgent had come up, and she said not to worry, that Mum had been asleep all day. I hung up, and never told anyone that I wasn't there. In my letter to Bear, I said what happened the day before. That Mum had said she loved me. That I'd been holding her hand when she passed. I knew I had good reasons for not being there at the end, and that was that.

Except that it wasn't. Months after we'd buried her, I couldn't stop thinking about her last day on earth, and how I wasn't there. I was sure I wouldn't have regrets, and now, here I was, having them.

I thought of phoning the care home, seeing if I could speak to the manager, or to Marie, to ask who *was* with Mum when she died. Don't tell me she died alone, please don't. Would they even remember? There had probably been so many deaths since then. I wanted to ask if anyone had finished cutting Mum's nails. But I never mustered up the nerve to make the call.

TWENTY

LIVERPOOL, DECEMBER 2023

All the work Helena had sent to me so far had been digital things I could do from home. But today I was on my way to meet her for a real-life job, and in my old stomping ground, no less.

She'd called yesterday, apologising for the short notice, but she'd only just realised she needed another pair of hands. 'It's in Liverpool,' she'd said. 'A place called Hoylake?'

My heart stuttered. 'That's where I come from.'

'Jesus, really? Oh yeah, you introduced yourself to everyone at uni as being from "Liverpool, the posh bit". Ha! I'd forgotten that till now.'

So had I. 'Ugh, how embarrassing.'

'We were young and fabulous. So listen, it's kismet then, you back in your old hood. All expenses covered, and the pay's great.'

Great pay was music to my ears. Murray and I were getting close to our cottage goal of fifty grand, and every penny counted.

How strange it was to be on the familiar train to Liverpool, knowing I wouldn't be seeing Mum at the end of it. I'd done this journey two or three times a month to visit her for years. Then, when I was in Hoylake and on my way to a café to meet Helena, I realised that I was really near Mum's care home. Though it would clearly be quite weird to turn up unannounced, six years after her death, it seemed like kismet, to borrow Helena's word, and minutes later, I was standing at the door. The messy front garden made me think of Mum's frown, her telling me to have a go with secateurs when no one was looking.

Back then, I'd known the door code by heart. I couldn't remember it now of course, and anyway it was probably different, at least, I hoped so, for their security. I had a bit of trouble explaining through the unforgiving crackly speaker what I wanted, but after a confused exchange they let me in. The instant I stepped inside I was overwhelmed by the evocative smell of pine and old age. It was all I could do not to slip into my former routine: sign in and head for the smaller of the two living rooms in search of Mum.

The woman who'd been reluctant to let me in was sitting at the desk with a suspicious look on her face. But, incredibly, the woman next to her was Marie, Mum's favourite care worker! Kismet again. Weird to think of all the things I'd done since I'd last seen Marie, and she had just been sitting here. Well, she'd probably gone home occasionally, and had holidays and things, but she was still here in the same job. The minute she saw me her eyes lit up. I was really touched that she remembered me. She gestured to wait while she finished her phone call. Meanwhile the other woman pushed the signing-in book towards me with a 'you've got away with it for now' look.

There were Christmas decorations up and a large glittery tree near the entrance to the restaurant. Mum had come to us all the Christmases she'd been here, apart from the last one when she wasn't up for the journey. That had been difficult, me and Stella sitting by her bed, trying to be cheerful, offering her morsels of turkey from home which she had no appetite for.

Marie hung up the phone, then ran round the desk to hug me.

'Oh, Mrs Bright! How lovely of you to come and see us.'

She didn't need to know my new name, or, indeed, any of the things that had happened since Mum had died. She offered me a cup of tea, but my thrill at being recognised wore off pretty quickly once we were in the overheated living room, sitting as part of what I used to think of as 'the grim semi-circle' of extremely elderly people, who didn't seem to move from one month to the next. Marie asked after my kids, and told me of changes to personnel in the home.

'Marie, you know when Mum died?' I blurted.

'Yes, lovey?'

'I was wondering. It's silly really.' I suddenly couldn't ask the question, and extemporised hastily. 'Do you know what happened to her watch?'

'Goodness, it should have come straight to you. Didn't you get given her things? In a bag? The watch ought to have been with those.'

'Yes, of course, what am I thinking, I remember the bag. I'm being daft.' I really was.

She stood up, looking panicked. 'But, Mrs Bright, if the watch wasn't there that's terrible, I must look into it…'

'No, I'm sure it was. My memory, honestly!' It took a solid five minutes to talk her down from going through Mum's records, looking up whoever had been on duty that day, etc. I finished my tea, and got up to go, but was blocked by a fluffy-haired old lady who was holding on to her walker for dear life.

'Hello,' she said. 'I expect you'd like to know how your mum's getting on.'

Marie and I exchanged a wry smile, and she stepped in for

me in her practised way. 'That's nice of you, Joyce, but Mrs Hurst passed away several years ago.'

'I know,' Joyce said. She leaned forward and patted my hand. 'I've got a message from her for this lady.'

Jesus.

'There's no need,' Marie said smoothly. To me, she said, 'Joyce got Covid in that first wave, and came through it without any ill effects. Incredible. She'll easily get to a hundred.'

Joyce smiled again. 'Do you want the message, dear?'

Marie stroked Joyce's hand and said, 'She's all right, love. Thanks though.'

'Can I use the loo, Marie?' My eyes were blurry.

'Of course, do you remember where it is?' She pointed, and I stumbled in there, and had a little cry. Stupid! My guilt over Mum was making me so stupid.

But suppose...

When I came out I went back to the lounge as though I wasn't in charge of my feet. Some of the residents were being moved into the restaurant for lunch, but Joyce was still there. I sat next to her.

'What was the message?' I asked.

She looked at me blankly. 'What message?'

'From my mum,' I said, feeling quite desperate.

Her eyes were the palest blue and she seemed to have no eyelashes at all. 'I don't know her.'

I really was stupid. I returned sheepishly to Marie at the front desk.

'Got to go, have you?' she said, a little wistfully. I knew that feeling; it was always such a relief to get out of the home, away from the decrepit and dying. Even now, at pushing sixty, I felt incredibly youthful in comparison to the residents. In the time it took some of them to get upstairs, I'd be on the other side of Hoylake. I pulled the visitors' book towards me to sign out, and then had an urge to look at the last time I'd signed in. I asked

Marie if she still had the visitors' book from 2017, and of course, she did, retrieving it in an instant. How efficient she was. I easily found my final scrawled signature, 10th May 2017, the day before Mum died. Then I started flicking back through to see if my memory of how little I'd been there in the last year or so of her life was correct, and was brought up short by an entry in October 2016. *Rose Swift.* What?! *Visiting Theresa Hurst. Time in 1.15 p.m. Time out 5.45 p.m.*

Rose had never mentioned visiting Mum. I stared at the page. Rose hated coming back to Hoylake, actively avoided it. If only I could ask her.

Seeing her name made me brave. I said, 'Marie, you know Mum's last day? I wasn't able to be with her, but do you know if someone was?'

'Course I do, lovey.' She reached across the desk and took my hand. 'I stayed with her all afternoon, till it was her time.'

I nodded, unable to say anything, unable to stop the tears from spilling down my face.

'It was very peaceful. She went from being asleep to being gone. She wouldn't have known if you were there, lovey. And I know you'd have been there, if you could.'

I couldn't stand her being kind to me any more; I was so undeserving. I thanked her and we exchanged some pleasantries about how nice it was to see each other again, though I expect she was wondering what the hell all that had been about. There was no hug this time and I went outside feeling as if I had deliberately put myself into the path of a truck, and was then surprised to find I was injured.

I'd had a notion to pop in and see Stacey, who was living in her mum's old house nearby, but I'd run out of time. I hurried to the café, red-faced and apologising, but to my surprise Helena threw her arms round me. 'You've saved my life! Thanks so much for dropping everything.'

She ordered me a takeaway tea, and I asked whose party it

was. She named a very famous person. 'It's her grandparents. She's the one paying, she's spared literally no expense. And before you ask, she won't be there, she's in the States. But you might recognise some faces. It's close friends and family this afternoon. Then they're going on to late evening with hundreds more, but we'll be gone by then.'

I imagined an event of great excess and decadence. But I knew that not all Helena's clients were so fancy. Since working with her I'd discovered that she did this kind of job to fund less lucrative but more interesting work, such as a recent project in Burundi documenting women's reproductive health clinics. I wished I'd been able to be part of that. I needed to make myself indispensable today, pass my probation, so she'd hire me as her assistant for real.

We walked out into the cold winter sun, and she said, 'How are you with heights?'

I blinked at the unexpected topic. 'Heights?'

'Do you get vertigo, all that?'

'No, I don't mind heights. Small spaces, not very keen on those.'

'Good to know.'

I followed her as the pavement narrowed to accommodate a row of shops whose forecourts were covered with crates of fruit, some so overloaded that they were spilling out almost to the road. We turned into the next street, where the houses were fifty per cent bigger.

'So, I've been wondering for such a long time,' Helena said. 'Why did you leave?'

I spluttered into my takeaway cup. 'Well, uh, there were lots of reasons, I mean Richard and I had really grown apart, but also...'

'I'm so sorry!' Helena stopped in the street, and a young woman with a buggy had to negotiate round us. 'I meant, why did you leave university?'

'Oh!' We both started laughing.

'Neither of the leavings is my business. Of course, if you want to tell me why you left Richard feel free! But since we met, I've wanted to know. I'd not thought about you for years, then it all came rushing back. One minute you were there, and we'd signed up to do a placement together. The next, you were gone. I knew you were pregnant, but other students got up the duff and didn't vanish.'

We started walking again. 'It's hard for me to reconnect to that person back then. Do you remember Howard, our tutor?'

'Of course. I kept in touch with him for a few years.'

'He tried to convince me to stay. But Richard had asked me to get married, and I wanted to be able to devote myself to him and the baby. I didn't see how I could do that, and the degree as well.'

We turned into a street whose name I knew: Briar Tree Lane. Hoylake was already a bit posh, as I'd cringingly said in my student days. But even in Hoylake there were a few streets that were a cut above, as Mum used to say. And Briar Tree Lane was several cuts above.

Helena stopped in front of an enormous house behind a high brick wall, pressed a code into a keypad, and a solid metal gate slowly slid open. We went through into a beautiful garden, a world away from the ordinary one we'd just walked through. Like the hidden courtyards of Naples. An unsmiling security guard stopped us at the front door. Helena showed him ID and he nodded, stood aside to let us in. I felt very important.

The house was professionally decked out for Christmas in white and gold, like something out of an interiors magazine. There were a lot of familiar-looking people milling about, stylishly and expensively dressed, most in their sixties and seventies. Old people, I thought, then caught myself on. Did one ever stop feeling a particular age that was way younger than one's actual age? I'd got stuck at twenty-one.

Helena introduced me to a glamorous older woman. 'Kay, this is Delphie, our gorgeous hostess and ruby anniversary girl.'

I congratulated Delphie, and she laughed. 'I certainly deserve congratulations that my marriage has lasted so long! I could tell you some stories...' I wished she would, but she moved away to greet someone else. Forty years she'd been married. Incredible. I recognised something of what was going on behind her wide smile and glittering eyes. I'd been there myself, after a mere twenty-nine years.

We were shown into a quiet side room, and Helena started unpacking her equipment. 'We'll do the formal ones outside at golden hour, about three,' she said as she locked lenses onto camera bodies. 'But there's nothing to stop you taking informal ones before then, independently of me.'

I took out my camera, but she glanced it over, shook her head and casually handed me a Hasselblad that doubtless cost thousands. I knew I would find some inventive way to trash it, and gave it back to her immediately.

'It's too grand.'

She rifled through her bags. 'OK, use the body of yours but try this lens.'

It was an expensive make but not will-definitely-drop-it-down-the-loo expensive. I managed to put it on without breaking it.

She hooked a camera on each of her shoulders. 'Let's go.'

The next hour was a blur as I followed Helena round the party. She moved fast, taking a picture every couple of seconds, dropping into a chair for an up shot, or bounding up the stairs to get a higher vantage point. I was rather slower, but still took dozens. Sometimes people turned and mugged for the camera, though mostly they didn't notice us, but a few people – mainly the very famous faces – held up a hand to say 'no picture'. How I wish I could tell you who they were, but Helena swore me to secrecy.

We took a break before setting up the formal poses outside. We had thirty minutes before golden hour, that time before sunset when the light, as Vanessa often reminded my class, did ninety-five per cent of the work. Delphie's husband, a rakish-looking man in a white suit, handed us glasses of mulled wine and suggested we take a walk round the garden. It was astonishing, both in size and ambition, seemingly modelled on something like Versailles. Though winter, there were still some flowering shrubs, and I watched as Helena squatted down to take close-ups of plants. Over her shoulder, she said, 'You know that night we went out with your crazy cousin and you told me you were pregnant. Was that it? You left right after that?'

'The next day. I didn't feel I belonged any more.' I sat on a bench. 'Felt that I had no right to be there.'

'I did wonder why you didn't say anything.' She stood up. 'I was a bit pissed off for a while.'

'I'm sorry.' So I'd been right about her coolness at Stella's party, her reluctance to reconnect. 'It was crappy not to say goodbye. I can see how hurtful it was. But I couldn't face telling you I wasn't going to be able to do the placement. I wasn't being very "sisters before misters".'

She smiled. 'I'm sorry too. I feel bad that I pretended not to recognise you at your wedding.'

'I was surprised to see you at Stella's party after that, knowing I'd be there.'

'Well, you'd sent me that gorgeous student photo, and I knew I was being childish holding a grudge, just because you'd bailed out. I shouldn't have taken it personally. I was just so scared, being on my own at the start of that placement with Zander.' Helena sat next to me, and held out her hand for my camera. 'Truth is, maybe I'd have done the same as you, if I'd got pregnant. Sure, it was the 1980s, not the 1950s, but you know what, it wasn't as enlightened as all that, not for us girls from the provinces. I hardly knew any single parents back then, did you?'

'I didn't know any.'

She started flicking through the photos I'd taken of guests. 'After you went, Howard gave me your portfolio and I didn't know what to do with it.'

'Oh no, I'm sorry you had to deal with that...'

She waved her hand, to show it didn't matter. 'Actually, you've probably forgotten this, but your mum came in a taxi a week or so later, and collected your things. She was lovely.'

'I didn't know that.' Oh, Mum. She always tried to make things right for me. I could picture her, getting out at Euston, losing her nerve over the tube, splashing out on a cab.

'Got more out of her than that friend of yours, Rose. She said she didn't know how much you wanted to tell people.'

I'd never thought much about what it was like for Rose in her final year. We'd moved to London together, shared a house, then abruptly, I was no longer there. I don't think I'd ever asked her about it. I could hear Richard's voice. Ungrateful, take people for granted. Well all right, Richard, maybe.

'Some of these are good.' She gave me back the camera. 'Have you made up with Rose yet?' When I shook my head, she said, 'Something to do with your new man, perhaps? Did you drop her for him? Sisters before misters, remember.'

'Maybe. I'll probably never find out what I did wrong. I can't imagine her contacting me now.'

'She might be waiting for you to contact her.'

'No way. She's made that very clear.'

'What I mean is, once you've worked out the reason, she'll expect to hear from you.'

'You think?'

Helena shrugged, and we were silent for a minute. Then she said, 'Do you remember in our second year, taking cast photos for the drama society?'

'I've not thought about that for ever. What was it they put on, *An Inspector Calls*?'

'*Pygmalion.*'

'How'd you remember that? It was really fun, wasn't it?'

'The highlight of my degree. You were great at shooting the actors. I always thought you were the one who was going to be David Bailey.'

How lovely to think of a time at university that wasn't overshadowed by boyfriend dramas, that little line on the pregnancy test, David Endevane's closed-off face as I told him. I remembered instead the thrill of seeing our glossy black-and-white photos on the wall outside the little student theatre, young Robert-Smith-haired Helena clutching my arm in excitement. She was more brittle now, but underneath I could see the person I had liked back then.

'The clock has run out on me being David Bailey, but that's a lovely thing to say.'

'Even without that, you're having a terrific life, aren't you? A charmed life.' She took out a cigarette and lit it, which startled me. First Stacey with her vape, then Tim, now Helena: my generation seemed to be re-embracing smoking. 'At Stella's party, when your gorgeous grandson hugged you, I could have cried. I'd give anything to be at that stage.'

'Really? But to be at this stage I ditched my degree!'

'Yes, but you've had a lifetime to catch up. Now you can do whatever you like. Meanwhile I'm at the lethal menopause-plus-teenager stage. I'm so bloody knackered all the time.' Helena took a massive inhale of her cigarette. 'You were smart to have kids early. Now you've got the joy of grandchildren, plus a dishy new husband. You're rocking it, Kay.'

Well, that was an interesting perspective. On the one hand, I had certainly put in long decades of parenting. But on the other, it was very novel to have someone other than Stacey be envious of my situation.

'Haven't you got a fairly new dishy husband yourself?' I reminded her.

'The shine's worn off after nine years, I'm afraid!' She ground out her cigarette and kicked it under the bench. 'Gosh, I'm being indiscreet. But I feel like I know you. Shame we lost touch.' She squinted at the sky and said, 'Right, let's get set up. That flat lawn over there, in front of the trees.'

Watching her marshal a hundred people into place for the group photos was quite something. She was endlessly patient, witty and sweet. I checked the light meter for her, and stood at the sidelines, taking it all in. It was a shock when she turned to me and said, 'Right, ready for the ladder shot?'

'The what?'

She pointed at a tall step ladder, about eight foot high, that someone – a gardener, possibly? – was setting up behind us. 'They want some shots from above, old school. I was going to use my drone camera but when I opened the case yesterday, I discovered my last damn fool assistant broke it.'

'Seriously?'

'I don't think she did it on purpose, probably...'

'No, I mean you seriously want me to take some of the formal photos?'

'I'm petrified of heights.' She laughed. 'Remind me to tell you how I missed my big break, shooting for *Vogue* in the Tatra Mountains. Actually, no need; that's the whole story.' She handed me a camera. 'Go on, you'll be fine. Be quick, people are starting to look cold.'

This was a lot bigger a deal than taking informal snaps which Helena could simply discard if they weren't up to scratch. I hung the camera around my neck, took a breath, and climbed to the top of the ladder, hands trembling. It was true that I didn't mind heights, but the responsibility of getting a good photo made me nervous. Helena held the ladder steady while encouraging everyone to stay in position. At the top I squinted through the viewfinder at the smiling faces looking back up at me, and I could see immediately how to frame it. I adjusted the shutter speed and took six, seven, eight frames one after the other. Then I called, 'Last one – can everyone hold out their arms towards me?' I knew exactly how it would look. Everyone immediately complied – what a sense of power – and I took half a dozen shots before people started moving and laughing.

'All done, thanks so much, everyone,' Helena called.

The guests dispersed, and I climbed down the ladder on wobbly legs.

'Sorry I went off piste there,' I said, handing Helena the camera.

'Are you kidding?' Helena flicked through the pictures. 'These are great, well done. This one is absolutely charming.' It was the last one, and though everyone still had their arms in the air, people had started to relax, and at the centre, the anniversary couple had turned to look at each other, which they hadn't done in any of the other pictures. Maybe they were no longer in love, maybe they hadn't been for years – I thought of the expression on Delphie's face as she said 'I could tell you some stories' – but they sure looked in love in this picture. My tutor Vanessa often said, as a counter to the adage that the camera never lies: actually, the camera often lies, and we, the photographers, can take full advantage of that.

Our hosts thanked us and we left. In minutes we were back in Normal Land, like waking up after a dream. We took a cab to a hotel Helena had booked, where I'd imagined we'd spend the evening together, dinner and drinks, perhaps more revelations about the past. But she said she needed to go straight to her room. 'I have calls to make. Apparently Martha's walked out of a detention and is facing suspension. Just what I need.'

All day I'd been in awe of her calm confidence. Now, for the first time, she looked unsure of herself. She pressed the button for the lift, then paced away, headed towards the stairs, and as I was about to follow she came back and pressed the button again. 'Come on, come on.'

'Helena, I'm really sorry. Do you have to head home?'

'No, her father can sort it. I'm going on to Manchester tomorrow to do a shoot for Deutsche Bank. I can't drop everything whenever she's a mardy arse.'

I could see the weight she must feel of being the breadwinner. There were plenty of times when Stella had been in trouble at school – she constantly chafed against the rules – and I'd been there to talk her down, hug her, make things right. The children had been my domain when they were growing up. I'd sometimes resented it, but, with the benefit of not having to be so involved now, I could see that it could also be a privilege.

While we waited for the interminable lift I looked at my phone, and saw that Murray had sent a picture of himself, taken twenty minutes ago. He was sitting on our sofa, a smile on his handsome face. After being immersed in professional photography I could see numerous problems with the composition, but it was nonetheless the best shot I'd seen all day. The caption said, *Back from the fleshpots of Aberystwyth. Me and the sofa miss you.*

Helena said, back in brisk and confident mode, 'So, I'd call today a success, wouldn't you?'

'I loved it. Oh, I must give you back your lens.' I started looking through my bag, but she put her hand on my arm.

'Keep it, it works well for you.'

'Really? But...'

'I think we should make things official. You'll be my assistant?'

'God, really?'

'Yes, and maybe take smaller jobs off my hands entirely?'

'Am I good enough?'

'Fishing?' A slight smile. 'You still have that eye, Kay.'

The lift finally arrived and we got in. She added, 'Get whatever you want on room service.'

The thought of a meal in my room, and a night in a faceless hotel when I was only a few hours away from my love, seemed mad. I missed Murray, with a real pang of homesickness. I thought of Helena telling me I was rocking it, and she was right. I really did have it all. I put my hand against the door to stop it closing, and said, 'Actually, I'm going to head home.'

TWENTY-ONE
LONDON, FEBRUARY 2024

It was ridiculous to be shocked at the death of a person in their late eighties. No one went on for ever, after all. But when Richard phoned to tell me that Imogen had passed away, I reeled as though I'd been punched in the gut. She'd been a gentle, motherly and encouraging presence in the background of my life for so long. A childlike part of me had assumed she would always be there.

Her funeral was private, family only, but the celebration of her life was held two weeks later, at St Paul's Church in Covent Garden. The large space was near-full, with people from the many different worlds Imogen inhabited. When Simon got up to speak, his face sombre and anxious, I really felt for him. I'd always seen him as the person who I paid rent to, the person we were in the process of buying the cottage from. But today he was a son in mourning for a much-loved mother. Murray, next to me, shifted in his seat when Simon began to speak. I squeezed his hand, and he squeezed it back. He'd been even more wonderful lately, listening patiently to me reminisce about Imogen, the kindness she'd shown me. Shown both of us. How generous she was, how fun, how *alive*. It was hard not to think of her in clichés: the end of an era, they don't make 'em like that any more, but they were true of her.

Simon said his mother really had wanted a celebration, not sadness, and she hoped we would always think of her fondly. There were some wonderful speeches, revealing the Imogen I had known, as well as aspects to her that I had no idea about. For instance, I didn't know that she had lost a fiancé to the flu epidemic of 1957.

As Imogen's oldest friend, Alice had been asked to speak, and despite our many ups and downs, my heart went out to her as she made her way slowly to the front, accepting Simon's arm with ill grace as she negotiated the steps.

'Imogen and I met when working for Her Royal Majesty's household in the early 1960s,' she began. Richard and I glanced at each other and sat up straight. How often we had begged Alice to tell us some of her secrets from those days! We'd never prised anything more interesting out of her than the reveal that Princess Anne 'quite liked' blancmange.

'Of course, I am not allowed to talk about that time...'

Damn.

'But Imogen didn't stay long. She was a restless spirit, and the constraints inherent in cooking for royalty were not for her. She was interested in fashion and theatre, and art, and soon became a darling in those worlds with her keen eye, her championing of young artists. Some of you here, in this beautiful actors' church, will have benefitted from her support, her advocacy. How I loved meeting her at weekends, when we would go to the latest gallery opening, the most exciting plays and restaurants...'

It did sound fun. I fell into a reverie of Alice and Imo, young and gorgeous, Swinging London at their feet. Like in the picture I'd used in my display. By the time I met Imo in the late 1980s, her mini-skirted days were long behind her. Good Lord, when I met her, she must have been about the age I was now! How sorted she'd seemed to me then, and, yes, how old. The passing of time was, as Stacey would say, an absolute bitch. I was startled back into the present at the unexpected mention of my name.

'...and always such a good friend to my family, in particular, my daughter-in-law, Kathleen.'

Murray and I shared a look of surprise. I was astonished that Alice would mention me publicly, and without putting a truthful-but-snarky 'ex' in front of 'daughter-in-law'.

'Even in her last months, Imogen was still worrying about everyone but herself. She was so concerned about Kathleen being able to stay in her darling little cottage in North Wales. Many of you remember it, I'm sure, from when it was free in the past. So many happy holidays we all had there, before Kathleen moved in.'

Ah. The world made sense again. A public telling-off that only I would recognise as such. People were sending kind glances my way, and I shrank down into my seat. I could feel an inappropriate laugh bubbling up, and I pressed my lips together hard. God, Rose, why weren't you here? You and I would be crying together with the effort of not laughing, like we used to in school assemblies, pinching each other's arms in a doomed attempt to make the laughs subside.

'That's who Imogen was. Selfless. Kind to a fault.' Alice's voice broke. She was not much younger than Imogen, and must be memento-mori-ing like mad right now. 'I'm going to miss her more than I can say.' The heartfelt way she said this took away my desire to laugh.

She stepped down, shaking off various hands that reached out to help her, and walked back to her seat in front of us, head held high. Richard turned to me and blew out his cheeks in a 'Damn, I'm sorry, but you know what my mother's like' gesture. A lot to get from a cheek-blow, perhaps, but then, we had known each other for a long time.

Afterwards, several of us went to eat at Din Tai Fung across the piazza, one of Imogen's favourite restaurants. Murray made his excuses because he'd got a promising business meeting nearby. I didn't mind; I was keen to catch up with Stella, who was not long back from Naples.

We took up two large tables in the restaurant, with most of Imo's relatives on one, and most of mine on the other. Richard immediately took charge, ordering for our table. It was a trait of his that used to infuriate me, but today it was restful not to have to even look at the menu. The champagne came quickly, and both Alice and I raised an eyebrow at its inappropriateness, a rare moment of accord. But Richard reminded us of Imo's desire that we should celebrate her life, so we both shrugged, and took a glass. My God, was I turning into Alice? When she died, not that she ever would, there would be a vacancy in this ragtag family for an imperious matriarch. Maybe that would be a good look for me. But I would try to be kinder, more understanding of people's frailties. More like Imogen. My voice caught in my throat as we made a toast to her, and I sat back in my chair, feeling rather wrung out.

Alice turned to me, her face a simulacrum of concern. 'Your latest husband never stops working, it seems.'

I didn't need to answer this; I was an old hand at Alice. I didn't have the energy for a ruck, even a well-mannered ruck of the sort that she and I had perfected over the decades. I would be like Imogen, I decided. She never let other people's nonsense derail her. She sailed on, spreading loveliness and light, and...

'Talking of your husband,' Alice went on, 'he seemed awfully uncomfortable. Do they not teach them to sit quietly in the Antipodes?'

'Thanks for mentioning me in your speech, Alice. I did so enjoy you dragging me.' Hmm. Clearly I was still more Kay than Imogen. Work in progress.

'Oh!' Her face lit up. How she loved our genteel disputes. Maybe, at some level, I did too. 'I wasn't *dragging* you, Kathleen, whatever that means. I was, I am, genuinely grateful to Imogen for her kindness to you. She treated you like a member of her own family, didn't she?'

Gaslighting much? Alice *invented* gaslighting.

'And talking of family, why is dear Edward not here?'

Richard, hearing Edward's name, turned to us. 'The twins are starting their new school today.' He frowned at her. 'I already told you that. Do stop stirring, Mother.'

I goggled at him in surprise. In our many years together I had never known Richard speak so sharply to Alice. I wondered what the atmosphere was like back in the old homestead. Was Alice an irritant in Richard and Aileen's marriage? Mind you, Aileen was looking supremely unconcerned, as serene as the Buddha. At my wedding she'd shown not the slightest sign that there was anything odd about her husband walking his ex-wife down the aisle. Indeed, she had given me a conspiratorial wink. Was she the instigator of Richard's new backbone? Good for her.

'Ah good, the dumplings are here!' Newland cried, looking ready to kiss the waiter.

Alice turned to Richard to continue bickering, which was great news for me as I had Stella and Newland to myself for the rest of the meal. How delightful to see them loved up again. They kept smiling into each other's eyes, finishing each other's sentences. We talked about Nita, who was living at her parents' house with Piet so that everyone could look after her. Things were looking unexpectedly hopeful because she was in remission, and regaining some of her strength.

'Can you stay for a bit after?' Stella asked me, as Richard and Simon waged a polite-yet-manly tussle over the bill. It went on long enough that Alice took it from them with an exasperated sigh, and brought out her gold card. She never normally paid for anything and I decided to interpret it as a general apology.

Richard, Aileen and Newland mercifully took her away, though not before her parting shot; bending down to me under guise of buttoning her coat she said, 'I do hope you won't ruin Imogen's beautiful cottage now she's gone, Kathleen, with any "artistic" alterations.'

I hadn't been able to channel Imogen earlier but I caught Aileen's eye, and something of her unflappable serenity wafted my way. Be more Aileen, be more Imogen. One of Imogen's gifts was to see the emotional heart of people even when, or especially when, they behaved at their worst. Alice had just lost her dearest friend, and if anyone knew how that felt, it was me.

Instead of answering, I patted Alice's hand and said, 'I know you must be feeling really miserable about Imogen today, Alice, and I'm so sorry for your loss.'

Her expression faltered slightly, and instead of a final barb, she rested her hand on my shoulder and whispered, 'Thank you, dear.'

Well! I would need to channel my inner-Imo more often. I sat back, enjoying the rare glow of having said the right thing.

I said goodbye to Simon, and he thanked me for coming to the memorial – as if I would have missed it – and said, 'I'm terribly sorry. Are you all right?'

How sweet of him. 'Yes. Of course, I'll miss her terribly, but not as much as you. Are *you* all right?'

He said he was, and went off with his wife and daughters. Neither Murray nor I wanted to bother him about the cottage sale, though the timing was a little unfortunate as it was pretty much six months to the week since Imogen had negotiated us an extension. Murray, rightly, said he would wait a little longer before reminding Simon, but anyway, the 'Sold STC' sign had gone up outside Bryn Glas, gladdening my heart every time I saw it. I hoped Imogen would have been pleased to know that we were absolutely on target whenever Simon was ready to exchange, with more than fifty grand in the joint account and a healthy-looking set of accounts any business would be proud of.

After everyone had gone, I started a new tab and Stella and I ordered coffees and dessert. I wouldn't have minded another glass of wine, but ever since the hen party I'd not wanted to go past 'pleasantly tipsy', and I was close to that point now.

Stella grinned at me. 'Nice one, Mum. You really threw Grandma for a loop.'

'I meant it, though.'

'And she could see that, which made it even more delicious. She was bang out of order, mentioning you in her speech. Anyway...' Stella sat back. 'You want my news?'

'Of course I do!' Looking at her smile, I knew what she was going to say before she said it.

'I'm pregnant!'

'Oh, my darling girl, the best news ever!' I threw my arms around her and we both squealed. 'Tell me everything!'

'Gosh, it's been quite something. I'm a little over three months, so I'm starting to believe in it now.'

I looked at her stomach but she was slim as always. 'You can see it if I do this,' she said, holding the material of her skirt taut against her body. There was indeed a slight curve that hadn't been there before.

'This is so exciting! What does Newland think?'

'Over the moon. We're going to tell Dad tonight, and his parents tomorrow.'

How touched I was to be told first. I kissed her again. 'Newland's going to be a brilliant dad. And you're going to be the world's greatest mother.'

'I hope you'll help me in the early days. I'm a bit frit.'

'Course I will! Just try and stop me.'

'Edward said you were wonderful when the twins were born.'

I hadn't had this many compliments since... well, ever. 'I'm an old hand at being a granny, you know that.'

'It's so funny the way I got pregnant, do you want to hear it?'

'Um, didn't it happen the usual way?' I braced myself for whatever mad detail of millennial lovemaking she might be about to reveal.

'Yes, and that's the weird thing! We couldn't get pregnant, we tried for ages, so we were about to start IVF when we got the news about Nita's diagnosis. We put it on hold then, so I could go to Italy with her.'

I remembered her saying she was having to miss something important because of going abroad.

'And before that, I stayed with her a lot at Dad's, so I could go to chemo appointments with her in town.' Ah, and that explained Richard saying they were over at the house all the time; I'd thought it was because, well, never mind. 'Anyway, at our first IVF appointment I took the standard pregnancy test... and it was positive!'

'Sparkle, that is just brilliant.'

'You know, you're not the first person we told.' She looked up for a moment, trying not to cry. 'We told Nita the day we found out. I know it sounds ridiculous, but she seemed to get stronger after that.'

'Not ridiculous at all.' I held her hand.

We celebrated the best news ever with delicious little dumplings containing 'chocolate lava'. We speculated about how excited Richard would be when he got the news – a lot – and about how much knitting Aileen would be doing for the baby – a lot – and made many toasts with our coffee cups to each other, the baby and Newland.

'I can't wait to tell Murray,' I said, 'though do you want me to wait till after your father knows? Would that be politically sensible?'

Stella shrugged. She didn't care about the territorial sensibilities of our two dear alpha males, and quite right too. 'You know who I'd like to tell, because she was always such a friend to me.' I thought she was going to say Imogen, so was surprised when she said, 'Rose.'

'Yes, she'd be so into it, wouldn't she?' I was pleased to find that I had reached a place of acceptance where I didn't fall apart at the unexpected mention of Rose's name. The wound was closing up, and I could envisage a time, not far away, when it would be healed completely, leaving a scar, of course, but no longer painful.

I'd done what I could. I'd visited important people in my life, and dredged through events from my past, trying to work out if there were any repeating patterns. The results, as a scientist like Edward might say, were inconclusive. I'd certainly not always behaved perfectly, but who had? I'd definitely taken some people for granted, but who didn't sometimes do that? I was lucky enough to have plenty of people in my life who loved me and still wanted to hang out with me.

When we left the restaurant I had to stop myself from announcing the news to every stranger we passed. 'My beautiful daughter's going to have a baby!' We strolled together for a while, then she peeled off to meet Newland and get the train home. 'Look after yourself even more than usual,' I said as we hugged.

She smiled dreamily at me. 'You too, Mum.'

I was smiling myself, thinking about babies, as I walked in the direction towards our hotel. Then I was startled back into the present by my phone ringing in my pocket. Simon. Why was he calling?

TWENTY-TWO

LONDON, FEBRUARY 2024

'Kay, are you still at the restaurant?'

'I've just left. Is everything OK, Simon? Did you forget something? I can go back if you like...'

'Tell me where you are and I'll come to you.'

How weird. I looked around. 'I'm on Garrick Street, near a Waterstones.'

'Do you want to go inside, and I'll meet you there in five minutes?'

'Uh, sure, but...'

He hung up.

Puzzled, I went into the bookshop and loitered by the latest releases near the door. It must be to do with the cottage, though I was surprised he'd want to think about it today. I'd got slightly absorbed in the first pages of a new Anne Tyler novel when he hurried in, red-faced.

'Goodness, are you OK?' I asked.

'Ran here.' He took a moment to get his breath back. 'Kay, when I said I was sorry earlier in the restaurant, you thought I was talking about Mum, I think?'

'Er, yes. Weren't you?'

'Christ. This is so awkward. I've no idea what you do and don't know, but Mum would never forgive me if I didn't check. My wife thinks I'm crazy, I just jumped off the tube and...'

'Sorry, Simon. What are you saying?'

He took a breath. 'Kay, when I said I was sorry, I meant I was sorry because you didn't get the cottage after all.'

It took me quite a lot longer than it should have done to process these words.

'What?'

'You don't know?' He shook his head. 'Oh hell. I was afraid of that.'

'We didn't get it? But how? I don't understand. We've raised the deposit the bank asked for. The paperwork's in place. There's a "Sold" sign in the front garden, for God's sake. What's happened?' I felt sick, my legs shaky, and I looked around for somewhere to sit. I didn't want to collapse here, in between the tables of three books for the price of two.

Simon took my arm and led me to the children's section, mercifully free of children, where there were sofas. We sat down, and he looked anxiously at me.

'Murray rang me a few weeks ago...' he began.

Oh God. 'He didn't tell me.'

'He said he was still having trouble securing a mortgage...'

My mouth went dry.

'He asked for more time. He wanted another six months.'

'Simon, I had absolutely no idea.'

'I can see that. You're white as a ghost. Can I get you something, some water?'

I attempted my yoga breathing, though I still couldn't remember whether it was in or out through the mouth. Fuck it. I breathed randomly. 'Go on.'

He looked very worried. 'Mum was still alive then, of course. I was concerned about needing the money for the care home fees. I'm really sorry, but I told Murray I couldn't wait any longer. I didn't know, no one knew, that she would pass away so soon.'

'Of course you couldn't know.'

'To be honest, I did feel that I'd already been more than fair. I put it on the market the day after he called me, and it's been sold to a developer. They're going to put in a new kitchen and bathroom.'

My cottage was not my cottage any more. It was going to have modern, shiny fittings. The stained, lovely old cast-iron bath would go in a skip. Soon, other people would sit in my living room, walk up my stairs, open my back door, breathe in the scents from my herb patch, gaze at my Carneddau mountains.

'So the "Sold" sign isn't because *we've* bought it?'

'No.'

Silent tears began to pour down my face in a river. 'And Murray would have known that.'

'Yes.'

How well do you know each other?

'I'm terribly sorry,' Simon said. He looked like he might cry too. He offered me a tissue. 'Mum really wanted you to have the cottage.'

'Did she know, before she... did she know we didn't get it?' The cottage was no longer mine. It would never be mine. Oh, Imo.

'No, I didn't want to worry her. I think she knew something was up, though. She was lucid right to the end, and she asked a few times if everything was going smoothly. I'm a rotten liar, but I did my best.'

'Thank you. I'd have hated for her to worry.' I wiped my eyes. 'How long before we need to leave?'

Simon looked at his hands. 'Four weeks.'

I nodded. That was fair. I stood up, slightly surprised to find that I could. 'Thank you for telling me. Not everyone would.' I smiled. 'Not everyone did, in fact.'

'Will you be all right? Can I get you a taxi? Walk you somewhere?' Simon was the model of gentlemanliness, concerned about me even though he'd just lost his mother. To think I had once thought him rather wimpish, and Murray the epitome of manhood. I heard Bear's voice: Well, Kay, you really are the crown princess of idiots.

Outside the shop he was reluctant to leave me, but I put on a bright smile and assured him I'd be fine. Finally, we parted: him back to his family, and me to follow the tracker on Murray's phone. We'd set it up months ago after he got lost, giving us both a fright, on what should have been an easy mountain walk to the top of Tal y Fan. I'd never used it before, and it took me a minute to work it. Then I found him, only minutes away, in a street off Tottenham Court Road.

Could I cling to the tiny possibility that there was a logical explanation for why he hadn't got the mortgage, why he hadn't told me? I couldn't think of one. I thought of him shifting around at the church earlier, so uncomfortable that Alice had noticed. Did he suspect this was the day I would find out?

I went into a branch of the bank which housed our joint account, and asked the cashier to give me the balance. She tapped away at her computer, then looked up. And that's when I found out that the cottage wasn't the only problem, the mortgage wasn't the only problem, that whatever I had thought was the bad news today, it was as nothing compared to what was now coming down the pipe.

'It's empty.'

'*Empty?*' I stared at her. Intellectually, I'd known this might be the case. It was why I'd come in to check. But emotionally, I couldn't handle it. 'There should be more than fifty thousand pounds in there.' My knees felt weak again, and I staggered slightly.

She disappeared, and moments later she was at my side of the counter, taking my arm. 'Come in the back room with me.'

She escorted me into her office, past a few bank staff who stopped what they were doing to look at me. How often had they seen this, the duped, shell-shocked wife?

The cashier sat me down and gave me a glass of water. 'Do you feel faint? Can I call someone for you?'

'No thank you... that was our house money. Can you show me?'

She typed into the computer on the desk, then turned the screen towards me. 'The funds...' she read out, 'of £55,423 and 80p, were removed in a series of withdrawals over the last few days.'

He'd even taken the eighty pence.

'Does it say who made the withdrawals?'

'Mr Garland, the joint account holder. But if you think someone might have impersonated him, or if the account was otherwise compromised, I can contact our Fraud Team immediately...'

'There's no need.'

'I'm sorry. Can I help with anything else?'

Yes, do you know where I can buy a gun? 'No, thank you.'

Back on the street, my head feeling as if it had been detached from my body, I continued following the tracker, which took me almost to the end of Charing Cross Road. So he was still in London and not on a flight to Costa Rica or wherever it was that villains went once they'd secured the cash. The tracker soon announced that I had reached him, and indeed, there he was across the street, his back to me, standing at a cash machine. Wow, the tracking technology was excellent. If only I was in the right frame of mind to fully appreciate it. I slipped into a shop doorway and watched as Murray took out some money – clearly our fifty-five grand wasn't quite enough – then turned and walked purposefully up the road. I followed at a distance, onto Tottenham Court Road, then he took a right turn, went into a large building and disappeared. I stepped back to see what it was. A casino. I had no idea Murray was interested in casinos. But then, let's face it, I had no idea about anything to do with him at all.

The doorman smiled benignly at me as I went in, because I was a smartly dressed older white woman – quite the superpower, if I ever wanted to do something more useful with it than follow my husband. I couldn't think if I'd ever been in a casino before, but I knew what they looked like from films: card tables, a roulette wheel and fruit machines. It wasn't very busy, presumably because it was the middle of the afternoon.

I saw Murray at the far end of the large room, talking to a man. My heart was thudding out of my chest. Though it was quite a distance, I understood from the body language that Murray knew the man, and that they were having a bit of a joke. Then the man opened a door and Murray went in. The door was closed immediately behind him.

I approached the man, but he blocked my way. So much for my superpower of innocuousness. 'Sorry, ma'am, authorised personnel only.' He was absolutely enormous – about six foot eight, built like an American football player, bursting out of his sharp suit.

'Yes, of course. That man who just went in? Murray Garland?'

'I don't know anyone of that name.'

Perhaps they were obligated not to know. Or perhaps Murray went by a different name here. Did he? What were the implications of that? My overloaded brain filed that one under 'deal with it later'.

'That's fine. Would you mind passing him a message?'

'Sorry, ma'am, there's to be no interruptions once the game's in progress.'

'Of course.' I managed a smile. At least, I could feel my face moving the muscles generally associated with a smile. 'I'll, er, go over there and wait.'

The man nodded, like he couldn't care less.

I sat on a scratchy green velvet sofa in the central bar area, where I had a clear line of vision to the mysterious door. A waitress wearing a tuxedo asked what I'd like to drink, and I ordered a French 75. It would be good to, very quickly, be a little drunk.

What game was it? How long did it take? Or did they play more than one? Why was it in a side room? I focused on basic logistics, rather than anything more frightening. At the same time as I was telling myself this was a one-off, he'd popped in for a fun bit of relaxation after covertly removing all our deposit money, I was scrolling through my emails. Far away, in a distant part of my brain, an email I'd received almost a year ago, puzzled over, then forgotten about, was waving at me. There had been way too much forgetting about things lately. Things which later turned out to be important. With that in mind, I pushed away my cocktail after a couple of sips.

Thank you for renting with Drive Friendly... On your receipt, you will see tolls matched to your rental...

The start and end toll roads in Texas were listed for each of the separate charges, so it wasn't difficult to see on Google Maps where Murray had gone while we were on honeymoon. Most of his journeys were on the interstate roads 35E and 35N, to a place called Thackerville, about an hour north of Dallas, just over the border into Oklahoma. It was the work of seconds to look up what was there: not much, other than the Winstar World Casino, biggest casino in the United States. I nodded to myself, as though I had solved a tricky clue in a cryptic crossword. Most of his other journeys involved drives on Interstate 75, presumably not named after my favourite cocktail, into a different part of Oklahoma. Numbly, I noted that where they stopped, a place called Durant, was the Choctaw Casino and Resort. One hundred tables offering craps, roulette, baccarat, and 'the ever popular blackjack'. A poker room with thirty tables and its own dedicated staff. More than seven thousand slot machines.

No wonder Drive Friendly had sent me a polite but adamant reply that the toll road charges were not a mistake.

I put down my phone. There seemed little point looking up the last couple of journeys. The likelihood of them turning out to be to interesting state monuments or art galleries were slim. At least I understood, finally, why we'd gone to Dallas for our honeymoon.

I studied a colourful poster on the wall near the bar, for a gambling addiction helpline. *Think about your choices*, it said. Well, that was good advice for anyone, wasn't it? My mind felt very clear. Things were falling into place just about as fast as I could handle them. I sent Will a text, asking if he'd mind telling me exactly what Tim had been in rehab for. Then I messaged Murray:

Hello darling, wondering where you are?

When the waitress returned, she asked if there was anything wrong with my cocktail. I reassured her that it was delicious, but that I needed to have my wits about me. She laughed and said, 'I know what you mean, ma'am!' I asked for a lime and soda and the bill. When I saw how much the French 75 cost, I realised you could be a sucker in here without ever getting to the gambling tables. I watched a woman with big yellow hair pushing coin after coin into a noisy fruit machine, the lights flashing constantly, reflecting off her glasses. It paid out every so often but she didn't seem to notice, just kept feeding it as if it was a hungry pet.

The text had been marked 'read' for some time before Murray replied:

Hello! Where are you?

I pondered how to answer. It made sense, I decided, to keep my cards close to my chest. There were a lot of gambling metaphors, weren't there, now I thought about it. Luck of the draw. All bets are off. Hit the jackpot.

Betting the farm.

I'm still at the restaurant with Stella. Where are you?

At the meeting. Looking forward to seeing you soon.

I nodded. Yep. Look how easy he did it. I regretted that I didn't have quite enough padding from the cocktail to protect my heart. Well, one of us had to not be a liar and it looked like it was going to have to be me. I texted again.

Actually I'm in a casino just off Tottenham Court Road.

I pressed 'send', knowing, in a distant sort of way that I was setting light to my marriage. But could you set light to something that had already burned down? Even Filomena would have trouble hiding in the sand from this one. There wasn't enough sand in the Sahara.

I wasn't surprised when, a couple of minutes later, the door to the room opened, and Murray came out. His body language, even from a distance, was agitated; he spoke to the doorman, who pointed in my direction. I waved cheerily. Keep him on his toes. Murray walked fast across the room, trying not to look aghast.

'Kay!' Oh, to be inside his puzzled head right now.

'Hello.'

He sank onto the sofa next to me. 'What did you... how did you... did you *follow* me?'

He sounded annoyed. A little angry, even. Like I'd said to Stella, sometimes when people were scared, they covered it up with anger.

'Really, I think I should ask the questions, shouldn't I?' I was pleased at how calm I was being, and wondered how long the calmness would last.

Uncertainty rolled over his face. I could see him trying to work out what tack to take. Ratchet up the anger, or become helpful and deferential? The latter won out. 'Yes, of course. Er, what do you want to know? So funny you being here! My business associate comes here, he's a member, strange place for a meeting but he hires this back room, he's got some work lined up for me next month so it was worth it, honestly, the way some of these fellows do business, so old school, I've said it before, rich people are weird, but you know, it doesn't matter as long as the work comes in.'

He rattled to a stop, and we stared at each other. He looked the way he had the day of my exhibition, when he'd earnestly explained to me and Charlie why there was no problem with him borrowing Charlie's money.

If Helena could see me now, would she still think I had a charmed life?

'On a scale of one to ten, where one is extremely smart and ten is the dumbest person who ever lived,' I said, taking my time, 'exactly how stupid do you think I am?'

'What? Not stupid at all.' He reached for my hand and I let him hold it. 'You're the smartest person I know. A one, for sure.'

'That can't be true, can it?' I said. 'Because if I was in the least bit smart, I would have had an affair with you when we met, then left promptly by the nearest exit.'

'Oh now, Katie, what do you mean?' He looked really shocked. 'We fell in love! We couldn't wait to be married!'

I nodded. 'We rushed into it, didn't we, before we knew important things about each other.'

'I knew the most important thing: that I loved you.'

'And I loved you too.' We were both using the past tense, but in two different ways.

'Look, Katie, whatever you're thinking, I guarantee it's not like that.'

'What am I thinking?'

How well do you know each other?

Well enough to register every last little thought that crossed his face, Rose.

How did she find me? How much does she know? Does she know everything? Just the money, or the cottage too? Can I tell her this is my first time here? Why was I so careless after all this time?

'Listen,' he said. 'Why don't we get out of here? Funny old place. Let's go to our hotel.'

'You don't like it here any more? I'd have thought, from all the casinos you visited on honeymoon, that you were a big fan.'

He startled, but covered it up quickly. 'I like the occasional flutter, who doesn't? But there's no more to it.'

There was no more to it, apparently. Apart from one or two things. More than that – so many that a human brain could barely hold them all in their head at once.

1. The multiple trips to casinos on our honeymoon that he hadn't mentioned.
2. The wads of cash he sometimes had; the huge amount he splashed on the honeymoon.
3. The huge amounts he mostly didn't have, despite working all hours.
4. Taking money from me and Charlie.
5. The silent disappearances, there one minute, gone the next. Returning hours later. 'Went for a nice walk.' Sometimes in a great mood, often not.

6. Bear trying to protect Charlie's money for his education. Describing Murray as not being brilliant with money which, in hindsight, looked like the understatement of the century.
7. Murray not ever seeming to have evidence of the rent money from his house in Australia because, I now realised – better late than never, Kay – he no longer had that house. That it had long ago been sold.
8. That his financial chaos wasn't only down to poor bookkeeping. It was because he gambled with his wages.
9. Of course, there was also the small matter of the missing fifty grand, the cottage even now being sold to someone else.
10. Rose trying to warn me to take my time over getting married. Oh Rose, why hadn't you spelled it out? But maybe you had... In a shattering moment, I pulled something from the dregs of my stunned, overworked brain, buried so deep I could almost feel its tentacles ripping away from the walls as I yanked it. Rose saying, 'Listen, if I was to tell you something about Murray, would you want to know?' and me walking away, drinking and drinking so I couldn't hear it, couldn't remember it. You fucking drongo, Kay!

I sat still, processing it all, as every penny in every fruit machine in the casino of my life finally dropped. Murray stared at me, saying words, but I couldn't hear him. I didn't really need the final piece of evidence, the ping of a text, the one-word answer from Will – *Gambling*. But it was good to have it in black and white. So Stacey had been right, that Rose *had* said something about Tim. And Tim had guessed correctly: she'd suggested Murray had something in common with him. And Stella had been right that I had pushed Rose away, told her to... well, we all knew what I had told her to do.

I shook my head, shook it free of Will, of Tim, of Rose. There'd be time to think about that later. For now, I had to focus. *Man up, Kay!* Well, Anthony, I'm not sure manning up had worked all that well. I might try womaning up, for a change.

'Murray...' I said, and looked him in the eye. 'I know we've lost the cottage. I know you've taken our money. I don't need to know any more of the *what's* happened. I would, though, like to know the *why*.'

'Who told, how did you, what...?' he blustered briefly, then came to a standstill, and put his head in his hands.

I waited, and finally, so quietly I could barely hear over the noise of the fruit machines, he said, 'They won't give me a mortgage.'

'Who won't? Your bank? But you said it was fine.'

'My bank turned me down, but I thought it *would* be fine because there were a lot of others to try. But they all said no.'

As he talked, and I fired questions at him, I slowly realised that behind the scenes, behind my back, behind his cheery, can-do persona, Murray had been scrabbling round for months trying to convince someone, anyone, to give him a mortgage. But even our large deposit and tidy accounts weren't enough to wipe out the fact that he was too much of a risk. And why was he too much of a risk? Because – didn't see this coming, did you, Kay? – he had been declared bankrupt less than two years ago. There was no house in Australia, as I'd belatedly guessed. It had been taken by the government to pay off his debts. He'd left nothing behind. He owned nothing.

Too much of a risk. It was a rather fitting epitaph, wasn't it, to my whirlwind marriage.

Finally, as Simon's six-month deadline approached, Murray realised the only way we could get the house would be if we bought it outright, without a mortgage. An impossibly large sum. He asked Simon – 'on my knees' – for six more months so he could raise the whole capital. But Simon said this didn't seem like a real possibility, and that he couldn't wait any longer.

'You thought you could raise the whole cost of the cottage?' I blurted, in disbelief. 'From gambling?'

'Speculating.'

'Is that what we're calling it?'

'I promise you, Kay' – and he looked right at me – 'if Simon had said yes to more time, I was going to tell you everything.'

'Sure, because that's something you often do.'

'I was, I swear. Get us both working together on raising the whole amount, so we needn't be beholden to a bank, a mortgage. Free agents.' He shook his head. 'When he said no, there was no point telling you. I was trying not to get you involved in my mess.'

'What did Simon actually say to you? Apart from that he needed to sell it?'

Murray gave me his wryest smile. 'He said, given that no one would offer me a mortgage, I seemed to be "a rotten bet".'

Ah yes, another gambling phrase. The thought of the gentle, upright Simon saying this – having him, Imogen's son, be the witness to my absurd marriage, this insane *folie à deux* I'd got myself in – was the thing that finally broke apart my calm. I felt, all at once, an overwhelming urge to smash something. If only I was in my soon-to-be-lost home I would get down those hideous, expensive wedding plates from Aileen's daughters and I would smash every single one on the quarry-tiled floor, till it was more crockery than floor, till Murray, cowering under the table with his dustpan and brush, would beg me to stop. I thought that maybe for now, I would throw my drink in his face, but I'd finished my lime and soda, and my cocktail cost too much to waste. I was going to have to be very careful with money from now on. I had nothing to throw but my words, and I did so, at top volume.

'You bloody idiot! You said last time that you didn't want to pull me into the mess, when you took mine and Charlie's money. Remember? And I said then, don't do that, don't do this big man thing of shouldering the burden. It's utterly toxic, and it always creates an even bigger mess than the one you're trying to hide.'

The waitress materialised by our sofa. 'Ma'am, is everything all right? Do you need assistance?' As she spoke, she was sliding her walkie talkie out of her pocket.

I looked at Murray. The brown eyes I'd thought so lovely were large pools of horror. I didn't want him to be thrown onto the street by a burly bouncer. Not until I had finished wiping the floor with him.

'I'm fine,' I assured her. Just turns out my husband's a fucking asshole who's ruined my life, nothing to worry about.

She did that 'uh-huh' thing people do when they don't believe you. 'Please try not to shout, ma'am, we have a strict "calm and quiet" policy here. I'll be right over there if you need anything.'

She went away, but not very far, and I saw her exchange a glance with a bouncer. I expect they'd seen it all.

'*Please* can we go somewhere else?' Murray said. 'I can't bear to have my guts ripped out all over this hideous orange carpet. If I'm going to be eviscerated, at least let's do it somewhere with decent decor.'

'I think this is the perfect place. You're obviously fond of casinos, and I'm starting to see the appeal. Strong drinks, waitresses who keep an eye on you. The last vestiges of our money are here too, floating somewhere out there in the ether.'

'Kay, you have to know how desperately sorry I am. I really thought I would get it sorted today.'

'Yes, go on, what was today's big plan? Not to be confused with all the previous big plans.'

'If I'd only had a bit more time...'

'Haven't we heard that one before? Just tell me, Murray. Tell me why you stole that fifty grand we both worked so hard to save.'

'I didn't steal it.' He looked so sincere. 'I knew I could triple it today. Then I could take it to Simon, say we're cash buyers, have this for now, we'll get you the rest in a few weeks...'

I took a slow sip of my cocktail. Thought about meeting Murray at that dinner, almost a year and a half, or a hundred years ago. The frisson between us. The first time we made love. His face at our wedding. The affection and support he had always shown me. Scrape the surface of all that loveliness, and what was underneath?

'I take it that this plan didn't exactly work out?' I shook my head. 'Given that it was entirely based on you winning at gambling?'

'Speculating.'

'You're a gambler, Murray.'

'I am a speculator, an entrepreneur.'

'You're an addict.'

'I am bloody well not! Gamblers do it day and night, they can't control it, they lose...'

He stopped.

'They lose all their money, you were going to say?'

'I was going to say, they lose more than they win.'

'Uh-huh.' There he sat, in a casino in which he had just lost every penny of our savings, pretending not to be a gambler. He made Filomena look like a model of facing up to things. If he'd buried his head in the sand any deeper he'd have made his way back to bloody Australia. Which might have been for the best.

'Even if you'd somehow been able to double or triple our fifty grand, what was the plan? You know it's too late. You know someone else has bought the cottage. You knew all this time that the "sold" sign wasn't about our offer.'

'It's only sold subject to contract. If I'd given Simon the money, I knew he would agree.'

'Everything you say makes you sound even more deluded.'

'No, Kay, cash talks, people respect it, they...'

'Yes, talking of cash, why were you at a cash machine outside?' I asked. 'Given that you've already spaffed fifty-five grand.'

'For the bar tab, tips, that sort of thing.'

'Not because tens of thousands were gone and you thought another two hundred quid would somehow make a difference?'

The yellow-haired woman finally stood up and wandered away. It was a relief to not have the tinkling and crashing in the background. And it meant that when Murray said, 'You don't understand. I was this close' – he held his fingers a centimetre apart – 'to turning it around,' I could hear him loud and clear.

I knew that soon, I was going to have quite the cry. The end of things was horribly sad, and I'd had my share of the end of things lately. It was the nature of being human, wasn't it? Things ended. That's how it was. But also, sometimes, other things began. I thought of Stella's smile, the new life she was making. I thought ahead, to the time I'd spend with her in those early weeks, looking after her, holding her child.

If I was to be granted the same lifespan as Imogen, I had about thirty years left. It was time to do something different with them.

It was time to go.

'Darling.' I touched Murray's cheek, and he jumped in shock at the tenderness of the gesture. 'There was something very important that I didn't know about you, wasn't there?' He started to protest, and I said, 'And something very important that you didn't know about me.'

'What don't I know about you?'

'Quite a few things, as it turns out. But the main one is, I can tolerate a lot, but I can't tolerate being lied to.'

'Honestly, whatever you're thinking, it's not right. I promise you.' He reached across for my hands, and this time I let him hold them.

'Don't make it worse. Don't make me list the lies.' I smiled, though it wasn't easy, it's not easy to do anything really, when your heart's breaking. 'I could have forgiven you for the stealing, even for losing the cottage. I made vows to you that I wanted to keep. We might have been able to rebuild my trust. But not for this. You're not admitting it, you're not taking responsibility for it, you're still lying.'

'But, Katie, it's...'

'The jig is up, Murray.' I said this firmly, in my Quiller Queen voice, the one that brooked no argument.

How handsome he was, how dashing. I'd loved that face. I thought of his vows at our wedding: Let us be friends and lovers, and grow old together. We'd been lovers, and it had been beautiful. But one out of three wasn't great.

Finally, I let go of his hands, stood up, put on my coat.

'This is it, isn't it?' I said.

'This is what?' he said softly.

'This is the other shoe.'

He didn't reply.

TWENTY-THREE
WINCHESTER, MAY 2024

I was startled awake by the car door opening. At least, I thought I was awake. But maybe I was dreaming, because settling into the passenger seat next to me was Rose.

'Fancy meeting you here,' she said.

I sat up, blinking in confusion. My phone, propped up on the steering wheel, said it was twelve thirty, which meant I'd been asleep for more than an hour. I felt stiff with cold. Was she really here? She looked older. Perhaps because her face was rather drawn, or more likely because her hair was very short and, crucially, no longer blonde. She and I had agreed a long time ago that we wouldn't go grey till it was absolutely unavoidable. How had she reached that point already? We weren't even sixty.

I tentatively touched her arm, to see if she really was here, sitting in my car, in her street, in the middle of the day. It seemed so, but it was quite hard to believe.

'You got my note,' I said, stupidly, because not only was it unlikely that she'd be here if she hadn't, but I had posted it through her front door just a couple of hours previously. Unless she now owned a dog that ate the post, it wasn't possible for it to have got mislaid.

Also, she was holding it in her hand.

'I've been waiting for you for a while, soft lad,' she said.

How I'd missed hearing her calling me a soft lad. My eyes filled with tears. It really was her. 'Waiting for me to wise up, you mean?'

'You might say that.' She smiled. 'I couldn't possibly comment.'

I'd been out here in my car since ten this morning, going over my short note to her for the hundredth time.

Dear Rose,

I understand now. I'm pretty sure you tried to warn me. I'm sorry I didn't listen, but I'm ready to now. There's a story you've not told me about Tim, isn't there? I'd like to hear it.
 I miss you. I love you. I'm sorry to have been a bad friend.

I forgot-you-not.

Kay

I hadn't said I was outside her house. I decided to leave it to fate. If she wanted to see me, she'd notice that I'd hand-delivered the letter. And if she didn't, I would drive back to Helena's studio and never speak of it to anyone. I put the blue flower brooch in the envelope, went on shaky legs to her door, and posted it through the letterbox. The bay tree by the front door was doing a little better than last time, I was pleased to see.

Back in the car, I sat with my eyes fixed on the house. I knew she was in, because half an hour before I posted the note, she and Graham had come back from a grocery trip, two carrier bags each. They didn't glance my way. Perhaps I had a future in espionage, what with trailing Murray, and now holding a stakeout.

But maybe not, because at some point, I fell asleep.

There was so much I wanted to know, but it was too overwhelming her being here, willingly sharing my airspace.

'How are you? How's Graham? How are the boys? What have you been doing for the last year?' I gabbled.

'I'm fine, chick. I've gone grey.'

'It suits you.'

'You don't like it.'

'I just haven't got used to it yet. Go on, how's everything that isn't hair?'

'Graham's fine. He thinks my hair is cute.' She threw me her old, challenging look, and I couldn't have been happier to see it.

'Cute's good.'

'It's the best I'll get now, I'll take it.'

'You're completely beautiful, Rosalie, you know that.'

She rolled her eyes. 'Graham's properly retired, busier than ever with volunteering. Thinking of getting an allotment. What else? His dad died last year.'

'I'm sorry.'

'Don't be. It was a long life well-lived. The boys are fine. You've seen Will and the baby, I believe?'

'Yes. Will said you were in hospital...'

'We'll circle back to that, as the tech bros say. Let's see, what else? Jay's engaged to his girlfriend. They're both happy.'

'And are you?'

A brief silence. Then: 'I've had my moments. Had a rotten falling-out with my best friend, and it's been very hard.'

'I'm sorry I was such a shitty friend,' I said. That, when all was said and done, was the most important thing I wanted her to know.

'What makes you think you were shitty?' She held out the note. 'You said it here, too.'

'I don't know. Everything. I was so awful, you wouldn't come to my wedding, and when I came here, you sent me away. I took you completely for granted, thought you'd always be around no matter how dreadful I was.' If I could have got down on my knees I would have, but there wasn't space what with the brake and accelerator. 'I've been doing a reckoning, trying to find out if I am generally a shitty person.'

'Have you now?' Her wry smile was back. 'And are you?'

'To be honest, the results are a bit mixed. God, I've missed you so much!'

'I've missed you too.'

'But, you can't have done. It was you who...' I almost said 'fell out with me', as if we were at school. 'You stopped talking to me.'

'Yes, Kay, because you told me to.'

'I most certainly did not.'

'Your exact words were: "I don't want to speak to you again".'

'I beg your pardon?'

'Yeah, it's OK, I guessed pretty quickly that you hadn't remembered.' She nodded. 'It did not make sense that, after saying that, you then sent five million texts and messages with the sole aim of trying to get me to speak to you.'

'When the hell did I say...' But of course: the bloody hen do.

'You blimming well meant it at the time, though you were extremely bevvied. But look, don't beat yourself up, that wasn't the reason I faded out.'

'Are you willing to fade back in now, Rose?' I managed not to clutch her arm, though I very much wanted to.

'I don't know, chick. It was rough back then, handling roller-coaster-Katie.'

I winced, because she never called me Katie – it was Murray's thing.

She went on, 'I've hated us not being friends, and that's an understatement, but I had to make the break for, well, my own sanity. If we're going to try to mend bridges, I need to know you're ready to hear some not-great stuff.'

'I am, I swear. I've heard a lot of not-great stuff recently. I'm hardened to it.'

My phone started rattling on the dashboard; it was on vibrate. I turned it off, but Rose had seen the name of the caller. 'Murray?'

'For weeks he's given me space, but for some reason he's chosen today to message non-stop.'

'Asking for space, huh?'

'Yes. I've left him. One of the shorter marriages of the twenty-first century, up there with Britney Spears.'

She blew out a stream of air. 'Well, that's something.' I could see her thinking, the cogs turning. Finally she said, 'I really have missed you, soft lad. Let's see if I can fade back in.'

Had I ever felt such relief? 'Shall we go in your house?'

'How much petrol you got?' Rose gestured to the dashboard.

'Um... Two-thirds of a tank?'

'Let's take a little drive.' She put on her seatbelt.

'Sure.' I started the engine. 'Where are we going?'

'End of the street, then left.'

I pulled out into the road.

'So tell me about leaving him.'

'Two months ago,' I said, but couldn't say more for a moment. I pretended to be focusing on the not-very-tricky manoeuvre of turning left.

'It's tough, chick, because you really loved him.'

'Still do, Rose, against my better judgement.'

'You can't turn love off like a tap.' She touched my hand, and I wanted to stop the car, hug her tight. But I held back. I didn't trust the situation. She could disappear again. Friends you thought would always be there sometimes vanished; husbands weren't always above board. You couldn't be sure of where you were with people. I carried on driving.

'So go on,' she said. 'What did you find out about him?'

'Don't you know?'

She shrugged. 'Mostly educated guesses.'

'I'd like to hear them.'

She didn't hesitate. 'Gambler. Addict. Liar.'

Jesus. I was glad I didn't have to look at her. It was rough hearing it stated out loud, so clearly. And yet, it wasn't any different from what I would have said.

I told her what I knew, and what I had worked out. That yes, Murray was absolutely a gambler and an addict. But the lying was more complicated, because I wasn't sure if he knew what he was doing, or if he was neck-deep in denial. He had explanations for everything. The toll-road trips in Dallas were for business meetings which happened to be in casinos; the money he took from me and Charlie was to improve our mortgage chances; it was late payments, not lost bets, that caused his rocky finances.

It was laughable when you said it all together like that, but neither Rose nor I were laughing.

'If he'd be honest, that would at least be a starting point,' I said. 'But he kept saying he didn't have a problem, it was all a misunderstanding.'

'Kay, he may never admit it. Tim never did, not to me, anyway. It was his third wife who got him into rehab. A better woman than I.' She exhaled. 'I'm sorry. I did try to tell you. But you weren't ready to hear it.'

'Not at the hen do, I was in a right old state. But I've been wondering why you didn't try again?' I glimpsed the objection on her face – me telling her I didn't want to speak to her again – and added lamely, 'You could have written me a letter?'

'Like in ye olden days. The lost art of letter writing, explaining why your suitor is a car crash.'

'It didn't have to be on parchment. An email?'

'I honestly don't know if you'd have accepted it. You were swoony in love.'

I wanted to protest, but it was irrelevant, anyway. She hadn't written or called, and I'd probably never know why…

'Actually,' she said, 'I was in no state to write.'

Oh. Maybe I would know why. 'You weren't? Why not?' Was this to do with her stay in hospital? 'Were you ill?'

'Kinda. Stick a pin in that, will you?' She pointed at the road. 'Right at this roundabout. Tell me about meeting Tim.'

'Will told you?'

'Yes. Poor you. Tim's lousy company.'

I laughed. 'He's scintillating if you're into damp coursing. I was trying to find out why you'd mentioned him at the hen do.'

'Ah! Bit of the old Miss Marple. And did you work it out?'

'No. I thought you'd mentioned him because he was somehow back into your life.'

'Heaven forfend!'

'Well, quite. Then I wondered if you'd been comparing him to Murray, but couldn't work out why. I thought perhaps Tim had been an alcoholic.'

'Well done, he was. A multiple addict. So there you are, you got one of the clues.'

'Yeah, then I spent weeks checking Murray's moderate alcohol intake, thus completely missing all the other signs.'

Rose laughed. 'I bet Murray was confused when you kept knocking the gin bottle out of his hand. Where is he now?'

'In Sheffield, in a colleague's flat.'

'Take the road for the M3. So you're in Bryn Glas on your own?'

Of course, Rose knew nothing of my recent life. 'No, Imo died. And it's been sold.' I was pleased I could say this out loud without blubbing. But when we stopped at a traffic light, I saw that Rose's eyes were wide, her hands over her mouth.

'Imo was so lovely. And Bryn Glas was your special place. Why didn't you buy it? Don't tell me; he let it get away. Kay, chick. I'm sorry.'

The lights changed, and I drove towards the motorway slip road.

'Don't worry, I've had plenty of time to repent at leisure. Letting Murray take the reins on buying Bryn Glas is one of my biggest ever regrets.'

I'd learned too late how foolish it was to put some of my own self into bricks and mortar. Into a place I didn't even own, a place that slipped through my fingers. The day I left the cottage was one of the bleakest of my life, outside of bereavements. Murray had already moved out, and I packed up with help from Edward. While he lugged boxes into a hired van, I trailed round, touching walls and floors as if I could imprint the cottage on my hands. Edward was pretty worried about me that day. I was pretty worried about myself. After we closed the front door, I burst into tears at the thought of leaving behind the silver lion's head door knocker, and Edward removed it for me with my dad's old Swiss Army knife.

I didn't want to dump all this on Rose. Instead, I told her about my new living situation: a room above Helena's photography studio in Stoke Newington.

'Wow, you're so trendy, Kay.'

'It's tiny but it's got a dear little kitchenette and a bathroom. It's the bachelor gal in her twenties pad I never had. And Helena's letting me stay for free while I get myself together.'

'She sounds like she's been a good mate. You can't be all that shitty a friend after all.' I could hear the smile in Rose's voice.

'It's handy to be near Stella, too. She's pregnant!'

'Never!'

'I know! My baby is having a baby! I plan to be extremely over-involved.'

'That's bloody brilliant, that is. I can't wait to get her some adorable little babygros.'

No one was as good to tell things to as Rose.

Once we were on the motorway, she took out a tissue – 'just in case' – and asked if I was ready for her Tim story. When I nodded, she said, 'Right. Well, you already knew he was a shit. Now you know that he was also addicted to gambling, and an alcoholic. I was too embarrassed to tell anyone.'

'Even me?'

'Especially you. I couldn't bear for you to see me in that situation. I almost didn't call you that night he threatened Jay. I sometimes wonder what would have happened if I hadn't.'

'I'm sure you'd have found another way to get out.'

'Maybe. Maybe not. You were there at the right time.'

I thought of my lonely and anxious drive there, Rose's frightened face, the sleepy boys in the back of my car, the long drive back.

'Murray does, unfortunately, have some things in common with Tim,' Rose said. 'But not everything. Murray's a genuinely nice bloke, isn't he? Bear's only real complaints about him were around money.'

I was mightily relieved to hear her say that. My impression of Murray had changed rather a lot since we married, but I couldn't reconcile the man he was with the man Tim was. 'Did she ever tell you about Murray's gambling?' I asked.

'No. Shame, we could have had such fun comparing notes. But occasionally she said something that made me wonder.'

'So… you and Tim?'

'Well, I suppose it would be called financial abuse now. He was in charge of the household budget, and sometimes he didn't give me enough for food for the boys. Anything I earned, you remember I had little jobs here and there, in that bakery, and as a teaching assistant, I had to hand over to him, and he invariably lost it on some stupid bet.'

How could I not have known any of this, for all these years? 'I just cannot believe it.'

'There's a little more to come, so give your incredulity somewhere to go.'

'I wish I could have helped more.'

'You did help. You'll see. Let me quickly get through this bit. So he was big into sports betting. He drank when he won, but he mostly lost, and drank then too. And though Sober Tim wasn't great, he was a saint compared to Drunk Tim. He often threatened to hit me, and though he didn't, that's not the only way you can hurt someone. I'm going to skip over that.' She dabbed her eyes with her tissue.

I thought I'd known how bad her marriage was, but there was clearly so much she hadn't told me.

'Then he raised his fist to Jay and I woke right up.'

'He was so scary that night.'

'Yeah, well. All in the past. Or so I thought.'

'What do you mean?'

'Stick a pin in that too, will you? Anyway, was any of that like your experience with Murray?'

'It sounds just horrendous with Tim. But no, nothing like that with Murray.'

'Thank goodness. I'm extremely glad for you. What about these: mysterious financial transactions. It not being clear where money is coming from or going out to. Spending time away from the home and being vague about where he's been.'

'Oh.'

'Resonates?' I could feel her eyes on me. 'Stay in the left lane, we're taking the M25.'

'To London?'

'Magical mystery tour, chick.'

I did as she asked. 'So, when did you first guess about Murray?'

'I knew something was off straight away, but I didn't know what. That night we met up with him and Charlie, the night you two scorched the restaurant with your chemistry, I felt really strange. Sick. I couldn't work out what the hell was going on. I didn't want to ruin your night, you were so smitten.'

'I remember you went home early.'

'It was such a weird feeling. There were a couple of things he said, when you were asking him about his work. I can't remember what now, but more than once, the hairs on the back of my neck stood up. It was such an instant physical reaction.'

'Bloody hell!'

'When I got home I was queasy all night, thought I was coming down with something. Next day I was fine. Then it happened again next time I met him, when the four of us went out to celebrate your engagement. I barely made it through that evening. It was like my body knew something that my brain didn't.'

'I've been getting that a lot lately.'

'It's a menopause superpower, innit?'

'Is it?'

'Well, it's not in the official list. Davina never mentions it. But seriously, I think it's to do with getting older, being more aware of your reactions to things. Anyway, that second time with Murray, I recognised it. It was the feeling I used to get with Tim, when we were in public together. This terrifying, sick-making adrenaline.'

'My *God*, Rose.'

'When you live with an addict there are signs you know

instantly. Addicts can be such exciting people to be with. But they can also create a living hell.' She put the seat back, and stretched out her legs. 'Anyway, when I got home I was in quite a state. I told Graham, because he was obviously very concerned. Murray's lovely, I said to him, don't get me wrong. But something hidden underneath is giving me the frighteners. Anyway, after that I did some digging.'

'What sort of digging?'

'Just the basic due diligence I think you failed to do.'

'Bloody hell!' I seemed to be saying this rather a lot today.

'Eyes on the road, please, Miss Kay.' She laughed. 'Our kids, they google anyone they're about to date as a matter of course. We could learn from them. Our generation takes everything on trust.'

'It's nice to trust people, though?'

'Mmm, lovely. Seriously though: how well did you know each other?'

'Yes thanks, Rose, that mantra's been going round my head for months.'

'It's a fair question, isn't it? And here's another: why did you get married so quickly?'

'Well we weren't kids, were we? When you know, you know.'

'Yeah, that's what you kept saying. I've always wondered, whose idea was it to marry so quickly?'

'Well, both of us seemed to...'

'Come *on*, Kay.' Rose was impatient. 'By your own account you took two decades to leave Richard. You worked in Quiller Queen for twenty-five years. You're wearing a cardigan you bought with me in Camden Town in 1987! You never rush into things.'

I glanced down at my cardigan. She was right.

'What I'm getting at is, Murray wanted to, didn't he? Here we are, M25, head towards Heathrow.'

'Where are we going? I don't have my passport.'

'Nowhere exotic, don't worry.'

'Of course he wanted to marry quickly.' Our third date. Him going down on one knee. Why wait? he said. When you know, you know.

'Did you not wonder why?'

'Well... it was love, why wait...?'

'Yes, you've got that down pat. Do you want to know the probable reason?'

'Not really.' My stomach felt hollow. 'Yes, of course. Go on.'

'Like I say, I don't know any of this for sure. But I've done a little research. I looked at the Australian equivalent of Companies House. I searched the address of their house to see who owned it. And I talked to Charlie.'

'You *did*?'

'I didn't tell him anything, don't worry. Just popped in to see him in Oxford. Asked how it came about, them moving to the UK. Look, it all might be a coincidence, right? Charlie said he was interested in that particular course, and his dad was right behind it, seemed pretty keen to get out of Australia.'

'Declared bankrupt.'

'Ah, so you know that. Good. Yes, they lost the house, and whatever business Murray was running got shut down. Looks like he left a mess in Oz, and wanted a fresh start over here.'

'And so,' I said, glad I was facing ahead and not having to see her face, finally letting the penny drop that had been quivering over the edge, 'Murray needed to marry someone British.'

'If he wanted to apply for a spouse visa and stay here, yes.'

Neither of us spoke for a while. I carried on driving along the motorway as though everything was fine, as if my beautiful love affair hadn't been a complete and utter sham, a massive betrayal. A sick joke. My poor, battered ego, would it ever recover?

'Here's the thing, and I'm not saying this to make you feel

better,' Rose said, finally. 'I don't doubt for one minute that he genuinely adored you. Maybe he did want to get married quickly, but I'm sure he lucked out with meeting you, he really did fall for you.'

'You can't possibly know that, and nor can I.' I was aware that I was going to start crying soon, and consequently might be a bit of a driving hazard.

Reading my mind, Rose said, 'Am I still insured?'

We were always insured on each other's cars, it didn't cost much extra – thanks, middle-aged white lady privilege! – and it meant that whoever drove somewhere didn't also have to drive back. At renewal I'd almost taken her off the policy, but it was too much like accepting that we'd never make up. One day, when I wasn't in a complete mess, I'd appreciate the way I'd held the faith there.

'Stop at the next services and I'll take over,' Rose said. 'Listen, Charlie was convinced his dad was madly in love with you. Said he'd known him with other girlfriends – sorry – and that he had never been remotely like this before.'

I held it together till we reached the services, then I let it all out. Rose put her arms round me, though I couldn't properly appreciate the miraculous nature of her being there because I was so desolate at having fallen for the wrong person. He was the biggest arsehole this side of Sydney, so why did I still miss him so much?

Rose held me for a long time, Disney-style, saying nothing, but when I at last stopped weeping, she said, 'Busting for a pee.'

'Me too,' I said, snivel-laughing.

We used the loos, and got coffees and muffins, then Rose took over at the wheel.

'So,' she said, when we were back en route to wherever it was we were going. 'Was it a nice wedding?'

We both started laughing. I was pleased to find that I could. 'Very nice, till you fucked it up.'

'Sorry about that. I was so close to coming in, you know.'

'You were?! You were there?'

'Long story.'

'We have time, from the looks of it. Go on,' I said, sitting back in my seat. It was nice to be driven. Especially by Rose. It was like old times, me and her, on our way somewhere. 'Tell me. Tell me everything. Start with the hen do. I'm ready.'

TWENTY-FOUR
ROSE'S LAST ENCOUNTER WITH KAY: NORTH WALES, APRIL 2023

Rose took a French 75 over to Kay, who was sitting on a banquette with Stella. They were with some of Kay's friends from her photography course – Carys, Emily and Padma – and they were all laughing together. Rose wished her conscience would let her enjoy the party, take pleasure in how happy her friend was. But she knew she had only one more shot at trying to convince Kay to slow things down.

Rose's early unease, following the dinner when Kay met Murray, had developed into full-blown anxiety. These last few months Kay had been wilder, more impulsive than Rose had ever seen her. Whenever Rose mentioned how fast things were moving, her friend behaved as if it was all a big cosmic joke. Murray was very attractive, certainly, and clearly mad about Kay. But right from the beginning, something, not just the speed of it all, had felt off. Rose had reluctantly, painfully, come to accept that she might know what that was.

Stella moved along to let Rose in, and she squeezed next to Kay and handed her the glass. 'Brilliant, thanks!' Kay said. 'I've already had two, but they don't seem to be having any effect.' She undermined this slightly by spilling some of the new drink onto her knees. 'This is mad, isn't it?' She put her arm round Rose. 'I'm too old to be getting married again, aren't I?'

'Not too old,' Rose said, seeing an entry point, 'in fact, what's the hurry? You're still a slip of a girl.' She took a slug of her own cocktail. She was going to need plenty of courage.

Kay threw back her head and laughed. 'Ooh yes, I'm an ingénue.'

'But really, chick. Tell me, why's it all so fast?'

'It was fast when I married Richard too. No time to think, that's how I like it!'

'And you're pregnant this time, are you?' Rose said, nudging her.

Kay roared. 'Wouldn't that be awful! Well, it makes no sense to wait. What are we going to do, date for a few years? Introduce each other to our parents? We're not kids. And we really love each other. When you know, you know.'

'I'm only thinking, why not push it back a little?' Rose persisted, cringing at how obvious she was being. 'Give you a chance to get to know each other better.'

Kay turned to look at Rose properly. 'You're really stuck on this, aren't you?' She downed the rest of her cocktail and gave Emily, sitting on the edge of the banquette, her bank card. 'Can you get me another two of these, please? I'm *very* thirsty.'

'Have some of mine while you're waiting,' Carys said, handing Kay a vibrant blue cocktail, which looked like a bad idea in a glass.

Rose lowered her voice. One more go. 'Listen, chick, if I was to tell you something that concerns me about Murray' – this was a massive risk, because she didn't have anything concrete, just instincts, plus some circumstantial evidence that would not stand up in a court – 'would you want to know?'

'Absolutely not.' Kay pulled away, and swigged down Carys's blue drink in one go. 'Ugh, disgusting! Where's my proper fucking drink?' She heaved herself out of the chair and stumbled to the bar.

Rose watched her talking to the barman, laughing, her arm round Emily. This was hopeless, she was making such a mess of it. Stella touched her arm. 'Are you OK?'

'Fine. Just, your mum's getting into this thing quite fast, isn't she?'

'I know! And he's Bear's ex as well. Bit weird.'

Murray being Bear's ex didn't bother Rose. The younger generation were more concerned by these niceties. Her son, Jay, had told her he was worried about the age gap between himself and his fiancée, which turned out to be four years.

'I mean, it's good to see Mum so happy,' Stella said. 'But she's really hyper.'

'She was like this at university. First time round, I mean, when we were eighteen, nineteen.'

'Bit wild?'

'A little.' Rose remembered Kay losing her head over that pretty boy David Endevane, then announcing, a few months later, that she was marrying Richard. It hadn't escaped Rose's notice, though she'd never mentioned it, that Edward as a child looked rather like David. Her suspicion had been accidentally confirmed years ago by Bear. It had bothered Rose at first that Kay had confided in Bear and not her, but she reasoned that different friends served different purposes. Kay finally told Rose the truth the day they threw Bear's ashes into the sea at West Kirby, and Rose did a good job of pretending that she had never known.

Stella told Rose she had secretly invited Kay's cousin along tonight. 'They used to be really close, though they haven't spoken for years,' Stella said. 'But by the time she gets here Mum's going to be off her face.'

'I knew Stacey a little, back in the day,' Rose said. 'Maybe you should tell your mum before she gets here?'

But Stella was fixated on it being a lovely surprise. When Stacey arrived, twenty minutes later, smiling anxiously and holding her bag in front of her like a shield, Rose could see how utterly incapable the very drunk Kay was of handling it. She took one look at Stacey, turned her back and staggered away.

Stella brought Stacey over to the table, semaphoring for help. Rose did her best, apologising for Kay, saying she'd surely soon say hello properly.

They looked across to where Kay was wriggling about in an impromptu dance to a Taylor Swift song.

Stacey laughed. 'Looks like she's past the hello stage of the evening.' She nodded at Rose. 'Are you all right? You look even more worried than that night I showed everyone my boobs.'

'I'd like to hear that story,' Stella said. 'But yeah, we're both a bit concerned about how fast this wedding is happening. Oh Christ.' She jumped up, and ran over to Kay, who had fallen into a crumpled pile on the floor.

'I'm all right, I'm all right,' Kay yelled.

Stacey smirked at Rose. 'Looks like me and Kathy have swapped personalities. So go on, what's with this bloke she's marrying?'

'They only met in the autumn,' Rose said, then, because she needed to tell *someone*, if Kay wasn't willing to listen, added, 'You know, Murray reminds me of Tim, my ex-husband.'

'Bad sort, is he, this Tim?' Stacey said, leaning closer.

Rose immediately regretted saying anything. Stacey was likely to be incredibly indiscreet. She quickly backtracked.

'No, all I mean is, Tim was fun, like Murray, spontaneous, you know. And they look a little alike.' Rose told herself this wasn't exactly a lie. Tim was fun when they first met, and he looked like Murray in that they both had eyes, a nose and a mouth.

Stella returned, and suggested they join her mum. So they

all got up and danced, Rose trying to enjoy herself, Kay still behaving as if Stacey wasn't there.

When they flopped back into their seats, Kay opened some presents, mostly of the penis-shaped pasta and edible knickers variety. Rose did her best to join in with the general hilarity. Her own gift to Kay was understated, a brooch of blue forget-me-nots. Even if Kay never realised, Rose wanted to give her something that symbolised the importance of their long connection.

'Something blue, and old too,' Rose said. 'It's vintage. You know, what we used to call second-hand.'

Kay loved it, kissing her effusively, their earlier exchange apparently forgotten. The conversation naturally turned to the wedding, and to Murray.

'He's handsome, funny, kind, generous,' Kay said, slurring. 'And for some reason he thinks I'm great!'

'You are great!' Carys said.

'What's his favourite colour?' Rose asked, abruptly. She hadn't known that she was going to say that.

Everyone turned to look at her, and she hastily extemporised, 'It's a fun party game, asking the hen questions about their husband-to-be.'

Kay was frowning, but Padma called out, 'I like it. What's his favourite position?'

Everyone groaned.

'I couldn't possibly say before my wedding night,' Kay said, and there was much giggling. Everyone began firing questions.

'What's his favourite food?'

'What's his favourite drink?'

'What's his favourite film?'

Kay laughed. 'I don't actually know.'

'How well *do* you know each other?' Rose said, looking straight at Kay. It was easier to be bold in a group.

'I know his favourite colour, actually,' Kay said. 'It's red.'

She stood up. 'Going loo.' But her legs buckled under her and she sat back down with a bump.

'Oh, Mum, you're so hammered!' Stella helped her up and escorted her to the toilet. When they came back, Kay ordered three more cocktails, lined them up on the table, and drank them down one after the other. Only Stacey, who egged her on despite, or perhaps because of, being ignored, seemed to think this was a good idea; everyone else looked concerned, and after that, the evening got rather out of hand. Kay tried to dance on the table but broke the heel of her shoe and fell off, and the bar manager gave her a warning. She was nigh on incoherent by the time Rose got Graham's call.

He was at Murray's stag do on the other side of town, having been roped in to attend as Murray didn't know many chaps in the UK yet other than business associates. Rose retreated with her phone to a quiet corner, and listened as Graham told her that they had somehow ended up at the only casino in North Wales; that Murray and two of his colleagues had been sitting at the blackjack table for an hour; that they'd already blown through several hundred pounds.

How Rose wished her instincts had been wrong. The queasy feeling she'd had before returned, but worse, and she hurriedly told Graham she'd call him back, then ran into the bathroom to be sick. What the hell was the matter with her? She splashed water on her face, then once her hands had stopped shaking she booked an Uber, and messaged Graham to say she'd collect him shortly.

In the bar she found Kay, who was sitting on the floor showing the millennials how to do the row boat dance. 'Graham's, er, not feeling great. I'd better go.'

Kay staggered to her feet. 'I'll see you out,' she said, as though they were in her house. She clung on to Rose for balance, hobbling on one intact and one broken shoe. At the door, Rose kissed her friend on the cheek. She knew it was a stupid time to say anything more, but when else would she be able to? She and Graham were going on holiday tomorrow, and wouldn't be back till the day before the wedding.

'Kay chick, is everything really all right?'

'Why yes. I'm great. Neverbeenbetter.'

'You *are* great. I'm just worried about Murray...'

'Oh do you ever stop?' Kay said, swaying as if the force of her words had knocked her to the side. 'You've been non-stop nag nag nag about Murray from the moment I met him.'

'I have, haven't I?' Rose braced herself. 'And I'm really sorry. It's only... I have this feeling I can't shift...'

'I don't give a shift about your feeling,' Kay yelled. 'A shit, even.'

The nauseous feeling was coming back. Rose tried one last time. She could see Stella approaching from the other side of the bar, alerted to Kay's shout. In a low voice, she said, 'There are things about Murray that remind me of Tim, and I haven't told you this before, but Tim gambled all our money and we...'

'Fuck *OFF!*' Kay yelled, as Stella reached them.

'What the hell, Mum?' Stella said.

Kay put her face close to Rose's. 'Don't talk to me any more, all right?' she said, too quietly for Stella to hear. 'I don't want to speak to you again. I *mean* it.' She weaved away, back to the bar.

Rose couldn't have said any more, whether she'd wanted to or not. The bile rushed into her mouth and she closed her eyes, willing it to subside.

'I'm so incredibly sorry,' Stella said. She hadn't heard Kay's last words, but Rose being told to fuck off was dreadful enough.

'It's all right,' Rose managed to gasp. She stood at the door for a moment, watched as Kay raised her arms in the air as she reached the others and started dancing again. She went outside to find her driver, the air cold on her face like a slap.

TWENTY-FIVE
SOUTHWOLD, MAY 2024

I was so absorbed in – and cringing myself inside out about – Rose's recounting of the hen party that I scarcely noticed where we were going. We'd been driving for what felt like hours, through the whole of Essex and out into Suffolk. Then I saw a sign I recognised.

'Southwold?'

'Memory Lane time, innit, chick?'

'Jesus, Rose, this is a hell of a long way from Winchester.'

'And from Richmond.'

'What's Richmond got to do with it?'

She smiled enigmatically. She'd been driving and talking up a storm, but she didn't appear tired. If anything, she was energised. The face I'd thought older when she first got in the car seemed less lined, was now more like the image of her in my head.

'Pass me another muffin, will you?'

I did so. 'We ought to get something proper to eat. How much longer?'

'Are we nearly there yet?' Rose mocked me, biting into the muffin. 'Remember how knackering the kids were when they were young? But how joyful? I'd give anything to have them back at that age, for a little while.'

'Grandchildren are a blessing, wait and you see. I love hanging out with Jamie and Finlay. In the blink of an eye Janis will be a little kid. Loads of fun, then hand her back.'

'I'm sure you're right. And I'm looking forward to being an extra granny for Stella's baby too.'

My heart lifted. Did this mean Rose was back, properly back? Was she going to give me another chance?

She pulled over outside a large modern house, and I finally understood where we were.

'Hang on a minute, this is...'

She turned off the engine. 'It's the house you rescued me from.'

We looked at it together. I knew we were both thinking of her final night there.

'Who owns it now?'

'No idea. I've never been back before. It looks pretty much the same, doesn't it? I wonder if they kept my world-beating collection of coasters.'

'So look, it's lovely to be anywhere with you, Rose. But why are we here?'

'It was a long way, wasn't it?'

'About five hours, by my estimation.' My tummy rumbled. 'We must get some food.'

'It's not quite as far from Richmond. I reckon that's probably about four hours? But I thought you needed reminding of what you did for me, back then. For months, when things were getting bad, when Tim was out doing goodness knows what, you used to drive over here nearly every weekend, do you remember?'

'I remember.'

Friday nights, after I'd finished at Quiller Queen, I'd do the long drive up to Suffolk so Rose wouldn't be on her own with the boys. She never said much, I just knew something was wrong and she was struggling. Sometimes I'd bring Edward and Stella, other times Alice had them. Then I'd drive back down first thing on Monday to be in time for work.

'As we have just established,' Rose said, 'it was a blimming long way. You never complained once.' She started the engine, and drove towards the end of the street. 'There used to be a great chippy on the front.'

'I didn't know what was going on, you were very discreet, but I knew you needed company.'

'That last time when I called and said I was scared, you said, "I'm coming, hold tight." You waited outside till Tim left. I couldn't think straight. I was running from room to room, and you calmly took over, packed up our stuff, found passports and things that I was too panicked to think of, and got me and the kids out of there. You stood up to Tim, you sang songs with the boys so they weren't frightened. When we got to your house you cooked them cheese on toast and Richard made up the beds and you looked after us and...' Rose broke off, and pinched her nose, a gesture I hadn't seen her do since she was a teenager. She always insisted that it prevented you crying or laughing, though it never worked for me.

'I was glad I could be there for you. I'm only sorry you couldn't tell me everything that was really going on.'

'That's what I'm trying to say.' Rose turned the car onto the seafront. 'It's my fault you've got it into your head that you're not a good friend. But that's not true. Just because people don't always tell you everything, has nothing to do with it. They don't tell you everything because they value the way you see them: as the person they want to be.'

'Eh?'

'I'll be honest, I thought of calling quite a few people that night before I rang you. I didn't want you to think of me as an abused wife, a victim. I knew you were the person who'd come without question, but I didn't want you bloody well feeling sorry for me. I wanted to know that when you looked at me, you still saw me as me, the person you'd known since school. I didn't want that to change. I didn't want you to see me in a different way.'

This was such a new way of thinking about things that I didn't know how to reply. I felt as I had after my first therapy session, as if my head had been turned to a different angle.

'Look, the fates are shining on us,' Rose said. 'The Fish Plaice is still there!' She parked the car, then pressed the forget-me-not brooch into my hand. 'Take this back, will you? It was meant to communicate what I couldn't. That whatever happened, I wouldn't ever forget you, or our friendship.'

I pinned it to my coat. Then we went into the chippy and ordered the works – fish, chips, mushy peas, gherkins and tea – and took them onto the beach. Rose said she used to often come here with the boys for their dinner. I guessed she meant, out of the house, and away from Tim.

It was starting to get chilly, but I had a blanket in the car and we snuggled under it. We sat on the sand, our backs against the promenade wall, and watched the light fading on the water as the sun went down.

'Bliss.' Rose cut up a piece of cod with the inadequate wooden knife and fork. 'This is how I want to be remembered.'

'What, with ketchup on your cheek?'

She wiped it off. 'Relaxed, happy, reclaiming a place I once loved.' She raised an eyebrow at me. 'You know, I'm pretty sure that's why Bear never told you she was ill.'

'What do you mean?'

'I'm guessing – you know me and my educated guesses – but I imagine that what she most appreciated, in her last few weeks, was that with you, she could be normal, have fun. She didn't want you to see her as a sick person. In fact, as soon as you found out she was ill, she skipped town, didn't she? You're the friend who sees us for who we still are, underneath whatever else is going on. Sometimes that's what we most need. A person to pretend to be normal with.'

'Pretending isn't a good thing, though?'

'When things are at their worst, pretending to be normal can be all that stands between oneself and sanity. Bear's last real adventure was with you.'

I ate a salty chip while I thought about it. 'What would she have said about me marrying Murray?'

'I'm sure she'd have been shocked at first. *"Don't do it, Kay, he's a bloody idiot."* Then maybe, if she'd seen how much you two liked each other, she'd have said, "Give it a go then. Maybe you can knock some sense into him, even if I couldn't."'

'I couldn't, alas.' I pointed at the darkening sky. 'I wondered if perhaps it had gone tits up with him because somewhere up there, she didn't approve.'

'That's proper daft talk, that is, soft lad. She wouldn't want to mess things up for you, would she?'

'OK, since you're in Wise Woman mode, let's hear your take on this. I've been thinking a lot lately about my mum. About how I, well, I never told you this… I wasn't actually with her when she died.'

'So?' Rose shrugged. 'I wasn't with mine, either.'

'Yes, but I told you, and everyone, that I *was* there, though. I don't know why.'

'See? You don't tell me everything either!'

'I was there the day before. Even though I knew it was the end, I didn't go back and…' Would this ever stop choking me up? 'I never gave her a proper goodbye.'

'Wise Woman Rose says this is an easy one.' She took my hand. 'You *did* have a proper goodbye. So what if it was the day before? Maybe it wasn't perfect, like on the telly, or in books, where everyone says what they need to say and they walk off into the sunset.' She gestured at the sky ahead of us, the reds fading into greys. 'But real goodbyes can be messy. Sometimes we don't know that it's the last time we'll see someone. People fade away, or we don't hear from them for years then we think, oh, whatever happened to so-and-so and discover they died, maybe ages ago, and we didn't know, they were being dead all that time. Your mum might not have wanted you there right at the end, anyway, like Bear. She might have wanted you to remember her as she was. She knew you loved her.'

Maybe she was right. Maybe Mum and I did have a proper goodbye after all. The final minutes of someone's life weren't intrinsically more important than the weeks, months and years of relationship that had gone before.

I told Rose about seeing her name in the care home visitors' book. 'I never knew you'd visited her.'

'Ah, it was ages ago. Around the time Stella was ill, depressed, after university. You were so worried about her, and she needed all your time. You told me you'd not been able to get to your mum, that she might feel neglected. So I popped up to see her.'

'You hate going back to Hoylake.'

'Too bloody right.' Rose hadn't had a good relationship with her own mother. 'But I thought it would be a nice thing to do for you, and for her.'

I remembered Mum saying, the day before she died, 'I had company.' Was she referring to Rose's visit?

'It was the act of a true friend. Thank you.' I wiped my eyes on a napkin. 'Not sure how I managed these last months without you, Rose.' In fact, had I managed them? Not really.

'I wish I'd been able to handle things better, but I had such an intense physical reaction every time I thought about you, or Murray.' In a rush, she said, 'After the hen party I did hope you'd reflect on what I'd said, and contact me, but no. I was at a loss, because you'd told me not to speak to you again. Graham and I went on our holiday and I worried the whole time. I rang

Stella while we were away but lost my nerve. Then I thought, well I'll just have to try to talk to you at the wedding.'

'So you really had intended to be there?'

'Of course. I bought a new dress. Graham and I were outside Imogen's house for hours.'

'The whole time I was wondering where you were! So what happened?'

'The floodgates opened, is what. Every time I tried to go in I got these weird dizzying white-outs. Bizarre. Like a migraine. Shaking, sick, all sorts.'

'God, that's horrible. It sounds like a trauma response.'

'Put a pin in that as well, will you?'

'I've lost track of all the pins.'

'I'll get to them, I promise.' She closed up our chip boxes and put our takeaway cups neatly on top of them. 'There were so many messages coming in that I turned my phone off. I wanted Graham to go in and ask you to come outside. But he wouldn't leave me, because I was in such a state. I was sick so many times.'

'That is absolutely horrible, you poor thing.'

'It's a bit late now but I wish I'd apologised to Imogen's neighbour for the mess I made of his hedges. You probably don't need to know that. It got later and later, and finally I accepted that I wasn't going to be able to go in, that something was really wrong with me. A waitress came out, and I asked her to put my gift on the present table. Then we went home.'

'You left me a gift…?' But as I spoke, I realised what it was. Well, of *course*. 'It was unbelievably generous. Where on earth did you get so much money?'

'You'll like this.' She smiled, her old cheeky Rose smile. 'Post-rehab Tim has been extremely remorseful about the money he took from me. One of the reasons he's quite broke now, though he is working hard, is because he gives me money every month. His idea, not mine. Not much, but it adds up. I just save it, so I thought you might be able to make good use of it.'

It felt even worse that the money had gone, knowing now what it meant. How would I ever pay her back? 'Why didn't you put your name on it? I suppose you got Graham to write the notes?'

'He was a bit baffled by that but I thought, even if you guessed it was from me, you'd still have plausible deniability.'

'With Murray, you mean?'

'Yes, in case you did open it in front of him, despite instructions. I didn't want him to get angry or defensive, have it backfire. "What the hell have you been saying to Rose about me", kind of thing.'

'You really did think he was a bad lot.'

'I only had Tim to go on as a comparison.'

'You had Graham too! Murray is way more like Graham than Tim.' I thought about it. 'Apart from the lying and stealing.'

She smiled. 'That wasn't the only reason I kept it anonymous. I didn't know how welcome I'd be, or my gift. You'd said you didn't want me to speak to you, after all. I wasn't even sure I was still invited! If all the texts and calls were because you actually wanted me there, or were just trying to save face. Anyway, it was academic, I couldn't come in, I was in too much of a mess.'

'Jesus, Rose, I'm sorry. Why was it so important to give me the money?'

'One of the worse things for me, with Tim, was not having any independence. That's what money buys you. It was meant to be a safety net, in case I was right about Murray. Did you manage to hold on to it?'

Murray had taken it, then given it back. But it was, now, properly lost. Rose could hear my answer in the silence.

'Ah well, if he knew about it there's no way you'd keep it. At least I tried. I wanted to do something for you because I knew I wasn't going to be any good emotionally.' Rose took a breath. 'So here come the pinned bits. Are you ready?'

Oh God. I nodded. 'Go on, chick.'

'On the way home from not-the-wedding, Graham insisted I call my old therapist. He was pretty alarmed; he'd never seen me like this. Actually, I'd never been like this. Thank goodness my therapist was available. She said that my worries about your relationship seemed to have brought up a mass of unresolved stuff about my own marriage. I thought I'd worked through everything about Tim with her years ago, but it appeared not.'

'That's awful, I'm so sorry.'

'It's absolutely not your fault. May I recommend therapy, by the way? I know you've always been agin it but...'

'Way ahead of you. Been seeing someone for nearly a year now.'

'Wonders will never! Anyway.' She paused, then said, 'She advised against me being in contact with you for a while.'

'Hence that text.'

'Yes. I'm really sorry. I know how bloody awful it must have been to get that. But I was kind of hysterical at this point.'

'It was a remarkably calm text.'

'I asked Graham to write it.'

'Ah.'

'I was too busy lying in the back of the car freaking out to type.'

'Christ, Rose!'

'He was probably a bit brisk, because he just wanted to get me home in one piece. I said some stuff that frightened him. Just as well that it's a blur now. That's PTSD for you. You forget the worst parts.'

'Wait, PTSD?'

'Oh I'm all up with the therapy jargon.' She waved a hand to play it down, not fooling anyone. 'That's what my marriage left me with, apparently. Bit sceptical myself, it's what soldiers get, isn't it? I'm told that traumatic feelings can be suppressed for years. But something about your situation sent me right back to the worst of my own marriage, and I hadn't processed it then, because I was too busy surviving.'

What the hell had gone on with her and Tim? She hadn't wanted to talk about it the day she left, nor any time after. I knew her well enough to understand that she'd given me only the parts she thought I could handle. I looked at her enquiringly to see if she wanted to tell me more now, but she shook her head. She knew what I was thinking.

'When I was in the psychiatric unit last year, they said it's not a great idea to dwell on my marriage outside the therapy room.'

'When you were in the *where?*' Tears pricked my eyes. I could hardly bear to think about what Rose had been through this last year.

'My therapist recommended intensive treatment after the Tim stuff resurfaced. Only for a few days. They said I was having a crisis. Mental health, innit? It's very fashionable.'

'My God, Rose! You were sectioned? Because of me?'

'Not sectioned, I was admitted of my own accord. And not because of you, you egomaniac. Yes, the stuff with you got it rolling, but it would have come out sooner or later anyway, most likely when I saw Tim at Janis' naming ceremony last month.'

'Oh, Rose, I'm so, so sorry.'

'Please stop apologising. It was actually good. I'd avoided being in the same room as Tim for years, but I really wanted to be at the baby naming, for Will and Edith's sake. Thank goodness I faced things down before then; I barely felt a flicker on the day. And look, I'm fine now. I really am. I go to therapy every week and I can talk about this as though it's no big deal. I've processed it.'

She might have processed it, but I hadn't. I thought back to the day in Winchester, her crying through the locked bathroom door. 'Jesus, no wonder you didn't want to see me when I turned up...'

'That wasn't our best day, was it? Though you were rather heroic, bursting in, trying to protect me from Graham.'

'Poor Graham.' I couldn't help but smile when I thought of pushing past him, his bewildered face. 'He's not really like Tim, is he?'

'He really isn't. Anyway, the day after that, I went into treatment.'

'It's all my fault.' I honestly didn't think I could feel any worse. But Rose put a firm hand on my arm.

'It was a good thing. I mean it: you did me a favour. I only wish I'd been able to do you one in return. When I was past the worst, Graham said we should tell you about what I suspected about Murray. He said he'd phone you, if I couldn't, or write. Offered to take dictation, bless him.'

'Why didn't he?'

She shook her head. 'Remember, I didn't know anything for certain. It looked from Stella's Instagram feed that everything was going really well for you. You and Murray looking so loved up at her party; you and her in Naples...'

'I had no idea Stella was on Instagram.'

'Awkward,' Rose said with a smile. 'But then, you don't have it, do you?'

'No, but even I know that social media is hardly a factual document.'

'I didn't want to risk bursting your bubble. I knew how much you liked him. And if I *was* right, well... like I said, I'd been advised to avoid contact with you. I'm so sorry I had to hide away, and block your number, I hated it, but I knew every message would spark things up again. I had a bit of a turn when that text came out of the blue via your Stacey.'

'I'm sorry about that. I don't know why I let her.' I did, of course. I'd been desperate. How long ago that felt, now I was sitting side by side with my friend on a dark, cool beach, the truth unspooling between us.

'Stacey writes well, doesn't she? Or did you tell her what to say?'

'No, all her, and I only authorised the first one, might I add.'

'Listen, chick. It wasn't that I didn't worry about you, I did, but I told myself I was mistaken, that you were fine. I just didn't have the capacity to get involved. I couldn't be pulled in because it made me properly ill.' The wry smile was back. 'So much for wanting you to see me at my best!'

'This Rose is the best. All sides of Rose are the best.'

She put her arm round me. 'It broke my heart when you turned up that day. Graham said you looked desolate. I so wished I could see you.'

'What's different now?'

'My doctors recommended I only reconnect if something changed for you, or I'd had enough therapy to cope.' She smiled. 'Both those elements are now in place.'

'You've been through such a lot. You keep saying it's not my fault but I can't help feeling that it very much is.'

'I don't know how else to say this: I owe you, and that fool you married, a thank you. I was still lugging all the Tim stuff around in my gut, weighing me down. It's been painful but cathartic to get rid of it. I'm light as a feather now.' She pointed at the Styrofoam boxes. 'Apart from all them chips.'

We sat quietly for a few minutes, our shoulders touching, the sky now completely dark.

'Stars are coming out,' Rose said. 'Pretty. I hate driving at night, though.'

'I like it. It's my turn, anyway.' There was so much to think about, my head felt full to the brim. One revelation after another.

We watched a family walk past on the sand. Two little kids,

jumping and laughing, excited to be near the sea at night. A man and woman with them, holding hands. Behind us, the shutters went down on the ice cream stand.

'Will you stay in London?' Rose asked.

'I don't know. I miss Wales, the peace of it. I'm not going to make plans until after Stella's baby. I can stay at Helena's till then. I'm starting to earn a bit from photography, and I reckon I'll be able to get back on my feet soon.'

'After all this time, you're a professional photographer,' Rose said. 'What an exciting second life you're having.'

'I could do with less excitement. God, I can't get over that the mystery money was from you. So unbelievably kind, given what you were going through. A weird thing happened with it, actually.' I told her how I kept her money in a drawer, at which she mock-slapped her head in frustration. And how when I told Murray, he was insistent I put it into a bank account.

'A joint bank account, I assume?'

'No, we didn't have one then. He was very keen I should put it in my own account. I didn't, though, and months later he did help himself to it, so I don't know what that was all about.'

Rose thought for a while. 'No, I got nothing.' She shook her head. 'Gamblers are mysterious entities.' She gathered together the rubbish, in mum style. 'Let's head off, shall we? We've got a long drive ahead of us.'

TWENTY-SIX
LONDON, MAY 2024

We didn't get back to Winchester till gone midnight, so I stayed over at Rose's. After all this time, to be welcome in her home was hands down the nicest thing that had happened to me for ages. Welcomed not only by her either, but also by Graham, who'd waited up for us. Imagine if I'd known, when I was at my lowest ebb, that one day not so far away, Rose and I would be sitting in her kitchen at one in the morning drinking Graham's hot chocolate. It was lovely to be normal with him again, and also get the chance to apologise for implying that he was an abuser. He was so wonderful that when I was finally alone in the spare room, I couldn't help but weep, not just at his kindness but also at the loss of my own husband, who I'd once thought was also very kind.

In the morning Graham cooked an excellent breakfast, then left Rose and I to catch up properly on the smaller events of our recent lives. Yesterday was for the big stuff, but the small stuff was as important: the glue that connected friends. I left mid-afternoon, with many promises to meet soon, and drove back to London, feeling lighter than I'd done for more than a year.

Helena's little flat wouldn't ever replace Bryn Glas, but in the busy heart of the city it was an oasis of peace and reflection. Getting parked in Zone E, of course, was quite another matter, and it took me forever to find a space. I was very keen to get in when I finally made it back to the flat. I raced up the stairs, and it wasn't till I reached the top that I saw with alarm that someone – a man – was sitting on the floor outside my door.

When he looked up, I was shocked to see that it was Murray. He was a shadow of his former self. He'd lost weight, and there were dark shadows under his eyes.

'Hello,' he said, cautiously. God, I could have done without this. I was all talked out after Rose, and not in the mood for conversation with my estranged liar of a husband, no matter that I had missed him last night.

'What are you doing here?'

'I heard this was an excellent place to sit, I've been checking it out.' He got slowly to his feet, stiff-limbed. His knee cracked as he stood. 'Wanted to see you, is all. Sorry to ambush you.'

'How long have you been here?'

'Since yesterday morning.'

'Nearly two days?'

'I'd wait an eternity for you, my love.' He grinned. 'Christ but you're a sight for sore eyes, Kay.'

I silently noted Kay, not Katie. Interesting. I could feel myself softening, bending towards him, and told myself sternly not to be such a sap. While you couldn't turn off loving someone, you could be sensible if it was bad for you. You couldn't just have sticky toffee pudding whenever you liked. You had to ask yourself each time if it was worth it. Murray was sticky toffee pudding. I smiled to myself because this analogy barely made sense, and Murray thought I was smiling at him, and held his arms open for a hug. I stepped into them, and it was lovely to be close to him, though I pulled away quickly. Sticky toffee pudding, Kay!

'Enough of that. We're separated. So you arrived yesterday

and slept in the stairwell, did you? What nonsense.' He had an overnight bag with him but there was no sign of a sleeping bag. I was sure he'd have got a hotel and come back this morning, but knew that he would never admit to it. Once a liar, always a...

'Actually, when I realised last night that you weren't coming back, I got a room at the Travelodge up the road.'

Oh. He was trying to blindside me with honesty, but it would take more than that to win me over. I got out my key.

'Is that the same door knocker as...?'

'Bryn Glas, yes. I brought it with me.' I gave him a challenging look. 'One small part of that cottage is still mine.'

I watched it land. He nodded, and briefly closed his eyes. Then he followed me into my little room. He hadn't been here before.

'Hey, this is nice.'

I'd brought in some plants, and a colourful rug to make it more homely, and put my favourite photos on the wall. I reckoned it looked a little like Astrid Kirchherr's flat in Hamburg, around the time she was taking the first iconic photos of the young Beatles. Maybe I should get my hair cut pixie short, like hers. Like Rose's. How often a woman's instinct at times of great change was to get a haircut.

'You're smiling enigmatically,' Murray said. He went over to the wall of photos, and pointed at one of my recent self-portraits. 'This is a gorgeous one of you, did you take it?'

'Yes. I realised I hardly had any nice photos of myself.'

'I'd love a copy.' Murray's eye was then caught by the old record player on the sideboard, which Helena had left behind. I'd bought a few LPs from charity shops, and Murray flicked through them. He held one up, a smile on his face. 'You've got Mississippi John Hurt.'

'Yeah, I guess I came round to it after listening to you play it. I like that one about cooking good biscuits.'

'"First Shot Missed Him"? Yeah, I love that one. Can I?'

I nodded, and he slipped the album onto the turntable and dropped the needle. As the first evocative finger-picking guitar notes filled the room, he went and sat on the bed because the only chair had my clothes thrown over it, bachelor style. There was a time when I would have cared about that, would have rushed to put them away. In the only gesture of hospitality I was willing to concede to, I put the kettle on the little stove. I could guess why he'd come, and him sitting there looking hopeful with his big brown puppy eyes, chatting about my photos and music, was only breaking my heart further.

'So was sitting outside my door for hours your idea of a grand gesture?' I turned down the volume on the record player. 'Because listen, pal, it isn't even close.' Murray had introduced me to this music and it was a bittersweet evocation of our brief, glorious life together in Bryn Glas. But I wanted it to be mine alone now, it wasn't for sharing with him.

'I'm all out of grand gestures,' Murray said. 'I'm here to give you your post' – he rifled in his bag and handed me some letters – 'and also to tell you something important. You don't have to do anything with the information, I just want you to know.'

'A text or call wouldn't have done?'

'I did try, but you weren't picking up,' he said.

That was true. I remembered all the calls he'd made yesterday. My phone was still turned off, in one of my bags. How nice it had been not to think about my phone for a whole day. To be out, alone – abroad, as the old-fashioned term would have it – with no one knowing where I was. I ought to turn it off more. I did grudgingly admire his restraint in not asking where I'd been. Imagine Richard's reaction to waiting for me for a night and most of a day! My mum used to say 'dirty stop-out' when I was in my teens; it applied to returning from an evening out at anything later than nine o'clock. Mum. I noted with pleasure that I was able to think of her fondly, without the immediate aftermath of guilt I'd had since she died. Something had shifted. Good old Louisa, and good old Rose.

'Well, go on then.' I took milk out of the little fridge. 'What's so urgent?'

'I wanted to...' Murray looked down at his hands. 'When you left, you said that I didn't love you enough.'

So we were going straight into it, were we? The big stuff. The day he left Bryn Glas. Just before he'd got in the waiting taxi, I'd said to him, 'Was it all a lie? Do you even love me?'

'I love you more than I have loved anyone,' he'd said.

'What rot. Did you marry me because you thought I had money? Because I really don't, you know.'

'Jeez, Katie, how could you even think that?'

'I don't know what I think. Maybe I think that I hate you.'

'You should do. I've ruined everything.' His face was blurry with tears too. 'You don't have to believe me, but I really loved living here with you.'

What I'd actually said, after that, was not 'You didn't love me enough', but 'You didn't love me enough to stop gambling.'

I pointed this out to him now, and he nodded.

'That's what I've come here to say. I do love you enough. I know I have a problem, and I want to stop.'

'Well, great. Excellent to accept there's a problem, but words are easy, aren't they?' I got mugs down from the shelf. 'You've always been good with words.'

He looked up, straight at me. 'I've started rehab.'

'You have?' Another way that he was like Tim! I hadn't expected that. Good. But a couple of sessions of rehab weren't going to make much difference.

'I'm in outpatients for now, I have to go four times a week. But they think I need intensive inpatient treatment.'

'That'll be very expensive, won't it?'

'It is.' And he allowed himself an enigmatic smile of his own. 'But my last big blow-out was pretty lucrative.'

'Well, that's great news, apart from how you're paying for it. Do you want me to look after the money so you don't accidentally, er, spend it?'

He opened his eyes wide. 'Would you really do that?'

'I want you to get treatment, and you don't have a great track record of hanging on to large sums. So how did this come about? Before you left, you were still insisting you didn't have a problem.'

'It was finally accepting that I'd lost you, that we had broken up,' he said. 'I was pretty sure that you did love me, and I really loved you, so I had to face it: there must be something seriously wrong with me.'

'You really were in denial about being addicted?'

'Apparently. One of my counsellors says I told myself, very convincingly, that my gambling was occasional, under control, that it was no different from speculating in business.'

I wasn't sure what to say. I'd assumed he'd carry on the same path, so rehab was a curveball, but I was too tired to think about what, if anything, it meant for me. I was grateful for the distraction of the kettle, which started screeching.

'I don't have fancy coffee, do you want anything?'

'Yeah, I'll have tea.' He smiled at my surprised face. 'Started drinking it after you left. It made me— No, that's way too stupid, Murray, don't fucking tell her that.'

'Go on, tell me, you drongo.' I couldn't help feeling affectionate towards him, despite everything.

He looked pleased at my use of his slang. 'All right. It made me feel like you were still around, if I was making tea for you. Then I thought I might as well drink it, feel close to you kind of thing.'

Wow. OK, that was sweet, but I wasn't going to tell him

that. I handed him a mug. 'So you've been getting treatment for how long?'

'Six weeks. Took me a couple of weeks after I left to get it together.'

All this time, and he hadn't mentioned it. 'So why are you telling me now? You still haven't said why you're here.'

'Ah yes. It's because an inpatient place has come up, a cancellation because, well, Jesus, because the person who was going to take it, they, er, killed themselves.'

'Oh God, Murray.'

'Yeah, bit of a facer, that. Pretty weird taking their place. And terrifying. So it starts next week, and they tell me I'll be there at least a month. Not sure what I'm in for once it starts, and I wanted to let you know, I suppose. And tell you that I'm really sorry, beyond sorry, though I know that doesn't begin to make up for any of it.'

He paused, and I thought he was going to beg for forgiveness, and I wasn't ready to give it, but he pointed at his tea, and said, 'You're not gonna approve, but I have sugar in it.'

I handed him the sugar bowl and watched in horror as he stirred in four spoonfuls. 'You don't like tea, you like sugar.'

'If I'm giving up one vice, I need to replace it with something, right?'

I thought of Tim coughing up nicotine, saying that you couldn't give up everything. How many more things, I wondered, did they have in common?

We sat next to each other on the bed, side-by-side, holding our mugs of tea like middle-aged students. Middle-aged, who was I kidding. We might be the 'don't look it' generation, but we were nonetheless not far off pension age. You'd think we'd be old enough to have made sense of everything by now, but it felt as if we were only just getting started.

'I've made up with Rose,' I told him. 'That's where I was yesterday.'

'Ah what wonderful news! You missed her so much.'

'Can I ask' – I wasn't sure if I wanted to know the answer to this, even now – 'when did you realise it was because of you that Rose cut me off?'

He focused on his sickly sweet tea for a moment. 'I suppose, on one level, I knew straight away.'

'On our wedding day?'

He nodded. 'I mean, of course I hoped it wasn't anything to do with me. I didn't know for sure. But in my darker moments, I probably knew.'

'Wow. OK.' I would need to think through the implications of that. But not yet. Not till I was alone, and feeling stronger. Or maybe not alone, maybe in conversation with Louisa. Or Rose.

'We talked about Bear. Ursula,' I said.

Murray smiled, and pointed at the wall, to my photos of Bear. Some were from when she was young, but the most striking was one that I took in Venice, in the half-light at the Gritti Palace, where we'd had a memorable and difficult final meal together. The shadows on her face accentuated her hollow cheeks. She was turned towards me, her hand slightly blurred in front of her mouth because she was gesticulating, her eyes bright in the candlelight. She was very alive, but a few weeks later she'd be dead.

I hadn't used it in my display for my degree as it had always made me too sad. But somehow, since coming here, I'd made my peace with it, and liked having her up there, looking at me.

'I've never seen that picture before. It's stunning.'

'It is, isn't it?' Why be modest? I was a professional photographer, don't you know. 'Rose and I wondered what Bear would say, if she could see you and me now.'

'She'd probably congratulate you for getting there so much quicker than she did. Took her nearly ten years to realise what a lousy bet I was.'

'Lousy bet, huh?'

'Once you start on the gambling analogies, there's no going back.'

'I know, right? I've noticed how many there are.'

'So Rose guessed about me, did she?' Murray said.

'Apparently, for people who know the signs, you were lit up like Piccadilly Circus.' I could feel the tension radiating off him, and wondered what it had cost him to seek help, and then to come and tell me. How bad had things got, these last weeks, that he had no option but to let everything collapse into the truth?

'Do you want to tell me what happened, then? After you left?'

He shook his head. 'Kay, it was bad. I can't lie. I was really angry.'

'With me?'

'With you? Christ, no. With me, for fucking things up. Furious for several days. Then so miserable I thought I might die. I sat in that crummy flat in Sheffield, boxes everywhere, I couldn't even bother to unpack. I had a few pretty dark nights, best not dwell on that. Then Charlie was unlucky enough to phone me. Crikey, the ear-bashing he gave me when I told him you'd gone. How could I let you go, you were the best thing that had happened to me since his mother, what sort of idiot was I, etc. He did shake some sense into me, actually.'

'How so?'

'He didn't know why you'd gone, though he did say, is it about money and I said kinda. He said I ought to do anything I could to try to get you back.'

'Did he?' I thought of Charlie the day of my show, his face as he wrestled with trying not to drop his dad in it too much. How generous he had been, letting me into his life. He still needed stable parental figures, and I would be that for him, if he wanted. 'Tell him he can call me if he needs anything while you're away. And he's welcome to stay here during reading week, or whatever. The sofa pulls out.'

'Oh, mate, thank you.' Murray rubbed his eyes. 'He said to me, "You might fail, but you'll never forgive yourself if you don't try." Soon as I put the phone down I emailed a clinic. Saw an emergency counsellor there two days later.'

'Blimey, that was fast.'

'Counsellor's a good bloke.' Murray took a big gulp of tea. 'Now I see him twice a week, and there's a group, and I also have sessions with a fellow who used to gamble and turned his life around, he's tough. I know it's early days. They keep telling me that. Can't expect everything to get sorted quickly.'

'Have you told Charlie you're getting help?'

'Not yet, but I'm going up to Oxford to see him after this. Thank him for pushing me. Explain everything.'

'Do they tell you to do this, at rehab? Kind of twelve step thing, go round apologising?'

'Nah, this is all me.'

I wanted to tell him how great he was doing, how proud I was. I could feel pressure, coming from me, not him, to give him a crumb of hope that maybe, if he really did get better, we might try again. But there were too many obstacles in the way. And there were things I needed to know, but whose answers I was scared of. I felt stiflingly hot, all at once, and wanted to get out of there.

'Shall we go for a walk?'

'Yes, sure.' He got up immediately.

Once outside, we walked in the direction of Springfield Park, in step as we had always been. We walked past shops which were becoming familiar to me: the Polish supermarket where I bought pickles and cheese, the little baker's which served delicious babka.

'This is a great area, isn't it?' he said.

'I really like it.'

'I can't tell if it's gentrifying or not.'

'Some streets are, like this one, and others not yet.' Before I lost my nerve and we started chit-chatting about the shocking price of a flat white, I said, 'So, can I ask you something? Two things, in fact?' I didn't look at him as I spoke; walking side by side was good.

'Please do.'

'You wanted to get married very quickly.' I swallowed hard. Did I really want to know this? But yes – woman up, Kay! In the last couple of days I'd lived through the hardest parts of Rose's life. This should be a lot easier. It was only my pride at risk, after all. 'That was because you wanted to get settled status here, wasn't it?'

'I'm not going to come out of this very well, but I'll tell you the truth.'

'You're not coming out of any of this very well, darling.'

'Don't spare me, will you. OK.' He took a breath. 'I'll just tell you what happened, best as I can. Things had gone to shite in Oz. Lost the house. Made a dick-up of everything. You know this, right? I made sure Charlie wasn't affected, but he was ready to leave, he'd always wanted to come to the UK, his mother's homeland. When he got offered the place at Oxford, he was scared of being on his own. So I thought, why not go with him? New start for us both.'

'You didn't push him into it?'

'Not at all. He made all the college arrangements. Once we were here, it was complicated getting any kind of visa given my finances. Then a bloke I knew through work, Andrew, he said…'

'Real work, or gambling?'

I could feel the heat of Murray's eyes on at me. 'Real work. What do you mean?'

'I've been wondering if there was any real work, or if your only income was through gambling?'

He stopped in the street in front of a Turkish barber's. 'Christ, Kay, I'm not that bad! You saw the invoices, you think I made the whole business up? I only wish I was that smart.'

'I don't know how much of anything was true or real.'

He nodded, then closed his eyes for a moment. 'I get that. I've got no right to expect you to believe anything I say.' We started walking again, and he went on, 'No, the business is real all right, and when I'm on top of it, I do it well. It was what I'd been doing in Oz, and I started it again with a new name. Not completely legit, probably, but I needed income fast. When you and I met, I hadn't gambled for months. I didn't fall off the wagon, if that's what we're calling it, until our honeymoon.' He looked like he might cry.

We went through the black metal gates of the park. It was pretty in the sunshine, though I came here every day, whatever the weather. I liked the café, you could sit inside by the floor-to-ceiling windows if it was cold, or outside if it was warm. I liked the large pond surrounded by tall trees, and the panoramic but utilitarian view towards the east, of tower blocks and pylons. Most of all, I liked seeing families with young kids, teenagers, older people, all just doing their thing. It gave me a rare feeling of normality during these strange, dislocating days.

We started to walk round the pond. 'Go on,' I said, 'you were saying about getting a visa.'

'Yes, my colleague Andrew. He knew a woman called Oriana, British woman, very well-off...'

'Oriana de Damas!'

'Crikey, Kay, how do you know that?'

'Her name was in your accounts.'

'Jeez, that's right. Well, she wanted to get married to avoid having to give half her fortune to her ex-husband. I never really understood the legal bind she was in, I was just happy to be along for the ride. Mutually beneficial arrangement. It didn't hurt that she was super-wealthy. I was thinking all my ducks were lined up in a row.'

'So what happened?'

'You know what happened, Katie. I met you.'

'Oh.'

'Meeting you wrecked my brilliant arrangement, and I didn't even care. Oriana was mad, I can tell you. I had to return her first payment almost immediately. But it couldn't be helped, I fell madly in love.'

'I'm feeling sorry for her now.'

'Don't be, she married Andrew instead and by all accounts they're pretty happy. He was probably a better husband than me, let's face it.'

'Good point. So what you're saying is, you did want to marry, but it didn't have to be me.'

'Damn right. I know I went at top speed with you, and that was because I was worried I'd have to leave Charlie on his own here. I might not have been the best father, but I love him to bits. He's still young, he doesn't have a mother, I want to be there for him. But it was you I wanted to marry.'

'I wasn't rich in the slightest.'

'Strangely enough, I didn't care.' He stopped by a jasmine bush and held out a branch of it towards me, not picking it, just offering it. 'I turned out not to be a very good gold digger, after all.'

I sniffed the flowers he was holding, then looked up at him. Our faces were close, but he waited for me to make the move, and I couldn't stop myself. I was addicted to him. I leaned in, and our lips met. A small, gentle, uncertain kiss. I moved away straight after, afraid he would sense how much I had missed him, how much I'd missed kissing him.

'All right,' I said, trying to sound brisk. I sat down on a bench looking out over the water. 'So tell me this: what the hell happened to our cottage?'

He sat next to me and hunched up into his coat. 'Dreading this. Worst day of my life. Letting you down, it was unforgiveable, and I don't expect you to.'

'It wasn't losing the cottage that was unforgiveable, it was...'

'Me lying about it till it was too late.'

'Well, yes.' God, he really was in some kind of process if he got that.

'Everything went out of control. It was hell. Couldn't get a loan, had no reserves after the honeymoon. I know, I know.' He held up his hand. 'It wasn't necessary to spend so much on it. But I loved you, cherished you. I wanted to be able to pay for everything, like a proper husband. I knew I could get money easily, anyway, so I went back to the casinos, won loads, then it all started again. Couldn't hang on to it, lost it all.'

I watched a thirty-something couple walk past with two dogs. Did they have one each, I wondered, or did they share them both?

'I could probably have got a mortgage in my name, you know. Richard would have underwritten it. You should have told me straight away, after the first bank said no.'

'Shoulda. Didn't though.' He puffed out a long breath of air. 'Are those the two things you wanted to know?'

'No, those were all one. The other thing that I can't understand, no matter how I look at it, is about the money you took. The cash in my T-shirt drawer.'

He looked confused. 'You know this. I took it to show that we had a larger deposit...'

'No, I don't mean then. Back when I first told you about the money, you said I should put it in a bank account. You kept on at me about it. I cannot work that out at all.'

'It's pretty simple.' He rubbed his forehead, as if he wanted to rub the thoughts away. 'I was trying to protect your money.'

'From who?'

'From me, of course.'

'Oh, Murray.' That, more than anything else, gave me a glimpse into the war that raged in him, his gambling side versus his careful side. I leaned against him and he put his arm round my shoulder.

'I might not have been able to face it head on, but I knew there were times I couldn't be trusted around money. In fact, I twice cancelled being the joint account holder with Charlie. But other times I could always justify why I needed it, more than the person whose money it was. I'm told that rehab will give me strategies for dealing with those weaker moments.'

'So you told me to put it in a bank so that you couldn't get hold of it?'

'Yes.'

'And that's why you originally refused to set up a joint account with me?'

'Oh man, yeah, no way could I trust myself with that. As you saw, only too well. I wanted to protect you, and protect our marriage. From myself.' His voice faltered. 'Didn't work, but that's because I'm an asshole, not because it wasn't a good idea.'

I stood up, feeling the need to move again, and we walked back towards the park's entrance.

'Can I tell you the absolute worst thing in all this?' he said.

'I can't take any more shocks, Murray.'

'It's kind of a nice thing really, if that doesn't sound like a paradox. I've always loved the way you look at me. As if you can see me, all of me, and like what you see. The worst thing was when we were in that awful casino, and you looked at me differently for the first time. I suppose that's why I didn't tell you about the banks, the money. I wanted to be the man you wanted me to be.'

I stopped walking and stared at him. 'That's so weird. Me and Rose were talking about the same thing. She said both she and Bear saw me as the friend who you want to see at your best. I'd thought I was awful for Bear not wanting me to know that she was ill, but actually with me she could behave like it wasn't happening. She liked the version of herself that she could see through my eyes.'

'Wow, exactly, I completely get that. The friend who sees you as you want to be seen. Same for me.'

We started walking again, and he went on, 'Ursula definitely felt that with you, I know it. You absolutely were that for her, and her last weeks were happier because of you.' His voice cracked, and he cleared it. 'She was so knackered when she got back from Venice, but happier than she'd been for months.'

'You saw her when she got back?'

'Of course! Those last few weeks I stayed at her place, pretty much looked after her, shared it with her teacher friend. It made things better for Charlie that I was there.'

'You were there when she died?'

'I was.'

'Why did you never tell me this before?'

'I don't know, sweetheart. Because it's bloody sad, I suppose. But I'm sorry I didn't – I should have. One of the last things she said to me was that she'd had the time of her life in Venice, with you.'

I pinched the top of my nose, like Rose did, but it didn't work, as I'd always known; a tear slid down my face. His eyes were also watery, and we held hands, and the day swirled round us, and I couldn't tell you if it was the start of something, or the end.

On our way back, he asked about my work for Helena, and I made him laugh with stories of the photoshoot last week with an old lady's prized Pomeranian dogs who would not sit still. Once we were in the flat, he said he ought to head to Oxford before it got too late. While he freshened up in the bathroom, I looked through the letters he'd brought. Mostly bills, apart from one, in a heavy old-fashioned cream envelope. It was from a solicitor, dated a couple of weeks ago.

Dear Mrs Garland,

I'm writing to inform you of a bequest from the late Ms Imogen Gray, which she hoped you will receive as a token of her great love and friendship. Please can you contact my office at your earliest convenience, to arrange to collect the cheque? It is for the sum of £100,000.

Ms Gray's wishes were that you would keep a substantial part of it towards purchasing Bryn Glas, if it is on the market, should it, for whatever reason, not be currently in your possession. Ms Gray feels that you are the rightful custodian of the property. However, she does not want you to feel obligated to use the money in this way, and states that if you wish to blow the whole thing on Parisian couture, she would cheer you on.

Yours sincerely,

Martin M. Claymore, solicitor

I'm sorry, *what*? I stared at the letter, unable to believe my eyes. For the second time in my recent life, someone who loved me had given me a financial safety net. Or in this case, a hundred safety nets. Imogen, you astonishing, crazy, wonderful friend. What an act of faith, an act of love. How late in the day must she have amended her will to put this in? Had she sensed from Simon, in her final weeks, that there was a problem with us buying the cottage? Did she know all along that Murray wasn't quite the steady provider I had assumed he was? I would never know. But perhaps I would, one day, be able to go back to Bryn Glas. The developer that Simon had sold it to might agree to sell it to me. Or maybe I would use the money to live somewhere else, perhaps near Stella and the baby. Maybe I would take Rose and go travelling somewhere amazing. After I'd paid back her ten grand, of course.

Rose. I couldn't wait to call her, tell her about Imogen's gift. Ask what I should do with the money. Start making plans. I wished Murray would hurry up. I was positively itching to speak to her, hear her voice. Now that I *could* speak to her again, I didn't want to waste any time *not* speaking to her. I texted her, a methadone substitute for actual conversation, at least for my generation. Our generation.

Hey chick, the most incredible thing!

I only had to wait a few seconds for her reply.

Call me immediately!

She was *back*. I replied:

Give me five minutes. I have so much to tell you.

The loo flushed in the bathroom, and without thinking too hard about it, I put the letter in the cutlery drawer. One day I might tell Murray about it, but not now. I didn't know what would happen to me and Murray, or if there would be a me and Murray, and it felt rather early in his addiction treatment journey to put such temptation in his path.

He came back in and hoisted his bag on his shoulder. 'I'll be off then.'

I kissed his cheek. 'Good luck with Charlie, and with the rehab.'

'Thank you, Katie. I know this is ironic under the circumstances, but are you OK for money?' He saw my expression, and said hastily, 'All above board – I'm working all hours, and thanks to your business systems there are no problems with cash flow. I can put some in your account.'

'Don't worry.' I laughed. 'I'm fine for money.'

He stood at the door, and I was transported back to our wedding day, the way he had stood looking at me in Imogen's garden. He looked at me then, and now, as if he liked what he saw.

'Hang on a minute,' I said. 'Just stay like that.'

I grabbed my camera from the table, with its excellent new lens. I wanted to record him, this handsome man in my doorway, his bag not the only weight on his shoulders. I took a few quick frames then lowered the camera. Done. We smiled at each other. I could already see exactly where on my wall I would put the photo, and how it would look.

A LETTER FROM BETH

Dear reader,

I want to say a huge thank you for choosing to read *The Friendship List*. If you enjoyed it, and want to keep up to date with all my latest releases, just sign up at the following link. Your email address will never be shared and you can unsubscribe at any time.

www.bookouture.com/beth-miller

Those of you who've read my earlier book, *The Missing Letters of Mrs Bright*, will probably have noticed that this new one features some of the same characters a few years on. If you haven't read *Missing Letters*, it explores what Kay, Rose, Bear and Stella got up to back in 2018, around the time that Kay left Richard. Both books are standalone, and can be read in any order.

I hope you loved *The Friendship List* and if you did please let me know what you thought, either in a review – I read them all – or you can get in touch through my website. I love hearing from readers.

Thanks,

Beth

KEEP IN TOUCH WITH BETH

www.bethmiller.co.uk

facebook.com/bethmillerauthor
x.com/drbethmiller

ACKNOWLEDGEMENTS

This book took quite a while to be born, and I was lucky to be surrounded by wise, talented, sparky writers whose feedback and support helped steer it safely into the world: Liz Bahs, Melissa Bailey, Sharon Duggal, Jules Grant, Anna Jefferson, Kate Lee, Katy Massey, Charlotte Mathieson, Erinna Mettler, Jacq Molloy, Lou Tondeur and Laura Wilkinson.

Thanks also to Saskia Gent, my first reader, unfailingly generous as usual, and to Mark Radcliffe, who reminded me to keep the writing going while teaching.

Two top-notch Bookouture editors were involved: first Maisie Lawrence, who got the ball rolling after it came to a stop, then the creative and encouraging Harriet Wade, who remained calm even as I lost the plot – literally, sometimes – over yet another edit.

Finally, thank you to John and my amazing grown-up children, who were great cheerleaders when things went well, and excellent sources of distraction when they didn't.

PUBLISHING TEAM

Turning a manuscript into a book requires the efforts of many people. The publishing team at Bookouture would like to acknowledge everyone who contributed to this publication.

Commercial
Lauren Morrissette
Hannah Richmond
Imogen Allport

Cover design
Alexandra Allden

Data and analysis
Mark Alder
Mohamed Bussuri

Editorial
Harriet Wade
Sinead O'Connor

Copyeditor
Laura Gerrard

Proofreader
Becca Allen

Marketing
Alex Crow
Melanie Price
Occy Carr
Cíara Rosney
Martyna Młynarska

Operations and distribution
Marina Valles
Stephanie Straub
Joe Morris

Production
Hannah Snetsinger
Mandy Kullar
Ria Clare
Nadia Michael

Publicity
Kim Nash
Noelle Holten
Jess Readett
Sarah Hardy

Rights and contracts
Peta Nightingale
Richard King
Saidah Graham

RAISING READERS
Books Build Bright Futures

Dear Reader,

We'd love your attention for one more page to tell you about the crisis in children's reading, and what we can all do.

Studies have shown that reading for fun is the **single biggest predictor of a child's future life chances** – more than family circumstance, parents' educational background or income. It improves academic results, mental health, wealth, communication skills, ambition and happiness.

The number of children reading for fun is in rapid decline. Young people have a lot of competition for their time, and a worryingly high number do not have a single book at home.

Hachette works extensively with schools, libraries and literacy charities, but here are some ways we can all raise more readers:

- Reading to children for just 10 minutes a day makes a difference
- Don't give up if children aren't regular readers – there will be books for them!

- Visit bookshops and libraries to get recommendations
- Encourage them to listen to audiobooks
- Support school libraries
- Give books as gifts

There's a lot more information about how to encourage children to read on our websites: **www.RaisingReaders.co.uk** and **www.JoinRaisingReaders.com**.

Thank you for reading.